THE SCOUNDREL SCOT

ALSO BY VANDA VADAS

The Pirate Lord

The Prodigal Laird

THE SCOUNDREL SCOT

Highland Hearths Book 1

Vanda Vadas

THE SCOUNDREL SCOT

HIGHLAND HEARTHS BOOK 1

ISBN: 978-0-6481871-2-7 (eBook)

ISBN: 978-0-6481871-3-4 (Paperback)

Cover Design by Damonza

Copy Editing by Jessica Fogleman

For my grandchildren
May books be your lifelong friends,
And may reading light your way, always.

CHAPTER ONE

Scottish Highlands, Summer 1743

I'M NOT A lunatic! Get me out of here!

The memory of that chilling plea froze Lady Helene Beckett's blood. Try as she might, she could not unsee the fear and terror of abandonment in her younger sister's wide, long-lashed eyes. Nor could she forget the harrowing words, 'Don't leave me,' screamed at her back when she exited down the long corridor of the asylum.

Helene suffered pain as if someone had carved her heart from her chest. In truth, she didn't deserve to draw breath, but she'd pledged a promise through the barred window of a locked door, and a promise made must be honoured. One she'd fulfil before she drew her last breath. The next time she entered that hell-hole of an institution it would be to see her sister freed, to take her by the hand and start their lives somewhere, anywhere, anew.

Well-laid plans required careful forethought. Deception remained her trump card. She would bear the shame because of it. No other course of action had presented itself, which had led to this very moment, with Helene seated inside a carriage heading into the wilds of the barbarous Scottish Highlands.

Despite the presence and protection of a retinue of the king's men on horseback outside the carriage, fear of the unknown—and of what she must do—sent a shiver through her. She pulled the woollen blanket on her knees closer to her middle and gazed through the window to the dismal weather beyond.

Mist shrouded the peaks of rugged mountains. Woodlands and moors grew lush from rain. Fine, persistent rain. Clean and uncontaminated. If only she could stand beneath the heavens and be soaked in its purity like a kind of lustration. Wishful thinking, for even if it were holy water, it would never wash her conscience clean, and if she were to receive forgiveness from the highest order, still it would not alleviate her long-endured nauseating guilt.

'Is something the matter, my dear? Ye look as pale as the day is grey.'

The question jolted Helene from her dark despair. She looked at Viscountess Sutton and her daughter, Agnes, seated opposite her, and summoned a well-practised smile. 'Not at all, Lady Sutton. If I appear out of sorts, it's only because I've never travelled for so many days and on such uneven ground.'

The viscountess presented as a classic auburn-haired beauty. Long-distance travel in the confined carriage did not lend itself to the wearing of London's glamorous wide skirts, and yet she still appeared the picture of tailored perfection dressed in a simple, practical fine woollen gown and cloak.

She leaned forward to pat Helene's hand. 'Ye needn't worry, lass. We've not much further to go. I ken ye're a long way from yer kin and home, but ye'll be welcomed and looked after as one of our own at Drumocher Castle.'

Helene smiled. 'Thank you. Agnes has told me much about your sister and her family. I look forward to meeting each member of your clan.'

Agnes, a mirror image of her mother, giggled. 'Remember

what I've told you about my cousin Lachlan being quite the ladies' man? Well, you're sure to catch his eye.'

'Agnes!' chided Lady Sutton. To Helene, she reassured, 'My nephew is a man of principle, but if he puts a foot wrong, ye only need tell me or his mother and he'll soon ken his place.'

Agnes's sweet laughter filled the plush interior of the carriage. 'And this coming from a Scotswoman who captured the eye of a notorious English rake and who ultimately married him? Sound advice, Mother, if not hypocritical.'

'Yer father was, and still is, an honourable man!'

'Indeed he is, but that didn't stop him putting a foot wrong, did it?' Agnes winked at her mother. 'One stolen kiss when you were a lass—so you told me—and, well . . . here we are.'

Lady Sutton's cheeks flushed red. 'That one kiss redeemed his ways, and as I said, yer father is an honourable man.'

Agnes grinned and tucked her hand into the crook of her mother's arm. 'Then there's still hope for Lachlan. He and Cuthbert are one and the same. Are they not?'

'That ye should talk about yer brother and cousin like that! Really, Agnes.'

'I say it because it's true, and because I do enjoy teasing you.'

Her mother's lost-for-words expression set Agnes off again. Only when Lady Sutton's chagrin relaxed into a broad smile did Helene enjoy a genuine laugh. She'd almost forgotten how to do that until the day she'd met and befriended Agnes, who radiated verve and an infectious zest for life.

Cheerful gaiety subsided into amiable conversation, as it had during their journey. They'd all but exhausted what there was to know about Helene—or rather, what she'd been willing to divulge. Some matters—family matters—were best kept private. Agnes and her mother, being of polite society, knew better than to overstep the mark or appear too inquisitive.

Lady Sutton's high-spirited mood increased with every mile they came closer to their destination. She spoke of happy childhood memories growing up in the Highlands and the mischievous adventures she and her twin sister, Caitrin, had pursued.

Understanding the Scottish accent proved to be a challenge for Helene, and the more animated the viscountess became, the faster she spoke. She trilled the *r*'s in words and delivered a sing-song intonation driven with as much lively energy as her facial expressions. At one point she paused to take what Helene believed to be a breath, but instead she looked at Helene expectantly, as if awaiting a response.

'Ye're not following me, are ye, lass? Ye look a wee bit perplexed.'

'I confess I don't know at what point I stopped comprehending what you've said, in favour of enjoying *how* you've said it.'

'Ne'er ye mind. Yer ear will soon grow accustomed to the way we speak here in the Highlands.'

'Only if the words are spoken slowly, as you did just now.'

'Understanding my mother's thick Scottish brogue is like running a race and struggling to keep up with the leader,' Agnes explained. 'As you know, Cuthbert and I were born and raised in England; however, people do find it a curious thing to hear a mother speak in one accent and her children in another.'

Again, Lady Sutton's chatter took off at a gallop. Had Agnes not interjected here and there with words clearly enunciated in the king's English, then the conversation would have been entirely lost on Helene. She envied their close bond, their jovial banter, and the love in Lady Sutton's eyes whenever she looked at her daughter.

Helene closed her mind to crippling memories. God rest her own mother's soul.

As they crested the top of a rise, Agnes blurted, 'There it is! In the distance! Drumocher Castle.'

'Och!' exclaimed Lady Sutton. 'My heart beats so.' She took a lace handkerchief from her embroidered reticule and dabbed her eyes. ''Tis too long since I last saw my sister. And to think we nearly lost her to a fever.'

Agnes took her mother's free hand in hers and murmured heartfelt words. The consoling gesture took Helene back to the asylum when she'd sought to reassure her sister in the same fashion. Her resolve turned as hard as the stone fortress. To the impending task at hand. Catch the MacLanoch laird's philandering eye. If all went according to plan, Helene would hurt no more than his pride.

Lachlan MacLanoch closed the last of the ledger books. With all accounts now reconciled, he slumped back in his chair, figures and forecasts still spinning in his head.

The business of rearing and selling black cattle was by no means without its challenges. He massaged first the ache behind his temples and then the knotted tension in the back of his neck. On one side of the desk lay a parchment scroll from which he read the fresh list of grievances between disgruntled kinsmen. Far easier as laird to soon settle their disputes than to draw his broadsword against anyone who dared steal from his livelihood or threaten his clan.

The estate's coffers retained ample reserves to ensure those who served him would not go without food, shelter, or his protection, be they residing within the castle walls or eking out a living on his lands.

While the cattle grew fat on rich summer pastures, crops flourished down in the straths. For the time being, he was without major worry or concern and looked forward to the imminent arrival of his auntie and two cousins travelling from London. He pondered the woman in their company, a stranger to Lachlan, yet a guest and contemporary of his twenty-year-old cousin Agnes.

Cuthbert, older brother to Agnes, had written in advance of their visit with news of Lady Helene Beckett accompanying them. Of marriageable age, she'd caused a stir by refusing the hands of some of London's wealthiest and most influential suitors.

Privileged, conceited arrogance. Cuthbert's words when describing her in his missive.

In need of stretching his long legs, Lachlan pushed up from the chair and went to the library's rain-streaked window. The unusual cold snap saw a breeze kick up, strong enough to pleat the loch's inky surface like the folds of his kilt. Beyond the castle, fog blanketed the moor, shifting here and there as if it were a wraith on the move. Not the finest of Scottish summer days to be welcoming visitors.

Before he turned to stow the ledgers under lock and key, something in the distance caught his eye. A fleeting dark flash of movement amidst light rain and swirling fog. He stood watchful, waiting, until out of the thinning mist, travelling along the castle's approach, came a rider.

The tall horseman carried himself upright in the saddle, and a hooded dark cloak concealed his body and the thoroughbred's rump. Even in the inclement weather, polished stirrups shone silver against black leather riding boots. Had the sun been out, Lachlan might have seen his own smile reflected in the windowpane. He knew of only one man who cut such a gallant, noble figure.

Cuthbert.

A sudden squeal of feminine delight pierced the outdoor air. At the same time, a knock came upon the open library door. Lachlan turned towards it. 'Mother! Come in.'

Caitrin MacLanoch joined her eldest child at the window. 'Cuthbert has yet to dismount, and already yer sister runs to welcome him.'

Lachlan laughed and laid an arm around his mother's shoulder. 'She's spent the last hour keeping watch from the curtain wall.'

From their vantage point, they observed Cuthbert slip from his saddle and toss the reins to a waiting groomsman. Grizel, a lithe young woman of sixteen summers, threw herself into her cousin's waiting embrace. He lifted her high and swung around in circles, sending her into fits of laughter and merriment. The hood from Cuthbert's cloak fell back to expose fair hair tied at his nape. When at last he set Grizel upon her feet, she took his hand and tugged him out of the rain towards the keep's entrance.

'Well then.' Caitrin patted her son's hand. 'Let's go welcome yer cousin. He'll be in need of warmth and food. Cook has prepared the midday meal.'

'More to the point,' warned Lachlan, 'he'll need saving from Grizel's incessant chatter.' He set away the ledgers and accompanied his mother to the blazing open hearth in the great hall.

There, Cuthbert removed his sodden cloak and handed it to a servant. He greeted Caitrin with open arms and drew her into his embrace. 'Auntie. Such a pleasure to see you again.'

'And ye too, dear nephew.' She switched to Gaelic. 'I hope ye've not forgotten the Highland tongue, lad.'

He replied in kind. 'Not forgotten, but 'tis rare I've the opportunity to speak it.'

Caitrin pulled back, a picture of surprise. 'My sister doesnae speak it to ye and Agnes?'

'Only when it be the three of us. 'Tis not fair to speak the Gaelic in front of Father. Ye ken he doesnae understand it. Besides, I've nae peers in London with whom to practise.'

Grizel's eyes lit up. 'Dear cousin, ye can practise with me all the while ye're here.'

Cuthbert switched to English, cultured and refined. 'Thank you, but it's far less taxing on my brain to think and converse in English.'

When Grizel opened her mouth to reply, Lachlan leapt to Cuthbert's rescue. 'Sister, I'll not have ye box his ears. Ye can talk the heads off Auntie Elspeth, Agnes, and her guest when they arrive.'

His sister skewered Lachlan with a death stare, which he ignored in favour of embracing his cousin. 'Good to see ye. I've missed yer pretty face.'

Cuthbert slapped him on the back and fired a teasing rejoinder. 'It's only pretty because you're used to looking at your own ugly face in the mirror.'

Lachlan roared with laughter and gestured towards the dining room.

During the meal, Cuthbert regaled them with news of London and answered Grizel's volley of questions about society, gossip, and fashion.

Caitrin asked, 'And what of the young lass travelling with my sister and Agnes?'

'Lady Helene Beckett,' answered Cuthbert. 'Her father is the Earl of Penforth.'

'He's a Whig?' asked Lachlan.

Cuthbert nodded. 'My father's good friend. Helene would be refused any association with you or our family if her father thought you supported the Jacobite cause.'

Lachlan agreed. 'There's much to be said about the company one keeps. I'm careful not to engage with Jacobite insurgents.'

'Very wise, else you'd have the wrath of the English at your door.'

'Aye,' said Caitrin. 'We're ever mindful of resentful clans who speak ill of us because we dinnae engage with partisans of the exiled Stuarts. We MacLanochs keep to ourselves, but our ties with the English through my sister's marriage has always raised the eyebrows on some and the hackles on others.'

Grizel fidgeted in her seat. 'All this talk makes me worry for the women's safety. I hope their carriage willnae be set upon without yer protection, cousin.'

Cuthbert pressed one hand to his chest and feigned a wounded heart. 'Sweet Grizel. Upon my life, I would never abandon a woman to the perils of danger. Rest assured we travelled here under the protection of the king's men. Sanctioned by King George himself. For this reason, I was able to leave my mother and sister and Lady Helene in safe hands and ride ahead to advise they'll arrive later this afternoon.'

Grizel smiled with excitement. 'I cannae hardly wait to greet them. I'll go now, Mother, to alert the housekeeper.' She stood and lifted the hem of her skirt to avoid tripping over it as she ran from the dining room.

'The king?' queried Lachlan.

'Yes,' said Cuthbert. 'It was a condition of Helene's father that we travel into the Highlands under the protection of a retinue of redcoats. Seems the earl has clout *and* the king's ear. No pressure, cousin, but she's yours and mine to protect.'

Helene. Lachlan was at a loss to understand why Drumocher Castle was her choice of destination. What young woman in her right mind, one with privilege and connections, abandoned the Season in London when it was in full swing? He found it difficult to believe she'd turn her back on high society in favour of spending time in the rugged Highlands. More to the point, why would her father allow it? There was more to this than Lachlan could fathom. Already she had his attention, but not his trust.

His mother voiced his next concern, asking Cuthbert, 'The soldiers. Will they make camp here?'

'No, Auntie. From here, the men will reach the nearest military garrison by nightfall.'

Caitrin gave a sigh of relief. 'Well then, before our guests arrive, I've a few last-minute preparations to oversee.' With a parting smile, she exited the dining room.

Lachlan adjourned with Cuthbert to the library, noting the way his cousin flopped into a chair in front of the fire. His head tipped to one side, supported by his hand with elbow bent on the chair's arm. The heavy sigh he expelled—the sigh of one burdened with a world of worries—had him sink deeper into the armchair.

'Wine or whisky?' asked Lachlan.

'Wine.'

Lachlan poured and handed Cuthbert a glass of claret before seating himself with a dram of whisky. *'Slàinte mhath.'*

'And to your good health too.' Cuthbert raised his glass and took a deep swallow of the red.

''Tis good to have ye visit us. I've missed ye this past year, and I'm verra sorry I couldnae spare the time to join ye in London for a while.'

'No apologies required. Our visit to the Highlands is long overdue. Besides, your mother was poorly, and you were needed here to ensure her recovery. She looks well, I might add.'

'Aye. The fever almost took her. She gets tired quickly, but in time her full strength will return.'

After a silent pause, Cuthbert's tone turned jovial. 'Your

non-attendance at the start of the Season's balls and social gatherings was noted by certain women with whom you are, shall we say, intimately acquainted.'

Lachlan sipped his whisky. 'Is that so?'

'On the other hand, I was not deaf to the whispers of those who exalted over your absence.'

'Namely?'

'Mothers who rejoiced knowing their debutante daughters would not fall prey to the charms of the Scoundrel Scot.'

Lachlan turned his head sharply towards his cousin. 'The Scoundrel Scot?'

'Their words, not mine.'

'I dinnae dally with debutantes!'

'Apparently, they believe you do.'

'An assumption that doesnae sit well with me.'

'Wipe the scowl from your face,' laughed Cuthbert. 'We're self-confessed rakehells, and now you suddenly develop a care and conscience for your reputation?'

'I'll concede there be nae difference between myself and the English libertines. We both bedded aristocratic ladies whose husbands failed to satisfy their needs, but ye ken verra well 'tis a rule of mine to leave debutantes and virgins well alone.'

'Those mothers and domineering matriarchs couldn't care a whit about your rules. To them, you're a savage Highlander and a threat to any mother's virtuous daughter, but don't let that stand in the way of our womanising wagers. In so saying, I propose a toast.' Cuthbert raised his glass. 'To next year's Season. We'll pick our prize and see which of us will be the first to bed her.'

Lachlan shook his head, knocked back the whisky, and laid the glass next to the bottle on a rosewood table between their armchairs. 'I've nae appetite for any future wagers. Even if I did, we both ken I'd win.'

Cuthbert's laughter ricocheted off the library walls. 'You're the most arrogant Scotsman I know.' He took a swallow of red and pointed a finger at Lachlan. 'Correction. I pronounce you the most arrogant *man* I know.'

'I'm a MacLanoch. What do ye expect? And dinnae forget the same blood runs through yer veins.'

'Well, thank God my mother married an English viscount, else I might have turned out like you. Wild, arrogant, and as scandalous as these Highlands you call home. I'd not trade a genteel life in London for anything in the world.'

'Genteel?' Lachlan quirked a brow and said with a wry smile, 'Dinnae ye mean ye're a regular Don Juan living under the guise of an English gentleman?'

Cuthbert shifted in his chair and rolled his shoulders as if to shrug off the truth of it.

Lachlan poured himself another dram. 'I'm just glad my luck with the ladies didnae drive a wedge between us.'

Cuthbert downed his wine, only to then stare into the empty glass. His lips compressed into a thin line and a troubled expression marred his fine aristocratic features. 'With all sincerity, and jesting aside, I hope nothing but the border ever separates us. No matter what the future holds.'

The pensive admission gave Lachlan pause. 'Sombre words. 'Tis not like ye.'

Cuthbert twirled the glass stem between his fingers. 'We're kin. That will never change, but it would destroy me if anyone were to cause a rift between us.'

The confession took Lachlan aback. 'What? A woman? Is that what ye're referring to? If it's our history of rakish rivalry that be playing on yer mind, I'll have ye ken I'll ne'er let a lass drive a wedge between us.'

'I pray nothing and no one stands between us.'

Those ominous words shifted something in the air, the

room silent save for the pop and crackle of the fire, rain tapping the windows, and the drumming of Cuthbert's manicured fingernails against his empty glass.

'Did ye not hear me?'

Cuthbert lifted his gaze to Lachlan. 'Do I have your word on that?'

'I cannae believe ye're asking it of me. Aye! Ye have my word.'

'Just making sure.'

A spark momentarily returned to Cuthbert's pale-blue eyes and disappeared in a flash. There was something about him in his manner and conversation that seemed oddly out of place.

Lachlan rose from his chair under the pretence of reassessing the dismal weather outside. At the window, he looked sidelong at his cousin sitting forlorn, shoulders slumped, and the empty glass tilted in his slack hand. It was a curious if not worrying image of a man who was otherwise nothing less than the life of any gathering.

There was power in a pause, and by giving Cuthbert space to his thoughts, Lachlan hoped his cousin might voluntarily speak of what had deepened his frown and induced his thirst for claret. The longer the silenced stretched, the more Cuthbert hunched his shoulders, resembling a man defeated and without purpose.

A pitiful sight.

Lachlan's patience ran dry. 'I ken ye too well not to ken something weighs heavy on yer mind. Will ye not tell me what it is?'

Cuthbert set the glass aside, made a half-hearted attempt to rise from the chair, and slumped back down into it. 'The deuce and all! I can't lie. Not to you.'

'What are ye talking about? What lie?'

Cuthbert levelled his gaze at Lachlan. 'You're right.

There'll be no more salacious wagers between us. At least not that which has us vying to bed another woman.' He heaved a deep sigh. 'Father has given me an ultimatum.' He buried his face in the palms of his hands.

Lachlan went to his side. 'It cannae be that bad.'

'You've no idea!' Cuthbert sprang to his feet and took to pacing the floor. He stopped abruptly, hands on hips, looking out over the misty moors. His shoulders lifted, his back expanding with each deep draught of air he took into his lungs.

'Out with it, man,' said Lachlan.

Cuthbert swung around. 'If I'm not married or at least engaged by this time next year, Father has threatened to cut me off and leave me penniless.' He slapped a hand to his forehead. 'Christ! I sure as hell don't want a wife! I'm not ready for marriage!'

He resumed pacing the floor like an animal committed to eternity inside a cage. For all that Cuthbert had been born to privilege, his future was not secure unless he married with the hope of producing an heir.

Lachlan sat forward on the edge of his seat.

'What is it?' Cuthbert helped himself to more claret. 'You look like you've been struck with an epiphany.'

'Lady Helene!'

'What about her?'

'Marry Helene.'

Cuthbert choked on the sip he'd swallowed. He drew a square of folded pressed linen from his coat pocket and dabbed his mouth. 'Marry her? What the deuce? Are you mad?'

'Not mad. Practical. She'd be yer perfect match. Similar upbringing and connections. Yer fathers are in thick with each other and of a like mind. In fact . . .' Lachlan stood.

'I hate it when you do that,' said Cuthbert.

'Do what?'

'Run a hand over your chin. Means you're overthinking something.' Cuthbert used the kerchief to wipe his brow.

'I had questioned why a lass of her station would make the arduous journey north to Scotland. To a stone-walled castle with no prospect of invitations to grandiose balls or social frivolities. Wouldnae the Highlands be anathema to her ilk?'

'Obviously not.'

'Then perhaps it's London and the marriage market she wishes to escape, or . . .'

Cuthbert rolled his eyes. 'Or what?'

'Do ye not think yer father and hers have set ye both up?'

Cuthbert's face was a picture of confusion. 'Where are you going with all this?'

'Given yer father's ultimatum and her father's decision to let her travel to the Highlands, do ye not think it possible both men hope for a match between ye two?'

Cuthbert flinched as if Lachlan had slapped his face. In the next moment, he threw his head back and sputtered, through uncontrollable laughter, 'Most intriguing, but you couldn't be further from the truth.'

He poked a finger in Lachlan's shoulder, and his face lit up with the dawning of a new idea. 'We'll make Helene our last conquest. Our last prize.' His eyes glittered with predatory excitement. 'Don't think for a moment she, or I, regard each other as marriage material, and besides, the chit thinks herself too good for any man. For us, that makes the thrill of the chase even more challenging.'

'Enough!' Lachlan took the glass from Cuthbert's hand and set it out of reach. 'Ye're spewing nonsense. 'Twould be a conflict of interest. Ye said yersel' that we're to protect her. Not ruin her.'

'I'm not suggesting we wager who'll be first to bed her. More like, sample her. Stealing a kiss will suffice in claiming victory.'

'Och! Ye've imbibed too much of my finest red. Let me make myself clear! Helene is nae prize to be had. If ye'll not consider her for yer bride, then neither will we dally with her and tarnish her reputation.'

Cuthbert strolled back to the window, where he stood looking out, hands clasped behind his back. 'The women will soon arrive. Before they do, I'm sure you'll shave the stubble from your face and run a comb through that mop of thick hair. I've no doubt you'll present yourself to Helene not as some Highland heathen, but as the honourable laird of Clan MacLanoch. Protector of your family, your clan, your livelihood.'

He turned and walked casually towards the library door. With hand on handle, he looked over his shoulder at Lachlan. 'If you won't play our game one last time'—he shrugged—'well then, you'll have to protect Helene from me.'

It was impossible for Lachlan to take his cousin seriously. 'Ye jest. Aye?'

Before leaving the library, Cuthbert flashed Lachlan a smug smile. 'One last thing. May the best man win.'

CHAPTER TWO

HELENE STARED IN awe through the carriage window as the brooding bulk of Drumocher Castle loomed large.

'Do you see it, Helene?' asked Agnes.

'Yes. I do.'

A wide expanse of hewn stone rose from steeply sloping ground like a sheer cliff face. At either end of the wall stood a strong tower, one four storeys tall, the other five. A series of slits and four pointed windows pierced the tower walls.

Uncontained excitement had Agnes point and say, 'See that glorious stretch of water nestling beneath the castle?'

'Very impressive,' marvelled Helene.

'It's a fine walk along the loch's shore. Perhaps tomorrow we can take a stroll. You'll never have taken air as clean and as fresh as you will here.'

Outside, the rain had stopped. As the carriage rolled closer, the bustling activity around the castle's curtain wall came to a standstill. People turned towards a sight sure to raise the hackles on any Highlander.

Redcoats.

Helene's nerves drew tight. 'Lady Sutton. How might the laird's clan receive me?'

Winged eyebrows shot up beneath a green silk bonnet. 'Whatever do ye mean?'

'Already I see the way they stare at the soldiers. Will they view me with the same contempt?'

'Ye might be what we call a Sassenach, but ye're a guest of mine and Agnes, and more importantly, a welcomed guest of the laird of Clan MacLanoch. Ye'll be shown the respect ye deserve.'

'Helene,' said Agnes. 'Have you forgotten that Cuthbert and I are half English?'

'That's different. You're relatives. I'm a complete outsider.'

Her friend laughed. 'As they say here in the Highlands, dinnae fash yersel'.'

The carriage had not quite reached the castle, and yet it slowed to a halt. There came the sound of galloping hooves. A conversation took place beyond the women's sight. To Helene, the indistinct exchange between a redcoat and a Scotsman at least sounded civil.

Through the window on her side, she observed the redcoats on horseback assemble in a group. Two coachmen, both soldiers, walked past the window towards the back of the conveyance where riderless horses, some carrying military supplies, had been tied for the journey. Within minutes, all the redcoats, with the remaining two packhorses in tow, turned their horses' heads away from the castle.

'What's going on?' asked Helene. 'Why have we stopped short of the castle's entrance, and why are the soldiers leaving?'

Lady Sutton peered through the window. 'I've nae idea. A handover, perhaps?'

Never one to await her fate, Helene decided it best to act and investigate. In the same moment that she half stood, leaned in, and turned the carriage door latch, it swung open, pulling her with it. She stumbled forward and out of the carriage, colliding with the solid strength of a man. The momentum forced the Scotsman back a step, with arms wrapped tight as a vice around Helene's waist and back.

Winded, she made the most unladylike grunt against the curve of his neck. Embarrassment held her fast until she heard, 'Are ye all right, lass?'

His breath brushed her ear as soft as a butterfly's wings, the sensation not in the least unpleasant, but to find herself in a situation so intimately aligned with a man? It was the stuff of scandal and ruined reputations. Neither of which she cared about. As for the genuine concern in his deep-toned words? *Pah!* Her acquaintance with men thus far proved they cared not for her well-being, but rather her sizeable dowry. Who was to say this broad-chested Scottish brute was any different?

'Lass?'

Agnes's tittering in the carriage restored Helene's wits. That, and the realisation she held the stranger in a tight embrace.

'No. I'm not all right,' she hurried to say. 'Something hard causes me discomfort.'

He set her feet on solid ground and let go. Helene made to draw back as fast as she'd fallen, unsuccessful in her attempt. His hands shot to her upper arms to steady her once again.

'Nephew!' said the viscountess from inside the carriage. ''Tis a blessing to see ye once again, but what on earth is going on?'

So, this was the laird of Clan MacLanoch? He stood taller than Helene and spoke over her head.

'Yer escorts are eager to reach their barracks before nightfall and have therefore refused our hospitality. I cannae say I'm disappointed. 'Tis not a good marriage between redcoats and Highlanders, and while I'm grateful to them for yer safe passage here, 'tis best for all they dinnae linger.'

'Aye. Well then, unhand the lass. 'Tis not the way of a proper introduction.'

'Cousin,' teased Agnes with a giggle. 'We've yet to set foot inside Drumocher, and already your hands seek to seduce my friend.'

'Agnes!' her mother fired back. 'Where *are* yer manners?'

Their conversation at her back caused the burn of a blush to creep up Helene's neck and cheeks. To the Highlander, she said, 'We seem to be stuck.'

'Aye, lass. Like bairns fused at birth.'

She braved a tilt of her head, their faces inches apart, and looked for the first time into a gaze filled with flecks of gold and brown.

In one transitory moment, his eyes dilated and darkened. His grip tightened on her arms, gaze dipping to her mouth.

Helene's pulse jumped, emboldened by an element of triumph. Were these signs to suggest she'd already sparked Lachlan MacLanoch's interest in her? Dare she believe she'd witnessed an inkling of potential, or perhaps a kernel of what might develop between them in the coming days, if only feigned on her behalf?

She whispered a polite command, their lips a breath apart. 'Pray, unhitch me, Laird MacLanoch.'

He seemed not to hear her. Then, 'Aye.'

His gaze fell to whatever the cause of their physical connection, giving Helene the briefest moment to study a handsome face fraught with a furrowed brow.

'My baldric,' he said by way of explanation.

He wore a leather cross-piece over his right shoulder, which reached down to the opposite hip holding his sword. The buckle on the baldric had caught on the weave of her woollen cloak.

'I'm trying to be careful, lass. Dinnae want to ruin yer fine clothes, mind.'

She said nothing, instead watching his large hand with long nimble fingers work to unhook the pin of the buckle from the cloak.

Once freed, he said, 'There now. A few pulled threads, 'tis all. I'll have the housekeeper mend it.'

He made no attempt to set distance between them. Another positive sign that, despite Helene's flirtatious inexperience, she used to her advantage by slowly meeting and holding his gaze. 'Thank you, laird.'

'Lachlan.' He took two steps back, held his right hand over his heart, and bowed. 'Lachlan MacLanoch. At your service.' He righted himself and gestured to the stone fortress. 'Welcome to Drumocher Castle.'

Helene dipped at the knee and inclined her head. 'Lady Helene Beckett.'

A quick glance at her surrounds and she saw a clansman seated aloft on the box seat, reins of the horse-drawn carriage in hand. Two other mounted clansmen waited at the ready, their eyes darting between Helene and their laird.

Lachlan MacLanoch approached the carriage, reached in, and kissed the back of Lady Sutton's gloved hand. 'Welcome, Auntie. 'Tis indeed a pleasure to have ye return to Drumocher. Mother eagerly awaits yer arrival.' He set her hand free and shifted his gaze to Agnes. 'Despite yer mischievous tongue, ye've grown more beautiful since last I saw ye.'

Agnes responded with a cheeky grin.

'Hurry along now, nephew,' said Lady Sutton. 'With no stepping block in sight, you'll have to assist Lady Helene back into the carriage. And do be quick about it. I grow more anxious by the minute to see my sister.'

The laird extended a hand in invitation towards Helene.

She went to him like an obedient wife, all too aware of the heat of his touch through her kid gloves. It caused her a sudden lapse in concentration so that when he said something, she grasped not one word. 'I beg your pardon?'

'When I lift ye into the carriage, mind yer head and be careful not to trip on yer skirts. Aye?'

She dipped her head in understanding.

He moved behind her, hands spanning her waist. In the next instant, he lifted her as if she weighed nothing at all and held her steady while her leather soles found purchase on the carriage floor. Agnes caught her hands, guiding her inside to sit on the velvet cushioned seat.

The laird nodded when Helene thanked him, but something shifted in his expression.

''Twas a rash move to alight the carriage before ye entered the gates of Drumocher. What were ye thinking, Lady Helene?'

The question took her by surprise. 'Curiosity got the better of me. Like your auntie, I had concerns over why the carriage had stopped.'

'Concerns?' His eyes darkened and his tone took a slight turn. 'Ye doubt my ability as laird to protect my kin? And ye?'

'No. I . . . I was concerned for our safety,' she countered. 'Our escort looked to be abandoning us, so I decided to take matters into my own hands.'

'And yet ye weren't abandoned. Nor will ye be whilst under my protection. 'Tis a promise I made to yer father and a promise I make to ye. Ye ken?'

Helene sat as still as a chastised child. 'I meant not to offend you, laird.'

'Nae offense taken. 'Tis turbulent times here in the Highlands, and curiosity, without regard to caution, can be a dangerous thing. Ye must be ever mindful of that.'

Helene squared her shoulders. 'I shall. Thank you.'

He gave a curt nod and closed the carriage door.

Agnes huffed. 'Well! I know my cousin to be a proud man, but I did not expect that performance from him.'

'Aye,' agreed her mother, dismayed. ''Twas most peculiar. I dinnae wish to make excuses for my nephew, but—'

'Please. No need to apologise.' Helene smiled to reassure the viscountess and Agnes. 'He's right. I should not have assumed there to be anything wrong. From what you've told me, Lady Sutton, your nephew has had much to contend with of late, what with his mother's recent ill health and a clan to care and cater for.'

The carriage lurched forward, the wheels rolling at a steady pace. Lady Sutton smiled as if in appreciation of Helene's understanding, then her spirits seemed to soar again at the prospect of reuniting with her sister. While Agnes engaged her mother in conversation, Helene peered through the window. She made a quick study of Lachlan MacLanoch riding a short distance from, and adjacent to, the carriage.

He sat tall and proud in the saddle. Hair the colour of her Baltic amber teardrop earrings sat level with his linen stock tie. A breeze fingered wavy locks, brushing the layers back from his face enough for her to observe him in profile. A nose as straight as his dialogue and instruction; a strong chin and jawline that looked to be hewn from the same granite as Drumocher's foundations. He was every bit the Highland laird, armed and dressed in belted plaid, crisp linen shirt and necktie, waistcoat and a brown woollen hip-length coat.

Helene's gaze sank lower, to the leather knee-high riding boots over long woollen socks. Seeing exposed skin between the top of his boots and the hem of the skirted plaid immediately brought his scent to mind. Fresh. His face soap-shaven. The aroma still lingering in her senses. How different he smelled compared to some of the intolerably cloying odour equalizers worn by London's nobility.

Lachlan MacLanoch smelled clean, natural, as if having bathed in a stream beneath a summer sun. Curiously, the very image of him doing so sent her stomach aflutter.

She lifted her gaze to catch him staring back at her. The scowl he wore wiped the smile from her face, and she pressed back against the plush squabs, no longer within his view.

Fool. You completely misread him.

His eyes had dilated when they'd stood face-to-face. She knew now the reaction was not because he'd seen something he liked, but because she'd angered him. Further validation of that had shown in his tight grip on her arms. Why then had her parted lips held his gaze if for no other reason than to contemplate kissing her?

They'd only just met and already she'd offended him. Something she must quickly remedy if her plan was to succeed.

The carriage rumbled through the castle's wide entrance, beneath the outer and inner portcullis, and into a bustling stone courtyard. Two carts lined the perimeter, one filled with hay, the other with chickens squawking in their caged confines. A series of rough logged structures hugged the castle wall. Within each, people busied themselves plying their trade, key to castle and clan needs and function.

In one, a cooper taught his apprentice the craft of barrel-making. In another, several women clad in dark-brown homespun sat at a spinning wheel, their feet working the pedal while joining more fleece to yarn. Next to them, a blacksmith toiled over an anvil, forging a weapon of lethal proportions. A stark reminder of the barbarous Highlands. Who would the blade claim as its first victim? Helene shuddered. Poor wretch, whomever it might be.

All this was a far cry from the prestigious New Bond Street

in London where the purveyors of luxury items peddled their wares in a more sophisticated manner to serve the beau monde.

A young woman's happy squeal had Lady Sutton and Agnes exchange a knowing look. Simultaneously, they grinned and said, 'Grizel.'

'The laird's sister?' Helene enquired.

'Yes. Sixteen and garrulous,' explained Agnes.

'My niece is an excitable delight,' said Lady Sutton.

The carriage had barely come to a halt when its door opened, a stepping block put in place, and there, proffering a helping hand, was Lady Sutton's son, Cuthbert.

'At last,' he beamed. 'Mother. Agnes. Lady Helene. How thrilled you must be to have finally arrived. Come, Mother. Let me assist you first.'

Next, Cuthbert helped his sister alight the carriage. She swept instantly into the welcoming arms of her cousin Grizel, and then towards the unfolding joyous reunion between her mother and widowed auntie, Caitrin MacLanoch.

Cuthbert returned for Helene, took her hand in his, and gave it a squeeze. Something was wrong. It was written on his face. In his narrowed eyes and deep frown. In the way his lips pressed together to form one severe thin line.

She hastened to ask, 'What is it?'

In a hushed voice, he said, 'There's been a change of plan.'

'Oh?'

'Lachlan has refused to play my little game.'

Helene's stomach dropped; she feared her quest had ended before it had truly begun. Despair must have shown on her face, for Cuthbert was quick to reassure her.

'You needn't worry. All is not lost. *Yet.* However, it seems my cousin is more intent on protecting you and your virtue, rather than making any attempt to seduce you. Regardless, you and I will proceed as arranged, only now you must do whatever it takes to weaken his resolve. Lead him astray, as it were. Hoodwink him into believing he has your interest and undivided attention, then turn him down and focus your efforts on me.'

Helene didn't try to understand the mind of a rake, nor what could only be egotistical games of one-upmanship. She kept her eye on the monetary prize, something Cuthbert reminded her of with his next breath.

'I'm paying you handsomely to follow through.'

Helene grimaced when his grip on her grew fractionally tighter.

'Fail me,' he warned in a whisper, 'and you'll not leave here with my promissory note. Understand?'

She heard for the umpteenth time her sister's scream inside her head. Helene had made not one promise, but two. She would honour both.

'Yes,' she whispered emphatically. 'Whatever it takes.'

CHAPTER THREE

HELENE HAD NOT spent what seemed like an eternity cooped up in a carriage traversing the countryside only to discover the laird of Clan MacLanoch had suddenly developed a moral conscience. Stalwart determination would not be thwarted just because he'd sworn to her father that she'd be well protected. Her father had read aloud to her that oath, pledged in the laird's own hand. Without it, the earl would not have consented to her visiting the Highlands.

It went without saying that virtue and reputation were key for an eligible, unmarried woman of good fortune. It therefore begged the question, what recompense had the laird guaranteed should he fail to keep good on his promise? Helene's father had not conveyed to her that part of the agreement.

Regardless, it remained a moot point. Her father had played into her plans, and that was all that mattered. If in fulfilling her one objective she returned to him safe but with the faintest whiff of scandal, then so be it. It didn't matter. She cared naught for, and did not seek, the good opinion of London society, or whether she was, or was not, deemed to be marriageable goods. If she secured Cuthbert's promissory note, she'd have money to be used as she wished.

As for her dowry? Her opinion on the matter was both

cynical and realistic. Marry, and her husband would do with her dowry as he wished. She'd not receive control over one penny of it. If she chose spinsterhood, her father would mete out an allowance as he saw fit. Either way she'd have no control over how and when *her* money would be spent.

Helene turned her mind to the art of flirtatious behaviour. A novice she might be, but she'd wield inexperience to her advantage like a weapon. All she need do was trip like a child learning to walk in hope of the laird taking her hand to guide her. If Lachlan MacLanoch determined not to seduce her, then she'd set about seducing him. She the spider. He the fly. He was no different to every other man who weakened to lustful temptation.

Helene glanced over Cuthbert's shoulder to see the laird swing out of the saddle. A stable lad instantly took up the halter of the horse and caught the reins the laird tossed him. Helene took stock of what she must do. Cuthbert's sudden firm grip on her hand came as a sober reminder that failure had no place in her plans.

'Mind your step,' he warned, commanding her focus. 'I wouldn't want you to trip.'

'Aye, lass,' said the laird on approach. 'Lest ye fall into the wrong hands.'

Cuthbert gave a startled laugh. 'Ah, cousin. Impeccable timing, as always. Who better than the laird of Drumocher to formally welcome the lovely Lady Helene Beckett?' He stepped aside and out of their way.

The laird appeared wary and switched his gaze from his cousin to Helene. 'I've already had the pleasure of doing so.' He seemed to notice the hand she rubbed. 'Are ye all right, lass?'

'Yes. Of course. Would you be so kind as to help me down?'

Before she could reach for him, he took her by the waist

as he'd done before, forcing her need to grip his shoulders. He lifted her from the carriage, setting her down and clear of the muddy ground surrounding the stepping block. Helene searched the planes of his face, taking in the shape and serious set of his mouth. She held on to him longer than propriety required.

Of course, he could have removed his hands from her waist, and yet, curiously enough, he didn't, instead waiting for her to initiate their separation. When she did, Helene averted her gaze to pretend interest in her surrounds and took in the portcullis under which they'd entered the courtyard.

He followed her gaze, explaining, 'We've accessed Drumocher from the north via a passage beneath the lord's tower.'

'The lord's tower?' asked Helene, marvelling at the imposing height of hewn stone.

'Aye. A private set of principal rooms, including the lord's hall and three storeys of family bedchambers. Ye've been assigned a chamber there.'

Her gaze fell to his face. Sudden awareness, together with his steady regard, left her with a feeling of unease. Not because she feared for her personal protection, but because, for the first time in her life, a sensation akin to pins and needles afflicted her body in the most private of parts. She flinched at the shock of it.

'Ye needn't have cause for concern, Lady Helene. This tower and its chambers are secure.'

Oh dear. How to explain? Helene swallowed and dragged her gaze from his. Another mistake, for he interpreted her dismissal of him as a personal affront.

'Ye doubt me again, lass?'

She looked him in the eyes, quick to placate any misunderstanding. 'No. Not at all. I merely wished to ask'—she pointed to the north and north-west walls—'where those two sets of external stairs lead.'

He considered her for a moment before indicating with a nod of his head. 'Over there, adjacent to the lord's tower, are stairs leading into the great hall, and the stairs there'—he pointed to the second tower to the west—'lead into the kitchens.'

'I see.' She refrained from asking what occupied the levels on the tower above the kitchen. There'd be plenty of time to explore.

'Come,' he said. 'My mother and sister anxiously await yer acquaintance.'

To her side, Helene caught the hint of a smile tug at one corner of Cuthbert's mouth. He sent her a scarcely perceptible nod, as if secretly approving of her discourse and coquettish ploy to feign attraction to and interest in their host. It made her feel dirty, unclean, as if he were a brothel-keeper pushing his whore towards the next client in line. And just like a whore, her reward was monetary gain from Cuthbert's purse.

Helene had long absolved herself of any guilt, safe in the knowledge she'd hatched a plan born of moral conviction, of a fundamental sense of doing what was humane and what was right by her sister. There was no price she wouldn't pay to secure her sibling's freedom from an institution destined to mistreat, destroy, if not kill her.

Cuthbert's smile twisted into a smirk. The smirk of a shallow rake. Was it his plan to best his cousin—by duplicitous means—in the art of seducing a woman? If so, how abhorrent to think a man would go to such great lengths to save face when his masculinity, pride, or ego was at stake. In this case, it served her purpose.

Helene moved forward with the laird at her side, mindful of the gathering crowd's curious stares. Any grave fears she harboured in thinking the clan displeased over having a Sassenach in their midst was quickly put to rest when a woman, unmistakeably Lady Sutton's twin, standing on the threshold of the lord's tower lifted her arms in greeting and beckoned Helene forth.

'My mother,' whispered the laird, by way of preparing her for their meeting.

Helene spared him a glance and was taken by his expression—filled with as much pride and affection for his mother as was spoken in his words. This quality of character surprised Helene. It struck something deep inside her, almost endearing the laird to her. What was it her mother had always said? *If a man is good to his mother, he'll be good to his wife.* Most inconvenient. She wasn't here to form attachments. He was a rake and no better than his cousin.

The young *excitable delight*, as Lady Sutton had described her, turned from her conversation with Agnes and looked towards Helene. Her eyes lit up like lanterns, and she went at once to stand at her mother's side.

'Your sister?' Helene enquired in a whisper to the laird.

'Aye.'

'So beautiful.'

'And wild,' he said under his breath moments before making introductions. 'It is my great pleasure to introduce ye to my mother, Lady Caitrin MacLanoch, and my sister, Grizel.'

Spoken with the love and devotion of a laird prepared to lay down his life for kin. *Blast the man!* Rakes weren't meant to show any manner of decency. They had a reputation for debauchery, breaking hearts, and ruining, without a care, virtuous women.

This introduction made things even more difficult. Helene had a conscience even if *he* did not. She hadn't expected to feel so culpable over her reasons for being here. Duping the laird was one thing, but to deceive his mother and sister?

No turning back now. Besides, what man seeks his mother or sister's comfort when he loses a conquest to another hell-raiser? When all was said and done, his wounded pride and deflated ego would prevent him from discussing the loss with anyone, save Cuthbert.

Helene dipped a low curtsy as Caitrin MacLanoch welcomed her with a gracious smile. The woman stood tall and straight. Braids were arranged in an elegant upswept hairstyle, and softly curled copper tendrils decorated her oval face. A finely knit capelet adorned a tartan olive-green dress trimmed in colours to match her hair. And her eyes, a shade lighter than her dress, focused kindly on Helene. She was, without doubt, a sophisticated woman of Highland aristocratic status.

Beside her mother, Grizel curtsied in kind. Inquisitive innocence danced behind eyes the colour of an autumn oak leaf. She had a dimple in her right cheek and a smile to brighten the darkest room. Long wavy hair cascaded down her back and shoulders in a shiny curtain, the copper colour a touch darker than her mother's.

'And this,' said Lachlan to his mother and sister, 'is Lady Helene Beckett, youngest child and only daughter to the Earl of Penforth.'

Only daughter? The woman behind the scream in Helene's head begged to be acknowledged.

'Lady Caitrin. Grizel. It is my honour to make your acquaintance. I come as a stranger to you and your clan, so it is with much gratitude that I thank you for taking me in as your guest.'

'Och! Such a wee, sweet lass ye be,' said Caitrin. ''Tis our great pleasure to have ye here. That ye would make the long journey is something to be admired. 'Tis not all young English ladies who'd feel safe, let alone have the desire to set foot in the Highlands.'

Helene pretended a sense of enthusiasm. 'Agnes has always extolled the wonderous beauty of the Highlands so much as to make me want to see it for myself. As for my safety?' She tipped her head at the man beside her and affected a smile of appreciation. 'I needn't worry on that account. Your son has solemnly sworn to protect and keep me safe.'

'Lachlan is a man of his word.' Caitrin laid a possessive hand on his arm. 'Isn't that right, son?'

'Aye.' He looked pointedly at Helene. 'As long as the lady trusts and abides by the laws of the realm, then her safety is guaranteed.'

'Perhaps then,' ventured Helene, intent on holding his gaze, 'you might, this evening, take a moment to sit with me and fully explain these laws of the realm. I'm in unfamiliar territory, and I wouldn't wish to step outside the mark. At least, not intentionally.'

The laird studied her with quiet regard. 'Aye. 'Twould be in yer best interest.' He looked skyward and squinted against the fall of light rain. 'Well then. Best we all move inside before this drizzle becomes a downpour.'

As the MacLanoch matriarch lifted her skirts to turn and do as her son had suggested, Helene could have sworn she caught just the hint of a smile on the older woman's lips. Certainly, before Caitrin had lowered her lashes, there'd been a tinge of amusement in her kind, shrewd eyes.

Helene mused over the point as she went with the women inside. The laird and his cousin followed behind, conversing in hushed Gaelic. *That* was something else she pondered, curious about the nature of their exchange, what with Cuthbert sounding jovial and the laird, terse.

Helene glanced around the tower's ground-floor entrance.

Weaponry, mounted stag heads, and intricate tapestries depicting hunting scenes adorned the interior stone walls. A wide staircase dominated the centre of the room and led to the first floor.

On the wall at the top of the stairs was a pair of three-quarter-length portraits. The first caused Helene to draw in a sharp breath. It had to be Lachlan's late father, dressed in full traditional Highland regalia. He looked proud, commanding. So striking in looks was Lachlan's resemblance to his sire that it held Helene in awe.

The woman in the portrait to the right smiled down at her. The same serene smile to have greeted Helene moments earlier. Caitrin MacLanoch. Just as elegantly dressed in person as was breathtakingly immortalised in pigmented oils in the ornate gold-framed painting.

'He might look fearsome, lass, and indeed he was,' whispered Caitrin to Helene, 'but he was the fairest of men with a good, kind heart. Just like my Lachlan.'

Helene acknowledged Caitrin's comment with a smile. How else could she be expected to respond? She had no first-hand knowledge of the late laird's character, nothing by which to draw an accurate comparison with his son. How could she tell Caitrin, if the woman did not already know, that her son's byname among the ladies of London's elite was the Scoundrel Scot? Was his womanising a learned behaviour passed from father to son? What wife and mother could be proud of that? The shame of it! Better Caitrin be left in the dark about her son's rakish reputation. It was not for Helene to wound the feelings of a doting widow and mother.

'Gather round,' said Caitrin, taking her sister's hand in hers. 'Ye and Agnes will remember the way to yer bedchambers.' She looked pointedly at Grizel. 'Lass, be a dear and accompany Lady Helene to her chambers. Refreshments and belongings will be sent directly to each of ye. Ye'll all have time to rest a wee bit before the evening meal.'

Lady Sutton said, 'If I've a mind for conversation before the meal, will ye be up to welcoming me in yer private quarters?'

'Aye, Elspeth. That I will. Lord knows I've been craving yer company for more months than I can count.'

Helene had taken an instant liking to Caitrin. She was all grace and poise and spoke with a humble heart. These sisters, twins, demonstrated a connection born of sibling love and respect. Such a pity that so many miles separated one from the other.

Cuthbert executed a bow. 'If you'll all excuse me, I'll go directly to the library and write to Father. He'll want to know we've arrived safely at Drumocher.' His eyes came to rest on Helene. 'With your permission, I'll do likewise in writing post-haste to your father.'

'Thank you, Cuthbert. Please let him know I'll write to him in due course. Once I'm settled.'

He favoured her with an obliging smile in reply. A smile reserved only for one of intimate acquaintance. She knew it to be a mask worn to conceal the deceit of his true intentions. A deliberate act to goad his cousin as if he, Cuthbert, was making progress in their rakish rivalry.

Helene was at once embarrassed by his public show of false affection and schooled her expression to show no more than gratitude for his offer to write to her father. Guilt, and only guilt, caused a blush to heat Helene's cheeks. She prayed the prevailing silence was not evidence of her blush being otherwise ill-interpreted by those in the room.

Cuthbert climbed the staircase and disappeared into a corridor. *Damn the man!*

Lady Sutton gave a polite cough and declared, 'I could do with a cup of tea.' Her face suddenly lit up as it does when one remembers something joyous. 'In my luggage there is a tea chest. Indian tea, I might add. Imported by the East India Company. A gentleman who goes by the name of Thomas Twining sells London's finest. Dearest sister, shall we have ourselves a long-overdue blether over a cup of tea?'

Caitrin laughed, the sound richly melodic and pleasing to Helene's ear. 'Ye have indeed adopted the ways of the Sassenachs, Elspeth. Of course I'll share yer tea, but if it's not to my liking, then a dram of whisky will doubtless improve its flavour tenfold.'

Lady Sutton's look of horror drew a laugh from her family and Helene.

Caitrin winked at her sister. 'The fever might have temporarily stripped me of strength, but it willnae stop me from teasing ye.'

Lady Sutton blew out a breath. 'I should have kenned ye'd tease me so.'

'Aye,' laughed Caitrin. She gestured the ladies away. 'Now off ye go. Make yerselves comfortable, and should ye require anything, the servants will assist ye.'

Helene chanced to look at the laird and found him staring at her. She felt instantly warm, if not strangely uncomfortable beneath his lingering scrutiny.

As if sensing her disquiet, Caitrin came to her rescue, softly reclaiming her son's attention. 'Lachlan, I'll need yer arm for support. Will ye see me to my private quarters?'

'Aye. Gladly.'

He gave Helene a courteous nod, via way of excusing himself, and went to his mother's side. She tucked her hand in the crook of his elbow, and together they ascended the staircase. Lady Sutton and Agnes followed, with Helene and Grizel at the rear.

Helene touched her hand to the ornately carved wooden

banister. Well-worn it might be, but its polished shine stood as testimony to the immaculate upkeep of her surrounds.

The laird and his mother branched right along the landing at the top of the stairs and into a corridor towards another stairwell. The company of ladies broke left along the landing, where another stone stairwell awaited them.

Helene paused for a moment directly in front of the late laird's portrait. His straight nose, strong chin, and the determined set of his jaw were not the only physical attributes he'd passed down to his son. She might as well have been looking at Lachlan thirty years from now, for the same penetrating golden-brown eyes stared back at her. Did those same eyes see through her?

She prayed not.

CHAPTER FOUR

LACHLAN STOOD FACING the fireplace in the lord's hall. Here, he awaited the others before joining the clan for the evening meal in the heart of Drumocher. Mesmerising flames drew him deeper into thought about Lady Helene Beckett.

He replayed the moment the carriage door swung open and a face, lovely and as fresh as a new spring day, reacted in surprise, if not shock, at seeing him. In the trajectory of her fall, he saw the lifting of eyebrows, the widening of eyes, and her mouth dropping open.

Though she fell hard against him, her body was all softness and curves. Full breasts, hidden beneath a thick woollen cloak, pressed against his chest. Stomach as flat as the blade of his broadsword. If his hands could speak, they would tell of a trim waist, the swell of hips, and a fine-boned back.

On impact, her warm breath heated the flesh beneath his jaw. It shot a chilling shiver clear to his boot-clad feet, a sensation he hadn't experienced since slipping into the loch one winter when he'd been a careless, curious wee lad. Lesson learned, never to be repeated. But this? This tremor delivered a warning, a warning that if left unheeded might see him slip forever beneath a surface more impenetrable than the ice on that winter's loch.

Dangerous, and with no means of deliverance.

The omen was loud and clear. He must stay focused and overrule distraction, for hers was the kind of radiant beauty to bewitch mere mortals. If Cuthbert was correct in saying she believed herself too good for any man, then Lachlan would refuse her the satisfaction of perceiving him in any way enchanted with her.

It took one ego to recognise another, and she was sorely mistaken if she expected Lachlan to fall at her feet. He almost laughed out loud, thinking himself a hypocrite. Now he understood why, according to Cuthbert, females of the London set had dubbed him the Scoundrel Scot. He'd wooed women into his bed and gave them not a second thought the following morning. Like Lady Helene, he had neither the time nor the interest for matters of the heart.

Even if it had pleased him to do so, dalliance of any kind with this English lass was simply out of the question. She would return home in the same state as she'd arrived: safe and virtuous.

Caitrin MacLanoch's furtive smiles and surreptitious glances had said otherwise. It wouldn't be the first time his mother tried to matchmake him with a lass she deemed to be promising marriage material. If she had plans afoot between Helene and himself, then the dowager would have to weather another disappointment. A bride and bairns would have to wait.

Best to remain the unattached laird and to closely guard personal autonomy and the well-being of his people. If such a woman existed to whom he'd genuinely surrender his heart, then let it be God's will.

Until then . . .

He glanced up at the stag's head mounted on the wall above the fireplace. Seeing it, with its majestic antlers and rich red-brown coat, reinforced Lachlan's reasoning. Celtic tradition served to remind him the animal symbolised independence and pride, being king of the forest and protector of all other creatures. The noble beast's lifelike glass eyes stared down at Lachlan, calling to attention his one true priority. Clan MacLanoch. Its people and their welfare.

And yet, being in Helene's embrace had given him a measure of comfort. She'd held him long and fast in the same way he'd clung to his father when pulled from the icy loch and dragged to safety on that cold, wintry day.

Safe. Restored from harm. Alive.

He'd saved the lass public embarrassment and the indignity of an ungraceful fall from the carriage, preventing the possible snapping of an ankle or breaking a limb.

Granted, the king's men had safely delivered their charge hundreds of miles from her home and to within three hundred yards of Drumocher. Had Helene sustained an injury during their handover, then Lachlan would appear the incompetent dolt in her father's eyes. It would have been a blow to his pride and prowess as laird of Clan MacLanoch. Any incompetence on his behalf would be a slight on every Scotsman.

His word was his honour. Protect the lass at all costs. Damn but he didn't need the bothersome responsibility. More pressing matters were at hand than to keep safe and shadow the skirts of a privileged blue blood. He wished Agnes hadn't devilled him about agreeing to Helene's visit.

If only the inquisitive lass had stayed seated in the carriage instead of taking matters into her own hands. He hoped her thoughtlessness did not foreshadow future rash decisions. There was nothing to be done about it now other than to remind her to think before she acted. He'd enlighten her to ensure no misstep or breach of clan protocol when it came to her safety.

I'm in unfamiliar territory, she'd claimed. The irony of those words was not lost on Lachlan. He looked down at his open palms and shook both hands. The action did little to cast off the searing memory of how perfectly each hand had moulded to her waist.

'Curse the lass for a witch!' he said.

'I beg your pardon?'

Startled, Lachlan swung around to see his cousin leisurely seated, long legs outstretched and crossed at the ankles, along the window seat of the wood-panelled alcove. 'Christ, Cuthbert! Ye nearly scairt me to death.'

'Definitely not my intention. Besides, you can't go dying on me just yet. Not before I've won our very last wager.'

The cocky comment put Lachlan on the back foot. 'There is nae wager. We've already agreed on that.'

'Correction. You agreed. *I* did not.'

Lachlan crossed the width of the hall. 'What's wrong with ye?' he said in a terse whisper, worried their conversation might be overheard. 'Yer father threatens ye with an ultimatum for marriage, and suddenly ye want to destroy the reputation of a young lass who seeks neither yer attentions nor mine. I'll not let it happen. Not under my roof. Lady Helene is here as a guest of Drumocher, not as yer lecherous plaything.'

Cuthbert had the audacity to look hurt. He raised arched blond brows. 'Steady on. You're being a tad melodramatic. I hardly think stealing an innocent kiss brands me a lecher.'

'Neither does it make ye a gentleman.'

'A gentleman?' Cuthbert barked with laughter. 'Cousin, we are, by birth, gentlemen. I the son of an English viscount and you of the Highland gentry.' With a flourish of his hand, he emphasised, 'The *dhaoine-uaisle*.'

'Being of noble birth is nae guarantee of any particular merit.'

'Good Lord, cousin! You *have* mounted a high horse. Charm and good looks are all it takes to seduce a woman, so when, pray tell, did gentlemanly tactics tip the balance of your scales?'

From the moment an obstinate, self-willed Sassenach fell into my arms!

The self-admission caught Lachlan by surprise. God forbid he confess the words out loud. He drew breath and released it on an exasperated sigh. He went to the hall's open door and pushed it shut to keep their conversation private.

Cuthbert swivelled where he sat and swung his feet to the floor. He pointed a finger at Lachlan. 'If I heard correctly, you said, "Curse the lass for a witch." Does Helene already have you under her spell?'

'Spell? Dinnae be ridiculous!'

Cuthbert sat straighter and folded his arms. An enlightened smile spread across his face. 'Of course you are. Otherwise, you wouldn't deny it so vehemently.'

'I met the lass a matter of hours ago and ye think me smitten?'

Cuthbert shrugged. 'You'd not be the only man to have been smitten at first sight.'

'Have ye been drinking my red again?'

Cuthbert laughed. 'No.'

'Then I think 'tis ye who's taken with the lass.'

'Wrong again, but do indulge me.' Cuthbert leaned forward and cocked one eyebrow. 'Is she not the most exquisite beauty you've ever laid eyes on?'

Lachlan turned his back on Cuthbert and settled himself in an armchair near the hearth.

'A simple yes or no will suffice,' said Cuthbert.

'Nae!'

'No?' Cuthbert rubbed the heel of his hand on the glass

pane through which he could see the drizzle-drenched moors beyond. 'I fear your vision is as foggy as this window.'

'All right! She is pretty, but—'

'And those eyes! Emerald jewels if ever I saw a perfect pair. They're as piercing as a sword to the heart.'

'I pray I dinnae ken the pain of a sword through my heart.'

Cuthbert eyed Lachlan with a manner of reserve. 'When you do, figuratively speaking, you'll recognise it as Cupid's bow. Only then will you know you're truly in love.'

'Hah! What de ye ken about love?'

Cuthbert blinked once, then twice. Seconds before turning his gaze to the dismal day outdoors, he'd taken on the same troubled expression as he had in the library earlier today. Lachlan refrained from further goading his cousin in favour of asking, 'Ye speak as if from experience. Do ye keep another secret from me? Are ye in love?'

'Most definitely not!'

An adamant denial, spoken with his back to Lachlan. Would Cuthbert's eyes tell a different story? Gut instinct said his cousin had no wish to shed the weight of another matter. Perhaps he shouldered more than his father's threat of disinheritance if he were not married, or at least engaged, within the year.

To reach out to Cuthbert once more, Lachlan rose from his armchair and walked to stand behind his cousin. As he opened his mouth to speak, the door opened and swung wide. His mother and auntie glided into the room, arm-in-arm and in deep conversation. They went directly to sit near the warmth of the fire.

Cuthbert stood with a nod in their direction. Only then was Lachlan given the opportunity to fully appraise Cuthbert's attire, from his meticulously fashioned queue tied with a black silk ribbon, to his leather buckled footwear.

Without a doubt he looked the dashing gentleman, wearing a three-piece suit of coat, waistcoat, and breeches. The pale-blue pastel suit, with embroidered gold and silver thread, marked him a man of elegant status. The expensive addition of lace jabot, decorative cuffs, and silk stockings made him look like a contemporary of King Louis XIV in the Palace of Versailles.

For Cuthbert to flaunt his class distinction and fashion to excess, here in Drumocher, was not without purpose. The moment he turned his gaze towards the open doorway with an air of anticipation, that purpose became apparent to Lachlan.

Helene!

A smug, predatory smile lit Cuthbert's face. He gave Lachlan a sidelong glance and whispered, 'Don't get your hackles up. There's really no harm in pursuing *one* kiss.'

Had Lachlan not clenched his fists, his hands would have tightened like a noose around Cuthbert's neck. The sudden urge to wilfully harm his cousin was both alarming and wrong on so many levels. He found it hard to stand by and watch Cuthbert greet Helene, bowing low over her hand in his, and to hear flowery salutations in praise of her appearance.

She presented as a picture of elegant beauty, with hair piled and pinned up to accentuate the column of her slender neck. Her modest attire surprised Lachlan. He'd expected her to have dressed in a manner typical of London's expensive fashion. Instead, she'd chosen to wear something of simple design and comfort.

Understated though it might be, the low-cut bodice drew his gaze. There, her skin, white as winter's first snow, rose and fell with the gentle rhythm of her every breath.

Lachlan's body reacted to the memory of those breasts pressed against his chest. Curse the involuntary stirring in his groin! He would have looked away if not for Helene catching his eye. She fleetingly acknowledged him with a subtle nod and a polite smile before refocusing on Cuthbert and his idle conversation.

He had watched Cuthbert woo countless women over the years. All for the sake of a flippant wager. What then was so different about this moment that it should cause Lachlan this stab of envy?

He resented Cuthbert for not ceasing his petty game, for defying instructions to leave *this* lass well enough alone. She was not some trophy to be pursued like hounds excited by the scent of a fox.

If Cuthbert refused to desist, then why not bring an end to the chase and be the first to kiss Helene and claim victory? Be done with it. The idea held appeal. Following through would come at a cost, though. Lachlan would be damned if he'd compromise his honour for the sake of a mere kiss. He'd uphold his promise to Helene's father to protect and keep her out of harm's way. Right now, harm's way took the form of an overdressed, fair-haired rake.

Before Lachlan could intervene, his sister and Agnes swept into the room, joining Cuthbert and Helene in lively conversation. Grizel ran her hand along Cuthbert's sleeve in an enthusiastic exploration of the rococo-inspired cloth.

Lachlan turned away from their frivolous, fashion-inspired conversation, preferring instead to send his gaze to the cloud-covered mountains beyond the window. There, in the fading light, he looked for signs of the weather improving tomorrow. He breathed in and detected a distinct fragrance in the air. Violets.

'Lachlan?'

The soft voice had him immediately turn his head, there to see those emerald-green jewels Cuthbert had so aptly described.

'Is it all right that I call you Lachlan? Or would you prefer—?'

'Aye,' he replied, if not a little too quickly. ''Tis all right, lass.'

'Then you may call me Helene.'

Lachlan raised a brow. 'Might I now?'

She hesitated. 'Only if it pleases you.'

'It pleases me.'

Damn but her smile and colour-flushed cheeks pleased Lachlan too. Why then did something about those emerald eyes unnerve him? Perhaps because they had the power to hold him captive.

'Have ye settled in?' he asked by way of polite conversation.

'Yes, thank you.'

'And yer bedchamber is comfortable and to yer liking?'

'Indeed. The window affords a magnificent view of the loch, and the steep-sided mountains and wooded slopes make it quite picturesque.'

'Even more so with favourable weather.' Lachlan had not anticipated her prompt approval of his beloved Highlands.

'I'm sure it is. Cuthbert speaks fondly of the loch and its surrounding beauty. Weather permitting, he's keen to show me the quiet glens and hidden caves concealed behind waterfalls. I should very much like to see it all.'

So that was his plan? Coax her into the woods and take advantage of her beneath a canopy of leaves. *Damn him!* Already Cuthbert schemed to expedite wooing and winning Helene.

Lachlan's fingers clenched into a fist again when he glanced briefly at his cousin. 'Aye. The Highlands are all that and more, but be warned. The woods and the animals within can be as dangerous as they are bewitching.'

She tipped her head slightly to one side. 'Do you mean to frighten me?'

'I wish only to caution ye. We'll speak more of it during the evening meal.'

Lachlan rallied and readied his family to move towards the great hall. He offered Helene the crook of his arm, lest Cuthbert beat him to it.

Helene conceded how well Cuthbert knew his cousin, right down to the subtle nuances of body language and facial expressions. Lachlan had reacted to her presence just as Cuthbert had predicted: Standoffish, yet watchful. Confident, albeit with an air of rigid tension.

She'd caught the slight shake of his head as if in censure of Cuthbert's flirtatious approach when first she'd entered the room. The grudging admiration in the laird's narrowed eyes for the ease with which Cuthbert engaged her had turned to disapproval when she'd responded to Cuthbert's attentions.

In her peripheral vision, she'd caught the laird appraise her from head to toe. She'd whispered her observation to Cuthbert, whose opinion it was the laird found her pleasing to the eye.

Encouraged by this, and in the count of a heartbeat, she'd locked eyes with her host and had done her best to convey a coquettish smile. Alas, her luring attempt and subtle nod failed to entice his participation in her conversation with Cuthbert. A snub, no less. Any gentleman with a modicum of good manners would indulge her. *Arrogant man!*

Wounded pride would not deliver what Helene had come for, and she most certainly would not stand by and be ignored.

The arrival of Agnes and Grizel had given her the

opportunity to approach the laird. Dropping formality and speaking only his first name, without first being invited to do so, proved to be a bold move. Nonetheless, it had garnered his attention, his approval, and his acceptance to address her as Helene.

Using one's given name betokens familiarity, and it set Helene one step closer to achieving her goal. Only then could she return home with Cuthbert's promissory note and set her sister free.

When she'd mentioned Cuthbert's offer to walk her through the woods, Lachlan had furrowed his brow, hands clenched at his sides, and delivered a terse cautionary warning about hidden dangers.

Now, Helene smiled and graciously accepted and settled her hand in the crook of his arm. Muscles hardened beneath the jacket sleeve. Remarkably, he looked at Helene with no expression of having tensed at her touch.

Odd. She hadn't sensed the same kind of tension in him when she'd fallen from the carriage into his solid strength, and yet, just now, she saw a glimmer of awkward vulnerability in his eyes. She'd misread his reactions once before and might well have done so again. Time would tell, but one thing was for sure, she had influence over him, be it for better or for worse.

He led her and the family along a corridor and down several stone steps to a large wooden door. Lachlan unlatched the handle with his free hand. It opened inward to reveal a wide, spacious hall humming with conversation. People seated at rows of banquet tables immediately stood and quietened at the sight of their laird and his family.

It dawned on Helene that not once had she accepted the arm of any man other than her father or her brother. Had she done so in London, it would suggest something of an intimate nature, the forming of a couple, an alliance, as it were.

It followed, then, that entering the great hall on the arm of Drumocher's laird must surely send a powerful message to all who witnessed it. Not only was it a display of his acceptance of her in his stronghold, but it would be easy for anyone to perceive something more than friendship existed between the laird and herself.

Of course, there was not a skerrick of truth to the latter. They were no more than half-day-old acquaintances. She, a guest of Drumocher, and he, the obliging host.

Helene ruminated over him genuinely believing Cuthbert's intention to steal from her a kiss. It explained why the laird placed himself in her path: to protect her from and stave off the improper attentions of his cousin.

Another redeeming quality she begrudgingly admired about her host. If being a capable protector was his strength, then she'd seek to make it his undoing.

He seated her between himself and Agnes, with Cuthbert tucked away at the end of their table. Glass of wine in hand, Lachlan remained standing and addressed his clan in Gaelic. Helene understood not a word of it. When he spoke his auntie and cousins' names, they became the centre of attention, with warm smiles and respectful nods directed at each one of them.

He continued speaking in Gaelic and then suddenly paused. Helene glanced up to see his eyes upon her. The words *Lady Helene Beckett* passed his lips with what sounded like all manner of kindness and respect, and there was a halting intensity in his eyes. Something in their momentary connection struck her, something such as she could not describe, yet it felt not at all unpleasant.

She was the first to break from their gaze to see all eyes were now upon her. Lachlan continued in his native tongue.

Helene's sense of disquiet fell away when drinking vessels were raised and smiling faces resoundingly echoed his last word.

To her left, Agnes laughed and said, 'No need to look so ill at ease. Lachlan has welcomed my mother, Cuthbert, and me home to Drumocher.' She giggled, winked, and leaned closer to Helene to whisper, 'He welcomed you too, speaking very highly of the *beautiful* Lady Helene Beckett. Now the feast begins.' She raised her glass. '*Slàinte!*'

Beautiful? A wasted compliment paid many times over in her lifetime. She cared not for flattery coming from the mouths of ingenuine admirers incapable of seeing past her physical attributes and dowry.

Had Agnes not secretly interpreted what Lachlan said, she'd never have known. *Beautiful.* Why say it at all? Coming from a man who had no selfish agenda or reason to flatter her, it left Helene in a state of quandary.

She turned to Lachlan beside her. 'Thank you for welcoming me into your home.'

He nodded and raised his glass. '*Slàinte mhath!* Good health.'

Helene clumsily repeated the toast and sipped her wine. No sooner did she set it down than a servant refilled it. A procession of servants placed platters of food on their table and those of the clan.

'Please.' Lachlan gestured to the food. 'Eat.'

Her stomach rumbled in response to breathing in mouthwatering scents of rich, succulent meat, roasted vegetables, and freshly baked bread. She helped herself to the tantalising fare.

'This meat,' she said, chewing and savouring the flavour. 'What is it?'

His gaze settled on her lower lip. She held still when tentatively he raised his hand, met her gaze, then refocused on whatever it was to have drawn his interest. With one thumb he wiped her chin, slow and gentle.

Helene's tongue darted out to lick what must be the meat's juice dripping from her lip. In so doing, the tip of her tongue flicked the laird's thumb when he brushed it over her mouth. She jerked back, sensitive to the tingle of his touch. In an instant their eyes met, leaving Helene at a loss to know what to do or say.

'Venison,' he replied, tasting the juice on his thumb. 'Red, and roe deer.'

Helene averted her gaze and broke off a chunk of bread. She took a moment to settle her nerves. 'They roam your estate?'

'Aye. On moorland, woodland, and right up to the mountain tops.'

'Will I have the opportunity to see one?' She popped the bread in her mouth while preparing a forkful of vegetables.

'I hope so. 'Tis an unforgettable encounter when ye do.'

'Why?' Courage returned and she looked him in the eye. She hoped not to appear rattled by what had just passed between them.

'Red deer are majestic and make for an impressive wildlife spectacle, while roe deer'—he paused and ran his eyes over her face—'are striking and delicate.'

Helene swallowed to moisten the sudden dryness in her throat. 'Do either one of them have any natural predators?'

He glanced over her head in Cuthbert's direction. 'Nae, save for the men who hunt them.'

Helene sought to change the subject and so gestured to his empty plate. 'You've not eaten anything. Not hungry?'

'Famished.' He took a sip of wine before piling his plate with food.

'Are there poachers on your land?'

'Sometimes.'

'And the penalty if caught?'

'Depends on whether they are poaching for money or their pot. 'Tis in their interest as well as mine not to make an unnecessary kill.'

Guilt pressed upon Helene's shoulders. She was no better than the poachers, feeding off her host to line her coffers. What punishment would the laird deal her if he learned the truth behind her visit?

'Speaking of predators.' He stabbed a chunk of meat.

The action startled Helene. 'Yes?'

'Danger and treachery in the Highlands are nae different to the subtleties of London's society, courts, and ballrooms. One must know when to voice an opinion or remain tactfully quiet. Which path to tread and with whom. Do ye understand?'

'Precisely.'

'Then ye'd be wise to do as I say in all manner of things. Ye have my protection and that of my clansmen, but if ye were to wander and walk alone outside of Drumocher, I cannae guarantee yer safety.'

'Goodness! Whatever must you think of me? The only place I wander alone are the corridors and gardens of my father's estate.'

'Then use Drumocher as ye would yer father's home. Ye're free to explore it as ye wish. Wander outside its walls, alone, and ye risk all kinds of danger. The Highlands, like London, has its dark side.'

'Such as?'

'Ruthless men who'd do ye all manner of harm. Ye're a woman *and* a Sassenach. A prime kidnapping target for those who support the Jacobite cause. Then there are those who trespass on my clan lands for reasons of being pursued by the law, or perhaps they filch from my streams and woodlands or simply wish to provoke a skirmish.'

'I see. Thank you for the warning.'

'One more cautionary word.' He ran a hand over his chin and wore the expression of a man deep in thought.

'What is it?' Helene prompted.

He leaned in close to Helene and quietly said, 'My cousin.'

'Agnes?'

'Nae. Cuthbert. Be wary if left alone in his company. His reputation is such that—'

'I'm well aware of his reputation. And *yours*, Lachlan MacLanoch.'

With his face only inches from hers, Helene seized the opportunity to court triflingly with him and did her best to form a seductive smile. 'Am I to be wary if left alone with you?'

A muscle ticked along his jaw. 'I promised yer father ye'd come to nae harm while in my care. I'm a man of my word, despite what ye might think of me.'

'I didn't voice my opinion of you, only that your reputation, like Cuthbert's, is such that—'

'Yer innocence is safe with *me*, Helene. Of that ye can be sure.'

He did not pull back but rather held her gaze as if daring her to dispute his word and tear down his honourable wall.

His forthright declaration induced in Helene feelings of rejection. Nonetheless, it made her determined to succeed in the art of seduction. All walls were penetrable. It was simply a matter of locating its weakest point.

'I shall heed your warnings to the best of my ability. Should I falter in any way, then I trust you'll be there, as you were this afternoon, to catch my fall.'

CHAPTER FIVE

HELENE AWOKE WITH a start. Semi-darkness prevailed, and for a moment she didn't recognise her surrounds. Memory returned, grounding her inside a bedchamber at Drumocher Castle in the Scottish Highlands. She yawned and stretched both arms above her head while gently rolling her hips from side to side, content and sated from a good night's sleep.

Reality dawned and with it, guilt. Always the guilt. Here she lay, safe and comfortable in a warm, soft bed, knowing a meal of substance awaited her at her leisure. Not so for her sister, Prudence, confined to a cold, dank room with a hard bed on which to sleep. How hellish it must be to suffer the noise of insanity all around and the chink and clatter of sets of keys locking and unlocking cells. Meals were no better than pigswill.

Entitlement held no joy for Helene. With every waking moment, she despaired for poor, wretched Prudence. How could Father and her brother have agreed to lock her up with lunatics? What would Mother say if she were still alive? Prudence was neither mad nor mentally unstable.

Helene flung back the covers and padded on bare feet across the rug-covered floor to the window. She pushed the curtain aside to see the loch bathed in a pre-dawn silvery glow. Mist hovered above the water's surface, and fog hugged wooded slopes on mountains beyond. The stillness presented a picture of peace and stirred hope for her atonement and better things to come. Being here in the Highlands was all part of her plan to make right that which she'd done wrong by her sister all those years ago.

Already the courtyard below buzzed with a flurry of activity. Women drew water from the well, and several young lads scurried towards the kitchen tower with armfuls of brushwood.

The sun would soon rise, and what better vantage point to greet the day than from the castle's curtain wall? There'd be time to explore the castle and wander at will before joining Agnes and her family for the morning meal.

A basin provided a splash of water to her face, after she made use of the privy stool. No need to summon the attentions of a lady's maid. Helene preferred to dress herself. From the mahogany wardrobe she fetched and donned her woollen skirts, bodice, and shawl and pinned her hair with minimal fuss.

Servants were already afoot, evidenced by a lit wall sconce illuminating the corridor outside her chamber. Helene trod carefully up the ascending stairwell, its stone steps worn, steep, and uneven. One hand supported her on the wall to the left, the other on the central stone newel. At its summit she entered a small enclosed landing with a bench to one side. A cross breeze through two narrow slits kept the area well ventilated.

The door opened directly onto a narrow pathway behind a crenelated wall. She stepped outside, closed the door, and imbibed a lungful of cool, crisp air. A short stroll to one corner of the wall presented a view to snatch away one's breath.

Fingers of sunlight broke the horizon, and treetops sprouted through shifting fog. Birdsong emerged with the gradual light of day, and a horse whinnied from stables below. The sun rose gradually higher, its rays dissolving the mist and transforming the loch into a glittering pool of yellow-gold under what promised to be a cloudless sky. Helene wrapped tight the shawl around her, tipped her head to the sun's glow, and welcomed its warmth on her face.

The early hour heralded a good start to the day, and there, on the east-facing wall, she stayed until the sun broke free of the horizon. The rugged landscape took on a plethora of colour, with hues and shades of purple, green, and yellow reflected on the loch's calm surface.

Prudence. If only she too could witness this savage beauty. Despondent, Helene walked the perimeter of the wall where it led to the kitchen tower to the west.

She pushed through another solid door and breathed in the scent of freshly baked bread. It triggered her hunger, and her mouth watered. Locating the kitchen was easy enough. All she had to do was descend another turnpike stairwell and follow the smell and sounds of a frantic castle kitchen.

Never would she have thought to set foot in any of the servants' quarters in her father's manor, so it was not surprising that her presence here in Drumocher's kitchen raised more than a questionable brow. Natural curiosity had her stand to one side as silent observer, intrigued with the intonation of Gaelic shouts, commands, and conversation.

A small army of staff worked around one long central table, each with a dedicated task to scrape and chop vegetables, pluck lifeless fowl, scale fish, and cleaver joints of meat.

Two large hearths blazed, one with a cauldron slung on a hook over the open fire and another being prepared with a long pole on which a servant skewered meat for roasting. He took a large knife in hand, engaged Helene in eye contact, and sharpened the utensil on the solid stone wall. A shiver ran the length of her spine.

A slosh of water drew her attention to a servant scrubbing pots and plates in an oversized barrel. Another man poured away what looked to be dirty water through a sink built into an outside wall.

'Are ye lost, my lady?'

Startled by the matter-of-fact question, Helene turned to see a woman well into her years, hands on hips, standing behind her. 'You speak English?'

The woman looked taken aback. 'We're not as backward as ye might think, my lady. Aye,' she said with a half-hearted smile. 'I ken English. As do most of us.'

Helene was embarrassed for having shown such ignorance.

The cook wiped her perspiring brow with the back of one hand and added, 'Only when required of us, mind.' Her tone suggested speaking English was as much of an inconvenience for these Highlanders as it was to have Helene in their kitchen.

'I'm not lost,' said Helene. 'I merely wish to better acquaint myself with Drumocher.'

The woman raised greying eyebrows. 'Aye. Weel then.' She spread her arms wide. 'Here ye are amidst our humble preparations for the midday meal.' She dusted floured hands on her apron. 'Are ye hungry? Because if ye are, best eat yersel' something now. The morning meal is done and over with.'

'Already?' It was still early morning.

'Aye. The great hall is in use for other matters.'

Helene's confusion must have shown on her face.

'Our laird has a list of grievances between clansmen to deal wi' and settle before the midday meal.' The cook gathered a selection of bread and pastries on a plate. 'Do ye wish to be served in the privacy of yer bedchamber, or the lord's hall, my lady?'

Helene quite enjoyed these simple surrounds. 'Here will do.'

A pastry fell from the cook's hand to the floor. 'Here? In the kitchen?'

'Unless I'm in your way.'

'Nae,' said the cook, stooping to retrieve and replace the pastry with another. 'As ye wish.'

The cook spouted a string of words in Gaelic to an underling, who cleared space on a separate benchtop and fetched a stool for Helene. There she ate the freshly baked fare, thinking about Lachlan acting as judge and jury and presiding over what sounded like a court of petty sessions.

Before long she noticed the conversation between servants had died, and though each diligent worker went about their duty, Helene caught their wary, surreptitious glances. Again, her father and brother came to mind. They'd be horrified to see her eating in the company of servants. Strange, she felt oddly at peace here in the culinary hub of Drumocher.

At the same time, she remained ever mindful of the confronting disapproval. She finished her mouthful and stood to leave, aware her presence made these good people uneasy.

'Thank you,' Helene said to the cook. 'Which is the quickest way to the great hall?'

'By way of the servery, my lady, but 'tis for servants. I dinnae expect ye to—'

'Through the servery is fine.'

Chatter flared at her back the moment she left the kitchen, leaving Helene more than a little intrigued as to the content of their conversation. It mattered not, for she'd soon be a forgotten memory in this castle.

From the servery she entered a door at the back of the great hall, surprised to find it packed with people standing stock-still. Trestle tables and all seating had been removed to the perimeter of the walls. All was quiet, save for the strong Gaelic voice of one man.

Lachlan.

Helene threaded her way along one side of the wall and stood on a stool to gain a better view of the proceedings. At the head of the hall, Lachlan occupied a heavily carved, dark wooden chair set upon a dais. He cut a striking figure dressed in full clan kilted regalia, complete with plaid draped over one shoulder and fastened with a brooch. Sunlight caught the sparkle of a green jewel at its centre, like the one in the portrait of his father hanging in the castle's entrance.

To his left stood two men, and two on his right, clothed in similar attire. Helene recognised each man whom Lachlan had pointed out last night as his inner circle of advisers.

Another man of senior years and with a thick head of silver hair sat straight-backed at a desk not unlike her father's French provincial writing table. He dipped a long, feathered quill into an inkpot and scratched the nib across parchment. It seemed to Helene that he documented Lachlan's diatribe to a clansman standing at the foot of the dais.

The clansman nodded, replied demurely, and slunk away through a side door.

Helene swept her gaze over faces in the hall, and when she looked to the gallery opposite and above, she saw Caitrin MacLanoch, Cuthbert, and Grizel. None of them had noticed her presence. Agnes and Lady Sutton were nowhere in sight. Either they still lay abed, or it was not a requirement they attend these proceedings. Helene assumed the latter explained why she had been excluded from the assembly.

The scribe said something to his laird. Lachlan replied and then suddenly switched to English. 'Father Crawford. Step forward.'

Helene blinked, her curiosity piqued.

There came an unsettling murmur from the people as a man dressed in the cloth broke through the crowd to present himself. Helene picked him as being not much older than Lachlan.

'Welcome to Drumocher Castle,' said Lachlan. 'I understand ye to be travelling north?'

'Yes. To the next soldier camp. I am to replace their priest who took ill and died.'

'Ye travel alone?'

'No. My guide is readying the horses and wagon as we speak. We shall be on our way as soon as a certain matter is resolved.'

'Aye. I trust ye were comfortable enough in the guest quarters last night?'

The softly spoken clergyman nodded. 'I thank you for your hospitality, laird.'

To Helene, his refined English enunciation distinguished him as a man who hailed from a privileged background. She could not imagine what he'd done to warrant an audience with Lachlan.

Lachlan gestured to the crowd at large. 'Father Crawford, do ye see in this room the boy whom ye allege to have stolen a chicken from yer wagon?'

'Indeed.'

Helene followed the direction of Father Crawford's accusing finger to see a child with a mop of red curls. Her heart reached out to the lad, who looked no more than ten years old.

'Donnie Ewing,' said Lachlan. 'Step forward.'

A forlorn couple, who must surely be the boy's parents, stood directly behind him. He looked at them over his shoulder before doing as his laird asked.

'Did ye steal the chicken, Donnie? Answer me truthfully, now.'

'Aye. I did, my laird.'

'Why?'

'The last of our egg-laying hens was taken by a wildcat, and Pa doesnae have the coin to replace it, so I prayed hard and thought the Lord wouldnae mind if I took—'

'Stole,' corrected Lachlan.

'Aye.' Donnie bowed his head. 'Stole.'

Helene held in check her fear for the boy. What punishment would Lachlan mete out to a child? The lad stood still, bravely awaiting his fate, chin dipped to his chest with signs of a tremor in his left leg. Helene fought her every instinct to rush forward, scoop him up in her embrace, and run from the hall.

His mother swiped at a falling tear. The father hung his head in shame.

Helene held her breath. She prayed Lachlan would go easy on the lad. In suffering the humiliation of standing amidst accusing eyes, and after publicly admitting to his wrongdoing, then surely a verbal reprimand from his laird would suffice in teaching the boy a lesson.

'Donnie Ewing, ye stand before me having pleaded guilty to the crime of stealing a chicken, and from one of the Lord's servants no less. Theft is a serious crime, ye ken, one which carries a heavy penalty.'

At this, the boy nodded, still with his eyes downcast. He sniffed and wiped his nose with his sleeve.

'Look at me, lad,' said Lachlan.

The boy dragged his gaze from the floor to meet his laird's implacable eyes.

'Yer punishment, Donnie, is to lose the hand ye stole with. 'Tis I who'll use my broadsword to slice it from yer wrist.'

Helene gasped in horror. Heads turned in her direction, and Lachlan glared at her as if sighting his enemy down the barrel of a pistol. She gave an ever so subtle shake of her head, her way of pleading with him not to administer such brutal punishment on one so young. He ignored her, returning his attention to the boy.

'Do ye ken, Donnie?'

'Aye, my laird.' The boy's voice wavered. To his credit, he stood straight and as tall as his thin frame would allow. 'I'll ne'er steal again.'

'Aye. Good lad. Best we get it over and done with now.'

Lachlan vacated his chair and stepped down from the dais. 'A wooden bucket,' he called to a manservant standing against the wall. 'To catch the severed hand.'

Donnie thrust his right hand under his left armpit as if to hide the offending appendage. Helene's heart broke when he slid the hand ever so slowly across his chest, pressed a kiss to the palm, and let the arm flop at his side.

Panic set in. Would no one protest this outrageous penalty and step forward to challenge their laird? She looked to the gallery, at Cuthbert, thinking he might hold sway over Lachlan's reasoning, yet he showed stoic resolve in favour of his cousin's ruling.

Helene stared in vain at his mother, willing the MacLanoch matriarch to look her way. Surely Caitrin, if anyone, could make him retract his decision. Instead, she sat visibly proud of her son's handling of the grim situation.

Despicable!

Helene looked away in disgust. Her chest tightened upon hearing the hiss of a broadsword drawn from its sheath. Lachlan examined each side of the blade. Forged steel glinted in the sunlight streaming through slitted windows, portraying the weapon as even more devastatingly lethal. He ran a finger along an inch of the razor-sharp blade and viewed the cut to his flesh. Index finger and thumb rubbed together, smearing blood.

'The smithy made good with my new broadsword,' he said to Donnie. ''Tis a shame its first use will be to take off yer hand.'

Helene stifled another gasp. Was this the weapon she'd seen the blacksmith toiling over yesterday after having passed beneath Drumocher's portcullis?

'Are ye ready, lad?'

The boy's legs trembled even though he stood with back straight and chin up. 'Aye, my laird.' He lifted his arm horizontally to the floor as proof of his resolute obedience.

Helene's stomach lurched with visions of the blade falling like a guillotine, severing the boy's hand, and hearing it fall with a dull thud into the bucket below. She imagined blood spurting from his wrist only for him to suffer more intolerable, excruciating pain when a lit torch would seal the severed limb. She bore the boy's pain even before the deed was done.

Bile rose in her throat. She swallowed, the nausea overpowering, and jumped down from the stool. She carved a path through the onlookers to stand shoulder to shoulder with those at the front of the crowd.

Lachlan had positioned himself at right angles to the boy and tested the weight of the blade in his hand. He'd said he was a man of his word. An admirable quality of character for sure, but to inflict such cruel torture on a child?

Helene's heart thumped in her chest. Each breath came in short, sharp gasps. She froze, gripped by fear for the boy. Every fibre in her body screamed in outrage at the laird as he lightly rested the blade on the boy's wrist and then raised the sword high in the air.

'No!' Helene rushed forward and stood between the boy and Lachlan. 'I won't allow it!'

The crowd sucked in a collective breath before falling eerily silent. If Lachlan's narrowed eyes had the power to kill, she'd have dropped dead where she stood. He lowered the sword to his side.

'*Ye* . . . won't allow it?'

'I will not!'

Lachlan's chest expanded on a long, deep breath. Slow and steady, he exhaled. 'Step aside, lass.'

Helene shook her head. 'You will *not* harm this child.'

'Step. Aside. *Sassenach!*'

Her chin tilted in defiance of his minatory tone. An outsider she might be, and unaccustomed to their ways, but she would not stand by and watch a man butcher a helpless child. She stepped forward, bringing them face-to-face, and saw the tightness around his eyes. Though the heat of his anger seared her soul, she was determined to protect the boy.

Their eyes remained locked in a standoff.

'All right,' relented Lachlan, loud enough for all to hear.

Helene closed her eyes and sucked in a deep breath. Pent-up tension dissolved in an instant.

'If not the boy's hand, then I'll take yers.'

Helene's eyes flashed wide. His words, like a punch to her gut, left her suddenly giddy and cold. 'What?'

'Aye. Ye heard me. Ye'll take the place of the lad. After all, 'tis acceptable in the Highlands for someone else to take the punishment intended for another.' He addressed the crowd at large. 'Unless . . . there's anyone here today who'll pay for the boy's crime?'

Lachlan waited. 'Nae?' His eyes pinned Helene. 'Then *ye* will stand in for the lad.'

'Nae!' cried Donnie, insinuating his small frame between his laird and Helene. 'I cannae let ye do it, m'lady.'

Helene's swift reaction saw the boy safely within the

embrace of his mother. Despite his brave protest, Helene bent down before him.

'Donnie,' she said, taking the boy's hands in hers. 'Do you understand what you did was wrong?'

'Aye, m'lady.'

'And as God is your witness, do you swear never to steal again?'

He shook his mop of curls. 'Ne'er again. I swear it.'

'Do we have your word on that?'

He gave an enthusiastic nod. 'Aye! Ye do.'

'Good.' She thumbed away tears rolling down the sweet boy's cheeks. 'Honour your word, Donnie, because a man without his honour is nothing.'

Helene glanced up at the boy's father, wondering why he, of all people, hadn't stepped in for his son. *Shame on him!* He kept his eyes downcast with head bowed. Coarse, work-roughened fingers fumbled the rim of his cap. Losing a hand might be to the detriment of his livelihood, whatever that might be, but young Donnie would be there to take up the slack.

'Sassenach!'

Anger in Lachlan's voice at her back sent her mind reeling. *Choose*, it said. *Your hand or Donnie's?*

An internal war waged between seeing the boy's hand lopped off and calling on Lachlan's promise to protect and keep her safe.

One look at Donnie and Helene had her answer.

Another dilemma surfaced. How would she care for Prudence with only one hand?

One hand!

She would learn to manage. The disability paled in significance to what her sister had already suffered, especially now, ensconced in that madhouse.

Short of breath and feeling faint, Helene stumbled to her feet. She swallowed a sour taste in her mouth, helpless to control the shakes in her legs and the cold spreading through her body.

Scotland. Highlanders. Barbaric! Just as she'd been warned.

She glanced at the clergyman. God's representative. If this was His way of punishing Helene for her sins, then so be it. She squared her shoulders and positioned herself with one raised, trembling arm over the bucket. Mental numbness took hold, resigned to the reckoning she deserved.

'My right hand,' she said to Lachlan. *The one used to push Prudence down the stairs.* 'The hand that sinned.'

CHAPTER SIX

LACHLAN SHEATHED HIS broadsword.

He slipped one arm around Helene's waist and hurried her directly into the adjoining lord's hall. The lass was shaking beneath his touch. He gently eased her down into a chair, reached for a crystal decanter on the sideboard, and poured a glass of red wine. Dropping to his knees in front of her, he tipped the glass to her pale lips. 'Drink.'

She took only a sip and rocked back and forth, eyes downcast while nursing her right hand in her left. 'Should have taken it off,' she mumbled. 'My fault. Should have taken it.'

'Nae, lass. 'Twas not yer fault. 'Twas Donnie who—'

'My fault. I pushed . . . I pushed . . .'

'Aye! Ye pushed me all right, but I—'

Lachlan cut short his words. Helene seemed not to hear him. Her left hand viciously tugged the fingers on her right hand in much the same way one might remove a glove. This was not the outcome he'd predicted.

He cupped her face with his hands to gently tilt her head up. 'Lass, look at me.'

Emerald eyes glistened with tears. Even though she looked at him, he knew she did not see him. Regret sat heavy on his shoulders. He'd mismanaged her dogged interference. He'd expected her to back down and retreat from the threat of stepping in for Donnie. She owed Lachlan and his clan nothing. They were strangers and shared no blood or family ties. It made no sense for her to get involved.

'Lass,' he soothed, 'I shouldnae have pushed ye the way I did. I meant only to put ye in yer place. To remind ye 'tis not for ye to challenge my authority or clan law.'

Lachlan returned the glass to her lips. Another sip and he patiently waited, watching until her breathing slowed and the shakes subsided. To his surprise, she took the glass in hand and gulped the remaining wine. She shuddered with a reaction more telling than having whiffed potent smelling salts.

He set the glass aside, and this time when he looked into her eyes, he was struck by the full force of her loathing for him.

He stood and took a step back. 'Nae. Ye've nae right to be angry with *me*, lass.'

She gathered herself and dashed away tears on her cheeks. 'No right? How could you think to be so horrendously cruel to a child?'

It was an unfounded recrimination.

In the next instant, she was out of the chair and on her feet. 'He is just a boy!'

'A boy who needed to be taught a lesson.'

'By cutting off his hand?'

''Twas not for ye to interfere.'

She inched closer. 'If not me, then who? Not *one* of your people—'

'My *people*?'

'—stepped forward to take his place. Not even his father or his mother!'

Lachlan harnessed his anger. 'Ye've nae understanding of our ways and—'

'It was a chicken. A chicken!'

'Aye. And if the deed of theft went unpunished, then what else might he steal?'

She came face-to-face with Lachlan. 'You heard him. His father has no money to replace their egg-laying hen. The boy looks half-starved. Have you no compassion?'

Her accusations cut him to the quick. 'So ye're happy for him to steal a chicken, and with nae repercussions?'

'A stern talking to would suffice. Besides, if you don't have a care or show compassion for the people who work your land, then it's no surprise the boy turned to theft.'

Another verbal blow. Enough with her insults. Lachlan took rough hold of her shoulders and raised his voice.

'What then if he graduates to stealing cattle, sheep, a horse, or a weapon? What if he's caught by redcoats who show him nae mercy? Or if he finds himself being judged by an unfair and corrupt jury, or no jury at all? Will ye shadow him for the rest of his life and be there always to defend him? Will it be ye who consoles his ma and da when they hear his neck snap and see him swinging from a gibbet?'

Lachlan's tirade drew a gasp from Helene. Her face turned white.

'Aye! Ye didnae think about *that* before ye thought yersel' so high and mighty to interfere and challenge my authority. Do ye think me such a monster that I'd actually take off his hand? Or yers, for that matter?'

Helene broke free of his hold and shrank back from him. Mute, she stared wide-eyed at Lachlan.

'Christ, lass! There's more to me and my clan than ye ken. Why do ye think nae one volunteered to take Donnie's place?'

She shook her head, seemingly mystified.

'Did ye not try to understand my objective?'

She swallowed, again mute.

'Donnie had to be taught a lesson, and everyone in that

hall kens it. That's why nae one of them stepped forward to offer for wee Donnie. They trust my judgement, and they ken as well as I 'tis not enough to tell him what he did was wrong.

'For a boy of his age, words go in one ear and out the other. He had to experience the full ramifications of his crime. To stand accountable to me, his laird, and his clan and the man from whom he stole. To see the blade and have him suffer in fear at the thought of being crippled for life, marking him forever a thief!'

Helene's gaze dropped to her clasped hands, and she whispered something unintelligible beneath her breath. In that moment, she looked small, beaten, and fragile. Lachlan's fired-up heart skipped a beat. All anger fell away, as did the fight in his voice.

''Tis my hope the lad will think twice before stealing anything again. Sometimes words hold nae weight. Actions do. Best ye remember that. Far better for Donnie to feel the sting of shame and regret now, within the safety of Drumocher and among those who care about him, than to face unfair judgement and far crueller consequences, if not death, in the future.'

Helene turned her back on Lachlan and walked stiffly towards a window to stare beyond the castle walls. Was she already pining for her homeland?

Silence filled the space between them.

Lachlan was mindful of his long list of pressing clan matters to settle. 'I'll go now to deliver the lad his reprieve. 'Tis not fair to keep him waiting.'

Without a doubt, he saw Helene's shoulders sag in relief. Before leaving her in solitude, he offered her a word of advice. 'If ye think ye'll find our way of life offensive, then perhaps ye'd be better off returning to *yer* people across the border. 'Tis simple and quick to arrange. I've nae wish to be undermined a third time by a Sassenach lass who doesnae ken or respect me and the laws on my clan lands. I'll expect yer answer by tonight.'

Lachlan exited the lord's hall, surprised to find Caitrin MacLanoch standing in the small passage leading to the great hall. 'Mother?'

'The lass. Is she all right?'

'Aye.'

Caitrin raised her brows. 'Spoken with a heavy sigh, my son.'

Lachlan kept their conversation to a whisper. 'She's been here a short time and has already twice crossed me.'

His mother settled both hands on her hips and tilted her head to one side. 'God forbid a woman to possess the courage and tenacity to challenge ye.'

Lachlan raised a brow. 'Ye jest about something so serious?'

'I dinnae jest, and aye, she doesnae ken our ways, but 'twas refreshing to watch a woman, a Sassenach nae less, show some backbone and stand up to ye. A lass of her mettle and means is worthy of standing by yer side.'

Lachlan huffed out a sigh and ignored his mother's matchmaking assumptions. 'She's a guest here. 'Tis not her place to challenge me. Especially not in front of the clan.'

'Aye, but dinnae ye agree that she be a strong woman to display such courage and who kens it her moral duty to speak her mind on behalf of another, whether she kens that person or not?'

Lachlan acquiesced with a reluctant nod.

Caitrin leaned in closer to Lachlan. 'I cannae understand why Donnie's situation would compel her to take his place or sabotage her future prospects. What man in her social circles would marry a woman with one hand?'

'A dowry, Mother. A man in need of status and money will overlook far worse an anomaly in a wife.'

Caitrin looked grave and shook her head. 'Some dark place in the lass's heart triggered her compulsion to protect Donnie. I find that as disturbing as she was distressed by the proceedings.'

'Ye're overthinking this. She's a lass who doesnae ken how to mind her own business. I'll not stand for her meddlesome nature, and I've told her as much.' He read the question in his mother's enquiring eyes. 'If she cannae trust me, or abide by our ways and customs without interference, then I've told her she best return to England. I expect her answer by tonight.'

'You'll have my answer now, if you please.'

The soft voice had Lachlan and his mother turn to see Helene standing in the light of the half-opened doorway. When Caitrin made a move to leave, the lass stepped into the passageway.

'Don't go,' said Helene. 'I wish to apologise.' Her guilt-ridden eyes took in Lachlan and his mother. 'To you both.' She moved closer, wringing her hands. 'I had no right interfering in something that was none of my concern, and I sincerely apologise for any upset or embarrassment I might have caused you and those of your clan. I assure you it will not happen again.'

A satisfactory apology, and it seemed genuine enough.

'But . . .' she said.

That one word, spoken with the sudden upward tilt of her chin, set Lachlan on edge. It conjured dual emotions: surprise at feeling disappointment at the thought she might yet announce her departure, and bracing himself in anticipation of her laying a challenge at his feet.

Her stretched-out pause compelled him to ask, *'But?'*

Her arms fell by her sides. 'I make no apology for wanting to rescue a child from harm, regardless of whether I'm privy to that child's circumstances or not. I can't promise it won't happen again. If you can live with that, then I'd like to see out my stay here at Drumocher.'

The lass stood firm in the courage of her convictions. Damn but he admired her for that, *and* she'd cleverly turned the tables on him, forcing him to decide whether she was to stay or go.

'We both can live with that,' said Caitrin in an accommodating and sympathetic voice. 'Apology accepted.'

Lachlan narrowed his eyes on his mother. In turn, her expression dared him to overturn her decision. His gaze settled on Helene's face, and there he detected no hint of gloating triumph in the serious set of her full-lipped mouth. His mother might have voiced acceptance of Helene's apology and ultimatum on his behalf, but he saw the question clearly repeated in the lass's eyes. At least she showed him the respect of wanting *his* decision.

He gave it in the form of a curt nod, bowed by way of excusing himself, and turned to make his exit.

'Lachlan.'

He stopped without turning, wishing the effect of Helene having spoken his name did not feel like an intimate caress on his neck.

'I should like to witness the remainder of the hall's proceedings,' she said.

At this, Lachlan swivelled on the spot and stared her down. The question of trust hung unspoken in the air between them. Still, he relented, gesturing for his mother and Helene to precede him into the hall.

When the lass passed him by in the narrow passageway, her hand chanced to brush against his. Their eyes met in mutual awareness, fraying Lachlan's senses as if he were a skittish young colt.

All manner of Gaelic curses crossed his mind in an attempt

to gather his wits. When re-entering the great hall, inquisitive eyes flitted between himself and the Sassenach. He resisted a glance in her direction, safe in the knowledge his mother would have taken Helene under her wing, seating the lass next to herself in the gallery.

The proceedings resumed when Lachlan seated himself in his chair. He summoned Donnie forth. The poor lad looked fit to faint.

''Tis yer lucky day,' said Lachlan with a stamp of authority. 'Ye'll be spared the loss of yer hand, but thieve again and ye'll know what punishment awaits ye. Ye ken?'

Donnie threw himself at Lachlan's feet. 'Thank ye, my laird. I won't ever steal again. I swear it.'

'Dinnae be thanking me, lad.' Lachlan hauled the lad upright. ''Tis the Sassenach to whom ye owe homage. If it weren't for her, ye'd be nursing a bloodied wrist by now.'

Lachlan watched as all eyes, including Donnie's, swung towards the upper gallery to look at Helene. Relief and the indebted smile on the lad's face told Lachlan the boy had learned his lesson. He need not know the truth behind the set-up of his trial's proceedings, leastwise until he was grown.

In the silence of the hall, Lachlan looked up at Helene. The sight of Cuthbert seated next to her set Lachlan's teeth on edge. His gut tightened, causing him to shift fractionally forward in his chair.

'Donnie,' he snapped.

The lad stood to attention. 'Aye, my laird?'

'Go now with Father Crawford to the chapel. Make yer apologies to him and repent yer sins to God.'

'Aye, my laird.'

Lachlan nodded to Donnie's mother and father, their expressions grateful. They exited the great hall with their son and the visiting priest.

Lachlan turned his attention to settling all manner of matters, ranging from couples with irreconcilable marital problems to freeing the necessitous from their arrears of rent. All the while, the one person present whose watchful eyes and whose opinion of him mattered was Helene. Curse him for a fool.

In the grip of a moment's maddening weakness, he risked another glance up to the gallery to see Cuthbert lean in close to Helene. What did his cousin whisper in the lass's ear to make her stand with him and exit the hall?

Lachlan's hands slid along the length of the chair's ornately carved arms. Had he gripped it any tighter, the wood might have splintered.

❧

Helene, at Cuthbert's insistence, left Drumocher's sanctuary to accompany him on a walk alongside the loch.

Nature had indeed waved her lavish hand over widespread terrain, creating a fairyland rich in breathtaking beauty. Fresh air and revitalising sunshine provided a cleansing tonic after the draining intensity of what had happened in the great hall.

Even now she shuddered with visions of what might have been, from the bloody act of losing her hand and the aftermath, to how she'd have struggled to adapt and cope in saving and looking after poor Prudence.

In hindsight, she might not have reacted in any other way, unless, of course, she'd been privy to clan ways and Lachlan's approach in teaching Donnie a lesson. Her focus had been on protecting the boy, acting on instinct. But the penalty for her rash behaviour now put her on the back foot with Lachlan.

It was the second time she'd underestimated the MacLanoch laird.

Her downfall, and definitely not conducive to seducing him.

Not once had it occurred to her during their confrontation in the hall that he *wouldn't* go through with his threat of taking Donnie's hand or hers. She should have done as he'd asked and stepped aside, allowing him to preside over his clan, knowing what was best for his subjects, especially Donnie.

She'd let personal prejudice impede her ability to trust Lachlan. A mistake she must rectify if she were to work her way into his embrace. With that thought came the memory of the moment he'd berated her for interfering in Donnie's trial. His anger she could understand. The heat of that anger was one thing, but the heat of his touch on her person was another. It robbed her of breath, as did the shocking truth of what might become of Donnie if he were to steal again. Lachlan had acted with purpose. She had reacted in outrage.

'He *will* follow us.'

Cuthbert's voice startled Helene out of her reverie. 'Did you say something?'

'I said he, Lachlan, will follow us. Mark my words.'

'What makes you so sure?'

'I have my cousin convinced I'll ruin you with a kiss, if not ravish you beyond repair.' Cuthbert donned a wily smile. 'Lachlan MacLanoch, the great protector, will come to your rescue the moment Grizel informs him of our whereabouts.'

'But surely Grizel will not interrupt the hall's proceedings on my account?'

'Of course not. I've asked her to inform her brother when the proceedings conclude. I want him to fret over how long you and I have been out here alone. He saw us leave the hall together. That would have put him on high alert.'

Men and their mind games. It made no sense to Helene. Her gaze sought and marvelled at ancient oaks, ash, and beech trees to the left of the trail. She then glimpsed the vibrant blue-purple flowers beyond the trees. Bluebells. She felt suddenly homesick. The cry of two birds overhead turned her attention skyward. She stopped to admire their majestic wingspan and watch them circle high above.

Cuthbert paused in his stride to look up. 'Two golden eagles. Did you know they pair for life?'

Helene studied the man at her side. Handsome and fair-haired, he looked every bit the polished rake, with jacket and breeches cut from the finest cloth. 'You sound envious.'

'I am.'

A frank and astonishing admission and said without hesitation. 'Then why waste time on your philandering ways instead of seeking your one true love?'

Cuthbert gave a derisive laugh and continued along the path. 'It's not that simple.'

'And why,' Helene called after him, 'is the laird of Drumocher yet to secure a match?' No sooner had she posed the question than she regretted asking it. It made her sound . . . interested.

Cuthbert stopped mid-stride. After a few moments he turned, and that wily smile reignited. 'Because, Lady Helene Beckett, he had yet to meet *you*!'

Helene stiffened. 'Me?'

'Yes.' He pointed skyward. 'Like those golden eagles, I sincerely believe you and my cousin are well matched. You could live out your days in wedded bliss.'

Helene's bark of unladylike laughter sent a pheasant fluttering from the woodland's leafy underbrush. 'Don't be ridiculous,' she sputtered. 'I'm the last person on earth to attract his attentions. Besides, your brief is for me to seduce him, not marry him. I'm in no position to—'

'Exactly what position *are* you in, Lady Helene?' Cuthbert

stood with folded arms across his chest, pinning Helene on the spot with his quizzical stare.

His sobering confrontation had her raise her chin and eye him with silent regard.

'Still tight-lipped, I see?'

'We agreed never to ask each other or to explain personal reasons behind our mutual arrangement.'

'There's no harm done if I were to think through the matter out loud,' he said, as if in the throes of playing a guessing game.

He relaxed his pose, tapped a finger to his forehead, and glanced up as one does when deep in thought. 'A young lady of noble birth'—he pointed to Helene—'would want for nothing. She'd bring to the marriage table a handsome dowry. So, for what lucrative benefit would she secretly require additional funds?' His eyes narrowed beneath a wrinkled brow. 'My, but if this intrigue isn't besmirched with scandal.'

'Keep your voice down!' Helene hissed.

He humoured her request. 'My dear, unless the air whispers our conversation upon a sudden incoming breeze, there is no one within miles to hear us.'

'You and I struck a bargain exclusive of candour.'

'Indeed we did, and when you deliver your end of the bargain, according to my terms, then you shall have your just reward.' He placed his right hand over his heart. 'I shall, herewith, uphold our ruling. No more questions.'

Cuthbert made a grand gesture with the sweep of his hand. 'Shall we proceed along this path of peace and tranquillity?'

Conceited bore. The man was also mad! She and the laird, marriage material? *Absurd!* She fell in beside him as they continued their stroll along the trail. Was it Cuthbert's intent to play Cupid? *Ridiculous!* Helene suppressed another bout of laughter.

Yet it had her thinking. Was there not one lass in the whole of Scotland worthy of marrying the laird of Clan MacLanoch? Perhaps *he* was the unworthy one and no self-respecting lass would have him. It would explain why the Scottish scoundrel chose to dally with ladies across the border.

Good Lord! Marry the laird. Such an outrageous and unrealistic concept. She'd convinced herself Cuthbert had conceited motives in wanting her to entice and engage Lachlan on a physical level. Now he'd turned her thinking on its head with his talk of wedded bliss between the laird and herself.

In her attempt to understand men, Helene toyed with another idea. Perhaps the cousins had wagered on who would be the last rake standing before being imprisoned in the institution of marriage. Cuthbert's scheme might well be to have Lachlan ruin Helene, thereby necessitating their forced marriage.

Preposterous!

Lachlan MacLanoch did not strike Helene as a man to be forced into anything, let alone marriage. Pair that with her disregard for an unblemished reputation, and Cuthbert had a foolhardy plan. She would never marry, especially not the laird, even if he did make a sincere proposal. Helene was committed to one person only: Prudence.

Her head ached. Best not try to understand a man's mind. She took a deep pine-scented breath and cast her gaze over the silver-surfaced loch to the right of the trail. It reminded her of a giant mirror, and in its reflection she saw a few patchy cotton clouds. Waterfowl swam in between the reeds fringing the large body of water. A woodpecker's knock echoed from afar, and a red squirrel twitched its tail on a low-hanging branch.

'I owe you an apology,' said Cuthbert.

The admission startled Helene. She tripped and Cuthbert

caught her arm, preventing her from stumbling forward. She kept silent, though wary of what he had to say as they maintained their steady stroll.

'Yesterday,' he began, 'before you alighted the carriage, I spoke and behaved in such a way as you did not deserve.'

'Correct.' Helene rubbed her hand with the memory of how painfully he'd squeezed it. 'You behaved not as a gentleman, but rather as a brute and a bully.'

Cuthbert gave her a sidelong glance and grimaced. 'I'm truly sorry. I had not expected Lachlan to be such an arrant prig, or that he'd throw my plans into disarray.'

Plans? Despite her natural curiosity, Helene refrained from asking Cuthbert to explain himself. What she wanted from this business transaction was not his concern. Conversely, she did not wish to know about *his* plans for his cousin. The less she knew about Laird MacLanoch, the better.

As they rounded a bend in the trail, a large, thick-furred, whiskered animal leapt from the loch's bank to pause briefly in the middle of the path. A duck hung limp between its clenched jaw.

'Don't move!' warned Cuthbert.

The animal's piercing green eyes narrowed, threatening attack. In a flash, it disappeared into the woods with its dead meal.

Helene slapped a hand over her heart, and she expelled a pent-up breath. 'What was that?'

'A Scottish wildcat. Aggressive and adaptable hunters. Once thought to be man-killers.' He laughed.

'I can see why!'

'Consider yourself lucky. It's a rare sight to see one at this time of day, if at all.'

His sudden silent scrutiny of Helene left her feeling uneasy. 'What is it?'

He rocked once on his heels and gave her an appraising nod. 'I salute you and applaud your impressive performance in the great hall this morning. I would never have pegged you to be the epitome of pluck, nor stout-hearted and as resourceful as you are attractive.'

Heat rose in Helene's cheeks.

'And,' he added, with a shifty smile, 'congratulations on calling my cousin's bluff. Smart move. He played right into your hands. You will have earned his and the clan's respect, and he will admire your courage, even though you publicly dared to challenge him. I'd say you've already won him over.'

Cuthbert's apology was dumbfounding to be sure, but this last admission all but winded Helene. Indignant, she flexed her fingers before tightly clasping both hands behind her back.

'What you witnessed,' she insisted, 'was not a calculated performance, and I most certainly did not call his bluff. My actions were sincere and true.'

Cuthbert stood silent and inscrutable. In the next instant, he doubled over with loud laughter. 'My dear, you speak with determined conviction, but . . .' He dissolved into another fit of laughter. 'You cannot expect me to believe you'd have let Lachlan lop off your hand.'

Helene picked up a fallen branch and held it executioner style. 'Laugh again and I'll lop off your head.'

Sobering words which caused him to stare at her, stupefied. 'You mean to say you would have actually gone through with it?'

'What in God's name is going on here?'

Helene turned to see Lachlan jump down from his horse even before it came to a standstill. Cuthbert received a forceful shove to the chest, further distancing him from Helene and toppling him to the ground. Lachlan's gaze made a clean sweep of Helene from head to toe. 'Did he hurt ye, lass? Are ye all right?' Genuine concern for her lay bare in his eyes.

She sent the branch hurtling behind her into the woodland. 'No, he didn't hurt me, and yes, I'm perfectly fine.'

'Cousin,' said Cuthbert. 'It's not what you think.' He sounded calm, if not amused by Lachlan's reaction.

Lachlan stood with fists balled at his side. 'I round the corner to find the lass looking heated and displeased, defending herself with a stick, and ye expect me not to think the worst of ye?'

'Cuthbert's right,' insisted Helene. 'There was an animal of the like I'd never seen before. I was preparing to fend it off.'

Lachlan's eyes sharpened on Cuthbert. 'An animal. Aye. Of course it was.'

'A wildcat, if you must know,' said Cuthbert, standing to dust the dirt from his breeches, backside, and the elbows of his jacket.

Lachlan's brows rose in suspicion. 'Wildcats are mostly active at dawn or dusk, not in the middle of the day.'

'It was indeed cat-like and huge,' said Helene.

Lachlan cut her a glance. 'Then describe it.'

'You don't believe me?' She settled both hands on her hips and her voice grew louder. 'You think me a liar?'

'Describe it,' he repeated.

'Very well. It hissed and yowled through long-fanged teeth. Its coat had solid black and brown stripes. It had a thick banded tail, and its paws were bigger than a dog's. It had a dead duck in its mouth, poached, if not stolen, from your loch. Shall we hunt it down and have it stand trial?'

Cuthbert gave a snort of laughter.

Helene's eyes did not waver from Lachlan's hard stare. A muscle twitched along his jaw. She lifted her chin. 'Satisfied I'm telling the truth?'

'Satisfied.' He gave Cuthbert a stern, cursory glance. 'For now.'

A horse whinnied, announcing the arrival of Grizel and Agnes each on horseback. Grizel slid from the saddle with practised ease, whereas Agnes accepted Cuthbert's assistance in dismounting.

Agnes took Helene's hand in hers. 'It seems Mother and I missed quite the confrontation between yourself and Lachlan.' She looked suddenly mortified. 'But were you quite serious about stepping in for that lad and—?'

'Quite serious.' Helene retracted her hand. 'I confess to being ignorant about clan convention.' She gave the laird a sidewards glance. 'Nonetheless, Lachlan, his mother, and I discussed what happened. We've cleared the air, and Lachlan and I have come to an understanding.'

Grizel's face lit up with a smile. 'All of Drumocher is talking about ye!'

Helene's stomach dropped. 'I apologise. I meant no disrespect, and I—'

'Apologise?' The young girl's eyes gleamed with adoration for Helene. 'Nonsense! I ken ye dinnae understand our ways, but 'twas most valiant and courageous of ye to speak up in wanting to protect wee Donnie. Ye've inspired me to be assertive and speak my mind.'

'Haven't ye always done so?' snapped Lachlan. 'Whether yer opinion is sought or not.'

Helene sensed his anger was directed at herself for having made such an indelible impression on his sister, but the effect of his words visibly stung Grizel as if she'd fallen on the ubiquitous spines of flowering gorse.

She squared up to her brother, chin raised and shoulders pushed back. 'Aye, brother! But I wish to be *heard*. Not simply tolerated.' Her voice gained power. 'Women are not mere baubles used to decorate a man's arm or to forever be his caretaker. Nor should their body's sole purpose be to warm a man's bed or deliver him a bairn, an heir no less. We're capable of so much more, and our opinions and actions are worthy of any man's note. Even yers!'

Helene felt compelled to applaud Grizel but knew better than to meddle in their fractious sibling altercation.

No one looked more shocked by Grizel's articulate attack than Lachlan. He blinked, then blinked again as though noticing her for the very first time.

A pained expression, if not one of regret, sat between his gathered brows. He acknowledged her with a slow nod. 'Thank ye, sister. Heard and respectfully noted.'

Agnes broke the silence with a loud clap of her hands. She pointed to satchels tied to the pommel of each saddle. 'Cook has prepared us a sumptuous picnic. I'm famished. Shall we partake now of the feast?'

Lachlan met her request with a smile. 'Ladies, perhaps ye can find us an agreeable spot by the water. Cuthbert and I will be along shortly.'

Agnes eagerly led Grizel and Helene towards the loch's edge. Helene glanced over her shoulder, disturbed to see Lachlan's visage darken and his gaze skewer Cuthbert.

CHAPTER SEVEN

WITH THE WOMEN out of sight, Lachlan's hand hovered over his dirk. He harboured nothing but contempt for his cousin. 'Did ye touch her? Because if ye did . . .'

'Yes, actually, I did.'

Lachlan moved with lightning speed, giving Cuthbert no time to retreat. One hand grabbed a fistful of jacket, the other pressed the sharp blade to his cousin's throat.

Cuthbert raised his hands in calm surrender. 'She tripped. I steadied her with my hand under her arm. Or would you have preferred I let her fall flat on her face?'

'Dinnae play games with me. Or her!'

'Games?' said Cuthbert, unruffled. 'I fail to see how taking a stroll beside the loch with Helene is akin to a game.'

The way he spoke her name was too intimate for Lachlan's liking. 'Ye lured the lass here to take advantage of her. Did ye not?'

'Lured?' Cuthbert grimaced when Lachlan applied more pressure to the blade beneath his chin.

'Dinnae lie to me!'

'I simply offered her a reprieve from the tedious events taking place in the hall. You should be thanking me. She deserved respite and fresh air after the trauma you put her through this morning.'

Damn, but he was right! If not for the long list of urgent matters to resolve, Lachlan would have brought Helene here to the loch. Still, it galled to have his cousin point it out. 'Helene asked to remain in the hall.'

'Then why did she choose to leave with me?'

'Ye must have coerced her.'

'She has a mind of her own, amply demonstrated in Donnie's case.' Cuthbert let out a loud, impatient breath. 'Remove your dirk and stop behaving like a jilted lover!'

'Gentlemen, will you be much longer before joining us?'

Lachlan's gaze snapped towards the voice. *Helene.*

How much of the conversation had she overheard? It was the second time in one day she'd seen him with a blade drawn. Not quite the best of impressions, but then what did it matter? In her eyes he was a notorious rake, and he'd given her good reason to add barbaric Highlander to her sullied opinion of him.

He discreetly sheathed the dirk and let go of his cousin. 'Nae, lass,' he called to her. 'We willnae be too long. Give us a wee minute longer, and we'll be there directly.'

She pointed to indicate the direction they were to follow, then left.

Lachlan eyed Cuthbert, wary of having been played for a fool. 'If ye're telling me ye didnae do nor intend anything untoward with the lass, then I'll believe ye. But if ye continue goading me with threats of impropriety against her, then ye give me nae choice but to react as I did just now. Ye ken?'

'Completely, but you can hardly expect me to rebuff the lady if she seeks my company of her own volition *or* if she flirts with me.'

'She flirted with ye?'

Cuthbert shrugged. 'If you call tripping on purpose so that I might prevent her fall, then yes, I do believe she not only flirted with me but also craved my touch.' He smiled and winked. 'She has the softest arms.'

Lachlan suppressed the urge to redraw his dirk. He would not be baited and so relaxed his jaw from having clenched his teeth. The worst of it was not understanding the true catalyst for his anger. He refused to believe he envied Cuthbert for having spent time alone with Helene on their solo stroll, or because she'd chosen to be with, and flirt with, Cuthbert. His cousin saw it as sport in making it so damned difficult to safeguard Helene. *That* frustrated Lachlan to the point of making him want to lash out.

He tethered the horses to trees nearby and left enough slack in the reins so each animal could feed on the lush grass. He untied the first leather satchel. 'Catch this!'

Cuthbert grunted with the impact of the bag hitting his chest and almost dropped it. 'Careful. The food will spoil.'

Lachlan took the remaining satchels in hand. 'Let me remind ye of yer oath to Grizel yesterday when ye said, hand on heart, ye'd ne'er expose a woman to the perils of danger.'

'An oath I intend to wholeheartedly keep.'

'Best ye do!'

Cuthbert cocked his head to one side. 'I hardly recognise you for these threats.'

''Tis not a threat, Cuthbert. 'Tis a warning. Dishonour Helene and ye dishonour me, my family, and yer own. Do that and ye'll have me to answer to.'

'And what of your pledge to me never to let anyone drive a wedge between us?'

'Have ye ever known me to break a solemn promise?'

'No, cousin, I haven't. At least, not yet.'

'Then we understand each other. Just dinnae let it be *ye* who is the wedge.'

Lachlan strode off in the direction Helene had indicated and worked to discard his foul mood. He and Cuthbert had never had cause to argue like this in the past. It rankled to be at loggerheads with him now, and he loathed himself for having held his cousin at knifepoint. It need not have happened. If only Cuthbert wasn't so hell-bent on winding him up about who'd be the first to claim a kiss from Helene.

'Over here,' shouted Agnes, giving an enthusiastic wave and pointing to a grassy verge on the loch's bank.

Lachlan set the satchels down, from which Agnes took a woollen blanket and spread it on the ground.

Grizel thrust a pebble atop the loch's still water. It skipped the surface five times before sinking. Helene applauded and her melodic laughter was enough to lift Lachlan's spirits.

'Here,' said Grizel, selecting another flat pebble and handing it to Helene. 'Ye try.'

Helene shook her head. 'I don't know how.'

Cuthbert dropped his satchel. It fell with a thud on the blanket. He took the pebble from Grizel and, with Helene's permission, placed the flat stone in the crook of her first finger and thumb.

The intimate connection between them triggered a pulling sensation in Lachlan's gut. There he stood, forced to watch the two of them interact. Helene mimicked the way Cuthbert drew his arm back in demonstrating how to propel the stone forward.

'Go ahead, now,' said Cuthbert in a voice Lachlan recognised as one reserved for enticing a woman. The smile of encouragement Cuthbert gave Helene tested the limits of Lachlan's patience.

The stone left Helene's hand and plopped in the water not

three strides in front of her. She laughed at her failed attempt, and the colour of embarrassment infused her lovely face.

Agnes and Grizel encouraged her to try again.

Lachlan sprang into action to keep Cuthbert's lecherous hands off Helene. 'Allow me,' he said, and bent to select a stone from the shore.

He offered it to her, and the sensitive shock of her fingers touching his palm took Lachlan by surprise. He was helpless to mask his reaction when their eyes met in that moment of contact.

This was not the usual way of things. Not one of the experienced courtesans he'd bedded had possessed the skill to transmit such a sensual spark.

He dropped his gaze to that spot on the edge of her wrist where, beneath the skin, her pulse throbbed. It kept pace with his own heartbeat, and suddenly intense desire prevailed upon him, leaving him wanting to press his lips to her skin.

'What can you teach Lady Helene about skimming stones that I haven't already demonstrated?' challenged Cuthbert.

The jibe jolted Lachlan to his senses. He placed the pebble in Helene's palm. Emerald eyes held him accountable. Lachlan swallowed. 'All ye need is a steady arm and a keen eye.'

'And plenty of practise,' laughed Grizel.

'Aye, practise,' said Lachlan, his gaze fixed on Helene. 'Can ye whistle, lass?'

'Yes.'

'Then learning to skim a stone is much like learning to whistle a tune. When ye master it, 'tis a magical thing. Now,' he said, folding her fingers over the pebble, 'feel its smoothness.'

Lachlan moved to stand behind her. He settled one hand on her upper left arm and reached around her with his right hand to adjust the stone in her grip. 'Hold the pebble as

Cuthbert showed ye, with thumb and first finger, but be sure to rest the stone on yer second finger.'

'Like this?' she asked.

'Aye.'

Lachlan glanced down at her face in profile, a picture of fixed concentration. With his next breath he detected her natural scent. A scent infused with the soft notes of violets. The alluring heady mix had the power to affect him in the same way too much whisky fuddled the brain.

Gather yer wits, Lachlan! 'When ye look down on yer hand,' he said, 'it should resemble the shape of a backward letter *C*.'

'Or a *U*,' she said.

Her hair, the colour of a raven, distracted him. Was it as soft as it looked? It had a healthy shine under the afternoon sun, and wayward strands tickled his cheek.

'Aye,' he whispered close to her ear, small and delicate like her hands. 'A letter *U*, if ye prefer.'

He gently manoeuvred her to stand almost at right angles to the water's edge. 'Now pull yer hand and wrist back a wee bit. When ye flick it forward, give it a spin and release the stone away from ye in a straight line horizontal to the surface. If ye can manage that, it will skip and hop atop the water.'

Grizel appeared in front of them to exaggerate a position bent at the knees. 'It helps too if ye crouch down like this when ye toss the stone.'

Lachlan reluctantly let go of Helene and gave her a wide berth. 'All right, lass. Give it yer best shot.'

Helene threw the stone further than her first attempt, but it hit the surface hard, creating an impressive splash, and sank to the bottom of the loch.

'Small progress,' she said with a smile over her shoulder to Lachlan.

'Aye. And practise makes perfect.'

Cuthbert offered Lachlan a stone. 'You've had years and years of practise. Perhaps you could show us what you mean by perfect.'

'With that round boulder? Nae!' Lachlan cast his gaze over the small rocks at his feet, singled one out, and let it fly forth from his hand. It travelled far, and the times it skipped the surface were too numerous to count. Agnes, Grizel, and Helene applauded with a cheer.

Cuthbert stared at him, slack-jawed.

Lachlan reversed the challenge. 'Yer turn.'

Cuthbert shook his head and threw his hands up in defeat. 'I don't have the advantage of living near a loch on which to practise.' He pointed to one of the satchels with food. 'I propose we eat.'

Helene enjoyed a palatable picnic of bannocks, cheese, meats, and wine under a perfect summer sky. Had she not partially witnessed the altercation between Lachlan and Cuthbert, she'd never have known they'd crossed swords. Curiously, both men behaved as if nothing had happened.

Lachlan and Grizel had their audience in fits of laughter as they recounted childhood memories and shenanigans of growing up in the Highlands. Cuthbert and Agnes told of happy holiday visits to Drumocher and confessed to the joys of running amok with their cousins along castle corridors, exploring the deep cavernous craggy landscape, and of learning to swim in the loch.

'The Highlands are not without hardship, mind,' said Lachlan to Helene. 'Clan warfare is vicious—new grudges are formed, and blood feuds carry from one generation to the next. Then there's the winters, bitterly cold and unforgiving.'

Helene agreed that no matter where one lived, life and freedom did not come without a price. However, talk of clan warfare troubled her. She cast her gaze around them, wary of their vulnerability outside the castle walls. 'Are we in danger of being attacked?'

'I've nae quarrel at present with neighbouring clans, but MacLanoch scouts are ever present safeguarding our clan lands. 'Tis poachers, cattle thieves, and miscreants on the run that are top of my mind.'

'And redcoat deserters,' said Grizel, yanking a tuft of grass from its rich soil. 'They take what they want, *when* they want. If ye get my meaning.'

Lachlan bolted upright from his reclined position on the rug. 'Grizel?'

'Dinnae be alarmed, brother. My virtue is intact. Ye might think me naive to such things, but there's much to be learned from whispers in castle corridors.'

'Ye would tell me if ye see or hear something I ought to ken?'

'Aye.'

The girl was wise to her world. One surreptitious glance at Lachlan and Helene saw how his sister's words had rattled him. Despite the beauty of the Highlands, danger in all its forms lurked here, just as it did in the so-called civilised realms of London society.

'Speaking of cattle,' said Cuthbert. 'Does all go well at the shielings, Lachlan?'

'Aye. I've men patrolling the pasture perimeters.'

'Shielings?' Helene queried.

Lachlan lifted his arm and pointed to higher ground. 'In the summer, before harvesting, cattle are taken to where they graze on fresh pastures. They grow fat, thereby increasing their sale value. Drumocher draws an income from the sale of its cattle, and drovers walk them to markets in Lowland Scotland and beyond.'

Grizel was eager to elaborate. ''Tis mainly the womenfolk and girls outwith the castle walls and in the wider countryside who visit and live at the shielings. Some boys go to tend the herds, but for everyone 'tis a time of much fun and excitement.'

'Might we have the opportunity to visit these shielings?' said Helene.

Agnes looked aghast at the suggestion. 'I doubt very much you'd find comfort sleeping inside small huts with dry peat fires and heather for bedding!'

Helene looked to the mountains. A sense of strange longing overcame her. 'On the contrary, I'd welcome the experience.'

Agnes sputtered, 'Are you mad?'

'No. I simply yearn for something more than being forced to sit still and learn needlepoint, languages, and the pianoforte! The scope of my life is limited to mastering every nuance and trait of a marriageable young lady. Such a boring life pales in comparison to the entertaining stories spoken by each of you just now.'

Honesty forced Helene to admit she wished, if only for a moment, to shake off the oppressive guilt of having forever destroyed her sister's future and quality of life.

She took a deep breath and aired her frustration. 'I don't know what it is to run as fast as my legs can carry me, or to explore caves or learn to swim in a loch like you have! I've led a life mostly closeted indoors, and now that I'm here, in the clean-aired Highlands, I want to know what grass feels like underfoot, or to stand with bare feet in the shallows of a running stream. I want to immerse myself amongst the life and the benignity of nature's beauty. I'll never be granted this opportunity again.'

The gusto of her passionate outburst left her audience momentarily speechless.

Grizel's face lit up with a smile. 'Have ye ever slept on the ground with a blanket of stars above ye?'

'Good gracious! Never.'

'Would ye like to?'

Helene pressed her palms together, prayer-like. 'Most definitely!'

Grizel swung pleading eyes on her brother. 'I see nae reason why we cannae honour our guest's request. It's a pretty walk, and I for one would like to visit the shielings again. Will ye take us, Lachlan?'

''Tis not up to me. Ye best seek approval from Mother and Auntie Elspeth. There's also Helene's reputation to consider, and—'

'Come now,' interrupted Helene. 'We're far from the prying eyes of London's gossips. You'd be my escort in the capacity of chaperone and protector, just as you'd do so for your sister.'

Grizel grinned at her brother. 'Ye cannae argue with that. So if Mother and Auntie Elspeth approve, will ye take us?'

The laird turned his gaze to the sky as if making a study of the weather. 'It would take us the best part of a day to trek to the shieling grounds, and that's if we trek at a sprightly pace.' He glanced at Helene. 'Are ye fit enough to walk far and over uneven ground?'

Pride had Helene sit tall and straight. 'Do I look unfit?'

Lachlan swept his gaze over her. 'Nae, but it takes stamina to walk through dense woodland and take on the mountain's incline.'

Agnes gave an unladylike snort. 'It's not the same as taking a leisurely stroll in London's Royal Parks, Helene. It's a strenuous climb in the wilderness. I don't encourage it, and I most certainly will not join you if you go.'

'I'll be perfectly fine,' insisted Helene. 'In fact, I'd welcome the challenge.' She caught Lachlan appraising her footwear. 'My boots are sturdy enough.'

He raised a brow in question. 'If not, then have Grizel loan ye a pair. Ye look to be of similar size.'

Grizel slapped a hand on her brother's sleeve. 'Does that mean ye'll take us?'

'I dinnae see why not.'

Excitement surged through Helene. 'When? Tomorrow?'

'Nae. I've matters to address.' Lachlan looked to the sky above. 'Weather pending, we'll go the day after tomorrow.'

Cuthbert stretched long legs out in front of him. 'A sojourn at the shielings where the women are in charge is not quite my cup of tea. Nor do I desire trekking up a mountain and sleeping roughshod in a hut or under the stars.'

Grizel pulled and then threw a tuft of grass at him. 'Yer London life has sent ye soft, cousin. Won't ye change yer mind?'

'I think not. I'll stay put at Drumocher and keep an eye on things while you're away. I'm happy for Lady Helene to experience her heart's *desire*.'

Helene understood the underlying message in Cuthbert's comment and inflection. She was to use this opportunity to cosy up to Lachlan and seal her end of the deal.

Cuthbert tossed the grass tuft aside and stood. 'For now, my dear Grizel, I need you to give me some expert tips on skimming stones. I'll not have you or your brother best me on that front, and I'll be sure to practise while you're both away.'

It was all the encouragement Grizel needed. 'Ye'll ne'er best me, cousin!' She jumped to her feet and ran to the loch's edge.

'Agnes, come join us,' said Cuthbert.

'No, thank you. I'll pack away the remains of the picnic, and then I intend gathering wildflowers to take home to Mother and Auntie Caitrin.'

'As you wish.'

Helene felt the pull of Lachlan's gaze on her. He rose from the picnic blanket and offered her his hand. 'Might ye take a wee stroll with me? I wish to show ye something.'

She glanced up to see him towering over her, strong and commanding in stature. She placed her hand in his, and he pulled her to her feet with no more effort than if he were to gently pluck a flower from the woodland floor. He let go of her hand and indicated the way forward.

They walked a well-trod path along the loch's perimeter, surrounded by nature's conversations. Birds twittered, leaves rustled, branches sighed in the gentle breeze, and hidden insects chirped in chorus.

In this moment, all was peaceful and right with the world, and yet Helene's state of mind stood at odds with the surrounding tranquillity. She suddenly stopped, hands wringing, and gazed at the ground.

'What's wrong, lass? Something ails ye?'

'No.' She looked up at him. Guilt had her look away. 'No, I . . .'

'Something troubles ye, then.'

She could have laughed out loud. It wasn't just one thing, but many things troubling her. Strategic reasoning gave her courage to look him in the eyes and say what weighed heavy on her mind. 'You and Cuthbert quarrelled.'

He raised a brow at her direct statement. 'Aye. 'Tis not the first time.'

'Is it the first time you've held a blade to his throat?'

Anger flashed in his eyes, overtaken by regret sitting heavy on the planes of his face. It brought Helene undone. Lachlan and Cuthbert were cousins. Nothing could ever change that, but no matter what she thought of them, it pained her to have seen their close bond and friendship fracture because of her. The damage done was not part of her plan.

His shoulders lifted and fell. 'Aye,' he said on a sigh. 'I'm sorry ye had to witness that, but ye needn't worry. We've sorted our differences.'

His attempt at a smile to allay her concerns made it all the worse for Helene. 'If I'm right, you quarrelled because of me, and for that I'm sorry.'

'Why would ye think we quarrelled over ye?'

She shrugged. 'Intuition.' A lie. 'And because you weren't happy to find the two of us alone.' The truth.

'Aye, well, I did warn ye about Cuthbert. He's not to be trusted around beautiful women.'

It was the second time the laird had called her beautiful. 'Am I?'

'Are ye what?'

'Beautiful.'

His gaze made a leisurely sweep of her face and his voice softened. 'I wouldnae say it if I didnae mean it.'

The back of her hand went to her cheek. She blushed as if on fire. Never had the compliment felt so good nor sounded so genuine as it did coming from him. 'The day is warm.' It was the only way she could casually dismiss his effect on her.

'A stream lies ahead. The water is cooling and fit to drink.' He continued on, turning when Helene did not follow.

She asked, 'I'm curious to know what you both said to warrant your act of violence against Cuthbert?'

A muscle ticked along the edge of his jaw, and his broad chest expanded beneath his linen shirt and unbuttoned jacket. He went to say something only to snap his mouth shut. He did it again, his head cocked slightly to one side as if deliberating a reply. Dark eyes darted in the direction they'd walked and resettled on Helene's face. The intensity of his stare made it clear he did not wish to discuss the matter.

'I'm sorry. I shouldn't have asked.'

Helene walked on. His hand caught her arm and stayed her. He drew her closer to him, sliding his hand down her sleeve before letting go. Pleasurable sensation rippled through her.

'Aye, then. Ye shall have the truth. Cuthbert and I, we . . . we've had ourselves a yearly wager when attending the London Season.'

'At the gaming tables?'

He looked suddenly sheepish. 'Not those kinds of games.'

Helene waited.

'Each year we'd single out one of the married women of London society who was known to welcome lovers into her bed.'

Helene knew both men to be rakes but had no knowledge of how they went about seducing their prey. 'Single out?'

Lachlan grimaced. His chin and gaze dipped down. 'We'd compete for that woman's attentions. Whoever bedded her first, won the wager.'

Helene held her disgust in check. 'And how much money did you wager on each of these conquests?'

He shook his head. 'Money held nae incentive.'

Helene gave a snort of disbelief. 'What could possibly hold more incentive for a man than money when making a wager?'

He seemed unwilling to meet her gaze. 'Pride, personal victory, and ego.'

'Ego. Something you and Cuthbert definitely have in common!'

He at least had the decency to look anything but proud. Still, his admission angered Helene. Using women to slake their lust in the name of winning a ribald bet was a despicable act. Her anger ran deeper for reasons she could not explain. It wasn't as if the married women he spoke of weren't willing participants in the bedchamber. They no doubt enjoyed the game of seduction just as much as Lachlan and his cousin.

Helene couldn't keep the sarcasm from her voice. 'And might I ask which one of you has won the most wagers?'

She had her answer the instant Lachlan averted his gaze. Simultaneously, the motivation driving Cuthbert's ambitions took shape. His ego demanded he best Lachlan in the art of seduction, and by way of pretence and deceit, Helene would reap her reward for being the willing vehicle in winning that wager for him.

Hoodwink him into believing he has your interest, then turn him down and focus your efforts on me. Cuthbert's words. He wanted to rub salt in Lachlan's wound. He was using Helene to checkmate Lachlan. A win to be noted on Cuthbert's score card.

'I see,' said Helene, and let fly with her scorn. 'Well, with a skill like that you must be the envy of all men. If not envied, then despised. I can't imagine how the English peers of the realm take to having other men bed their wives, especially a Scotsman.'

His eyes sharpened on her, and he leaned closer. 'Scotsman. Frenchman. Englishman. What does it matter? Infidelity is infidelity, nae matter a man or woman's background or breeding.'

Helene tilted her chin a little higher. 'Cuckolds and cuckqueans. They deserve each other! Likewise with rakes and coquettes. They make an absolute mockery of the sanctity of marriage. Wouldn't you agree?'

How the laird of Clan MacLanoch chose to conduct himself in his pursuit of carnal pleasure was no business of Helene's, nor should it matter to her, and yet, it did. She'd openly judged and insulted him as if he'd been unfaithful to her. The realisation left her reeling and confused. Her heart raced when he dipped his face to within inches of hers.

'Point taken, Lady Helene, but ken this. I hold the sanctity of marriage in high regard.'

'I doubt that very much, given what you've just disclosed!'

His gaze fell to her lips and lingered long enough to make her believe he wanted to kiss her. Here then was her chance. Here was the opportunity to draw him in, to tempt him with a provocative pout. Her pulse leapt at the expectation of experiencing something more than the exchange of terse words. The scent of red wine laced his breath. Now to taste it. Burgeoning desire caught her off guard, and her eyelids fluttered closed.

Soft words feathered her face. 'If not me or Cuthbert, those women would have bedded another. They were willing pawns in our game. A means to an end.'

Desire withered in a flash. Helene opened her eyes and recoiled from him. 'That end being a vainglorious boast of sexual conquests!'

'Judge me as ye wish. My point in telling ye all this is to let ye ken Cuthbert keeps pushing to make *ye* our next conquest. He pushed one too many times, which forced my blade to his throat.'

'But I don't fit your wager criteria,' she retaliated. 'I'm not married.'

'Rules of any game can change at a moment's notice. In yer case, I dinnae like his rules, therefore I refuse to play his game. As I said, he and I have reached an understanding in that ye're not to be toyed with. He'll give ye nae further trouble.'

Helene gave a curt nod.

His eyes darkened. 'There be something else ye need ken.'

'And that is?'

He closed the space between them and slowly bent his

head to within a breath of her parted lips. 'If I were married, I'd give my wife nae reason to stray.'

The husky, sensually spoken innuendo reignited desire in Helene. She stood immobile and trapped beneath the intensity of Lachlan's heated gaze. All coherent thought left her but for one thing. *Kiss him. Now.* Not because she had to, but because she wanted to.

Too late. He stepped back and gestured the way forward. 'Splendour awaits ye.'

CHAPTER EIGHT

LACHLAN FOLLOWED HELENE as she carefully picked her way along the path ahead. The slender-built lass possessed strength of will, courage that counts, and an ability to coax secrets from him.

An donas dubh! Never in his twenty-eight years had he confessed as much to Drumocher's family priest, so what had compelled him to spill the truth of his sins to this lass?

He cared not a whit for another person's opinion of him, except for immediate family. Still, it set his teeth on edge to have watched Helene stand in judgement of him. He cared about her, not *for* her. Begrudgingly, this Sassenach raised more than his interest. *Hell.* He'd almost kissed her!

According to Cuthbert, the lass believed all men to be unworthy of her. Be that as it may, she'd intimated to Lachlan he was at least worthy of her kiss. He'd recognised the signs in her quickened breath, the way she leaned in closer, gaze falling to his mouth. When her eyelids fluttered closed and her lips parted, he'd been at risk of crushing her in his arms and tasting what was so tempting and willingly on offer.

But the lass was not to be interfered with, and this overriding restriction was his saving grace. If he were to take advantage of her vulnerability, it would add strength to her already stained opinion of him. Besides, what man compromises his honour for the sake of a mere kiss?

'Can ye hear it?' he said at her back.

She stopped and turned. 'Hear what?'

'Listen.'

Helene tilted her head to one side. Deep concentration gave way to wide-eyed recognition. 'I hear running water.'

'Aye. There's a fork in the path ahead. We'll need to break left, away from the loch.'

Lachlan reached her side, and together they walked to a point where they veered off along another path. Thick tree roots ruptured the ground, forcing the need to proceed with care.

The lass rejected Lachlan's helping hand, and he could not help but admire her independence to forge on unassisted. Her determination boded well for their trek to the shielings. She lifted the hem of her skirts to step clear of nature's stumbling blocks, giving Lachlan a glimpse of shapely stockinged calves above laced ankle boots.

Rustling sounds from the underbrush drew her closer to him. 'What was that?'

Lachlan smiled at the fright in her voice. 'A mountain hare or pine marten. Perhaps even a fox. Dinnae be scairt. They'll scarper from us.'

Vegetation became denser, the air moist beneath a canopy of trees, and the path's gradual descent meandered between a small ravine-like formation.

'The sound of water grows stronger,' Helene observed.

Lachlan kept a close eye on her when they turned a corner along the path. She reacted just as he'd hoped, speechless with mouth agape, head tilted back, and eyes focused on water spouting from high up a jagged rock wall.

Water plunged into a crystal-clear pool strewn with smaller

rocks on its bed. From there it cascaded down a series of smooth stair-like stones worn from centuries of continuous fast-flowing water. Like an adder on the move, it meandered through lush woodland.

'How utterly beautiful,' said Helene with a sweeping gaze of their surrounds.

She trod carefully to the edge of the pool and ran her hands over a large, moss-covered boulder. 'It feels like velvet.' She turned to look with a smile at Lachlan over her shoulder. 'So green. A rich shade I've never seen before.' She bent down beside the babbling stream and laughed the instant her hands touched the water. 'Chilly and fresh!'

'Aye. 'Tis indeed bracing. Grizel and I each used to visit here often when we were bairns. We'd climb up those rocks and scoot over as close as we could to the waterfall. Then we'd splash about in the pool of water.'

'I envy you for having such a wonderful childhood playground,' said Helene with a wistful smile. 'So very different to mine.'

There followed a melancholy silence between them, save for the settling sounds of nature. Helene turned her face to the tree canopy overhead, and her chest expanded with a lungful of fresh air.

'The perfume of pines. So delightful and invigorating.' Again, she cast her gaze wide. 'A deep and soul-easing peace resides here.'

It gave Lachlan great pleasure to know she shared his appreciation of his Scottish homeland, but the flash of disturbing sadness he'd seen in her eyes came as a stab to his heart.

'Why are ye not yet married, lass?' The question was out before he gave thought to ask it.

She turned her head sharply to look at him.

''Tis a personal question, I ken, but yer a bonnie lass from an upstanding family. Why would ye choose to spend time here in the Highlands in lieu of the London Season?'

'If it's good enough for your cousin Agnes, then it's good enough for me.'

'Aye, but she's not the one who's refused the hand of London's most coveted suitors. Did ye reject them because ye dinnae think them worthy of ye?'

Helene remained silent for so long that Lachlan regretted the directness of his interrogation.

She spoke in a flat voice. 'I've no need of a husband.'

'Nae need?' Lachlan's laugh was one of disbelief. 'Lass, ye either marry or see out yer days as a lonely spinster. I hardly believe ye'd forgo a fortunate life of elegant frippery and endless balls in favour of the latter.'

Her eyes narrowed on him. 'And you draw that assumption about me based on what? Gossip? Has Agnes said—?'

'Nae. Not Agnes.'

'Then who?'

'Cuthbert.'

Helene rolled her eyes. 'Well now. He's a reliable source.' She planted her hands on her hips. 'Yes, I've refused several suitors, and with good reason. Aside from that, you know nothing about me, and yet you assume my life's ambition is to secure a wealthy husband, bear his children, and enjoy life's finery.'

She was right. Lachlan knew nothing about her other than what Cuthbert had told him. If she had been at last year's Season, or even the one before that, then why hadn't he noticed her? Probably because he'd been too damned busy chasing and charming the skirts off an adulterous wife in a bid to win a pathetic wager with his cousin!

'I'm sure yer father wishes to see ye happy and comfortably settled in marriage.'

'He *and* my brother, though not for reasons of love or compatibility or my personal happiness.' There was a sardonic twist to her smile as she shook her head. 'Their priority is to marry me off to someone of my station or above. A man with money, title, and useful family connections. Isn't that the way of it with fathers and their daughters?'

Her words rang true in part. It was what Lachlan's father would want for Grizel. It was what he and his mother wanted for Grizel.

As if reading his mind, she cocked her head to one side and asked, 'Is your sister free to marry a man of her choosing?'

'Within reason.'

She gave a derisive snort. 'Let me rephrase the question. Would Grizel have your blessing and consent if she were to fall in love with, and wish to marry, a Jacobite? Or perhaps the son of one of your tenants?'

Her question hit a raw nerve, and he responded with a resounding, 'Nae!'

Her face was a mix of triumph and contempt. 'Just as I thought. On that count you and my father and brother are one and the same. We women are nothing but puppets, our strings pulled by the men who seek to manipulate and control us.'

'I'm sorry ye feel that way.'

'Don't be.'

Helene plucked a large leaf from a nearby tree and crouched down beside the stream. She lay the leaf atop the water, watching in silence as it drifted away on its solo expedition. 'Like the women in your games of seduction, I too am a pawn, albeit an unwilling one, in my father's quest to marry me off.'

'Ye may well have a cynical view on marriage, but in these turbulent times, I for one do not wish to see my sister married to a man who doesnae have the means to provide for or protect her. I daresay yer father only wishes the same for ye.'

Helene remained crouched, turning only her head to look at Lachlan. 'And if your sister detests or doesn't love the man of your choosing? What then?'

'I can only hope she trusts me enough to secure her a good match. If love comes of it, then all the better. But I wouldnae force marriage on her.'

Helene picked up a large stone. She tested its heaviness in one hand as if weighing up the merit of his response.

'If ye had a daughter, what would ye wish for her future?' Lachlan caught something akin to regret in her eyes before she turned her gaze downstream.

'I shall never have a daughter, or any children for that matter, but I *will* have—'

She broke off suddenly and her hand fisted around the stone, turning her knuckles white. In a flurry of movement, she stood and with great force hurled the rock away from her. It landed in the water on the opposite side of the stream. The sound and size of the splash frightened a stoat from the underbrush, the bushy black tip of its tail flicking in protest as it bounded away.

The lass was a most perplexing enigma. Her words and sudden outburst suggested she wrestled with inner demons. It triggered in Lachlan the need to reach out, if only to lend her his ear, but her stiff back and clenched hands warned him off. Perhaps with time spent together at the shielings, he'd get to know and understand her a little better.

'Come, lass. We'd best be going now.'

Her head tilted towards sunlight filtering through the canopy, and the small breadth of her back expanded with another breath of fresh air. Fingers unfurled at her sides, and both hands shook off whatever had caused them to clench.

She turned to face him. 'Thank you for bringing me here.'

Her smile radiated gratitude, and in that moment, Lachlan's heart smiled too.

As they neared their picnic site, Grizel approached them at a run. 'It's Agnes! She's hurt her ankle.' Grizel stopped to catch her breath. 'She tripped over a fallen branch and fell most awkwardly.'

Lachlan wasted no time in sprinting to the spot where Agnes sat on a patch of grass, her face contorted in pain.

Cuthbert took the reins of a horse and swung up into the saddle. 'We must leave. Agnes can ride with me.'

'Aye. In a minute,' said Lachlan. 'Agnes, do ye mind if I take a look?' She winced when he gently touched her stockinged foot. 'Do ye have any numbness or tingling, lass?'

Agnes shook her head.

''Tis a good sign, then. Yer ankle doesnae look *off* either, so I dinnae think it's broken. When ye tripped, did ye hear a popping sound, or a crack?'

'No.'

Lachlan placed his hands directly over her ankle bone. 'Does it hurt here, or feel tender beneath my touch?'

Agnes swiped away a tear. 'No.'

Lachlan tested the soft part of her ankle. 'What about now?'

She sucked in a breath. 'That hurts!'

He removed his hands. 'Seems more than likely ye've sprained yer ankle rather than broken or fractured it. Ye'll need rest and to keep yer foot elevated.'

'How long will it take to heal?'

'If it's a minor sprain, it could take between two to four weeks. Any worse than that, then ye'll be off yer feet for a month or two.'

'Weeks! Months! But I don't want to be confined indoors.

How shall I pass the hours on my own with you all away at the shielings?'

Cuthbert exaggerated having taken offense to her question. 'Sister! You'll have *me* to keep you company, as well as Mother and Auntie Caitrin.'

When Agnes groaned, Cuthbert teased, 'Don't be like that. We'll teach you how to be proficient at whist, or we can play gammon, as they call it here in Scotland. You could of course immerse yourself in Drumocher's well-stocked library.'

Grizel took Agnes's hand in hers. 'I'll stay with ye.'

This cheered Agnes no end. 'Oh! Would you?'

Grizel glanced up at Helene. 'That's if ye dinnae mind. I'm sorry not to accompany ye to the shielings, but I dinnae feel right abandoning poor Agnes given what's just happened to her.'

'I can stay too,' said Helene. 'I need not go to—'

'I think you should!' said Cuthbert.

'The lass can make up her own mind,' objected Lachlan.

'Of course she can. I just want to emphasise the opportunity might not present itself again. You will keep her safe, Lachlan, and you, Helene, will find the scenery to be simply breathtaking.' He smiled down at her from his seat in the saddle. 'You'll not reap a better reward.'

Agnes echoed her brother's sentiments. 'Don't stay on my account, Helene. My ankle will mend soon enough. If it's something you wish to do, then do it. Leave the Highlands with no regrets.'

Deep down, Lachlan embraced the prospect of spending time alone with Helene on their trek to and from higher ground. This self-admission caught him off guard. It was the first time he'd been genuinely interested in and drawn to a woman since— He quickly buried that thought. 'What say ye, lass?'

'If it's not too much trouble, then I'd like to visit the shielings.'

''Tis settled.' Lachlan carefully lifted Agnes and seated her on the horse behind her brother. Grizel attached the picnic satchels to her own saddle, mounted her horse, and set off at a trot behind Cuthbert.

Lachlan readjusted the saddle on the remaining horse and held out his hand to Helene. 'Ye'll ride with me.' The uncertainty in her eyes amused him.

She folded her arms across her chest. 'I can walk.'

'I ken ye can walk, but we're going to ride back to Drumocher.' His hand beckoned her forth.

One more moment's hesitancy and she complied. Lachlan hoisted her up onto the horse and then swung into the saddle behind her. His hands came around her waist to gather up the reins. He urged the horse forward to follow the others.

Helene said not a word. Just as well. Lachlan was preoccupied with the mesmerising column of a pale slender neck perfumed with the scent of violets. His fingers twitched with the need to unpin glossy blue-black hair and let it fall about her shoulders. A matter of inches separated her rigid back from his chest, and yet the warmth he enjoyed had nothing to do with the late-afternoon sun. He resisted all temptation to lean forward and align his body with hers. Best he steer clear of wayward thoughts and think about something else.

Cuthbert.

Having threatened him with violence to back off from Helene was one thing, but for Cuthbert to capitulate to the point of pressing Helene to travel alone with Lachlan to the shielings was another. For the first time in his life, instinct had Lachlan mistrusting his cousin. Keeping Helene at a safe distance from Cuthbert was for the best.

'Those tenants. The ones who couldn't afford their rent?'

Helene's question startled Lachlan. 'Aye. What of them?'

'You showed great kindness in waiving whatever they owed.'

''Twas not so much kindness, lass, but compassion. I ken we all fall on hard times, but as laird I cannae show weakness by wiping the debt completely. 'Twould send the wrong message to all tenants and set a precedent. Their debt will be paid, if not in coin then by some other means.'

'How?'

Lachlan liked that the lass showed interest in understanding the reason behind his ruling. 'Come spring, the cottars might gift me a lamb or a calf, or bags of wheat at harvest time. Whatever they can afford, and equal to their debt, will suffice.'

She fell silent again. Lachlan tilted his head to the side to see her look of deep contemplation.

'Donnie,' she said in a soft voice. 'I'm glad you sent him to the chapel with Father Crawford to ask for God's forgiveness.'

'I doubt there's anything a wee child could do that God could not forgive.'

Helene's stiff spine softened. Her shoulders sagged forward, and her chin fell to her chest. 'Some sins can never be forgiven.'

So faint were her words that Lachlan felt sure she did not intend for him to hear her. He didn't comment or pursue the conversation further, instead taking his cue from her silence, lending his support as a prop when she slowly leaned back against him.

Intriguing mystery, thicker than a winter morning's fog, shrouded the lass. For Lachlan, their time away at the shielings couldn't come soon enough.

When Helene leaned back against the laird, it was because she suffered a moment's weakness and craved human comfort. As his arms closed loosely about her waist, his touch came as a stark reminder to set aside self-pity and focus on the task at hand.

Seduction.

Had Agnes not injured herself, then this opportunity for close contact with Lachlan might not have presented itself. Helene used it to her advantage and settled her forearms on the outside of his, gently pressing inward so that his arms hugged her waist.

She heard a slight catch in his throat, yet he did not pull away. His breath on her neck made her skin tingle. Her eyes closed and she rested her head against his shoulder as if drowsy from fresh air and exercise.

'Mo maise.'

Whatever he'd whispered in Gaelic sounded like a softly spoken endearment. Her eyes remained closed, and she opened up her senses to the surrounds, from the sun on her eyelids and the constant twitter of birds, to a mix of floral perfumes and Scots pine. Above all that, her senses filled with the man at her back. A pillar of solid strength. Warm. Protective. She could smell the wool in Lachlan's plaid kilt, the smoky scent of hearth and home, and something so masculine as to make her breathe and draw him in.

Their bodies moved as one, in sync with the horse's restful clip-clop gait. Helene knew herself to be in danger of never wanting to be separated from the here and now. How ironic. She, the seducer, was being seduced. She remained this way until Lachlan spoke as one does when gently waking another.

'Helene. We're home.'

She couldn't bring herself to stir. Her time here in the

Highlands had been so short, and yet, in some strange way, she did feel at home. In his arms.

'Lass, wake up.'

Warm lips moved against her cheek, sending the most pleasant shiver down her left side. Her eyes opened just as they passed through Drumocher's yawning gates and overhead portcullis. Ahead, a stable-boy came running, arms outstretched ready to take the reins and care for the horses. Cuthbert dismounted, scooped his sister into his arms, and made for the lord's tower. *Poor Agnes.* Her resting face suddenly contorted from the pain she suffered.

Grizel dismounted, as did Lachlan. He reached up to Helene. Large hands spanned her waist, igniting in her body another bout of giddy sensations. She braced herself against his shoulders, and when he set her on solid ground, he eyed her in such a way as she could not decipher. She ruled out having upset him because he still held her firm about the waist.

His gaze fell briefly to her mouth, and then, as if gathering his wits, his arms dropped to his sides. 'I'll see after Agnes.'

'Yes, of course.' Helene's gaze followed his every stride.

Grizel hailed another stable-boy and instructed him to return the food satchels to the kitchen. She stared at Helene with the hint of a mischievous smile.

'What?' asked Helene.

Grizel glanced at her retreating brother and then back at Helene. Her smile grew wider. 'Nothing. Come on. Agnes will want our company.' She hurried towards the tower's entrance and disappeared inside.

Helene had taken only a few steps when something even more puzzling than Grizel's curious behaviour brought her to a halt. Courtyard activity had stalled. Clan men and women stood motionless, seemingly fixated with her.

She turned on the spot. Slowly. Cautious. The subject of

their scrutiny. Narrowed eyes put her on high alert. It would seem her presence here in the Highlands, and perhaps her bold actions in the great hall this morning, had been severely judged. Was this some sort of silent retribution?

Helene turned towards a noise at her back and saw a tall, stocky man approach. He stopped, leaving a distance between them as long as the sword he held. A leather apron covered his sleeveless tunic and leather boots, and a girdle sat about his waist.

Helene recognised the smithy. Her gaze fell to the weapon he carried, which sent her heart hammering against her ribs. She'd seen one too many blades for today. One swallow was not near enough to moisten a throat parched and dry, and she became short of breath.

Run! She should turn and run towards the safety of the keep. *Impossible.* The brawny man ensnared her with eyes as grey as the steel he forged.

Lachlan! Would he hear her if she screamed his name? She looked up at the tower from one window to the next, eyes darting back to the smithy when he raised the sword high with the blade's tip pointing at the ground. With a forceful downward thrust, he stabbed it into the ground and let go of its hilt. It stuck out of the earth like a loyal sentinel by his side.

Helene expelled a lungful of air, and her knees almost buckled beneath her. All around her people stared, tormenting her sense of unease while she waited for . . . she didn't know what.

The smithy stepped forward. Helene took a step back. His gaze fell at her feet, and he removed his flat knitted bonnet in a gesture of supplication. He repeatedly scrunched the rim of the woollen cap in both hands, and upon lifting his gaze to meet Helene's, she saw that his eyes had softened to the grey hues of post-storm light. She relaxed a fraction only to flinch when she heard a shout to her left.

'M'lady! M'lady!' A child ran towards her from the castle's entrance. He skidded to a halt, cap in hand.

'Donnie!' Helene felt genuine joy at seeing the lad again.

He acknowledged her with a wide grin, then turned sheepish eyes on the smithy. The two exchanged words in sombre Gaelic before Donnie explained, 'M'lady, this man is my uncle, and he—'

'Your uncle?' Helene looked from man to boy.

'Aye. Hamish Ewing. My da's older brother. He has something to say to ye.'

Helene gave Hamish her wary attention. He looked her fair-square in the eyes and launched into Gaelic with no hint of threat in his throaty intonation. She was helpless to understand him. When he'd said his piece, he addressed his nephew with a few more words in their mother tongue.

Donnie looked up at Helene. 'My uncle thanks ye for what ye did for me today. He cannae understand why a Sassenach lass would do such a thing for a Scottish bairn. Ye're not of our blood or culture, and he says it took great courage to stand up to the laird.'

Humbling words. It was the last thing Helene expected to hear.

Hamish Ewing replaced his bonnet, gripped the sword's hilt, and yanked it out of the ground. He held the hilt close to his heart and spoke again in Gaelic to Helene. She awaited Donnie's interpretation.

'My uncle says for as long as ye're on Scottish soil, he'll have yer back. He'll stick his neck out for ye just as ye did for me. Ye're kin to him and my family now.'

Helene was left speechless. She blinked back moisture in her eyes and smiled her thanks to the smithy. He gave her a slow nod, touched a hand to Donnie's shoulder, and then returned to his anvil.

All around her people continued to stare, but just as a pendulum swings, so did their demeanour. Women acknowledged Helene with a smile, and men respectfully touched the brim of their bonnets or tipped their heads in her direction. One by one they went about their business, the courtyard returning to a hive of activity.

'Ye've earned their respect,' said Donnie.

Helene favoured the lad with a kind smile. 'That's not what I set out to do.'

'Ye have it all the same, and *I* need ye to ken how verra grateful I am to ye. Ye're as brave as a Highland warrior, and I'm forever in yer debt.'

'There's nothing brave about what I did, Donnie. I just couldn't let . . .' Helene tamped down the emotion welling in her throat. 'You owe me no debt. Just keep your promise to stay out of trouble and never steal again.'

'Aye. I promise.' He pointed. 'That be my ma and da standing outside the gates.'

Helene saw Donnie's parents acknowledge her, each with one hand raised in a wave.

'Do ye see the wooden cage they carry?' said Donnie.

'Yes. What's inside?'

'A rooster and four chickens. A gift from the laird to replace the ones we lost to wildcats.'

Helene looked sharply at the lad.

Donnie's gleeful smile faded. 'Did ye not ken?'

Helene shook her head. 'Lach—I mean, your laird said not a word about it to me.'

Donnie shrugged. 'Must have slipped his mind, or maybe he's yet to tell ye.'

Lachlan had had plenty of opportunity to do so. 'Well, that was most generous of him. I'm happy all has been resolved.'

'Aye. Well, I must be going now. Thank ye again, m'lady.' He donned his cap and went directly to his parents.

Helene returned their parting wave and reflected on the day's events. Lachlan sat top of mind. Her opinion of him had shifted. He might be a rake by reputation south of the border, but she'd seen first-hand that there was more to him than met the eye. It was hard not to acknowledge an undeniable curiosity to discover more about the MacLanoch laird.

CHAPTER NINE

HELENE WOKE WITH the dawning of a new day. She wrapped a blanket about her shoulders and padded barefoot to the window to watch mist eddy round the loch's bank.

After making use of the chamber pot, she tugged on the woven bell-pull to summon a servant. It wasn't long before there came a knock on the door. Helene welcomed the maid's assistance in getting dressed and having her hair securely pinned in preparation for the long trek to higher ground with Lachlan.

'Would ye like me to bring yer breakfast here to yer room, m'lady?' asked the maid.

'The lord's hall will suffice.'

'Verra well. I'll inform the cook.' The maid curtsied and took her leave.

Helene retrieved a small brush, pocketed it in her cloak, and set the garment to one side on her bed, there to collect prior to her departure to the shielings.

The long table in the lord's hall had been set for her and Lachlan's family, yet it was no surprise to Helene she was the first to arrive for the morning meal. She told herself it was because she simply wished to seize the day and venture deep into the Highlands.

Lady Sutton and Caitrin MacLanoch still lay abed and were not likely to rise before Helene and Lachlan set off this morning. For that reason, the older women had wished Helene well before retiring last night, and Caitrin had lovingly put the word on her son to take good care of their guest.

As for poor Agnes, she had a sprained ankle to contend with. Helene would keep her promise and visit Agnes in her bedchamber before heading off.

While awaiting her meal, Helene set about examining the room in more detail. Ancestral portraits lined the walls, including two beautiful full-length portraits, one of a woman, the other of a man who bore a striking resemblance to Lachlan. His grandparents, she supposed.

Situated between the two portraits sat a massive oak sideboard. Helene ran her fingers over the date carved into the ornate wood—*1645*. Two tall silver candelabras sat either end of the sideboard, with a silver urn positioned in the centre. Helene saw her reflection in the lovingly polished piece.

Her gaze fell to the large woven rug underfoot, timeworn and faded in places. How many generations of MacLanochs and their guests had partaken of meals at the scarred dining table with its twelve matching leather-upholstered high-back chairs?

She turned to the mantelpiece above the hearth and touched the smooth curves of the mahogany clock. One hundred or so years of family history furnished this room.

'Time is ticking, is it not?'

Cuthbert's voice startled Helene. She swung around to see him with arms folded and casually leaning against the door-frame.

'Ticking too fast,' she replied. An image of Prudence in the asylum came to mind.

Cuthbert went to her side and said in hushed tones, 'I

didn't get a moment alone with you last night to ask how things went yesterday?'

'With what?'

'You and Lachlan, of course. When you went for a walk by the loch. Alone.'

She whispered back, 'He didn't kiss me, if that's what you're asking.'

'There's time yet, and you'll have plenty of it when you're away at the shielings.' He winked. 'I'm quietly confident my cousin is taken with you. He's defended a woman's honour many times over, but none so passionate as he has done for you.'

Cuthbert rubbed the curve of his jaw. 'I tell you, blood is *not* thicker than water. My cousin dispelled that medieval proverb when he drew his blade on me.'

'If I do kiss Lachlan and he denies it, how will I prove it to you?'

Cuthbert snorted a laugh. 'If he kisses you, then it's not something he'll be able to hide. Believe me, I know my cousin better than he knows himself. Honour might be his strength, but it's also his downfall. Experience has taught him that.'

'How so?'

Their conversation was interrupted by a polite cough at the hall's entrance, where servants awaited permission to enter with trays of food. Cuthbert waved them in. No sooner had Helene seated herself at the table than Grizel arrived.

When Lachlan entered the room, Helene swept an appreciative eye over the commanding figure he cut in his traditional attire. He wore a brown linen waistcoat with hand-sewn long buttonholes. The garment was laced at the back. A neatly tied cravat around his neck looked as clean and crisp as the shirt worn beneath the waistcoat. His belted plaid hung down from the back of his waist to the ankles of leather knee-high boots. She looked away lest he sense her staring at him.

Morning pleasantries were exchanged, and Grizel launched into excitable chatter about all manner of things. Especially about the shielings. Helene could not fathom how the young girl managed to talk and eat so efficiently at the same time. Lachlan and Cuthbert exchanged a knowing look, suggesting they were of the same opinion. Helene felt ashamedly pleased to think Grizel would remain at Drumocher to keep Agnes company.

Lachlan pinned his gaze on Cuthbert. 'My council of men will look after things while I'm away, and ye know where to find me should the need arise. I'll expect we'll be gone for a matter of days, unless'—he glanced at Helene—'unless the lass here misses her creature comforts and wishes for an early return.'

Helene raised her chin. 'Oh, ye of little faith.'

The laird laughed, much to Helene's delight. She smiled back at him, conscious of Cuthbert's assessing eyes.

''Tis time we get going,' Lachlan said to Helene. 'We've a way to travel.'

'I just need to fetch my cloak and check in on Agnes. Will you accompany me, Grizel?'

'Aye. Of course.'

'I'll see ye in the courtyard, Helene,' said Lachlan.

'And I wish you a pleasant trip,' said Cuthbert.

Helene didn't need to think twice about the underlying message in Cuthbert's wink.

❧

Lachlan was standing in the courtyard conversing with a group of clansmen when he saw Helene approach. His men were quick to greet her. They wished him and Helene a safe journey to the shielings and then dispersed.

Lachlan acknowledged the woollen wrap around Helene's shoulders. 'Ye look good draped in plaid.' Her shy smile suggested his compliment pleased her.

'Thank you. Grizel loaned it to me. She was right in saying my cloak would be heavy and too cumbersome to carry.'

'Aye. We use the plaid in all weathers, and ye'll need it at the shielings. Nights can turn chilly.' Lachlan glanced down at her feet. 'Would they be a pair of Grizel's boots?'

'Yes.'

'Well, ye'll be pleased for having worn those instead of yer own.'

She cast a scrutinous eye over him. 'Why so many weapons? Do you expect to fight an army along the way?'

Since she last saw him at their morning meal, he'd added two scabbards to his leather belts; one held a sword and the other, his dirk.

'Precaution and protection. A man doesnae go unarmed here in the Highlands.'

'I see. And the bundle you carry over your shoulder?'

'A wee drop of wine, and Cook has prepared us a bite to eat along the way.' Lachlan looked towards the steep slopes they must climb. 'Are ye ready, then?'

At her nod, they set out together on foot towards the loch, starting along the same path as the one they'd walked yesterday. The hour was still early, and when they reached the calm body of water, Lachlan pointed to the lifting mist. 'There's our sign for the promise of a fine day.'

He diverted along a different path to where the mountains loomed. Skylarks, with their streaky earth-toned plumage, flew all about them. Their unending repetitive song filled the air.

Lachlan and Helene toiled up the mountainside along a well-trod path. He noted her expressive reactions when taking in her surrounds: a smile for the long-eared, high-leaping mountain hares running their erratic path to escape human intrusion; the way her jaw dropped in awe when she glimpsed through the canopy of trees a silent gliding eagle lording over all in the sky above.

When they walked beside a stream, she stopped suddenly and turned an ear towards the soft whistle of an otter, then laughed at the silly antics of the animals frolicking in the water. At intervals, she bent to sniff the scent of wildflowers or trail fingertips over mountain heather.

Her earthy, tactile interaction with nature was not lost on Lachlan. He'd been wrong to think she sought only to live a shallow, frivolous existence as a pampered titled wife. How might she fare if she were to marry a Highlander?

The question caught him unawares, and before he could give it due consideration, Helene said, 'Tell me more about the shielings.'

He was taken with her interest and curiosity—if it were indeed genuine—in wanting to learn more about his people and culture.

'Cattle are driven along a wider path to the pastures, with some horses and a few sheep and goats. 'Tis the women and girls who go with them, but a handful of boys under the age of fourteen go to help look after the herds.'

'The men play no part in this?'

Lachlan smiled inwardly at the astonishment on her face and in her voice. 'The young folk and women shelter in small huts, so the men go to the shielings a few days beforehand to make any necessary repairs. They gather sufficient heather for bedding and ensure enough dry peat is available for the fires. Then they return home.'

'And how long do the women stay at the shielings?'

'Between nine and ten weeks.'

Helene took hold of Lachlan's wrist and halted their progress. 'For so long? But what do the men do during all this time?'

The pressure of her hand on his wrist slackened the instant Lachlan glanced down. When she let go, he chided himself for having enjoyed her touch.

'The men have their work cut out for them. They repair or rethatch cottages, cut and dry peat for winter fuel, make brogues for the winter, and if they have the skill for it, they'll take to weaving and tailoring. Then there's farming work to be done during the summer months.'

She seemed to mull over what he'd said. 'So, in being governed by the seasons, you all make the best use of time and resources, even if it means being separated from loved ones.'

'Aye.'

Lachlan took the lead as they climbed a steeper woodland path. He reached back to assist Helene. 'Take my hand, lass. The ground is softer here.'

'I can manage, thank y—'

Lachlan reacted with quick reflexes and grasped Helene's hand in the moment she slipped and lost her footing on the exposed soil. He lifted her up to stand with him on level ground. Colour drained from her face.

'Are ye all right, lass?'

She seemed not to hear him and stared trance-like at the pathway below. He looked for, and spied, a fallen tree. 'Come. Take a seat over here.'

'No! No, I'm all right. Really, I am. Let's continue.'

'Are ye sure?'

She pushed him away to dust off her skirts and resettle the skew-whiff plaid around her shoulders. 'So clumsy of me. If not for you, I'd have looked like one of those otters sliding down the muddy river embankment.'

There was fear beneath her nervous laughter. Lachlan sensed she dealt with something she'd prefer not to disclose, and so he let it go.

They'd walked not five minutes more when he stopped and took Helene by the arm to prevent her from taking another step.

'What's the matter?' she asked. Then, 'What's that high-pitched noise?'

Lachlan knew very well what made that sound, and it was close. If Helene's near fall had rattled her, how might she then react when confronted with what could possibly be a disturbing find?

CHAPTER TEN

THE FRANTIC CALL sounded again. Helene edged closer to Lachlan. 'What *is* that?'

''Tis a roe deer in distress.'

'A deer? Then we must find it.' Helene made to rush forward and search for the animal.

'Wait!' Lachlan held her back. 'Where there is a deer, there could well be a buck. Stay close behind me.'

She did as he said, and together they followed the deer's call. Helene swept her gaze from left to right, through the trees and at ground level, searching for the animal.

Lachlan stopped and pointed.

A set of antlers bobbed up and down in the underbrush, about one hundred paces from where they stood. Helene's gasp caused the buck to raise its head. The mighty animal stepped forward into a small clearing and stared them down. Two roe deer ventured forth behind him. They appeared edgy, each stamping its forefoot.

Helene looked on in awe. Lachlan had been right. The proud stag was indeed majestic, and the two does, by comparison, were striking and delicate.

A rustling noise came from beyond the underbrush, followed by the heightened urgency in the distress call. It further agitated the stag. It made an aggressive snort-wheeze and stomped a hoof. The does looked to be on the point of flight.

Lachlan slowly withdrew a pistol from the folds of his kilt.

'What are you doing?' whispered Helene in horror.

'If I dinnae scare them off, the buck might attack and we'll ne'er get close enough to the injured doe. Brace yersel' for the noise of the pistol.'

Helene slapped her hands over her ears. The sudden movement was enough to frighten the animals and send them bounding away seconds before Lachlan pointed the firearm skyward and fired.

The shot echoed around the mountains and left a ringing in Helene's ears. She opened her eyes to see the pistol's smoke dissipate, while the pungent scent of gunpowder irritated the inside of her nose.

Lachlan returned the pistol to the makeshift pocket inside his kilt. 'Perhaps ye'd best wait for me here, until I locate the deer.'

'Certainly not!'

Helene lifted the hem of her skirts and quickly picked her way over the woodland floor. Lachlan's curse came from behind before he reached her side. In moments they stood where the stag had emerged.

What Helene saw tore from her a cry as desperate as the wounded deer's. It looked to have misjudged a jump over several criss-crossed felled pines and had caught its back legs between broken intersecting branches. Its body dangled over the fallen trunk of the tree with its head and forelegs resting on the ground.

Instinct kicked in, and Helene moved to free the weary animal.

'Stay back!' ordered Lachlan.

'I will not!' She had no luck in shrugging off his restraining hand.

'We cannae save it.'

'We need only lift its legs over the branches to set it free.'

'Aye. That I will do, but its life cannae be saved.'

Helene's gaze snapped from Lachlan to the doe. Its large dark eyes seemed to plead for help just as Prudence had begged Helene not to leave her at the asylum. Soul-crushing helplessness left her feeling wretched.

'Then . . . we must do what we can to lessen its pain,' she urged.

He let go of her arm. 'Aye. Leave it to me.'

Lachlan administered gentle strength to disentangle the deer from its bonds and lay it on its side on the ground. The animal struggled in vain to stand and cried even more from each painful, pathetic attempt.

Seeing it disabled and defenceless was, for Helene, confronting and too close to home. She recognised panic in the doe's wild-eyed stare and felt the pain of its erratic, jerky movements. She knew what must be done even before Lachlan voiced it.

'Lass, both its forelegs are broken. It willnae survive in the wild, and predators will . . . Well, 'tis far kinder to put it out of its misery.'

Helene hugged her waist. 'Yes, I know. Please, make it quick and as painless as possible.'

Lachlan crouched down behind the deer and gently stroked a hand along the fur on its neck. The doe let out an exhausted grunt and lay still, as if understanding this was its last day.

'Dinnae watch, lass.'

Helene turned her back on the disturbing scene and steeled herself for what was to come. She shut her eyes and said a quick prayer for one of God's most beautiful creatures, yet nothing prepared her for the loud snap of the deer's neck being broken.

A premonition left Helene ice-cold. She sucked in a deep, shuddering breath. *Prudence.*

''Tis done,' said Lachlan. 'She's in no more pain.' Then, 'Are ye all right?'

No. She wasn't. Even if Helene had words to voice what she'd seen in her mind's eye, she could tell no one. Least of all Lachlan MacLanoch.

A warm hand rested on her shoulder.

'Ye're as stiff as a board.' Lachlan turned her to face him. 'Christ! Ye look like ye've seen a ghost!'

The idea of losing her sister sent Helene's body into a quivering mess. Had Lachlan not drawn her to his chest and held her tight, she'd have collapsed to the leaf-littered ground.

''Twas the right thing to do,' soothed Lachlan. 'Ye needn't be upset, lass. Its life will not be wasted.'

Lachlan spoke of the deer, of course, but its premature death mirrored Helene's worst nightmare of losing Prudence to the convulsive condition of the falling sickness. Every hour endured in that asylum, and without the proper care and attention she deserved, ate at Helene like a rat gnawing its way through her stomach.

She took the much-needed comfort he offered her and wrapped her arms around his broad back, her cheek pressed against his solid chest. 'I'm sorry you had to be the one to end the deer's life.'

'Better me than to have left her here to die a slow death.'

Die a slow death. God forbid anything happen to Prudence before Helene returned to London with the means to bribe a warden and buy her sister's freedom.

Lachlan drew back slightly, his hands still spanning her waist. Helene glanced up, and there, in his frown and in his gold-flecked eyes, she saw something akin to confusion. His fingers slid slowly, if not reluctantly, from her person, and he separated himself from her by taking a backward step. He took the bundle from his back containing their refreshments. 'Would ye care for something to eat? A bannock or—'

'No. Thank you. I've no appetite.'

Lachlan took a drink of wine and returned it to the bag. 'This is yers to carry for the next mile or so.'

Helene took it without question and slipped the strap over her head. Lachlan leaned over the lifeless animal, lifted it by the hooves, and slung its carcass around his shoulders.

'What are you doing?' she asked.

'Ye'll see soon enough. Come now. We must press on.'

They trekked through the woods until a small stone cottage came into view. The door had been left wide open, yet no one was in sight. On approach, Helene saw chickens roaming free, and two goats were tethered to a post within the perimeter of a low stone wall enclosure.

Lachlan called out in Gaelic. A faint reply led them around the back of the cottage, where a man and a woman worked, backs bent, tending a vegetable plot. At the sight of Lachlan, the older couple dropped their tools and slowly straightened to eagerly greet their laird and landowner with a flurry of Gaelic, humble gestures, and elated smiles.

Lachlan reciprocated in kind and indicated the deer slung around his shoulders. Helene assumed he explained to the cottars the circumstances leading up to the animal's death. It was only when the woman clapped her hands together and then flattened them over her belly that Helene understood what Lachlan had meant when he'd said the animal's life would not go to waste. It would provide many a nutritious meal for these folk who eked out a living from the land.

This gesture of thoughtful kindness further softened

Helene's heart towards a man whom she'd believed to be a notorious libertine.

'Helene, this is Aila and Ross. They dinnae speak any English, but they wish ye to ken they're honoured to meet ye.'

Ross, barefoot and clad in knee breeches and a mud-smudged linen shirt, removed his knitted bonnet to reveal a head of thinning silver hair. He gave Helene a toothy grin, while Aila managed a stiff curtsy. She wore a linen kertch around her head, and the apron protecting a brown serviceable woollen gown was smeared with the soil she tended. She had the kindest blue eyes that shone bright with the wisdom of her years.

Helene smiled at the crofters. 'Thank you. I too am pleased to make your acquaintance.'

Lachlan translated her reply. Ross replaced his bonnet and said something to Helene, gesturing towards the cottage. Helene looked to Lachlan to translate the Gaelic.

'They've invited us to join them for a wee dram.'

'Whisky?' Helene hadn't meant to sound so shocked.

'Aye.'

'Isn't that reserved for men?'

Lachlan laughed. It was the kind of laugh to warm a person from the inside out. 'Not in Scotland, and certainly not here in the Highlands. 'Tis a drink for one and all.' His expression sobered. 'Have a wee sip. Ye'll offend them if ye say nae.'

'Well'—she smiled in acceptance—'I don't want to do that.' *Nor displease you, for that matter.*

If by drinking whisky it would impress Lachlan, then Helene would imbibe a dram or two; anything to get on his good side in the lead-up to coaxing from him a kiss.

As they rounded the sidewall of the cottage, Ross pointed to a wide, flat boulder with a dull crimson surface. He said something to Lachlan, who laid the deer's carcass upon the rock. It was the crudest form of a chopping block Helene could ever have imagined, but it only served to strengthen her admiration for people like Aila and Ross who lived and worked within their means.

Helene stepped across the threshold into an abode lit only by the light of day. The air carried a pungent scent from the dwindling peat fire in the centre of the room, and a cast iron cauldron slung over the fire wafted remnants of a previous meal. Two rabbits lay lifeless on a rustic table, along with bunches of herbs and garden-grown vegetables. Ingredients destined for the cooking pot, no doubt.

'Helene.'

Helene turned towards the gentle voice of Aila, who pointed to two wooden stools. The old lady led by example and sat down on one. Helene removed the leather satchel from her shoulder and settled it beside her feet on the straw-strewn earth floor.

Ross busied himself at a wooden chest and promptly produced four small drinking receptacles. Grey eyes sparkled as he spoke in Gaelic over raised cups.

Lachlan responded with words now familiar to Helene's ears. *'Slàinte mhath!'*

She repeated the spoken Scottish toast but hesitated in downing the liquid in the same customary fashion as the others. Hers was a cautionary approach to the potent drop, regardless of her somewhat amused audience.

Helene brought the amber liquid to her nose and took a whiff. 'It smells like the peat fire, with woody hints of cedar and pine.'

'Aye. So it does,' said Lachlan, lifting a quizzical brow. 'Ye didnae tell me ye're a connoisseur of whisky.'

She laughed. 'I'm not. Although my father did teach me a thing or two about wines.'

Fumes from the whisky caused the roof of Helene's mouth to tingle. She let the liquid touch the tip of her tongue before drinking it in one swallow. A burning sensation followed in its wake, and with the intake of her next breath she coughed, eyes smarting.

Helene glanced up at Lachlan and at the cottars, each one of them awaiting her verdict. The mirth in their expressions did not go unnoticed. She used her hand to wave air into her throat and said, in a hoarse voice, 'It felt like I swallowed fire.'

Lachlan translated her words through his broad grin, which sent Aila and Ross into fits of laughter.

Aila rose slowly from her stool and busied herself at the wooden chest. By the time Ross retrieved the whisky jar, insisting they drink another dram, Aila had returned with a plate of coarse bread and chunks of cheese.

Helene took a bite of cheese and savoured its taste and texture. 'Did you make this, Aila? It's delicious.'

Lachlan translated the question and compliment and answered on Aila's behalf. 'The womenfolk at the shielings make cheese and butter to see them through the winter. This cheese was delivered early this morning by one of the herd boys.'

'And the bread?' asked Helene.

'That's Aila's doing. She bakes it here.' Lachlan pointed to the hearth around which they sat. 'If ye dinnae mind, Helene, I'd like to spend a moment talking with Aila and Ross on several matters. I dinnae mean to exclude ye from the conversation, but it willnae take long.'

'Of course. Go ahead. I understand.'

Helene sipped the whisky as if it were wine. She had no wish to endure another heart-stopping sensation of liquid fire. Nor did she want to offend Ross by refusing the refill.

She fell into her own comfortable silence while Lachlan

conversed with the cottars in Gaelic. Her gaze wandered around the room, taking in the stone-walled house and the timber beams supporting a turf-and-heather thatched roof. A small vent in the roof above the fire was the only means by which smoke could escape, unless, of course, the door was left open. Even with lit tapers, the cottage would be dark and smoky during winter nights.

A neatly folded blanket lay in a heather-filled box-bed situated in one corner of the room. Beside that sat a chamber pot. A spinning wheel and a well-used dresser with four drawers occupied the opposite corner. Various trinkets rested on its scarred, unpolished surface.

It occurred to Helene that the sum total of the couple's worldly possessions were likely contained within the walls of this sparsely furnished dwelling. Even the goats and chickens seemed to have been assigned a space to bed down at the other end of the dwelling. What struck Helene most about the cottars was that they appeared happy and content.

All this was a far cry from the lap of luxury in which Helene had been raised. Something she'd taken for granted, until now. It was a most humbling experience sitting with this couple, sharing a meagre meal, and drinking whisky from origins of what could well-be an illicit distilling enterprise. If that were the case, then it was Lachlan's concern, perhaps one he turned a blind eye to. Either way, it was none of her business and a subject she'd not broach with him.

Whether or not he'd explained her breeding and background to Aila and Ross, they showed no sign of resentment or prejudice towards her. Shamefully, no English person of her ilk would reciprocate the same manner of kindness and hospitality towards these gentle Highland folk.

With her next sip of whisky, Helene sensed a shift in the air. She had no understanding of Gaelic, so why had Lachlan and the cottars lowered their conversation to a reverent hush? Helene bent her head and saw through lowered lashes their solemn expressions.

Something else was said between them, with Aila and Ross giving Lachlan a gentle nod accompanied by a smile. They both glanced at Helene, and then back at Lachlan. Conversation paused.

Concern had Helene ask, 'Is something wrong?'

It was a few moments before Lachlan would look at her. When he did, she saw sorrow in his eyes.

'Nae, lass.' Another pause.

Unconvinced, she handed him what was left of her whisky. 'You look like you could do with this.'

'Are ye sure ye dinnae want it?'

'Finish it off. You'd be doing me a favour.'

His lips twitched before downing it. ''Tis time we leave.'

Ross collected the drinking cups and placed them on the table. Helene retrieved the satchel and took her cue from Aila, rising to her feet.

The old lady smiled and set about rearranging the plaid around Helene's shoulders. Next, she unpinned the large silver brooch from her own timeworn shawl.

Helene stared at Aila's hands. Hands with thin, wrinkly skin stretched over bony fingers and enlarged knuckles. Hands that told a story of a hard-working life, requiring strength when challenged and being tender when needed. With the dexterity of youth, she fastened the intricately patterned brooch to Helene's plaid, displaying it beneath her throat.

Aila spoke as gently as the gnarled hands she'd placed either side of Helene's shoulders. The old lady had gifted Helene a personal treasure. When Aila had said her piece, she took two ends of her own shawl, and in lieu of her brooch, she tied them in a knot. The humbling gesture of giving away the prized Highland ornament brought tears to Helene's eyes.

'Lachlan, tell Aila I can't accept this.'

'Nae.'

'You must. Why would she give it to a stranger? She doesn't know me. I'm nothing to her.'

'Ye didnae know Donnie, and yet look what ye did for him.'

Helene looked down at the brooch. 'So that's what all this is about? News travels fast.'

'Aye. To Aila and Ross, ye're the Sassenach lass who showed great courage in standing up for one of their clan.'

The smithy immediately came to mind. 'Are Aila and Ross also related to Donnie?'

'They ken young Donnie. He's not a blood relative, but any member of the clan is considered family. The brooch is a token of their appreciation and in honouring what ye did for a bairn that isnae yers.'

'But the brooch looks to be an heirloom, something to be bequeathed to her own daughter or relative.'

A momentary shadow flickered in Lachlan's eyes. 'Their last living relative, a granddaughter, is . . . nae longer alive.'

'Oh!' Helene looked from Aila to Ross. 'I'm so sorry.' She touched the brooch with the greatest respect and took Aila's aged hands in hers. 'Thank you, Aila. I'm grateful. Truly grateful, and I'll wear it with pride.'

Lachlan's translation put a smile on the old woman's lined face. She said something to Lachlan, glancing between him and Helene. He bore the look of someone who'd just been told the impossible.

'What did she say?' asked Helene, curious to know what Aila had said to put colour in Lachlan's cheeks. He would not meet her eyes.

'Nothing that would interest ye.'

He couldn't have been more wrong, especially when Aila gave them both the biggest grin and Lachlan's colour deepened.

So, the laird was prone to blush? An enlightening discovery, and one that led Helene to believe Aila might have implied or referenced a connection between Helene and Lachlan. All the signs were there to explain his self-conscious reactions, his hasty farewell, and his long strides exiting the cottage into the afternoon sunshine.

Helene thanked Aila and Ross for their hospitality and followed Lachlan outside. She turned to wave the cottars a final farewell before the woods hid them from view.

The ensuing silence between herself and Lachlan gave Helene time to formulate the beginnings of a plan. A plan that just might elicit from the laird another endearing blush.

CHAPTER ELEVEN

JOYOUS SHOUTS GREETED Lachlan, with Helene by his side, when they entered the shielings. Their unexpected arrival drew a crowd, causing an excitable commotion among the women and young girls. Herd boys ran from all directions, bursting with boisterous chatter at the sight of their laird and his accompanying stranger.

Lachlan spoke Gaelic for the benefit of the elderly women who did not understand English and introduced to one and all his Sassenach guest. Discussion sparked amongst the crowd, and they stared, somewhat bewildered, at Helene as if she were some far-off exotic curiosity.

Lachlan noted her look of apprehension and the way she inched closer to his side. He winked to lessen her fear. 'Ye've nae need to worry, lass. These are friendly folk, and they've already heard of ye.'

'How?' The confusion on her face gave way to understanding. 'You don't mean—?'

'Aye. Seems yer legendary heroics in my great hall live larger than my victories as a fearsome Highland laird.'

Helene laughed at the feigned affront to his dignity.

Lachlan caught his breath. The sweetness of that laughter enchanted him, and not only himself, so it seemed. Highlanders were naturally wary of the English, and so Lachlan took heart in seeing these hardy people take to Helene.

The clan's acceptance of her pleased him in a way he hadn't expected. It was the type of hoped-for acceptance any man might wish for from family and friends when settling on a lifelong mate.

It was yet another realisation to leave him uncommonly rattled, and one he dismissed by concentrating on faces he recognised and enquiring about their families. After ten minutes or so, Lachlan brought the chatter to a close, mindful of clan folk having to perform certain chores before dusk settled upon the glen.

As the people dispersed, Lachlan arranged for Helene to sleep in the largest of the stone-made huts. Its occupants, Greer, a matronly woman of middle years, and her cheerful daughter, Mairi, who was of the same age as Helene, insisted Helene have the cottage to herself.

'I won't hear of it,' said Helene. 'I'm grateful for the accommodation and would be honoured to be a guest in your home.'

The Highland women looked to their laird for his approval. When Lachlan shrugged and smiled, Greer and Mairi took Helene under their wing to acquaint her with their modest lodgings.

It was inconceivable that a woman of Helene's gentle breeding and background would consider visiting, much less living in conditions she'd surely deem to be unclean and primitive. It would be the roughest sleeping conditions she'd have experienced in her life, an encounter to test her true mettle.

He predicted that, come morning, she'd insist they return at once to the comforts and cleanliness of Drumocher. If she chose to stay, then Helene was either an extraordinary lass or she had a well-guarded reason for being here.

Lachlan used his free time to wander about and assess

life at the shielings. It gave him the opportunity to talk to the women who'd been coming here year after year. He listened with genuine concern for the lives and the welfare of his tenants and subtenants who cared for his herds as payment for rent and other dues.

Summer grazing was essential to their survival and in seeing the beef cattle grow fat on nature's bountiful lush grass. Come late autumn, each animal would fetch a good price at the October tryst held in Crieff.

Down by the river, he chatted to a few boys who pointed to the fringes of the dairy herd where a calf, born to one of the cows earlier in the day, suckled its mother's milk. Lachlan praised their efforts in caring for the herd and then moved on to talk with the milkmaids, the cheesemakers, and the cooks.

Light was fading by the time he returned to the upland area where women prepared the evening meal. He found Mairi bent over a peat cooking fire and asked as to the whereabouts of Helene.

'She went to the river to freshen up, but she should be well on her way back by now.'

Lachlan swept his gaze down along the winding banks of the river and spied her near a copse of trees at the water's edge.

At that moment, a warning shout went up from the glen. He caught sight of a fox making a brazen attempt to attack the newly born calf. A quick-thinking lad with an accurate aim hit the fox in the head with a rock.

The fox, momentarily dazed, got up and ran away, but the commotion was enough to spook the herd and send them charging along the river's edge towards Helene as she knelt in their path.

Horrified, Lachlan shouted to alert Helene and ran headlong down the slope towards her, sickening dread spurring him on.

'Helene!'

He yelled her name again. Pointless. She was out of earshot. His lungs burned from exertion, heartbeat thrashing in his ears, torn between yelling at her to wade into the fast-flowing river, or run as fast as she could uphill and away from the oncoming stampede.

'Helene!' He ran harder, gaining ground and closing the distance between them.

She looked over her shoulder, sighted him, and stood, waving and walking a few steps away from the water's edge. She smiled that smile he'd come to know and appreciate. A smile that had awakened something dead inside him.

'Run, Helene! Run!'

Frantic, Lachlan pointed to the cattle charging at her. If she were to run now, she'd still have a chance to cross their path unscathed. If not . . .

The muscles in his legs burned white-hot. 'Stampede!' he yelled, pointing to her left.

Whether she heard him first or the hundreds of hooves sounding like a rumbling storm, she snapped her head towards the oncoming threat.

Lachlan was close, but he'd not get close enough in time to save Helene. It was a physical impossibility. He knew it now. The herd would reach her before him. Breath bottled up in his lungs with the crippling feeling of being powerless to protect her.

❧

Helene stood paralysed with fear and stared death in the face.

If death was one to mock, then it did so now, presenting her with two choices. Die drowning, because she couldn't swim, or be trampled into the ground beneath the weight of rampaging bovines.

She hadn't time for anything but two regrets: leaving this world having failed on her promise to keep Prudence safe, and having agreed to deceive the MacLanoch laird, whom she now believed to be a good man. The kind of man she could—

'Helene!'

Her name, yelled with a sense of desperation and hopelessness, had her turn to see Lachlan sprinting towards her, one hand outstretched, face contorted with a mixture of terror and grief. Did he truly care for her?

Helene pretended he did and closed her eyes to pounding hooves.

The moment of impact hurled her into the cold, fast-flowing river. Under the water she went, dragged down by the heavy weight of her sodden woollen skirt. Over and over, she tumbled in an undercurrent as forceful as the rushing water.

Something wrapped around her face, blocking all vision and escalating the threat of suffocation. Survival instinct had her swiftly push over her head what must be the plaid from her shoulders. In so doing, it ripped the pins from her hair, sending the dark tresses swirling about her face like long tentacles.

Arms flailed and legs kicked in a desperate bid to save herself from drowning. The current carried her along, tipping her over and granting her a gasp of air before sucking her back under.

Something latched on to her wrist and gave her a vigorous tug. She breached the surface and gasped a lungful of air. Before being sucked back under, she glimpsed her lifeline.

Donnie!

The image of him, panic-stricken, strengthened Helene's will to live. Her fingers locked around his arm lest he let go of her. She kicked for all she was worth and used her free hand to propel her way to the surface.

Air! Blessed air. She took in a lungful and opened her eyes to see Donnie's frantic face. In a cruel twist of fate, the sucking undertow pulled him down. Helene gripped his slender arm tighter, determined not to let go.

He surfaced, gulping life into his lungs. Suddenly, Helene slammed into a large rock jutting out in the middle of the stream. Weak, her movements feeble, she wedged the boy between the rock and her battered body, safeguarding him from the current's pummelling force. Pressed against the rock, he started retching water.

'Spit it out, Donnie,' said Helene in between her own bouts of coughing up water. 'All of it.'

He tried to speak.

'Save your breath. Can you climb on top of the rock?' He did so and lay down to rest. 'Help will come soon,' she assured him.

The continuous rush of water threatened her grip on the rock and pounded her back, spraying fan-like up and around her body. Water rained down on her, hampering her view of anything beyond the rock itself. She could only pray Lachlan would soon find them.

The lad began to shiver. 'Are you holding up, Donnie?'

'Aye, m'lady.'

'What were you doing in the river?'

'I'd been hunting rabbits downstream and saw the herd stampeding towards ye. I was close enough to run and shove ye in the water.'

Helene suffered chills colder than the water. 'That was you?'

'Aye.'

She lashed out in anger at his foolish actions. 'You could have been killed!'

'Aye! And ye too!'

The shocking truth of it unnerved Helene. 'You risked your life to save mine, and for that I thank you.'

'Are we square now?'

Helene glanced up to see his proud grin. She smiled at him. 'Yes, we are.' She paused to catch her breath. 'I'm going to call out for your laird.'

'Me too.'

'No. Conserve your energy.'

Helene shouted Lachlan's name. Nothing.

Minutes passed. Fatigue set in. Failing strength caused her grip to loosen on the rock, and the cold water at her back sapped her of breath. If the current swept her away, then at least Donnie would remain safe until Lachlan found him.

'Be brave, m'lady. For just a wee bit longer. The laird will find us soon enough.'

Had the boy sensed her weakening state?

'Aye,' she said in as cheery a Scottish accent as she could manage.

A bout of dizziness caught her off guard, and her grip loosened on the rock. At the same time, something pressed against her back. Something solid. Something strong. Something that moved.

Someone, not something.

Strong arms came under Helene's armpits to hold her above the water, and large hands with fingers splayed anchored their bodies to the rock.

Warm lips moved against her ear in an urgent whisper. 'Helene!'

Lachlan!

Donnie shouted with glee, 'M'lord! I knew ye'd come for us!'

Relief flooded Helene with more intensity than the undercurrent pulling at her feet and swirling around her skirt.

'I can only take one of ye at a time,' yelled Lachlan above the roar of the water.

'Take Donnie first,' rasped Helene.

The lad slid from the rock onto his laird's back, enabling Lachlan to lift Helene into the position Donnie had occupied, and with no further risk of being swept downstream. All she need do was hold still and hug the rock. It was there she stayed, watching Lachlan carry Donnie out of danger to the riverbank, where a small group of clan folk gathered.

Until the moment Lachlan walked out of the river and set the lad down, Helene had been too weary to notice that he wore only his linen shirt. The wet thigh-length garment stretched across his broad back. It clung to his tapered waist and the muscular curve of his buttocks.

When he set Donnie down, a woman—whom Helene recognised to be his mother—placed her shawl around the boy's shoulders. She raised a hand to acknowledge Helene and then immediately led her son towards the shielings.

The remaining women watched their laird return to the river, while covering the eyes of curious young girls who were too young to see a semi-naked man.

Fading light did precious little to hide the outline of his frontal modesty. Ingrained propriety urged Helene to close her eyes or look away. Instead, intrigue and natural curiosity compelled her to admire and appreciate his physique, his strength. To take stock of him having fought the river to reach her and Donnie, and a second time to take the lad ashore. Now he came for her.

She climbed upon his back, arms locked around his neck and legs about his waist. The instant his feet found purchase on the riverbed, Lachlan shifted her from his back to his chest, gently cradling her in his arms. Helene buried her face in the warmth of his neck, thankful to be safe.

She drew herself closer to him, pressed her cheek to the play of muscles beneath the wet linen shirt, and breathed in his scent. His heartbeat thumped in her ear.

Lachlan bent on one knee to seat her on the grassy embankment. Helene reluctantly let go of his warmth and fended off the cold by wrapping her arms about her chest. It was then she remembered. 'Aila's brooch! Grizel's plaid! They're gone.'

Lachlan pressed both hands to her shoulders and stopped her efforts to stand. 'We'll look for them tomorrow.'

'By then it will be too late!'

'Nae. We must get ye into some dry clothes and in front of a warm fire.'

Lachlan said something in Gaelic to the women and girls, who hurried off in the direction of the camp. He then spoke to a couple of herd boys and pointed to the river's edge. They returned with Lachlan's discarded coat, plaid, boots, sword, and dirk, then retreated along the path where the cattle had bolted.

Alone now, Lachlan worked Helene's arms into his coat before dressing and buckling the plaid around his waist and cinching the weapons belt in place. He pulled on his woollen socks and boots and crouched beside her, rubbing her back.

'Ye're shivering. Have ye the strength to stand and walk? If not, I'll carry ye back to camp.'

Helene craved his embrace, but he'd already expended enough energy on her behalf. She drew his coat tightly about her. 'I can walk.'

He assisted her in standing and slid a steadying arm around her waist. Night was closing in, and the air had turned cool. Helene gave thanks for the man at her side, for his warmth infusing her body, and for the gift of second chances. They walked on, her skirt waterlogged and her stockinged feet squelching inside her boots.

'The cattle, what's become of them?' she asked.

'They're being rounded up as we speak. Any strays will be captured tomorrow.'

Lachlan's arm grew tight around her waist. Just shy of the camp, he said, 'Ye should have waited for me to take ye to the river.'

His sharp tone took Helene by surprise. 'You were otherwise occupied, and I didn't want to interrupt—'

'And ye chose to bathe in a dangerous bend in the river.'

'I didn't bathe. I washed my face and hands beside the river. Not *in* it.'

His voice took a terse turn. 'Do ye nae ken anything about rivers?'

'It's not a subject covered in advice and etiquette manuals.'

Helene hoped he'd find humour in her sarcastic retort. Instead, it had the opposite effect. He grew even more agitated, and his arm around her waist held her tighter to him.

'Ye should have thrown a wee branch in the water to observe what happens! If it was pulled under or swept quickly downstream, ye'd have kenned not to enter the river.'

'As I said, I didn't enter the river.'

'Or ye could have dropped a rock in the water to gauge its depth.'

He wasn't listening to her. 'I'll remember that for next time!'

Lachlan steered her behind the privacy of a tree and turned her swiftly in his arms. 'Next time? There won't be a next time!'

Water still dripped from the russet hair plastered to his forehead and cheeks. A deep scowl marred his handsome face, and he unleashed what must have been bottling up inside him.

'If not for wee Donnie, ye'd be dead! He cannae swim and

neither can ye. The two of ye could have drowned, and I might have been hauling not one but two corpses from the river.'

'I'm sorry! I didn't mean to—'

'And what would ye have had me tell the lad's ma and da?'

Horror struck Helene with a vision of Donnie's lifeless body being carried in Lachlan's arms. She had no words for that.

Lachlan did. 'I'd have had to tell them his wee life was taken because of the ignorant stupidity of a Sassenach lass!'

Helene shoved Lachlan away. 'I did nothing wrong! I could have been beside the safest part of the river and still be in the way of the stampeding cattle. Or was I responsible for that too?'

'I promised yer father I'd protect ye and keep ye safe from harm. How am I to do that if ye wander about at will, and with nae regard for yer safety?'

'Oh! So it's my father you're worried about. Not me! Well let me assure you, my father would perhaps see my death as a convenience, not a loss. One less female in the family to worry about!'

The words were out before Helene could retract them. She hoped her slip of the tongue escaped Lachlan's notice.

He stepped forward and took her face firmly between his hands. His chest expanded and fell with every deep breath, and his heated gaze flitted between Helene's eyes and mouth. 'If ye had been killed, I'd have been . . .'

The raw tightness in his voice set Helene on edge. Still, she stood her ground. 'You'd have been what?'

His mouth came down on hers. Hard. Urgent. Pressing the heat of his anger against her lips. There he held her, unrelenting in his kiss.

He'd caught Helene off guard, rendering her too stunned to resist.

He broke the kiss before she had time to process or even protest the injustice of his words. Her eyes snapped open, his face a mere inch from hers. Thunderclouds in his eyes had yet to clear.

His hands still cupped her face. Slowly, his lids closed and his forehead lowered to rest against hers. In the ensuing moments, the shock of Helene's near-death ordeal took hold, stripping strength from her body and mind. Layered over that was something far more dramatically impacting on her senses than having nearly met her maker.

Lachlan had kissed her.

Deed accomplished. Sweet mercy!

Even more so, she'd not expected his lips on hers to have had such a rousing, heady effect. Her blood danced in her veins.

She heard him speak her name, not in anger, but with reverence, seconds before she collapsed in his arms.

CHAPTER TWELVE

LACHLAN SAT OUTSIDE the stone hut before the open fire, elbows resting on his knees and face buried in his hands. Try as he might, he could not unsee the horror of this afternoon's events. The stampede, Helene standing in harm's way, and Donnie putting his young life at risk to save the Sassenach. The two of them could have drowned before he'd intervened. His hand went to his stomach to settle another wave of nausea. How would he have explained her death to her father?

Then came the guilt for having laid blame at Helene's feet. She was as innocent as the newborn calf that had given rise to the whole unfortunate incident. The hand on his stomach clenched into a fist. If only he'd escorted her to the river.

The kiss he'd forced on Helene was born of anger over his failings to keep her safe. He swallowed past the thickness in his throat, a consequence of his shame.

His head drooped lower. He'd broken his word not to kiss her, and because of it he'd brought dishonour upon himself, his family, Cuthbert's family, and worst of all, Helene and her family. He'd inflicted a stain on her virtuous reputation. Self-loathing stripped him of his pride and dignity. Helene was sure to tell his mother and auntie. How he'd face their disappointment, he did not know.

His threat of violence had curbed Cuthbert's attentions towards Helene. Contempt hurled at his cousin now sat squarely on Lachlan's shoulders.

Good God! Helene. What must she think of him?

Damn him for giving credence to the byname the Scoundrel Scot. She'd surely want to leave for Drumocher at first light and prepare to return to London.

Lachlan's head snapped up at the sound of the cottage door opening. He shot to his feet in anticipation of seeing Helene. Greer appeared first, with an encouraging smile and a nod. In her hand she held Helene's wet clothes and proceeded to drape them over a length of rope strung between wooden poles staked into the ground close to the fire. Next, she went to the cooking pot to stir its simmering contents above the fire.

Mairi emerged from the hut with her arm in the crook of Helene's elbow. Relief surged through Lachlan to see the Sassenach on her feet and dressed in warm dry clothes, borrowed from the womenfolk. At least she wouldn't catch a chill. The fire's flickering flames illuminated her natural beauty, and her hair, still damp, had been neatly combed. It fell like a dark velvet curtain well past her shoulders and framed a face left pale from her harrowing near-death experience.

She looked vulnerable, but Lachlan knew better. Her actions thus far demonstrated the strength of mind and resilience to overcome adversity. She was kind, and a lass with principles and a strong sense of what she believed to be right and wrong. Admirable qualities, without a doubt. She seated herself on a stool the furthest away from him.

'Are ye feeling better, Helene?' It was all he could think to say until which time he'd apologise to her in private for the way he'd behaved before she'd fainted in his arms.

'Yes, thank you.' A toneless response without meeting Lachlan's gaze.

Very telling. Her opinion of him had sunk lower than the dirt beneath his boots. He deserved nothing less. His heart beat a dull thud inside his chest, and the need to repair her trust in him, if only to salvage his pride, burned brighter than the fire's flames separating them.

Never, until now, had he wanted to strive so hard for anyone's good opinion, and it rankled knowing that, in Helene's eyes, his word was as hollow as the log upon which he sat. He could not deny having taken a shining to the lass, and it mattered to him that they'd fallen out so early in her visit to Drumocher.

Mairi placed in Helene's hands a bowl of steaming stew. Lachlan had no appetite for food; nonetheless, he accepted what Mairi offered him, something to focus on instead of Helene.

Her presence drew the company of others. They engaged her in conversation about all manner of things, from the afternoon's drama to life in London. The herd boys sat at Lachlan's feet, begging him to retell stories of clan battles and victories, asking questions about cattle droves to markets in the Lowlands and eager to hear about the border reivers.

All the while, Lachlan stole surreptitious glances over their heads at Helene, listening to her animated voice and watching the lift and curve of her lips when she smiled and the graceful movement of her hands, as expressive as her face when she talked. Now and then her slender fingers combed her hair as a means of drying it in the heat from the fire. His fingers itched to perform the task for her, to cup his hands at the nape of her neck, testing the weight of those silky tresses. As the evening wore on, colour returned to her pale cheeks.

'M'lady. Will ye promise to stay with us here in the shielings?' asked Mairi. 'At least for the next two or three days?'

Helene's gaze fell to her lap, and her fingers picked at the fabric of her skirt.

Lachlan held his breath, wondering if she'd speak out against him. Her silence said she wished to return home because of his dishonourable behaviour. There was no question Lachlan should do right by her and take her back to Drumocher tomorrow. For selfish reasons, he wanted her to stay, and so he spoke up for her.

'I ken 'tis been a trying day for ye, Lady Helene, and I'm truly sorry for the frightening and . . . *unexpected* mishaps ye suffered this afternoon. Nothing of the sort will happen again. My wish is for ye to stay, as Mairi has asked, and enjoy what the Highlands and these good people have to offer ye.'

A larger crowd had gathered around them and stood silent, intently watching and listening in on the conversation. All eyes were on Helene, awaiting her response.

She lifted her gaze and seemed to consider the people about her. With a tilt of her chin, she announced, 'Well! If you all pegged me to be some lily-livered Sassenach who runs at the first sniff of discomfort or danger, then you'd be wrong. Of course I'll stay.'

Her mettlesome announcement drew a cheer from the crowd, and in his mind's eye, Lachlan reached out to embrace Helene. She was indeed a braw Sassenach.

She met his gaze for a matter of seconds before Donnie and his mother distracted her. They exchanged a few words before the lad joined the herd boys at Lachlan's feet.

It wasn't long before the singing started. Songs Lachlan remembered from when he was a boy. Memories stirred, triggering a range of emotions. Happy mountain sojourns with his father, learning the lie of the land, hunting, fishing, and swimming in the burns. Learning how to swing a broadsword and strike a lethal stab with a *sgian-dubh*.

He cast his gaze over the gentle folk around him. It was at this very shieling, in wilder times, when he and his father's men had fought off a hunting party whose aim it was to assault the women and girls and then make off with cattle and produce.

His eyes lit on Helene. He would do anything to protect her and keep her safe.

The hour was late, and one by one, families returned to their shelters or to sit for a while longer around the peat fires dotting the landscape. Helene stood and, accompanied by Mairi, retired inside the stone hut. Lachlan thought himself a fool to hope she might at least turn and bid him goodnight. He'd find the opportunity tomorrow to apologise for the upset he'd caused her.

Greer gave the remaining herd boys their marching orders, reminding them they must soon swap shifts with the boys keeping watch over the cattle and goats. 'That wily fox might return,' she warned. ''Tis up to ye to prevent another rumpus, ye hear?'

When the boys scattered, she pulled her arisaid tightly about her and smiled at Lachlan. 'The lads have made ye a lean-to shelter, m'lord, just as ye asked. I ensured they used fresh new heather. Ye should be comfortable enough, but if ye're not, there's me and plenty a family here who'd be honoured to give ye sole use of our dwelling.'

'Thank ye, Greer.'

'Good night, m'lord.'

Lachlan eyed the lean-to, perfectly positioned beside the door of the small cottage where Greer, Mairi, and Helene would sleep. If there was any threat of someone getting to the women, they'd have to first deal with Lachlan.

He remained seated in solitude, staring into the fire. Mesmerizing flames flickered like fingers beckoning his return to the past, trapping him in a time when he'd given his heart to a bonnie red-headed lass.

A block of peat turf shifted, and the fire hissed. Lachlan's attention snapped back to the present. He stood and shook his head to rid himself of painful memories, bracing himself for the usual follow-on feelings of humiliation and deep hurt synonymous with betrayal, and for the memory of the shame her actions had thrust upon her grandparents, Ross and Aila.

To his surprise, he felt nothing. His pulse was steady and calm. His mind clear, his heart open and free. The past remained in the past, dead and buried, along with the lass who'd been his betrothed.

He walked with a sense of light-headedness to stand beneath the overhanging branches of a lone tree and leaned against its solid trunk. When, or at what point, had he finally let her go?

The snap of a twig had him whirl around.

'Helene!'

'Lachlan.'

She stood within arm's reach. Long, dark hair hung over one shoulder, now tied in a loose plait. Her arms hugged her waist, and he noticed her bare toes peeking out from the hem of her skirt. She looked every bit the wild Highland lass, sending his pulse racing.

'Helene. I'm verra sorry for the way I treated ye this afternoon. The stampede . . . 'twas not yer fault and—'

'Neither was it yours.'

'Aye, but I should have been there to protect ye. If I'd lost ye . . .' He left the sentence hanging in the air.

'I know. You'd have had my father to answer to, and I'd not wish that on anyone.'

'That's not what I meant.' It was one thing trying to

process developing feelings for Helene, but it was another to articulate it.

She took the few steps to stand toe-to-toe with him. 'I didn't seek you out for an apology, but rather to thank you for saving my life. And Donnie's.'

'Och! Undeserved thanks. If not for Donnie, ye'd not be here at all, and ye cannae begin to imagine the guilt I feel because of it.'

'Yes, I can,' she said softly. 'I'm no stranger to guilt. I bear the burden of it every day of my life.'

The confession was another layer to her he wished desperately to understand. She spoke again before he had the chance to encourage her to confide in him.

'If not for *you*, Donnie and I might both have drowned.'

A cow lowed in the distance, filling the pause between them.

'My anger towards ye, lass, and that kiss. Forgive me, I shouldnae—'

She cut him off with a finger to his lips and whispered, 'Forgiven and forgotten, and no one need know.'

The soft pad of her fingertip fell away from his mouth and she retreated, a shadowy figure in the night, back inside the hut.

Lachlan stood for a time thinking about that life-changing kiss. Helene might be quick to forget, but he had not.

❧

Conflicting emotions kept Helene awake. For one, she could barely contain her relief and joy at achieving, far quicker than expected, what Cuthbert had tasked her to do. She had no reason to stay any longer at Drumocher.

Her monetary reward would not only buy her sister's freedom from the asylum, but it would be enough for the two of them to begin a simple, quiet life together deep in the English countryside. Their father, in time, would surely come around to the idea of Helene devoting her life to Prudence, and to giving her the proper care and attention she deserved.

Why, then, did the thrill of success taste bittersweet? Lachlan had made her task easy, and Helene could find no justification for thinking she'd done wrong by him. She hadn't had to trick, entice, deceive, seduce, or coerce him into kissing her. It had just happened, entirely his doing, brought on by self-inflicted anger in thinking he'd failed to protect her. He'd given her the perfect excuse to leave Drumocher, and he wouldn't care that she'd return to London in haste. She meant nothing to him.

This train of thought did little to ease her conscience, much less her confusion, for she'd not factored into the bargain her immediate attraction to the laird of Clan MacLanoch. That kiss had left her wanting, if not wondering how it might be between them if his kiss had been born of desire.

She swept selfish thoughts aside and formulated a plan. On their return walk to the castle, she'd ask Lachlan to arrange her journey to London. An excuse of homesickness would suffice. Of course, he'd assume her reason for leaving was because he'd taken certain liberties with her innocence.

No need to use the threat of divulging the truth of his indiscretion to his mother and auntie, as it would only evoke shame and disappointment. Even if he were to deny his actions, Viscountess Sutton would believe Helene's word over her nephew's, given her knowledge of his scandalous reputation in London.

Helene was certain Lachlan would do right by her and honour her wish, just as she'd obliged his wish to stay at the shielings for several days.

Here in the darkness of her earthy surrounds, she rolled

onto her back and lay in reasonable comfort with a well-worn quilt tucked around her for warmth. The creaky cot upon which she slept was a far cry from her walnut four-poster bed with canopy, finials, and superfluous plump pillows. A luxury she'd soon live without. A luxury she'd happily do without.

If her father and brother could see her now, they'd think of her as having fallen from grace and living amongst peasants and squalor. Should they in any way interfere with her plans to escape to the country and care for her sister, then Helene would bring to light the very existence of Prudence, her condition, and her whereabouts.

London society would see it as a scandalous revelation, ruinous for her father's good name. As for her brother? No family of worth would allow their daughter to marry a man whose sister resided in a madhouse.

Helene closed her eyes to the memory of her mother, who would surely have given her nod of approval, validating each step Helene took to ensure Prudence's survival and safety.

This rationale brought peace of mind, and it wasn't long before Greer's soft snores, together with Mairi's even breathing, lulled Helene to sleep.

When she opened her eyes, daylight streamed through the one tiny window in the cottage. The mouth-watering scent of freshly baked bread wafted through cracks in the wooden cottage door. Cows bellowed in the distance, and lively chatter and laughter outside the cottage boded well for a cheerful day.

Helene rose from the bed and neatly replaced the cot's quilt, a duty otherwise performed by household maids back home, but a task Helene carried out with a sense of novelty and self-satisfaction. She didn't expect her Highland hosts to wait on her hand and foot.

The thought of facing Lachlan gave rise to a fluttering in her stomach as she smoothed and straightened the shift she'd slept in. She dressed quickly and used a hairbrush to tame her sleep-mussed hair before tying it back in a thin strip of cloth given to her by Mairi last night. After a quick splash to the face of cold water from a basin, she stepped outside into glorious sunshine.

A hive of activity dotted the landscape, with women, young girls, and herd boys all going about their morning routine. Even though the hour was early, Helene must surely be the last to rise.

Greer looked up from the cooking fire, where she used a spurtle to stir a pot.

'Good mornin', m'lady,' she said with a smile. 'I hope ye had a restful sleep.'

The kind woman need not know the truth, nor the cause of Helene's restless night. 'Yes, I did. Thank you.'

'Weel then, if ye're feelin' hungry, sit yersel' down and I'll serve ye up a bowl of hearty brochan.'

Helene had no idea what that was until Greer set a tray on her lap with a spoon and bowl. 'Porridge.'

'Aye. If that's what the English call it,' said Greer.

Helene picked up the spoon, ready to take her first mouthful.

'Wait,' said Greer, placing another smaller bowl on the tray. "Tis fresh buttermilk. Dip each spoonful of brochan in the buttermilk before ye convey it to yer mouth.' She winked. "Tis the old-fashioned Highlander way.'

One mouthful and Helene closed her eyes to the tantalising texture of creamy, buttery-flavoured oatmeal. 'It's delicious, Greer. Thank you.'

"Tis my pleasure, m'lady. When ye've done wi' that, there's fresh bread to be had wi' a chunk of cheese, if it so pleases ye.'

Helene savoured another mouthful of Highland goodness before asking, 'Where's Mairi?'

'Ye just missed her. She's gone down to the stream with

some of the other lasses. They'll be making salted butter for the whole of the shielings.'

Helene planned to visit them as soon as she'd eaten. 'And the laird?' she asked, casting her gaze ahead.

'Right behind ye, lass.'

Lachlan's deep voice so startled Helene that the food tray almost toppled from her lap. She gripped the tray with one hand and turned to see him drape something over the drying line, next to her clothes from yesterday's near-drowning. When he stepped aside, her mouth fell open.

'Grizel's shawl! You found it!'

He sat down on the log beside her. 'Aye. 'Twas caught up in the branches of a fallen tree in the river, along with this.' He reached into his coat pocket, took Helene's free hand, and placed something in her open palm.

'Aila's brooch!' She flung her arm around Lachlan's neck, drawing him close.

A sudden awkwardness overcame her during the pause of that embrace. When she drew back, slowly, it was to stare into the darkened depths of Lachlan's eyes. Eyes with the power to trap and hold her still, so that she daren't look away. He blinked, breaking the spell, and her gaze fell to the barely there flush beneath the unshaven shadow on his face.

Had her reactionary behaviour to the retrieval of Aila's brooch made him blush? She hoped so. It was far more empowering to have triggered his response because he was attracted to her or experienced some degree of nervousness around her, rather than because she'd embarrassed him.

Best to think it the latter and err on the side of caution lest she embarrass herself. She subsequently resisted the urge to touch his cheek and test the sensation of his stubble against her palm.

'How can I ever thank you?' she said.

'Ye just did.'

There was something intimate about his softly spoken words and the way his gaze made a leisurely sweep of her mouth. It set Helene's stomach aflutter, and she could not pull her gaze from his face.

'Enjoying the brochan?' he asked, raising a brow.

'Aye.' Helene laughed at her response, suddenly realising she'd spoken in the Scottish affirmative, rather than English.

Lachlan grinned. 'We'll have ye speaking the Gaelic by the time ye return to London.'

Helene turned her attention to her morning meal in case her face betrayed her reluctance to see out the duration of her summer stay at Drumocher. With her last mouthful, she said, 'Mairi is making salted butter down by the river. I thought I'd pay her a visit and learn something of shieling life.'

If she was going to learn anything about country living, then the shielings were a perfect place to start.

Lachlan rose to his feet and took the tray from her lap. He set it down on a small stool beside the cooking fire. Helene looked around for Greer to thank her for the brochan, but her kind host had made herself scarce.

'This way,' he said.

They walked in companionable silence towards the river. Despite the weapons strapped to his body, Helene felt more than safe with the tall, strong, kilted man at her side. He walked with sure-footed strides and an air of confidence, a leader with the respect of his clan. Those who sighted him acknowledged his presence with a wave or a shout from afar. One little boy, who looked to be no more than five years old, raced towards them and clung to Lachlan's leg like a limpet to a rock. Lachlan stopped to ruffle the sulking lad's hair, picked him up, and sat him high on his broad shoulders.

As the trio walked on towards the river, the two spoke in

Gaelic and something was said to make Lachlan laugh. His reply did nothing to wipe the scowl from the boy's face.

Curious, Helene asked, 'What did he say?'

'Alistair has run away from his ma, who's set him the task of collecting kindling for tonight's fire. His preference is to play with his brother and the other herd boys, and he wants me to have cross words with his ma.'

Helene couldn't help but smile. 'Such a serious dispute. Whose side are you on?'

Lachlan feigned a look of alarm. 'His ma's! I told him as much, and he's none too happy with me.'

Now it was Helene who laughed. 'You, the laird of Clan MacLanoch, are not so fearless after all.'

Lachlan winked. 'You haven't met his ma.'

When they reached the stream, Lachlan took the boy from his shoulders and knelt before him. Their ensuing conversation put a smile on the lad's face, and his little chest stuck out like a proud peacock. He turned and ran off.

Helene remarked, 'Well! That was a turnaround in attitude.'

Lachlan stood up. 'Aye. I told him 'twas a man's responsibility to care for and look after his family, no matter the task. I also said that if he were to complete his chores, I'd teach him how to tickle fish so that he could provide a meal for his ma and brother tonight.'

Admiration and respect for Lachlan grew with every minute Helene spent in his company. As laird of his clan, he was protector and father to all, amply demonstrated in his kind behaviour and actions towards Alistair. How might he be around a child of his own?

The question stirred in Helene unfamiliar maternal instincts. If she were ever to want a man to give her a son or daughter, then that man would have to live up to the likes of Lachlan MacLanoch.

CHAPTER THIRTEEN

FIVE DAYS LATER, on the morning of their departure, little Alistair presented himself at Lachlan's feet and thrust his arms high as a signal to be picked up. He grabbed Lachlan's neck in a vice-like grip and burst into a babble of Gaelic.

'Aye,' promised Lachlan in their native tongue. 'Next time I visit I'll teach ye how to catch a rabbit.'

Alistair spoke again.

'What?' The boy's request took Lachlan aback. 'I'll not teach ye how to swing a broadsword. Ye're too young for that.' He set the boy down and ruffled his hair. 'I'll teach ye when ye've the height and strength to hold one in yer hands.'

The lad ran off, swallowed up in the crowd who'd gathered to bid farewell to Lachlan and Helene. Donnie wrapped his arms around her. A touching sight. The two had formed a strong attachment. Sad to think they were unlikely to ever meet again.

Mairi stood next in line to say her goodbyes and handed Helene a small woven bag. ''Tis a mixture of the herbs we gathered yesterday. Do ye remember my instructions on how to use them?'

'Yes, I do. Thank you, Mairi. You're most kind.'

Lachlan sensed something amiss with Helene. Her voice

had dropped to almost a whisper, and she gave him a surreptitious glance before pocketing the bag.

Yesterday, when he'd escorted the two women deep into the woods, he'd kept his distance, giving them space to chatter as lasses do. He'd assumed the herb gathering was for Mairi or Greer's use, but now, having just witnessed the exchange between Helene and Mairi, he passed it off as no concern, thinking the herbs were a tailor-made remedy for ailments of the female kind.

As they set off for Drumocher, Lachlan reflected on his time spent at the shielings, happy to see the lads and lasses looking robust, and satisfied with the well-being and happy temperament of the women, all thriving on Highland air and food. Stocks of cheese and butter, as well as generous lengths of linen and woollen cloth, would see the families through the harsh winter months ahead. Cattle, fat and glossy, were sure to fetch a handsome price at the late-autumn sales.

Observations of Helene sat uppermost in Lachlan's mind. The cottars and their way of life were well beneath her station, and yet she'd embraced them without judgement. It was unheard of to see a woman of her gentle breeding take up the long wooden stick with plunger attached to agitate buttermilk in a tall iron-banded churn. Her brow had glistened with sweat from the warm, heavy work, and yet she'd laughed and chatted alongside Mairi without complaint.

She'd watched with keen interest as the clan elders of the shielings sat hunched over their knitting, spun wool, or worked tapestries. The old women imparted their knowledge, technique, and experience, which Lachlan had gladly translated into English for Helene's benefit.

Her eyes and ears had been alive to the people about her, especially so when the singing started. From the herd boys along the glen, to songs sung by the cheesemakers, and those tending fires and preparing meals, but it was the singing of the dairymaids to have brought tears to her eyes. During the evening milking, each song would begin with one clear, angelic, if not haunting, voice. Others would join in and harmonise to create the most beautiful sounds. These songs, sung for generations, seemed to have made quite an impression on Helene.

'It's very moving,' she'd remarked.

Those wistful words, with an expression to match, were etched in Lachlan's heart and mind. He was glad to know the experience touched her as deeply as it had always touched him.

'What are you smiling at?'

Her words startled Lachlan, bringing him to a standstill. 'I was smiling?'

She stopped on the path a few paces ahead of him. 'Actually, you made a kind of snorting laugh sound. What were you thinking about just now?'

'Nothing.'

Helene's hand on his chest prevented his forward progress, and her raised brow said she didn't believe him.

'All right then. I was thinking about young Alistair, when I taught him how to guddle trout from the burn.' Lachlan was hard pressed to hide his mirth.

Helene stood there with both hands on her hips, head cocked to one side, and stared him down. 'I think it's not so much the act of guddling trout you laugh at, but rather the moment you hurled one from the burn and into my lap.'

Try though he did, Lachlan could not hold back a burst of laughter.

Helene shoved him playfully in the shoulder. 'All well and good for you to stand there and laugh, but it was not so funny for me to deal with a fish flapping about on my person.'

Lachlan doubled over, hands braced on his knees, laughing

as he said, 'I dinnae ken who was more terrified. Ye or the trout.'

'Me, of course!'

No sooner did Helene dissolve into laughter than Lachlan cut her off by taking hold of her arm. 'Listen!'

She went still. 'What's wrong?'

'Can ye hear it?'

'Hear what?'

Lachlan looked about him, at the sway of the treetops and a dense mist rolling in. He listened to a distant sound carried above the wind, a sound so ominous as to rival pounding surf against rocks in a violent storm.

'What is it?' urged Helene.

'A squall.'

Lachlan's gaze made a quick sweep of their surrounds. He knew every inch of the landscape, and if they were to flee the impending tempest, then they had no time to spare.

He grasped Helene's hand in his. 'Run!'

Minutes later, their lungs heaving from exhaustion, he pulled her into a crevice in the mountainside. He shifted his position, protecting Helene so that his back was to the opening of the crevice. Outside their rock shelter, the wind had whipped up into a frenzy.

There came the loud snap and crack of a branch. Helene jumped with fright and slapped her hands over her ears. When it crashed down close to the entrance of the crevice, she threw her arms around Lachlan's waist, her head pressed hard against his chest. He was quick to embrace and comfort her, for the worst was yet to come.

''Tis all right, lass. We're safe enough in here.'

Her body trembled against his. 'Storms! I fear storms.'

Lachlan pulled the vast length of his belted plaid around

himself and Helene, drawing it up over their heads. He inched her back as far into the crevice as they could go.

On cue, the rain arrived and struck with such force as to cause a waterfall at the opening of their shelter. Outside, the elements groaned, leaves thrashed about on their limbs, and the wind whistled through every splintered fault in the mountain's cleft.

The loud storm raged on, rendering conversation impossible. Lachlan kept Helene safe and secure within his arms, wrapped in the tight cocoon of his plaid. Inside the crevice, he stood as the buffer between her and the gusts of wind at his back. Her body flinched at the destructive sounds of nature's tempest.

He glanced down to see her eyes shut tight, prompting him to drop a soft, reassuring kiss on the crown of her head. Her frown fell away, and her tension seemed to ease.

Moments later, the wind and driving rain abated as abruptly as it had arrived.

'Is it over?' she asked without lifting her cheek from his chest.

Lachlan drew on his Highland experience and answered in truth, 'Nae, lass. 'Tis only just begun.'

She looked up, wide-eyed. 'But all is silent.'

He said in a voice so as not to alarm her, 'Aye. A temporary lull. The tempest is catching its breath. Listen.'

In the distance, wind howled across mountain tops. Despite it being mid-morning, light inside their safe haven turned ash-grey. Moments later, mist swirled about their feet, and outside their sanctuary the approaching storm whipped itself into a fury.

Emerald eyes darkened with fear, and she clutched him tight.

Lachlan took her chin gently between thumb and index finger. 'Ye're safe, lass. There's nae need to be scairt.'

'Kiss me.'

Her request took him by surprise, and his hand dropped from her face.

'Kiss me, Lachlan.' A desperate plea. 'Take my mind far from here.'

Would that I could. 'Nae, lass.'

There came the sudden roar of the storm outside.

Helene braced her hands on his shoulders, inched up on her toes, and pressed her mouth to his.

Lachlan took hold of her wrists and pulled away, the heavy plaid falling into place at his back. She'd gone completely pale, and he saw tremors in her hands and fingers, and her chin and lips trembled. Another tree splintered beyond their sanctuary, and she cowered back, wide-eyed, like some timid creature that had dwelled in the crevice for all time.

To his dismay, this lass, who'd showed stalwart courage under threat of having her hand lopped off with his broadsword, was terrified of a storm. He'd vowed to protect her, and would do so by any means, even if by way of a kiss to distract her from what he witnessed to be debilitating fear.

He took her face between his hands and commanded her focus. One quick brush of his lips over hers and she leaned into him. He slid one arm around her waist, pulling her hard against him. His free hand cradled the base of her skull, tilting her head as he bent to her mouth, pressing his lips firmly against hers. Her arms came around his waist, fingers splayed on his back.

His tongue traced her lower lip, and the vibration of her whimper against his mouth sparked a fire in his groin. Soft lips parted on a breath, offering him the opportunity to deepen the kiss, to touch the tip of his tongue to hers. She drew back, hesitating for only a moment before returning to his lips, her tongue mimicking his exploratory move, but with the stumbling innocence of a novice.

The lass was untouched. A profound realisation. Instinct, primal and protective, made Lachlan gather her tighter to him. He fed on the sweetness of her mouth like a man starved of affection, and the sensation of her tongue entwined with his was more thrilling than he'd ever encountered.

His hand shifted from her nape to the side of her neck. She literally took his breath away, causing Lachlan to tear his mouth from hers and inhale air. His gaze swept over her lowered lids, lips parted and mouth once again seeking his. When his thumb stroked her lower lip, her eyes flashed open, a window into her need for more than simply making her forget the havoc Mother Nature wreaked beyond their granite refuge.

She took his thumb into her mouth, sending Lachlan's heart into a pounding rhythm and igniting in him a hunger not to be denied. Once again, he stroked his thumb pad, now damp with moisture from her mouth, over her lower lip.

'Helene!'

Her name, drowned out by the storm, carried the same manner of urgency as he bent to kiss her, knowing he did so not just because she'd asked him to, but because he acted with selfish motives. The maelstrom outside faded from his mind, replaced instead by an all-consuming awareness of the woman in his arms.

Her sweet lips were more intoxicating than the most sinful of fruits from a tree. Helene had already stolen his soul. He knew that now. If she were to ask for his life, he'd give it. This was a moment to sustain him for the rest of his life. He'd take it and gladly bear whatever punishment God saw fit to mete out consequent to his ignoble desires.

He'd take whatever liberties Helene would allow him. Honour be damned!

Every part of Helene wanted Lachlan MacLanoch, and the throbbing between her thighs intensified with each wicked move of his tongue against hers. She pressed herself into his palm cupping her breast, shameless in the throes of experiencing new and thrilling sensations.

She dragged her sated mouth from his, drew breath, and then touched her lips to his neck where the blood pulsed fast and hot beneath his skin. The tip of her tongue tasted him, a mixture of rainwater and salty sweat.

The rhythm of his heart beat strong and steady against her hand upon his chest. In a bold move, she slid her hand sinuously down between their bodies to discover his swelling arousal.

Her gasp was as profound as the breath he expelled against her cheek. Encouraged by his lust for her, Helene took his mouth with hers and branded him with her own kind of kiss, a kiss as powerful as the squall at their backs. Pent-up yearnings for Lachlan, yearnings which she didn't know how to name, rushed forth in a torrent as strong as the river in which she'd almost drowned.

Her fingers interlocked behind his neck. Blood surged in her veins, and she ached for something more than his kiss, more than his arms holding her tight, and more than the friction of her body moving against the growing pressure of his maleness.

Lachlan broke the kiss and stared down at her, eyes burning with need, lids heavy with desire. Desire for *her*. His mouth moved, but Helene heard not a word above the noise of the storm.

'I want you,' she said, hoping he could read her lips.

Lachlan's hand went to her hair, his fingers spearing through the loose strands that had fallen free of their pins. His frown deepened, his expression serious, and the words he spoke were tossed about unheard in the air between them.

Helene took his hand in hers and, desperate to make him understand, placed it at the apex of her thighs.

In a swift counter-move, Lachlan cradled her head in his free hand and kissed her with the intensity of a lightning strike. His hand between her thighs moved in a sensual, circular motion. Exhilaration soared and the heat of her blood rushed into Helene's face. She felt no embarrassment and no shame.

His mouth left hers, and he turned her in his arms. Helene drew strength from the hard, virile body at her back, eager to follow his experienced lead. Large hands followed the curve of her hips, then slid lower as he bent to her ankles, before lifting her skirt up over her knees to her waist. He bunched the material in place with one hand and used the other to coax her legs wide.

Such was Helene's heated state of arousal that she was oblivious to the draughty cool air hitting her exposed flesh. Lachlan's hand, warm and rough, settled on the inside of her thigh. His thumb massaged slow circles on her skin, eliciting from Helene a moan and sending her delirious with anticipation of what was to come.

Why then did he pause?

His mouth moved against her ear, and she vaguely registered the inflection in his tone. Consent to continue? Yes, she wanted this, and to prove it she turned her head to one side, glanced up into his eyes, and lifted her chin to offer him her mouth.

His lips came down on hers at the same time as his fingers found and stroked the most intimate part of her body. Helene shivered from indescribable pleasure. One finger delved inside her, and then out again to gently flick her swollen nub. So exquisite was the pleasure that she flinched.

Her senses begged, *Again. Do it again.*

He repeated the pattern several times, sliding in, sliding out, his tongue working the same synchronised magic in her mouth. Instinct had her move her hips against his hand between her legs, desperate to appease the hungry ache building within.

When Lachlan broke the kiss, she drew in a much-needed breath and dragged her eyes open to see him looking down at her. Something about him watching her fall apart beneath his touch heightened Helene's arousal. Her skin burned as if with fever, and she conceived only one coherent thought. *Release.* Release from the storm building inside her. Release from the fire in her belly, and release from pleasurable agony when Lachlan slipped two fingers deep into her core.

Her body tensed as a feeling with almighty force peaked and burst in wave after wave of carnal liberation. Thrilling thunder pounded in her veins. Her senses soared, sweeping her higher than the mountain peaks and carrying her forward until slowly, like a feather falling in a lazy descent to earth, she returned to the present, her mind lucid enough to register peaceful silence. The tempest had abated, and in its place all was calm.

'Helene,' said Lachlan, his mouth hot against her neck. 'Helene.'

The deep timbre of his voice and the evocative way he'd twice murmured her name made Helene tremble. If not for his tight embrace, she'd have collapsed to the ground. If not for this scoundrel Scot, she'd never have known what was possible. This, *this* experience was the best pleasure of all.

CHAPTER FOURTEEN

IT WAS LATE in the afternoon when Drumocher came within sight. Helene had sensed a shift in the air between herself and Lachlan, and he'd initiated no conversation since leaving the rock crevice. She kept her own counsel and drew sensible conclusions about what had occurred between them during the storm.

Lachlan had obliged her in taking her mind far from the trauma of being caught up in the squall. For one with so rakish a reputation, he'd satisfied Helene to exquisite effect. She'd be selfish to expect anything more of or from him, and yet, in such a short time since meeting him, he'd moved her heart and mind to a place where she'd feel comfortable baring to him her soul, revealing secrets, and confessing the turmoil of her motivations in coming to Drumocher.

Would he listen with understanding and show her compassion, or would it rile him to learn she'd used him and her visit to his family seat for no other reason than personal gain?

Ironic that she should even concern herself with the latter, when he and Cuthbert used and seduced married women for the sole purpose of inflating their egos.

Helene had a conscience, even if Lachlan did not, and guilt tapped her on the shoulder for having enticed his part in their intimate liaison. It didn't bother her that she was, by definition, a ruined woman, but it was on account of her Lachlan had broken his promise and oath to her father to ensure, while under Lachlan's protection and care, she remain untouched. What mattered most was he'd protected her well-being and safety on more than one occasion and had saved her from drowning.

Words she'd said for all to hear in Drumocher's great hall came back to taunt her. *Honour your word, Donnie, because a man without his honour is nothing.*

Dread brought her to a halt. Lachlan valued honour above all else, and she'd been the one to strip it from him. It must surely be the reason for his silence.

'Are ye all right, lass? Drumocher is verra close, but if ye'd like to take a wee rest—'

'No. I'm fine.' She summoned the courage to look at him. 'Thank you, Lachlan, for . . . calming me during the storm.'

A muscle worked along his jaw. 'Nae need to thank me, but for both our sakes, speak of it to nae one.'

She nodded in understanding. They both would suffer damaging consequences should their secret liaison come to light. Still, Helene hoped Lachlan had taken some measure of pleasure from their intimate encounter. She turned to press on down the path.

'Tell me why ye're so afraid of storms?'

The question caught her off guard, so too his restraining hand on her arm. She saw genuine concern for her in the meeting of his brows and in the way his thumb gently caressed her arm. Golden-brown eyes probed her for an answer. She wished to confess all to this man to whom she'd fallen vulnerable. A man to whom she'd willingly commit for the rest of her life if only he would have her, and if she were free to do so.

Impossible!

'I did something unforgivable when I was a child of ten. My father banished me to my room for a week, but Robert, my older brother, believed the punishment not severe enough.'

Lachlan's eyebrows drew together. 'What did ye do that was so bad?'

In Helene's mind's eye she replayed her crime, and all over the possession of a stupid doll. The memory of it sickened her. Quarrelling with her younger sister over a doll. Shoving Prudence, taking from her the doll, and then walking away. A high-pitched scream, then turning to watch in horror as Prudence tumbled down the stairs. The loud thud of her head smacking the floor below and seeing her lying in a little crumpled heap. Unmoving. Lifeless.

Helene swallowed, incapable of confessing her shameful wrongdoing out loud.

'During that week, a storm loomed,' she said. 'Robert lured me outside to the grounds of Father's country estate. He tied me to a tree and left me there. Light rainfall turned into a downpour. There was thunder, and lightning struck the old oak within sight of where I stood. A large limb crashed to the ground.'

Helene squeezed her eyes shut and raised a hand to her ear. 'The noise. The smell of charred wood. I was petrified.'

'Did ye not call out for help?'

Her eyes flashed open. 'I screamed until I was left with no voice. No one heard me above the noise of the storm.'

Lachlan's expression morphed from concern to fury. 'Yer brother! How long did the cruel bastard leave ye there?'

'Until the storm passed and the rain stopped. But I deserved it. I deserved every wretched moment, and he was right. Not even that was punishment enough for what I did to—'

Helene tugged her arm free of Lachlan's grip. Coward that she was, she could not bear to think on it anymore. Prudence.

The trauma to her head. The seizures, the convulsions. Her sadness and suffering.

Lachlan was quick to restrain her again, forcing her to meet his eyes. 'The governess ne'er noticed ye were missing from yer bed?'

'Not until Robert smuggled me back into my room. The governess knew better than to question Robert, for threat of him having her dismissed on account of letting me escape the confines of my room.'

'Did ye tell yer parents what happened?'

Helene shook her head. 'Robert threatened to do something worse if I told them.'

Lachlan drew her into a tight embrace. 'I'm sorry for what ye endured. Kin are supposed to care for ye, not harm or threaten ye.'

Safe in his arms, she wanted to confess all. That her actions had destroyed her sister's life. Her future. That Prudence's condition had worsened to the point where her discreet carers in the country could no longer cater to her needs. Father would not have her return home, fearing embarrassment and bringing shame on the family name. Instead, he'd committed Prudence to a mental asylum.

Helene clung to Lachlan's warmth, his strength. It was she who deserved to be locked away. Years of pent-up grief and regret threatened to burst their banks, and it took every conceivable effort to hold the emotions in check. 'I'm sorry. I didn't mean to burden you with my troubles.'

'Ye've nae need to be sorry. Yer brother's heinous act was unforgivable. If ever I meet the monster, I'll—'

'No!' She drew back and forced a smile to her lips. 'It's in the past. Besides, I'll never again fear storms, for I'll be soothed by the memory of . . .' Awkward and shy, her cheeks flushed hot and her chin dipped to her chest.

'Aye, lass. I too shall remember. Always.'

Everything about the way he cupped his hand to her cheek and his gentle words and tone said he cared about her. Cared *for* her. And yet, it would be foolish to delude herself into believing intimacy ensured loyalty, connection, and a oneness with the laird of Clan MacLanoch.

She'd more than accomplished what she'd set out to do, and fool that she was, she'd developed more than a fleeting interest in Lachlan. Even more reason to fabricate a believable excuse to cut short her visit to Drumocher, call in Cuthbert's debt, and return home to London. To Prudence.

'Lachlan, I must lea—' The sound of galloping hooves forced them apart. 'Your sister approaches.'

Annoyance flashed in Lachlan's eyes before he glanced over his shoulder.

'Brother! Helene!' Grizel reined in her horse and promptly dismounted. 'The sentries along the castle's battlements spied ye at a distance, and I was too excited not to ride out and greet ye. I cannae wait to hear all about yer visit to the shielings.' She handed the reins to her brother. 'Do ye mind leading the horse while I talk and walk alongside Helene?'

Lachlan obliged.

Grizel cast them an appraising eye. 'I say, ye both look a little worse for wear. Are ye all right?'

Helene touched a hand to her untidy hair and spoke in unison with Lachlan. 'We got caught in a storm,' and, 'We weathered a squall.'

'Ah,' said Grizel, wrinkling her nose. 'That would explain the scent of wet plaid.' She possessively linked arms with Helene. 'How was it? Tell me in detail.'

Helene glanced nervously at Lachlan. 'Being caught in the storm?'

Grizel's shrill laughter rent the air. 'Nae. I can see ye

survived a wee squall. I'm talking about yer time away at the shielings.'

'I can assure you, Grizel, to my way of thinking, there was nothing *wee* about that squall.'

Helene shot a glance at Lachlan and saw his lips twitch. It warmed her to see he appreciated and understood the hidden context in her words.

He made a clicking noise to the horse, and together they all walked on.

'The shielings, Helene, do tell,' said Grizel.

'Not before I enquire after Agnes. Has her ankle healed?'

'Aye. She's much improved and hobbles with assistance.'

'Promising news,' said Helene.

'Now, what of the shielings?'

'Perhaps we should wait until we're with Agnes and your family, so I need not repeat myself.'

Grizel would not be swayed and made as if swatting midges. 'Nae! I cannae wait 'til then.'

'All right.'

Helene began with the unfortunate details of the injured deer on the day she and Lachlan trekked up the mountain. With mention of delivering the carcass to cottars Aila and Ross, Grizel came to a sudden standstill and her gaze shot to Lachlan. He returned her stare like a silent warning. It was a most curious exchange.

'Aila graciously gifted me this,' said Helene, brushing her hair aside and pointing to the brooch pinned to the plaid wrap Grizel had loaned her.

Grizel's eyes widened in surprise, and she shot another glance at Lachlan. The unusual interaction between brother and sister smacked of secrecy.

'Gracious indeed,' said Grizel. The light in her eyes reflected puzzling intrigue. She urged Helene onwards. 'Tell me more while I have ye all to myself.'

Conversation between Helene and her avid listener stopped when they walked beneath the raised portcullis and a throng of people surged forward to welcome home the trio.

Lachlan tossed the reins of the horse to a stable-boy and escorted Helene and Grizel up the stairs leading directly into the great hall. He signalled to a maid, instructing her to inform Cook of their arrival and to bring refreshments. His fingers uncinched the weapons belt and set it down atop a trestle table.

No sooner did they take their seats than a familiar voice boomed from the opposite end of the hall. 'Cousin! Lady Helene! Welcome back.'

Cuthbert.

Helene looked past him, towards the exit, and inhaled a calming breath in the hope it would settle her nerves. It didn't. She wasn't ready to face him, nor was she prepared for him to pull her aside and interrogate her.

And Lachlan. How could she bring herself to betray him so quickly after promising to keep their intimacy a secret? *A kiss. Reveal nothing more.*

Helene felt sick to her stomach. Betrayal and lies. They weren't within her moral makeup, but needs must.

❧

Lachlan's hackles rose on sighting Cuthbert. Instinct said to keep him away from Helene. There was something irksome about his cousin's confident stride, his tailor-made breeches, silk vest, and hair perfectly styled in a queue. Why would he dress as if he were at court?

By comparison, Lachlan could smell a mixture of his own sweat and the damp wool of his plaid, as his sister was so blunt to point out. His unshaven face and unruly hair left him looking more like a homeless Highlander than a laird.

When Cuthbert sat down opposite Helene at the table, his leer sent her gaze into her lap, where her hands flexed before repeatedly smoothing the folds of the skirt covering her thighs.

The memory of those naked thighs, soft and supple beneath Lachlan's palms, and the way she'd trusted him with her body, had forever changed him. So deep and profound were his feelings for her that, where once he'd threatened to harm Cuthbert should he so much as steal a kiss from Helene, any future threats Lachlan made would lean towards lethal.

A frightening and telling realisation. One that rocked him to the core.

All smiles, Cuthbert asked, 'How did you enjoy your sojourn in the hills? Did it prove to be all you both hoped to achieve? And Helene, did you accomplish your wish to stand barefoot in the shallows of a running stream?'

The lass had dipped more than her toes in a stream, but Lachlan was not about to let that discussion take place here and now. In a tight voice, he said, 'We'll talk about it later, in the company of yer mother and mine, and Agnes. Why not tell us how ye've occupied yer time in our absence?'

Cuthbert's smile broadened. 'I've mastered the art of skimming stones on the loch and therefore challenge you to a rematch.'

Music to Lachlan's ears. 'Challenge accepted.'

Grizel spoke up, her gaze darting between Lachlan and Helene. 'I for one cannae wait to hear more about yer time away at the shielings. From what ye've already told me, Helene, ye've had quite the memorable adventure.'

Cuthbert raised his brows at Helene. 'Well, that's pricked my ears.'

She stood abruptly. 'If you all don't mind, I'll take to my

bedchamber to rest before the evening meal. It's been a long day, and I'm somewhat fatigued.'

Lachlan came immediately to his feet. 'Aye, lass. I'll have a servant bring ye yer refreshments.'

Grizel, eager to please, said, 'And I'll arrange for the wooden tub to be brought and filled in yer bedchamber. After all that walking and being caught up in a squall, ye'll need a good, long soak.'

'I thank you both,' said Helene. She and Grizel headed for the door.

'Wait!' Cuthbert rose to his feet. 'How did you come by that brooch you wear?'

Lachlan wished he had insisted Helene remove the adornment before his sister and now Cuthbert had noticed it. But what explanation would he have given her for doing so, and without raising her suspicion or provoking questions?

Helene's slender fingers caressed the lovingly polished silver adornment. 'Aila, one of the Highland cottars, gave it to me.'

Cuthbert raised a brow. 'You must have made quite the impression for her to have relinquished to you such a personal heirloom.'

Lachlan didn't need to see his cousin's face to know the machinations of his mind. Cuthbert was too clever a man not to understand the significance of Aila's gesture.

'Enough now,' said Lachlan. 'Leave the lass be.'

'Of course.' Cuthbert inclined his head and made a sweep of his hand towards the hall's exit. 'Rest well. I look forward to hearing all about your . . . *adventures*.'

Lachlan swore under his breath and sat down at the table. He knew that with the women gone, Cuthbert would put the screws to him. Their conversation would not be so private, with servants busy in the hall setting up for the evening meal.

Two kitchen hands arrived to place wine, cheese, and bread

on the table and left with Lachlan's instructions to promptly provide the same for Helene in her bedchamber.

When Cuthbert sat down, he crossed one leg over the other, folded his arms, and wore a supercilious grin.

Lachlan poured himself a glass of wine and, after taking a sip, broke the temporary silence between them, demanding, 'What?'

'Helene and the shielings. Tell me something. *Anything.*'

'Did ye nae hear me? We'll discuss it tonight with the family present.'

'You're being evasive.'

Lachlan cut a chunk of cheese and took a bite. 'I'm not being evasive. I'm hungry, thirsty, and in need of a wash and a change of clothes.'

Cuthbert fanned his nose with his hand. 'You are a little on the ripe side, but surely you can talk, eat, and drink at the same time.'

'There's not much to tell.'

Cuthbert's sudden burst of laughter startled the servants nearby. 'You disappear to the shielings with a peach of a young woman, for longer than expected, and declare there's nothing to tell? *Something* happened. What did you do? How did Helene cope? Was she a benefit or a burden during your time away? And—'

Lachlan stabbed the knife he held into the wooden tabletop and at the same time said, 'Keep yer voice down.'

He immediately checked his temper, careful not to behave in such a manner as to have Cuthbert jump to conclusions about what had transpired between himself and Helene. He must protect her honour and reputation. At all costs.

He broke off a hunk of bread and said in a casual manner, 'The lass was in nae way a burden. Ye've seen for yersel' that she's of strong mind and will and possesses a good and kind heart. She didnae complain about anything or anyone. Not the arduous journey there and back or having to sleep in a stone hut on a bed of heather.

'She didn't baulk at having to eat from a crude wooden bowl or to drink water drawn from a stream. She tasted a dram of *uisge-beatha*, and the women and children took to her as easily as she did to them. There ye have it in a nutshell.'

Cuthbert spread his hands wide and shrugged. 'And here was I convinced she wouldn't be seen other than eating off fine porcelain plates and sipping champagne with England's elite. I find it hard to believe she imbibed whisky with uneducated heathens.'

'Dinnae speak so ill of my clan. They're honest and hard-working. The latter of which ye ken nothing about.' Lachlan took hold of the knife's hardwood handle. 'And ye underestimate Helene.'

'Clearly.' Cuthbert glanced down at Lachlan's hand. 'You might want to loosen your grip on that knife before your knuckles pop clear of your skin.'

Lachlan ignored the cynical quip in favour of steering the conversation clear of Helene. He yanked the knife out of the table and cut himself another chunk of cheese. 'How else did ye occupy yer time?'

'Thinking. I had plenty of time to think, and much of it done while skimming stones. Most therapeutic, you know.'

'Did ye draw any life-altering conclusions?'

'I most certainly did, dear cousin. All thanks to you. What you've just described of Helene, being so amenable and seemingly easy to please, serves to validate my decision in heeding your advice.'

Lachlan's guard went up. 'What advice would that be?'

Cuthbert whispered, 'To marry Helene.'

'Nae!'

Cuthbert stiffened at the sudden outburst. 'Was it not you who suggested her father and mine are in cahoots, hoping that here, away from London's distractions, she and I would forge a connection and in time marry?'

Lachlan stood up and bellowed, 'Clear the hall. Now!' Servants scurried away, slamming shut the doors behind them at either end of the hall. He sat down, rattled by his cousin's declaration. 'I was wrong to suggest ye wed her. She deserves better.'

Cuthbert's chin tilted a degree. 'You don't think I'm good enough for her?'

'Neither of us are good enough for Lady Helene.'

Cuthbert's face was all confusion. 'Who said anything about *you* marrying the chit?'

Lachlan leaned in closer and hissed, 'Curb yer disrespectful tongue and keep yer voice down! The walls have ears.'

In a sharp whisper, Cuthbert said, 'As you so rightly pointed out, she is the key to my problem. If I'm to marry at all, which is of course inevitable, it may as well be her. Doing so will satisfy my father's ultimatum and guarantee my inheritance. Upon his death, I'll rise to the rank of viscount. Helene will give me an heir and, God willing, a spare, *and* I'll be free to take as many lovers as I wish. It's the best possible outcome for all involved.'

It took every shred of self-control for Lachlan not to lunge across the table and throttle Cuthbert. 'As I said, she deserves better. She deserves a man who marries her for love, nae for convenience or connection.'

'Love? *Love?*' Cuthbert's laugh was as sardonic as his reply. 'That's hardly the way of the world, and you know it.'

'What I ken is that Helene is not what ye first described. She's not some highbrow lass with an offensive air of superiority. Nor does she think herself too good for any man. If she cannae wed for love, then she's nae desire to be bargained with like some prized breeding mare.'

Cuthbert pointed a finger at Lachlan. 'Now there's a conversation I wish I'd been privy to. Care to share?'

'Nae!' Lachlan took up his wine and took a deep swallow.

'If not me, then her father will marry her off to someone else. She'll have no say in the matter. You do realise that?'

Of course he did, but Lachlan would see her wed to God and cloistered away in a convent before he'd let any man claim her.

Cuthbert pushed his point. 'I'd be good to her. Treat her with respect. She'd want for nothing and have a good life with me. No harm would befall her. Surely you know me well enough to trust me on that.'

Lachlan set his wine down and clenched his hand into a fist beneath the table. Had he not done so, the glass goblet would have shattered within his grasp. 'Aye, Cuthbert. I ken ye well enough, and I do trust ye'd take good care of Helene, but ye dinnae love her.'

'An insignificant detail.'

'I won't allow it.'

Cuthbert rushed to his feet, palms pressed to the table. 'You won't allow it? Who the hell are you to dictate to me who I can and can't marry?'

Lachlan held his tongue, his eyes fixed on the scarred wooden table, fingers flexing beneath it.

'Does Helene know about Tibbie?'

'Nae.'

'Are you going to tell her?'

'Why would I tell her?'

Cuthbert sat down. 'The brooch. It would put the giving of the gift into perspective for Helene, because the only reason Aila would part with that brooch is if she thought you and Hel—'

'Donnie! Aila gave Helene the brooch in thanks for having the courage to defy me in standing up for Donnie.' It was at least half of the truth. No one, least of all Cuthbert, need know the other half.

'Balderdash! You're a fool if you expect me to believe that.'

Lachlan met Cuthbert's narrowed gaze. 'Believe what ye want. It makes nae difference to me.' He took up his glass, drained the wine, and reached for a refill.

'Slow down.'

'I'm thirsty!'

'And tetchy.'

Lachlan took a swig from the neck of the bottle and felt the unnerving eyes of an eagle on him. If he didn't up and leave the hall now, Cuthbert would stop circling him and swoop in for the kill.

'You seem unusually . . . different,' said Cuthbert. 'Your actions. Your outbursts.'

An observation Lachlan ignored and sprang to his feet.

'And for what reason do you so gallantly champion Helene?'

'So that she returns to her father in the same state as she arrived. Safe and virtuous.'

'Virtuous?' Cuthbert raised a brow. 'Why did you just look away the instant I said that word?'

Lachlan clapped his gaze on Cuthbert. 'I dinnae ken what ye're on about!'

Cuthbert folded his arms and studied Lachlan as if he were an insect stuck with pins under a microscope. 'My, my, cousin. If I don't but recognise the hallmarks of a guilty man. Unnaturally defensive. Shoulders drawn up. You've a harried look about you, and the wine bottle is damp from your sweaty palm. I must wonder if you've not already staked your claim on the emerald-eyed jewel.'

Lachlan snatched up his weapons from the table.

Cuthbert jumped to his feet and blocked Lachlan's path forward. 'Did you kiss her?'

Heart thumping inside his chest, Lachlan made a move to sidestep Cuthbert. Not fast enough. Cuthbert's face was inches from his.

'Did you? Kiss her?'

Lachlan's jaw clenched as hard as his fist around sheathed steel, and his eyes locked with Cuthbert's in a standoff. The walls of the hall closed in on him. Each burning breath laboured within a tightening chest. He shoved Cuthbert aside. 'Out of my way.'

'Cousin!'

Lachlan stopped short of the exit, standing with his back to Cuthbert.

'You made me a promise, remember? You said, "I'll ne'er let a lassie drive a wedge between us."'

Disappointment resonated in Cuthbert's accusation, causing Lachlan's shoulders to slump.

'If you did indeed kiss the lass, then I won't hold a blade to your throat as you would do to me. I'd shake your hand and congratulate you.'

'This is nae game or wager we play!'

'No. It isn't.' Cuthbert's sonorous voice had softened. 'But if you and Lady Helene have indulged in more than just a kiss . . . well then, I know you'll do the right and honourable thing by her. In which case, you have my blessing.'

Stunned into a state of confusion, Lachlan glanced over his shoulder to see Cuthbert smile, nod, and raise the bottle of wine in salute.

CHAPTER FIFTEEN

DURING THE EVENING meal in the lord's hall, Helene, together with Lachlan, recounted the events of their sojourn to the shielings. Details of their intimacy were memories kept under lock and key, although Helene was ever mindful of Caitrin MacLanoch's watchful gaze and lived in fear of the astute woman being a mind-reader. Her all-knowing expression gave Helene cause to worry.

'Well, my dear,' started Caitrin, 'despite facing down stampeding cattle and yer harrowing brush with death in the river, I'd say the clean mountain air agrees with ye. It's done wonders for yer complexion.'

Helene swallowed her last mouthful of pheasant, set down her cutlery, and graciously accepted the kind compliment. 'Thank you.'

'I concur,' said Elspeth. 'Ye might remember I observed ye looked as pale as the day was grey when we first arrived at Drumocher, and now ye've a rosy Highland glow about ye. Even yer eyes look clearer.'

A glow? Clear eyes? Helene stole a glance at Lachlan, who sat at the head of the table. Did he have any idea he was responsible for this positive change in her? A change that left her feeling guilty. She might look the picture of health, but what of poor Prudence stuck in her living hell?

'And as for ye?' Caitrin's eyes narrowed on her son. 'I ken something weighs heavy on yer mind.'

Cuthbert chimed in with a wink. 'I noticed that too, Auntie. Perhaps the root cause of Lachlan's, shall we say, *distraction* has something to do with a certain brooch.'

Helene saw Lachlan cut his cousin a scathing look, but the smile he bestowed on his mother was designed to set her at ease. 'My mind is merely occupied with business matters requiring my urgent attention.'

A shadow of concern fell on Caitrin's face.

'Ye've nae need for worry, Mother. They be small matters.' Lachlan pressed his gaze on Cuthbert. 'And fixed as easily as stamping out spot fires.'

If there were any two people to read between the lines, it was Helene and Caitrin. She'd picked up on the tension between the cousins the moment they met this afternoon. Whatever was discussed after she and Grizel had left the great hall had put Lachlan in a foul mood, but it seemed Caitrin MacLanoch was not so easily fooled. Her eyebrows furrowed, and Helene could see a question forming on the matriarch's lips.

'Cuthbert, ye referenced a brooch. Will ye tell me about it?'

With courtesy and casual ease, he deflected the question to Helene. 'I think that's your story to tell.'

'Shall I motion for tea, Mother? Aunt Elspeth?' said Lachlan. 'I'll have it brought to us now, if it pleases ye.'

Helene's gaze snapped to Lachlan. Clearly, he wished to avoid any further discussion concerning the brooch. What was it about the silver adornment that raised such a stir? First with Grizel, then Cuthbert, and now Lachlan's mother.

Helene had removed it hours ago, along with Grizel's plaid

wrap, when retiring to her bedchamber. It would seem Aila's heirloom held a story of its own. One seemingly shrouded in secrecy, like a forbidden subject undeserving of discussion, or a cursed object sealed in a box and never to see the light of day. Helene's curiosity was now well and truly piqued.

'In a minute, son,' said Caitrin. 'Let the lass speak.' She looked at Helene across the table. 'Does the brooch have anything to do with yer visit to the cottars Aila and Ross?'

Helene nodded. 'Aila gave it to me as a parting gift.'

In that moment, Agnes looked astonished. Lady Sutton's eyes rounded like saucers, and Caitrin's furrowed brows released, lifting in surprise as her keen gaze slid from Helene to Lachlan.

Helene felt as if she'd stolen from the poor. 'I didn't want to accept it, seeing it for the treasured heirloom it was, but Aila insisted, and I didn't wish to offend her.'

'I see,' said Caitrin, her voice soft, resigned, if not tinged with wonder. She reached for her son's hand beside her on the table and covered it with her own.

Awkward silence stalled the conversation.

Helene looked at Grizel, Agnes, Lady Sutton, Cuthbert, Lachlan, and his mother. Their expressions said they were privy to something she was not. *Enough!*

'What is it I should know about the origins of this brooch, or the intent with which it was given? If I should not have it, then tell me and I'll gladly see it returned.'

'No,' said Caitrin, waggling a finger at Helene. 'Ye must not return it.'

Helene noted the way Lachlan stared at his mother. It was the same stony stare he'd used to silence Grizel when she'd learned her brother and Helene had paid the cottars a visit.

Had Helene not glanced down in this very moment, she'd have missed Caitrin's almost imperceptible squeeze of her son's hand. The small reassuring gesture said she had his back. From what or whom did she protect him?

Helene met Caitrin's kind eyes. 'Why shouldn't I return the brooch?'

'I've already told ye, lass,' supplied Lachlan. He slid his hand from beneath his mother's and took up his glass of wine. 'It was Aila's way of honouring yer bravery and courage when ye challenged me in defence of young Donnie.'

He brought the glass to his lips. Helene deliberated over whether he'd reiterated the truth, or if he sipped the wine to swallow a lie. She need not be reminded of blood being thicker than water and that some secrets must remain secret. In her heart of hearts, she knew she did not deserve to keep Aila's precious brooch and would conveniently leave it where it presently lay—atop the dresser in her bedchamber—when she departed Drumocher. It would find its way back to the rightful owner.

Beside her, Agnes visibly shuddered and glowered at Helene. 'I just don't know how you did it. Sleeping in a wooden cot with heather as your mattress? Not my idea of clean, civilized comfort.' She poked her chin forward. 'And how could you have settled for meals any less than the quality to which you are accustomed? And you churned butter! That's what servants are for. Have you lost your mind?'

'Agnes! How dare ye,' scolded her mother. 'I willnae tolerate yer insolence and yer contempt of what it is to be a Highlander. Ye ken nothing but a spoiled, privileged life. If ye found yersel' cast out on the streets, ye'd ken nought of how to survive and protect yersel', so dinnae be so quick to judge those born to eke out a living on the land. If not for them, ye'd not be eating the food on yer plate. Best ye heed the voice of gratitude instead of churlish judgement!'

It was a just serve from Lady Sutton, after which the room fell deathly silent.

Agnes hung her head in shame. 'I'm sorry, Mother.'

''Tis not me to whom ye should direct yer apologies!'

Helene gave Agnes a sidelong glance and saw a flush creep across her friend's cheeks. The sudden outburst had taken Helene by surprise. As much as she adored her friend, she agreed with Lady Sutton. Agnes possessed a good heart, and with a likable, lively spirit, but she was also a product of her upbringing. Spoiled, entitled, and opinionated. Though never had Helene heard her speak words so pitiless and cruel. The slight on Highlanders and their way of life was a slight on her Scottish kin.

Agnes sank back in her chair, shoulders slumped and hands clasped in her lap. She shifted her sheepish gaze to encompass her Auntie Caitrin, Lachlan, and Grizel. 'I'm so *very* sorry. Forgive me. My comments were thoughtless and rude.'

Each of the MacLanochs nodded their acceptance of the apology, at which point Agnes turned to Helene.

'And I apologise to you too, my dear friend. If the truth be known, I lashed out in envy of you. In my eyes, you can do no wrong and you possess the qualities I lack. Courage. Compassion. Adaptability.'

The confession flabbergasted Helene, and she reached for Agnes's hand. 'It takes great courage to openly admit one's weaknesses, but let me assure you, I possess more flawed traits than you'll ever understand.'

Cuthbert tipped his head at Agnes. 'If I may offer some constructive, brotherly advice, try to move beyond your self-importance and your self-centred mentality.'

'I'm not perfect!'

'None of us are, dear child,' reassured Caitrin. 'Nonetheless, there are times when we must be brave and step outside our daily comforts. It is only when we are tested that we discover who we are, who we want to be, or who we want to become.'

Helene couldn't have agreed more.

Agnes nodded. 'Sage advice, Auntie.'

'Then perhaps ye could act on this advice and make the effort to visit the shielings when yer foot is completely healed. Ye needn't walk, of course. Ye can take the longer route and travel on horseback. 'Tis the same path the cottars take to transport their carts, livestock, and all essentials required to see out the summer amidst the pastures.

'There be a small hunting lodge owned by the MacLanochs not far from the shielings. 'Tis comfortable enough to overnight in if ye wish. Of course, ye need to convince my son to escort ye.'

Agnes inhaled deeply through the nose and exhaled long and slow through the mouth. 'Helene. Promise me something.'

Those words set Helene on edge, making her hesitant to ask, 'What would that be?'

'When my ankle comes good, then return to the shielings with me.'

Helene's belly contracted, her muscles tightening. She couldn't afford to stay one minute more in Scotland. Prudence was her priority. 'I—'

'Good! And Grizel,' said Agnes, 'I'm sorry I held you back from going with Helene and Lachlan. You must join us too.'

Grizel fidgeted with excitement in her chair. 'Of course!' Her head turned towards her brother. 'Lachlan! Ye will take us, won't ye?'

Helene sat forward in her chair and locked eyes with the laird, willing him to say no, or to at least defer the journey for when Agnes and her family revisited Drumocher. It took a grand amount of self-control to keep her rising panic in check.

'Please,' begged Agnes. 'I wish to turn over a new leaf.'

Lachlan seemed to give the idea due consideration. 'I'll not decide right now. Best wait until yer ankle is completely healed. Aye, lass?'

Relief had Helene reassure her friend. 'He's right. For your own safety. You don't want to do more damage to your ankle before it is completely healed.'

Cuthbert gestured towards the other end of the hall, to a plush padded sofa and a cluster of armchairs with a wooden games table at its centre. 'Well, now that we've eaten our fill, who's for a game of whist or cribbage?'

'I shall decline, for I'm a wee bit weary,' said Caitrin. 'Lachlan, if ye dinnae mind, I'd like a private word with ye. I willnae keep ye long. Walk me to my bedchamber, and there we'll sit for a while and share a wee dram. It will help me sleep.'

Aila's brooch was, without a doubt, the catalyst for Caitrin's need to corner her son in a private discussion. Helene could not help but suffer the intrigue of the matter. Best set it aside. She had other matters to address. As she stood along with the others to bid Caitrin goodnight, there came a whispered voice at her back.

'Am I right in thinking you're avoiding me?'

Helene bristled at the touch of warm breath on the back of her neck.

Cuthbert.

No one else would have heard him above the general chatter and commotion of chairs scraping on the wooden floorboards. Helene turned her head to the side and whispered back, 'What reason would I have to avoid you?'

His hand went to the crook of her elbow, and to avoid causing a scene, she did not protest when he led her away from the table.

Behind them, his mother and Grizel made slow progress

assisting Agnes, who hobbled one slow, painful step at a time in the direction of the armchairs and the card table.

'Shouldn't you lend your sister a helping hand?' said Helene.

'My mother and Grizel are managing well enough.' He spoke over his shoulder to them. 'Helene and I shall take the opportunity to stretch our legs and take a turn about the hall.' To Helene, he spoke quietly and quickly. 'I'll get straight to the point. Did Lachlan kiss you?'

The tip of Helene's shoe caught the edge of a woven floor rug. Cuthbert's steadying hand on her arm righted her.

'I'll take that faltering misstep as a *yes*,' he chuckled. 'And did he touch you?'

Heat ravaged Helene's face. The audacity of the man!

'I've never seen colour rise so fast in a woman's cheeks. Either you're embarrassed to have been asked the question, or Lachlan's kiss led to something more scintillating. Which is it?'

Helene stared wide-eyed ahead at the tapestry-covered wall.

'Speechless, I see. Well, never mind, my dear Lady Helene. Lachlan did indeed sample those luscious lips. That much I know.'

Helene's jaw dropped. 'He told you?'

Cuthbert's eyes lit up and he wore a triumphant grin. 'No, but your reaction just did.'

Helene tried without success to jerk her arm free of his hold. How she detested his gloating banter.

'Lachlan neither confirmed nor denied the same questions I asked of you. If he were innocent of any immoral or inappropriate behaviour towards you, then he would have flat-out denied it. The fact that he said nothing confirms he kissed you. My cousin is not one to lie. It's his weakness. His Achilles' heel. He simply doesn't have it in him.'

Cuthbert patted her hand as one would pet an obedient

pup. 'You've accomplished what I asked of you. The rest will simply fall into place.'

'The rest? Whatever do you mean?'

Cuthbert winked. 'He protects you as fiercely as a king protects his queen, and in the process of doing so, he's compromised your virtue. He must do the honourable thing now, and it's my hope he will soon make you his queen.'

'*Your* hope? What of *his* hopes?'

'I understand my cousin better than he understands himself. He thinks he knows what he wants from life, but I know what he needs. It's you, my dear. He needs you.'

Helene ground out hushed words through clenched teeth. 'Preposterous! He can't have me!'

'I'm willing to bet he already has.' He stifled a ribald snicker.

Bets! Wagers! So this was Cuthbert's twisted motive. Using subterfuge to trap Lachlan into tying the knot with a woman of Cuthbert's choosing.

'And what do you stand to gain?' she hissed.

'The satisfaction of being right and seeing my cousin happily married and settled.'

Such arrogance. 'And what am I in this game of yours? The lamb to lure the lion?'

'Precisely!'

Helene's cheeks burned hot with outrage. If not for being in the company of others, she'd have slapped Cuthbert hard across the face. Her next words delivered the impact her palm could not. 'I'm already spoken for.'

He brought them both to a shuddering halt and looked at her with mouth wide open, a picture of stupefaction. Then he cracked a smile and swatted the air as if batting back her words. 'I invested considerable time making thorough enquiries about you, and my sources inform me you are not yet spoken for.'

'Then you've been misinformed. My life is devoted to another.'

'You jest.'

'I assure you, I do not.'

'What's his name, his rank, his title?'

'My personal life is not up for discussion, and how dare you even think my future is yours to manipulate and command. Now, you listen to me! I upheld my end of the bargain and kissed your cousin. Tonight, I wish to collect what you owe me. At midnight, when all are sure to be asleep, you will deliver your promissory note to my bedchamber door. You'd best stick to your end of the bargain, for if you do not, I'll . . .'

Helene let the unspoken threat linger in the air long enough for Cuthbert to take the bait.

'You'll do what?' he mocked.

'Let's just say, I've done my due diligence on you, my lord.'

His chin rose a notch, eyes narrowing. 'You have nothing on me.'

Helene arched an eyebrow.

'You're bluffing.'

'Am I? Do you not think it incumbent upon me to have investigated the clandestine *affairs* of the man with whom I'm to do business?'

Cuthbert released her lightning-fast and took a step back, his face turning paler than the purest alabaster. She had indeed called his bluff, a bluff based on what she'd perceived to have witnessed in a quiet and dimly lit corridor of the most recent ball she'd attended in London. Judging by Cuthbert's mortified reaction, her eyesight had not failed her.

Helene used her bluff to advantage. 'I doubt your father would approve of such a, shall we say, controversial match.'

'What are ye two whispering about?' called Lady Sutton, having finally settled Agnes into an armchair and now shuffling a deck of cards. 'Are ye going to join us in a game of whist or continue to stand there engaged in subdued conversation?'

Helene forced a cheery tone. 'We'll be there directly, Lady Sutton. Your son was telling me what a master of the game he is, but I've just warned him that I've a knack of declaring the winning hand.'

Before gathering up her skirts to join the others, Helene inclined her head at Cuthbert and curtly whispered, 'Tonight. Midnight.'

~

Lachlan sat in an armchair beside his mother in her private quarters. A blanket covered her knees, and a low fire burned in the hearth, chasing away the night-time chill. They chatted and reminisced on all manner of things while savouring Drumocher's finest whisky, but idle chit-chat was not the reason his mother wished to speak privately with him. He waited patiently until which time she was ready to make her point.

'The Sassenach lass,' she began, and set about extolling the virtues of their English guest, recapping the day she'd arrived and moments henceforth. She declared her admiration of Helene's opinionated and bold behaviour and her curious nature to explore the Highlands and understand its people.

Then came the crux of her discussion. 'Ye're more than enamoured with her, aren't ye, son?'

Lachlan couldn't deny it. Not to his mother, a woman who possessed keen powers of observation and foresight, seeing through others as if looking through glass.

'Aye,' he confessed.

'I ken Aila honoured Helene's bravery on wee Donnie's

behalf, but she wouldnae parted with and pinned her brooch on Helene if not for one qualifying truth.'

Lachlan took a slow sip of whisky. 'Aye, there be that too.'

His mother's face brightened, and her hand went immediately to the triquetra pendant hanging around her neck, a symbol of hope.

'Tibbie,' said Lachlan, remembering Ross and Aila's granddaughter. Her name he hadn't spoken since her death five long years ago.

His mother drew in a sharp breath. 'If ye can say her name out loud, then ye must be finally free of her.'

'Aye. Wholly and solely free of her.'

'Because of . . . ?' She paused.

'Aye.' He smiled and nodded. 'Helene.' It seemed incredible to Lachlan the speed at which he'd developed feelings for Helene, given their short acquaintance.

'Och, son.' Caitrin reached for Lachlan's hand and held it tight.

'I had to tell Aila that—'

A wave of Caitrin's hand cut him off. 'Save it for the Sassenach. My ears dinnae need hear it, for I ken ye verra well. Speak yer truth to Helene. Though it be early days, ye've met yer match in her and she deserves yer honesty. Dinnae waste time. Dinnae let her look to another.'

Lachlan refrained from saying Helene had sworn off marriage and would bend to no man's will. 'Do ye approve of her?'

Caitrin's smile was serene and her green eyes shone brighter in the soft glow of the firelight. 'Ye dinnae need my approval, but for what it's worth, I approve, verra much so, as would yer father if he were with us today. God rest his soul.' She crossed herself. 'And I'll have ye ken *my* soul sings knowing Helene has reignited the light in yer eyes and stoked a fire in yer veins. She's demonstrated courage and a stalwart character. I think perhaps she's not so much the pampered society Sassenach, but a Highland lass at heart, and worthy of the MacLanoch name.'

'Aye, but am I worthy of her?'

'That ye are! Dinnae ye go doubting yersel'. Be warned, though, I see sorrow and pain behind her eyes. I've glimpsed the same tormented look as ye've carried these past five years. Just as well she's here for the summer. Time will allow ye to ken her better, scratch beneath the surface and discover what demons haunt her.'

His mother showed signs of growing weary. Her eyelids drooped and she stifled a yawn. Sleep beckoned. He stood and pressed a kiss to the back of her hand. 'I'll summon the maid to ready ye for bed. Thank ye for the chat. Sleep well, Mother.'

He turned to leave.

'Lachlan.'

He looked down at her in profile. 'Aye?'

''Twas yer grandmother, my mother, who once said to me, "Better ye follow where yer heart leads and face acceptance or rejection than to nurse a withered heart and spend a lifetime wondering what might have been between ye."'

Though her gaze focused on the hearth's glowing embers, Lachlan knew her mind was in the past, lost to a world of memories. A wry smile formed on her lined mouth.

She returned to the present and stared up at him. ''Twas those verra words that led me here, to Drumocher, to yer father. Had I not done so all those years ago soon after we quarrelled . . .' She giggled like a young lass. 'Weel, there's more to that courtship, of course, but that will have to wait for another day.'

Lachlan lightly rested a hand on her shoulder and winked. 'Father told me.'

His mother's eyes sparkled with mischief. 'Yer father was

prone to stretching the truth, so ye need hear my side of the story. Go now. I must rest.'

Lachlan dropped a soft kiss on the crown of her head, and instead of returning to the lord's hall, he repaired directly to the library. He'd have gladly joined the women in a game of cards and conversation, yet he had no stomach for Cuthbert's company. There was a marked and unpleasant change in his cousin since last they met. He behaved in the most inordinate way. Perhaps because Cuthbert's father was forcing him to secure a bride within the year.

Lachlan's gaze strayed to the dark of night beyond the library window. Marrying Helene would be no hardship. He grew pensive, calibrating his thoughts as if winding back the hands on a clock and recalling specific threads of shared conversations with Helene. *'I've no need of a husband,'* she'd said. *'I shall never have a daughter, or any children for that matter, but I* will *have—'*

Lachlan sat forward in his armchair, elbows on his knees, chin resting on fisted hands. What? What did she emphatically covet above marriage and a family of her own? And if achieved, would it banish the pain in her eyes and reset her world to spin on a fixed axis?

The lass was a complex enigma, and he wanted to understand her reason for snubbing notable offers of marriage and for stating she would never have any children of her own.

One theory had him surge to his feet. Could it be the lass was barren? That she refused to let her father and brother deceive her suitors and marry her off knowing she could not fulfil her wifely duty in giving her husband a child, an heir? Helene was not prone to deceit. From what he'd observed of her, she was all about the principle of the matter.

Lachlan eyed his reflection in the glass pane. A solemn reminder of *his* duty as laird to sire an heir in the name of securing Drumocher and future generations of the MacLanoch clan. If Helene were in fact barren, he knew with absolute clarity where his good intentions lay. Producing a MacLanoch heir would fall to his sister, Grizel.

One way or the other, it was a conversation he must broach with the lass. Surely, if she'd entrusted to him the intimacy and well-being of her body when weathering the storm, then she'd confide in him and reveal her secrets.

Tomorrow he'd take her aside, away from prying eyes, no ears alert to gossip. He'd follow his grandmother's advice and stand before Helene with an open heart, to reveal how his past had shaped his present and confess what he'd come to feel for her. He knew the emotion for what it must be and was determined to give it voice.

By placing his trust in her, he hoped it would give her the confidence to reciprocate. To be open and honest and consider a future with him. She could take however long she needed to think on it.

The hour was late and the household deep in slumber when Lachlan left the library. Sconces glowed dimly along the empty castle corridors. He came within feet of rounding a corner when hushed voices brought him to a halt. Hidden in the shadows, with his hands and back pressed to the wall, he peered around the corner in the direction of Helene's bedchamber and saw Cuthbert standing at her door.

Lachlan's hackles rose and his hands formed fists against the cold stone wall. All manner of mayhem broke loose in his mind, and suspicion took him to the darkest den.

His cousin was still dressed in his evening attire. Helene wore a silk banyan, hair cascading down about her shoulders. What in God's name was going on? Lachlan could only draw one conclusion. A clandestine tryst. Tingles racked his body, signalling dread.

A folded piece of parchment passed from Cuthbert's hand to Helene's. They spoke barely above a whisper, making it impossible for Lachlan to grasp their conversation. Pressure was building in his chest for not having taken a breath, and his heart ached from the thought of losing Helene even before he'd won her.

Losing her to Cuthbert cut deeper than if it were any other man.

Lachlan's body was so tightly wound it would snap. He must leave now. Before he lashed out, before he said or did something he'd later regret.

There'd be time enough tomorrow for confrontation and accusations.

CHAPTER SIXTEEN

LACHLAN HURLED THE stone from his hand with the force of his seething anger. The stone skittered at top speed along the loch's surface, disappearing into dawn's thick mist hovering above the dark mass of water.

He'd weathered a restless night. If he wasn't tossing and turning in bed, he was pacing his bedchamber floor, tormented by imaginations of Cuthbert engaged with Helene in an intimate foray. Kissing those sweet plump lips, fondling and sliding his hands over parts of her naked body he had no business exploring.

'Bastard! I'll snap yer bloody neck!' Another stone went hurtling towards the loch.

No matter how he tried, Lachlan failed to block images of Cuthbert with Helene. Had she invited him into her chamber, welcoming his touch? The latter was insanity. Helene wouldn't do that. Surely not. Not after allowing Lachlan certain liberties with her body when his touch had soothed her and taken her mind far from the terrifying squall.

They shared a connection, or at least that's what Lachlan chose to believe. Although, having seen her stand at her bedchamber door talking to Cuthbert, clothed only in her night-robe, her glorious mane unpinned and tumbling about her shoulders, made him question his understanding of her. Though she'd said she'd never marry, she made no mention of living the celibate life of a nun.

The possibility of each scenario and the conclusions he'd drawn last night had driven him to reach for a bottle of whisky and consume more drams than he'd cared to count. He'd hoped the amber liquid would have mellowed his mind and helped him see rationale and reason, or at the very least put him to sleep to escape self-inflicted mental torment, but to no avail.

He picked up a heavy-set stone and turned it in his fingers, inspecting it from every angle in the same way he still tried to make sense of what he'd witnessed last night. If nothing intimate or untoward had occurred between his cousin and Helene, then Cuthbert should have had no cause to visit her at midnight. Whatever discussion took place between them could have been conducted at a civilized hour during the day in respectable surrounds as would propriety demand. Not late into the night and on the threshold of her private quarters.

If Cuthbert had indeed compromised Helene, as Lachlan had already done, then it compounded Lachlan's failure to keep his word in promising Lord Penforth that his daughter would return to him as she had arrived. Virtuous and unsullied.

On impulse, Lachlan flung the stone from his hand with careless abandon. It fell into the water with a resounding plonk and sank to the loch's muddy bed, just as the blame of his misconduct and broken vow would fall firmly at his feet, his honour blackened. Ruined. In tatters. In this very moment, he hated Cuthbert. He hated himself even more.

A stone missile suddenly whizzed past him and skipped with precision along the loch's surface. Lachlan stiffened at the accompanying triumphant laugh behind him.

'I told you I'd been practising while you were away,'

gloated Cuthbert. 'But is this the reason for summoning me here? To challenge me in skimming stones?'

Lachlan whirled around.

Even at this early hour, Cuthbert's appearance was that of a freshly shaved, immaculately clothed English gentleman, complete with sword on hip. He cocked a brow. 'Good Lord! You look like hell, and judging by your dark glower, I'd say you'd prefer pistols at dawn over skimming stones.'

'Enough with yer drollery, Cuthbert. Ye're here because 'tis the truth I want.' Lachlan ground out the words with all the intensity of his reactionary ire. 'Spill the truth! And if ye dinnae do so, then so help me God, I'll plough my fist into yer pretty face and beat it out of ye.'

Cuthbert spread his arms wide and gave a wry smile. 'Well! Good morning to you too.'

Lachlan strode forward and roughly grabbed the lapels of Cuthbert's tailored coat. 'Nae! More! Games! I saw ye! At Helene's bedchamber door last night. What were ye doing there?'

Cuthbert's eyes widened in shocked surprise, then narrowed as he asked, 'You were spying on us?'

'I was not spying on ye!'

'Then why didn't you make your presence known?'

Cuthbert's unflappable attitude infuriated Lachlan. He gripped the coat tighter and gave his cousin a vigorous shake. 'I didnae ken what I might have been interrupting.'

Lachlan stared at Cuthbert's blank face for a long pause, awaiting an explanation. 'Answer me! For if not ye, then I'll confront Helene with the verra same questions.'

The strain of a dilemma showed in Cuthbert's eyes and in the way his brow furrowed in concentration.

'Choose!' shouted Lachlan. 'Will ye have me interrogate

and embarrass the lass, or will ye man up and admit yer dealings with Helene?'

A few moments passed before Cuthbert lifted and laid his hands over Lachlan's. With a gentle squeeze, he prised Lachlan's fingers from the coat and smoothed the lapels back into place. 'We had a manner of business to conduct.'

'Business?' Lachlan was outraged. 'At midnight? What kind of business might that be?'

'It's personal.'

'Oh, aye. I'm sure it was! And if it were the kind of business ye once referred to as *sampling* Lady Helene, then . . .' Lachlan took two strides back. The sword at his side was silent as it left its scabbard in an expert draw and found its mark perilously pressed to Cuthbert's throat.

'This is becoming a habit of yours.'

Lachlan begrudged his cousin's courage and inscrutability. The man didn't even flinch.

Cuthbert slowly raised his hands in surrender and inhaled deeply, resignation in his long, drawn-out sigh. 'I give you my word in saying I'm not guilty of that which you imply, and I can assure you, Helene has no amorous interest in me whatsoever, nor do I covet her.' He lowered his arms and indicated with a glance the blade under his chin. 'Come now, cousin. Do you not think your accusatory actions extreme and hypocritical, when we both know it is *you* who has sampled your charge?'

Lachlan's jaw ached from having clenched his teeth together.

'Your hand is trembling,' observed Cuthbert.

Lachlan glanced down to see his hand on the hilt of the sword did indeed tremble. Evidence of his self-loathing and guilt.

Cuthbert blew out a breath. 'It's time. A truce and the

truth. I need to hear it from you, just as much as you wish to hear it from me.'

Lachlan had been so blinded by his upset and rage that it was only now he registered familiar sincerity in Cuthbert's voice. There was a softening around his eyes, in his expression and open body posture. It was as if a veil had been lifted to reveal the Cuthbert of old.

With the relaxing of tensions between them, Lachlan sheathed his sword. Finally, he let down his guard, rolled his shoulders, and ran a hand through his hair. 'Aye. I kissed her.'

Their eyes locked, and a brief pause between them allowed for the weight of Lachlan's confession to take effect.

'Ah,' said Cuthbert, settling his hands on his hips. 'I'm hesitant to ask, being it none of my business, but did you indulge in more than just a kiss?'

The question nettled Lachlan. 'I didnae bed the lass, if that's what ye're asking.'

'But you're attracted to her?'

'Aye,' exhaled Lachlan, his shoulders slumping forward. 'From the first. 'Twas an instant gut reaction.'

'And am I right in believing Aila gave Helene the brooch for reasons other than rewarding her for championing Donnie?'

Lachlan nodded and gave in to that question too. 'Aye.'

'Hmm.' Cuthbert looked thoughtful. 'That can only mean you have genuine feelings for Helene.'

Lachlan choked on a laugh. '*Feelings?* Christ! The lass has utterly bewitched me.'

He took to pacing back and forth, eyes downcast with one hand rubbing his forehead. 'My mind is so addled I can think of nought but her. She only need walk into a room and I'm rendered tongue-tied. I pick up on her scent like a bloodhound in pursuit of a fox. I feel feverish. My heart pounds.

One glimpse of those mesmerising emerald eyes and I go weak at the knees like some love-struck milkmaid.'

Lachlan bent to retrieve a stone and hurled it in frustration over the loch.

Cuthbert quietly pointed out, 'You never spoke about Tibbie in those terms.'

It was the stark truth. Lachlan had always retained a clear head in her presence. Not once had he lost a wink of sleep thinking about or dreaming of her, as had occurred every night since meeting Helene. In fact, he could not even recall the colour of Tibbie's eyes. All that remained of her in Lachlan's mind was her betrayal of him, and even *that* no longer stung. At what point he'd forgiven Tibbie, Lachlan couldn't say. He'd once believed himself to have been in love with the fiery-haired lass. Apparently not. Perhaps it was not so much as having to heal from a broken heart, but rather that time had mended his wounded pride.

Lachlan admitted unto himself that a headstrong, opinionated, and independent Sassenach lass had overthrown his sensibilities. Like a surprise attack in the storming of a castle's defences, she'd taken root in his heart and bloomed like the heather on the hills.

'So . . . do you wish for a future with Helene?' asked Cuthbert.

'*Wish* being the operative word.'

'Well then, as I said yesterday, congratulations.'

Lachlan turned to see Cuthbert beaming with all the excitement of a child at Christmas. His behaviour was baffling. Since his arrival at Drumocher, Cuthbert's persona had been one Lachlan didn't recognise. He'd been difficult, antagonistic, and cunning in his attempt to use Helene as bait to force rivalry and a wager between himself and Lachlan. Now, he'd suddenly capitulated, gifting Helene to Lachlan as if she were Cuthbert's property to hand over.

'Dispense with yer good wishes, for the lass has nae desire to marry.'

'You've already proposed?'

'Nae.'

Cuthbert grimaced. 'I don't understand.'

'The lass has a cynical view of marriage.'

'How so?'

'She refuses to be a bargaining tool in her father's ambitions to marry her off for the purpose of a beneficial alliance.'

'Well, I for one can understand not wanting a lifelong attachment to someone with whom I share no connection. Then again, matters of the heart do not trump the forging of alliances when it comes to the retention or gain of titles, wealth, power, and position.'

'Aye,' agreed Lachlan.

Cuthbert shook his head as if baffled. 'So why the defeatist attitude if you have feelings for Helene?'

'I've learned my lesson ne'er to pursue or force marriage on a lass who doesnae wish it, and certainly not if there's nae place for me in her heart. 'Tis like the capture and caging of a bird, and I'll not do that to Helene.'

Cuthbert shrugged. 'A bird learns to live happily within its confines, though you needn't worry about clipping Helene's wings. There's nothing forced about the attraction between you both. In fact, it's almost sickening to observe.'

Lachlan lifted a single eyebrow.

Cuthbert rolled his eyes. 'Oh, come on, cousin! You're not blind to it, surely?'

'I fear the attraction is one-sided.'

'Good Lord, man! I never picked you to be such an imbecile. That spark, that connection I spoke of. You and Helene share it beyond doubt.'

Lachlan shook his head. 'Even if it were so, she doesnae

wish to marry anyone and said she's nae *need* of a husband. Nor does she want bairns.'

'But she told me . . .'

Cuthbert's unfinished slip drew a sharp look from Lachlan. 'She told ye what?'

'Otherwise.' Cuthbert swallowed and made a dismissive hand gesture. 'She simply told me otherwise.' He stared at his feet and tugged at one ear. 'This doesn't make sense,' he muttered.

Lachlan wasn't sure if Cuthbert intended for him to hear those last few words. All the same, Lachlan called him out on it. 'What do ye mean, this doesnae make sense?'

Cuthbert opened his mouth to say something only to snap it shut again.

'As ye said, Cuthbert, a truce and the truth.' Impatience seeped into the rising inflection of Lachlan's tone. 'Ye've heard it from me, now I'll hear it from ye.'

Cuthbert blinked rapidly and rubbed the back of his neck. He took a deep breath before clearing his throat and looked suddenly nervous. 'All right then, but you must understand that what I did, I did for you. I genuinely had, and still *have*, your best interests at heart.'

Lachlan's skin prickled with a sense of unease over what Cuthbert was about to disclose.

'Five years ago, after Tibbie . . .' Cuthbert cleared his throat. 'Well, it was several months after that, and at my prompting, you and I wagered our first bet, remember?'

How could Lachlan forget? Cuthbert had convinced him to attend the London Season, with all its frivolity, balls, and parties. At the time, it was just what Lachlan had needed. The perfect distraction to quell the damaging effects of duplicity, disappointment, and broken trust, and bury himself in the softness of a willing woman simply for the sport of it. 'Aye, I remember.'

'You won that very first wager, didn't you?'

Lachlan nodded half-heartedly.

'In fact, you won three out of the five years we wagered on a woman.'

'Meaningless beddings,' grunted Lachlan, shamefaced.

'Nonetheless, it's clear, women fancy you well and above me. And with good reason.'

Lachlan noted the way Cuthbert diverted his gaze when quietly muttering those last four words. He was going to ask Cuthbert what he meant, then passed it off as a lame attempt at paying Lachlan a compliment. 'Where are ye going with all this? Get to the point!'

Cuthbert sat himself down on the trunk of a nearby fallen tree, forearms braced on his thighs and hands clasped together as if in prayer. 'You're a good man, Lachlan, and I've always wanted for you that which you so admired about your parents, and what you had once hoped for in your life. It's what any person would wish for themselves. A marriage born of love, affection, companionship, and honesty, of mutual admiration and respect.

'Having each other's trust and sharing the ability to deal with a crisis or stress. Then there's empathy and sensitivity and . . . Well, given what Tibbie put you through, I understand the reasons why you turned your back on the notion of ever being blessed with what your parents shared. Nonetheless, I took it upon myself to prove you wrong.'

Lachlan's gaze sharpened on Cuthbert. 'What have ye done?'

Cuthbert wrung his hands together and stared at the moss-covered ground at his feet. His drawn-out silence was punctuated by the high-pitched call of an osprey perched on a limb overhead.

Lachlan's patience gave way and he shouted, 'What have you done?'

Cuthbert sprang to his feet and shouted back, 'I set you both up! All right? I set you up with Helene because I know, in my heart of hearts, *she* is your true match.' His chest rose and fell on a deep breath.

Lachlan's fierce and incredulous stare brooked no argument in insisting Cuthbert hurry to explain himself.

'I had hoped to introduce you both at this year's Season and to engineer opportunities to bring you together as much as possible so that you could both discover what *I* already saw. When your mother took ill and you cancelled your trip to London, I was determined to bring Helene to you, lest her father finally put his foot down and force her into marrying one of her many suitors.'

Cuthbert took another deep breath. Words sprayed from his mouth like a convicted man desperate to plead his case. 'She and my sister are close friends. I've had ample time and occasions in which to observe Helene, her character, her demeanour, her opinions, her beliefs, her likes and dislikes. And in knowing *you* as well as I do, it is my firm opinion she embodies all, and more, of that special someone of whom you'd approve, and whom you'd agree was your equal.'

Another deep breath. 'It was at my instigation, pending yours and Penforth's approval, that Agnes invited Helene to journey to Scotland with us and to holiday here at Drumocher in lieu of her being paraded at this year's Season.'

Seemingly exhausted from his outpouring of truth, Cuthbert sank down to sit on the log again, elbows propped on his thighs and forehead resting on the heels of his palms.

Lachlan's mind whirled. A set-up. Executed with good

intention, but now was not the time to deliberate the merits of the outcome. There had to be more to Cuthbert's confession. 'Go on,' he pressed.

Cuthbert raised his head to look at Lachlan. 'The reason I'd hoped you'd agree to one last wager between us was because I'd convinced myself one kiss from Helene would leave you smitten and wanting for more.'

Cuthbert had hit the mark on that count, but he'd deceitfully assumed the role of a puppet master, attempting to manipulate emotions and heartstrings without Lachlan's or Helene's consent. It triggered resentment and simmering blood in Lachlan's veins.

'When you refused to play the game, I forced your hand, goading you by saying you'd have to protect Helene from me. Shadowing *me* put you at Helene's side, in her company, her confidence, her conversation. In fact, I inwardly rejoiced when you made the journey together to the shielings. From what you've divulged of your feelings for Helene, it would seem you are now like a moth to the flame.'

'Aye! And my gut tells me I'm about to get singed.'

Sweat beaded on Cuthbert's forehead. He swallowed, evading Lachlan's direct stare. 'There's more,' said Cuthbert, wiping his brow with the back of one hand.

Lachlan gave a curt nod. 'Continue.'

'When Agnes extended the invitation to Helene to accompany us to Scotland, Helene declined and would not be swayed until I . . .'

'Until ye what?'

'Intervened. I had a quiet word with Helene on one occasion when she visited the house, encouraging her to change her mind, if only to make Agnes happy. It seemed her reluctance to visit Scotland far outweighed any loyalties in her friendship with my sister.

'When she would not be swayed, I asked what it would take for her to change her mind. "Considerable coin," she replied. I laughed, thinking her quick-witted, but no, she was damned serious. I agreed to her price under one condition . . .'

Every muscle in Lachlan's body tensed.

'That she allow herself to be seduced by you, if only in the form of a kiss. When you wouldn't comply, I had to change tactics. I insisted that if Helene were to claim her prize, she be the one to initiate intimacy with you.'

Simmering blood ramped up to a slow boil. In need of more answers, Lachlan kept his anger in check and his voice devoid of emotion. 'What did she know of our wagers or of your meddling little plan?'

'Nothing. I told her nothing, although she did, in passing, make a quip about our rakish reputations.'

'And just how much did you wager on my heart?'

Cuthbert gulped. 'A substantial sum.'

'She would already have a large dowry, so why would she be in need of money?'

Cuthbert shrugged. 'We both wanted something from the other and agreed not to question the whys and wherefores of our individual motives.'

Lachlan's hands balled into fists. 'Last night, at her door, what was the significance of the parchment ye handed her?'

Cuthbert released a shuddering breath. 'A promissory note. After the evening meal, when you escorted your mother from the room, I tricked Helene into admitting you both had indeed shared a kiss. She then called in the promissory note, insisting I deliver it to her door at midnight. A time and place when all would be abed. Or so we thought.' Cuthbert had the good grace to look sheepish.

Lachlan turned from his cousin to face the loch. The sun had begun its ascent, warming the air and thinning the mist.

Crisp scents of Scots pine and balsam fir filled the air, and a breeze set cone-laden branches in motion. For all nature's impressive tranquillity, it did nothing to ease Lachlan's misery.

Cuthbert pleaded at his back. 'Believe me when I say money is not the key issue here. My meddling little plan, as you prefer to call it, has worked brilliantly. A spark has ignited, the fuse lit between you and Helene. It's a relationship sure to flourish. I have every faith in it doing so, though I must warn you—Helene told me last night she is already spoken for. Personally, I don't believe it, but if there's an ounce of truth to it, then declare your hand or at least court her before we return to London by summer's end.'

The buzzing in Lachlan's head grew louder with every breath he inhaled. For the second time, a lass had taken him for a fool, and suddenly, in his mind's eye, he saw and heard Tibbie laughing at him for all his ignorance.

The buzzing intensified as images assailed him in short, sharp bursts. Of finding his then betrothed hiding inside a cave, deep in the woods. Her confession of love for the man who lay with his head resting in her lap, a wanted Jacobite rebel with no hope of surviving wounds sustained in a skirmish with redcoats. And days later, having thrown herself on a blade, Tibbie's body slumped over the man's unmarked grave.

Lachlan had been oblivious to the signs of Tibbie's betrayal, just as he'd been blind to Helene's deception. The difference being, if he didn't care for Helene so profoundly bone-deep, his devastated heart would feel no pain. He put a hand to his throbbing temples and winced from the pounding in his ears.

'Are you listening to me?' urged Cuthbert. 'If you've a chance at love, don't throw it away. Leave no room for regrets.'

The words reached Lachlan through the thick of his anguish. Anger soared with his elevated pulse, and the tight rein he'd held on his growing hostility towards his cousin finally snapped. He spun around, his fist connecting with Cuthbert's face.

The blow sent Cuthbert reeling backwards and to the ground. Lachlan stood over him and bellowed, 'Ye had nae right! Nae right to wager on my heart or Helene's! And dinnae be lecturing me on the merits of love when ye're nae expert on the matter.'

Cuthbert propped himself up on one elbow, shook his head, and gave a cynical chuckle. 'You're wrong about that.'

Strands of fair hair, having loosened from its queue, fell over Cuthbert's eyes. He spat blood from his mouth onto the ground and then used the back of his free hand to wipe his bloodied nose. A freshly laundered kerchief from his coat pocket served to wipe his blood-smeared face. He looked wretched, defeated, and forlorn, just as he had that day in Drumocher's library when divulging the marriage ultimatum his father had enforced on him. When he lifted his gaze, Lachlan saw once again in those pale-blue eyes that something seemed very much out of place.

Animosity towards his cousin gave way to pity. 'How could ye possibly ken how or what I feel for Helene when ye've ne'er experienced anything like it?'

One corner of Cuthbert's mouth lifted in a half-smile. 'On the contrary, I've experienced first-hand those things you mentioned, your gut reaction when you first met Helene and the debilitating dizzy ways she affects you. I know this because I share a deep and abiding love with someone. Have done so for years.'

Cuthbert's tone turned melancholic. 'But you see, in keeping up appearances, my love and I are like villains in a play and wear a permanent invisible mask. A mask we dare not remove except in the safest, most guarded, and private of moments.' He looked away. 'When the world is not watching.'

'Dinnae speak in riddles. Speak plain and true. Who is she? Name her.'

'Very well.' Cuthbert paused, then cut Lachlan a bitter glance. 'Unlike you, dear cousin, I'll never have the privilege or the right or the opportunity to marry and spend the rest of my life with . . . *him*.'

CHAPTER SEVENTEEN

Lachlan blinked, and then blinked again, unsure he'd heard right. 'Him?'

Cuthbert crushed the kerchief in his fist. 'Yes. *Him.*'

Shock washed through Lachlan in stupefying waves and his jaw dropped open. He'd known his cousin since they were wee bairns and as mischievous young boys. Throughout their adolescence, Cuthbert would visit and stay during summer before returning to his studies in England. They would play, explore, and run amok in and around Drumocher. They would swim in the loch, fish and hunt with Lachlan's father and clansmen, square up to each other in playful combat, neither of them holding back when old enough to use a targe and a dirk, or wield a sword.

Though Lachlan taunted Cuthbert about his pretty looks, his cousin had always been a strong and worthy opponent capable of holding his own. He'd matched and on the rare occasion bested Lachlan in strength and skill.

As men, together they had navigated the drawing rooms and ballrooms of London society. Cuthbert knew how to use with advantageous effect his wit, charm, and conversation and had mastered the art of luring women to his side.

So how was it that during all those years, months, days,

hours, and minutes spent in the close company of his cousin, Lachlan did not see or pick up on the cues, clues, and indicators of Cuthbert's core nature?

Speechless and confused, jumbled thoughts flew helter-skelter inside Lachlan's head. Nothing came to mind that his cousin had said or done to afford the slightest hint of him preferring the company of men over women.

'Christ! I sure as hell don't want a wife.' Cuthbert's words, spoken in Drumocher's library. *'I'm not ready for marriage!'*

Only now did Lachlan understand his cousin's vehement distress over his father's ultimatum to seek out a bride and marry. It would not sit well with Cuthbert to deceive and wed a woman, knowing she'd unwittingly be living a lie, and yet refusing his father's instructions would all but ensure his financial ruin.

Lachlan's stomach roiled with fear for his cousin. If exposed, the secret would have far-reaching consequences. It would bring shame upon Cuthbert's family, and his father would ostracize or excommunicate him, as would decent society. Even worse, he'd suffer the threat of verbal and physical abuse, if not death, if charged and convicted under criminal law and thrown into the notorious Newgate Prison.

'You're morally offended. I see it on your face,' said Cuthbert, his voice even and flat.

'Nae. 'Tis concern for ye and yer future that worries me.'

'Nonetheless, I'll make this easy for you.' Cuthbert's gaze dropped to the ground. 'Revile me, resent me, hate me for who and what I am—if you will—but hear me out before you send me on my way.

'My intentions in contriving an introduction between yourself and Helene were honourable and in your favour. Yes, I might have managed the situation better than I did, but

I know you'd have refused my request to bring Helene here as your potential match.'

Cuthbert met Lachlan's eyes. 'It was—and still is—my firm belief that you and Helene are well suited. For so short an acquaintance, she is smitten with you, even if she refuses to admit it, and by your own admission, she has bewitched you. I understand your anger over my interference, and I sincerely apologise.' He looked down at his feet and gave a sardonic laugh. 'Far better to ask for forgiveness than permission, and so I must ask for your forgiveness and—'

'Cuthbert!'

Cuthbert lifted his gaze slowly, and Lachlan saw for the very first time the true depths of his cousin's despair. Unhappiness and haunting loneliness resided in pale-blue eyes. Dark shadows sat beneath fair long lashes. Shadows born of the constraints in having to forever conceal his true self from the world at large.

For years Lachlan had tasked himself with filling his late father's shoes and carrying forward Drumocher's prosperity. Thorough dedication to the responsibilities and protection of family, the clan, and the running of a successful cattle business had left him blind to the subtleties of everything else going on around him, like Tibbie's betrayal, not giving Grizel consideration and respect for the blossoming young woman she'd become, Helene's deception, and now Cuthbert's unforeseen revelation.

Lachlan acknowledged and cursed his own shortcomings. He'd been solely focused on sustaining and growing Drumocher's wealth and resources. It was time to cast off the blinkers and devote more time and attention to those near and dear to him.

'I made ye a solemn promise,' he said to Cuthbert. 'One

I intend to honour. *Nothing* and *nae one* will drive a wedge between us.' He reached for his cousin with an open palm.

Cuthbert's wide-eyed surprise flicked between Lachlan's outstretched hand and his face. 'This, I did not expect.'

'I could say the same of ye and yer confession.'

Cuthbert laughed and accepted the helping hand.

Lachlan hauled his cousin up off the ground and to his feet, drawing him close in a strong embrace.

''Tis I who must ask for yer forgiveness, Cuthbert. I had nae idea of the personal struggles ye've weathered. I wish ye'd have told me sooner.'

Cuthbert pulled back and dusted himself off. 'I feared you'd think less of me as a man.'

'Nae. I think more of ye for having the courage to take me into yer confidence.'

Cuthbert's shoulders lifted and fell. 'I had little choice, given my bungled attempt at bringing the marriage bureau to your hearth.'

Lachlan narrowed his eyes in mock frustration. 'Aye. Ye took on the role of London's elite meddling matriarchs and sought to play matchmaker.'

'Cupid, if you will, and with some manner of success. You can't deny it.'

'Bittersweet success.' Lachlan quickly returned to the matter at hand. 'Does yer father ken yer secret?'

The question rendered Cuthbert visibly panic-stricken. 'No! Married or not, he'd cut me off *and* disown me. I've told only you. Please! Keep it to yourself.'

'Aye. Of course. Ye can trust me on that.'

Cuthbert's brows drew together in a tight frown. 'I fear there is one other who knows.' He met Lachlan's questioning eyes. 'Helene.'

Lachlan gave his cousin an incredulous stare. 'How would she ken about yer personal life?'

'I don't know. I've taken great pains to be discreet, but obviously not discreet enough. She threatened to expose me if I did not hand over the promissory note last night.'

Lachlan scowled. 'I didnae pick her to be as cunning as a fox.'

'Don't be so quick to judge her. I daresay it was her way of lashing out when I pressed my arrogance upon her. Until that moment, she'd kept the knowledge of my affair up her sleeve. I only hope she remains tight-lipped about it.'

'Aye.'

Lachlan felt uncomfortable voicing his next question, but still, he had to know. 'There's something I dinnae understand. Ye trounced me in two out of five wagers. Did ye actually go through with . . . ?'

Cuthbert grinned. 'I'm quite capable of performing in that arena. How else do you think I've earned my rakish reputation? Tongues wag as efficiently in ladies' parlours as they do in the men's smoking rooms. Best I keep up the façade and be known or perceived as a seducer of women, rather than . . .' He shrugged. 'Well, rather than the alternative.'

It was a conversation Lachlan never thought to have engaged in with Cuthbert. 'Might I ask who the lucky gentleman is?'

Cuthbert shook his head. 'That's one secret I'll never share. He and I have sworn mutual silence to not only protect ourselves but also our families.'

Lachlan nodded.

Cuthbert walked to the edge of the loch, crouched down, and scooped up a handful of water to rinse clean his mouth. He spat out the water on the ground to his side and then washed his kerchief in the cool water. He used the linen cloth to freshen his face and wipe away any remaining blood smears.

'I'm truly sorry for hitting ye,' said Lachlan.

Cuthbert glanced over his shoulder. 'Don't be. I deserved it.'

'If it's any consolation, ye still look disgustingly pretty.'

Cuthbert grinned. 'I'll have you know, just for the record, I let you win three of the five wagers because'—he stood and pointed to his face—'with these looks and irresistible charm, you never stood a chance against me.'

Lachlan winced. 'I'd have preferred ye take yer best swing at me than to suffer the demoralising pain of that truth. *If* 'tis indeed the truth of it.'

Jocularity aside, Lachlan voiced a more sobering truth. 'We must find ye a wife.'

'Not before you woo and win Helene. I will see finished what I started.'

Lachlan mumbled a curse and seated himself on the fallen log. 'Nae chance of that happening. 'Twas all a ruse on her behalf. The lass used and deceived me into believing there could be something genuine between us.'

Cuthbert perched himself beside Lachlan. 'I disagree.'

'She took payment from ye for having kissed me! What more proof could ye want?'

'Being paid to act on something is one thing. Owning and being in control of one's feelings is another.'

He was right. Helene had not been paid to give intimately of herself when they'd taken shelter from the squall. Her need for Lachlan to calm her fear, to soothe and satisfy her body and mind, was born of her own free will. Did that not say something about her feelings for him? Her trust in him?

Cuthbert added, 'I couldn't buy or force the state of attraction between you, but it was my sincere hope it would occur.'

He lifted his hands in joyous supplication. 'And hallelujah, it has!'

'*And* nothing will come of it.' Lachlan surged to his feet and scowled down at his cousin. 'She has yer promissory note and now I'm as good as in her past. She has nae more need of either of us.'

He strode to the loch's edge, swiped up a stone, and flung it into the water. Ripples formed from its point of entry and caused widening circular shapes on the surface.

'Wrong again,' said Cuthbert, following in Lachlan's wake. 'You are very much in her present, and if you play your cards right, she'll be in your future too.'

'She told ye she was already spoken for.'

'A lie to deflect from whatever it is she hides. A secret she withholds from her father. I of all people understand such a burden.'

'An elopement, then, with a suitor of lesser means. A man whom her father would ne'er give his consent to her marrying.'

Cuthbert shook his head. 'No. She told you she refuses to marry and that she has no need of a husband. Perhaps she finds herself in a predicament for which she needs the money.'

Lachlan felt the blood drain from his face. 'What if she suffers the shame of having been forced upon and now carries that man's child? It would explain why she doesnae want bairns. What if she intends using the money to—'

Cuthbert raised a hand to silence him. 'My, but you've a wild imagination! I don't know the full extent of what has transpired between you and Helene, intimacy or otherwise, but *think*, Lachlan. Think over your conversations with her. She must have said something that might lend itself to interpretation.'

Lachlan inhaled a deep, calming breath and tilted his head up to see the osprey, still perched on a limb overhead, staring down at them. In the next instant, it cocked its head to the high-pitched call of its mate and spread wide its wings to take to the sky. In flight, the large brown-and-white raptors held their wings with a noticeable crook at the wrist. Wild and free, they soared and dipped and glided on the breeze.

Lachlan lowered his gaze, his attention suddenly captured by a large trout breaching the loch's surface. Seconds after falling back into the water, one of the ospreys swooped down, legs and talons readied in a forward position. It hit the water with an almighty splash and grabbed its quarry. Wings flapped with the need to get airborne once again, lest the large trout match the bird weight for weight and drag it down to its death at the bottom of the loch.

The osprey's powerful wings lifted it from the water, overcoming the struggle. Curved claws grasped the thrashing trout in an unbreakable hold, carrying it off.

'Astonishing!' said Cuthbert. 'Now, there's a substantial meal to feed a few hungry chicks.'

Those words, and the scene he'd just witnessed, triggered in Lachlan a memory.

'You're doing it again,' said Cuthbert.

'Doing what?' said Lachlan distractedly.

'Slowly running your hand over your chin in such a way as I know you're deep in thought. What is it? What are you thinking?'

Lachlan paused before answering. 'When I rescued Helene from her near-drowning in the river, I wrongfully blamed and chastised her for having no regard for her safety and that she could have died. At the time, I was so fraught with anger and fear over the unimaginable possibility of losing her that I paid nae heed to what she said in retaliation.'

'Until now,' affirmed Cuthbert.

'Aye.'

'Well?'

'Helene said her death would mean her father had one less female in the family to worry about. As far as I ken, she has one sibling. An older brother, aye?'

'Correct, and her mother passed on years ago.'

'Odd that her father ne'er remarried.'

'Perhaps his heart remains true to his wife, with no other ever to replace her.'

Lachlan turned to his cousin in dismay. 'Ye sound like an idyllic sentimentalist.'

Cuthbert winked at him. 'It's all part of my charm.' On a more serious note, he said, 'As for Helene's comment? Well, truths are often spoken in the heat of an argument. She might have been talking about a cousin or some other relative for whom her father is responsible.

'Come to think of it,' continued Cuthbert, scratching his neck, 'Helene said she was spoken for, not promised or engaged to another. In fact, her exact words were, "My life is devoted to another." That could mean anything.'

'Aye. 'Tis a thread I need to unravel.'

After a pause, Cuthbert said, 'Fight for her, Lachlan. We're here for the summer, so you've plenty of time to elicit and cement her trust in you. Gain her favour. Leave no room for regrets.'

Lachlan nodded his agreement. 'I'll not tell her I'm privy to the transaction between ye two. I should like to think she learns to trust me enough to take me into her confidence, without having to force the truth from her.'

'Good move.' Cuthbert cocked his head to the side and pointed to his cheek. 'How do you propose I explain this to the family?'

Lachlan eyed the swelling and the emerging bruise where

his fist had connected with Cuthbert's jaw. 'I'm sure ye'll think of something, given all that charm ye possess.'

'Or I could just tell it like it is, saying we came to blows over a disagreement and I came off second best.'

'Ye might raise Helene's suspicions with that explanation, but our mothers and sisters will doubtless accept it and roll their eyes at the manner in which we men often settle our personal disputes.'

Cuthbert laughed. 'There's nothing like a vigorous tussle in the settling of scores. Let's be on our way. I need to clean up and change my clothes.'

As they made their way back to the keep, and considering all Cuthbert had disclosed about his dealings with Helene, Lachlan ruminated over something niggling away at him. What had Helene done as a child that still haunted her to this very day? She'd implied she'd done something to someone, describing the act as unforgivable, and carrying with it, so it would seem, everlasting consequences.

Rationale suggested this someone and the person to whom she claimed to be devoted were one and the same. Each stride lengthened in his haste to return to Drumocher, to seek out Helene, pry open her secrets, and win her over to the point where he was the only person in whom she placed her complete trust.

~

After breaking their fast, Helene, Grizel, and Lady Sutton settled down to a game of whist in the drawing room. Lady Caitrin opted for a book and sank into the comforts of an armchair close to the women.

Agnes reclined on a chaise positioned beside the games table, with both feet elevated to take the weight off her sprained ankle. 'How odd that we've seen nothing of Lachlan or my brother this morning. Did they take to the moors for an early ride?'

The same thought had crossed Helene's mind. Their early-morning disappearance, with no word of their whereabouts, gave her cause for concern. Especially so because of the palpable tension between the two men since she and Lachlan had returned from the shielings.

As dealer, Helene gave her attention to the cards and shuffled the deck.

Caitrin glanced up from her book in reply to Agnes's question. 'I've nae idea, although 'twould not surprise me if they had. 'Tis perfect weather for a ride. Perhaps ye young ones might take some fresh air once ye've digested yer morning meal.'

'How am I to do that in my condition?' said Agnes, gesturing to her injured ankle.

Caitrin winked at her niece. 'We've plenty of strong clansmen who'd be more than willing to be yer personal conveyance and carry ye to a comfortable patch of grass in the sunshine.'

Agnes giggled. 'You make it all sound so romantic, Auntie.'

Elspeth sent her sister a speculative glance. 'Is it yer intention to matchmake my daughter to one of yer MacLanoch clansmen?'

Caitrin raised a brow. 'Nae, but now that ye mention it . . .'

Helene and Grizel exchanged amused looks while listening to the sisters bicker about suitors for Agnes—Scotsmen and Englishmen alike—as if Agnes wasn't there.

'Mother! Auntie! Do stop,' protested Agnes. 'The order of the day, or at least for this morning, is cards. Being betrothed, and to whom, is the least of my interests.'

Helene dealt thirteen cards to each player and then turned

the last card face up. 'Trump suit for this first round is spades,' she declared.

In the prevailing silence, each player sorted their cards into suits. Helene worried herself over how to break the news of her intention to leave Drumocher and return home to London. Stating she was homesick would be a weak excuse, but she could think of no better or believable alternative. What would they all think of her after having travelled so far into the Highlands to get here? An early departure would make her look nothing less than flippant and just plain rude.

Now that she was in possession of the promissory note, she had nothing holding her here. Therein was another lie. Lachlan was here. If she were free to do so, she'd remain and relish every moment of his company. Even now she longed to steal away into his warm embrace, to savour his lips and to once again feel his hard body pressed against hers.

Butterflies took flight in her stomach with the memory of their time together when taking shelter from the squall. She could not conceive of the magic he'd wielded over her, making her senses sing and soar to heights she'd never known or dreamed possible. She became so lost in the memory of how and where he'd touched her that the cards in her hand blurred before her eyes.

'Are ye quite all right, Helene? Yer cheeks are flushed.'

Caitrin's observation startled Helene into placing the back of her hand to her cheek, mortified to think her body betrayed her thoughts. 'Flushed? Am I? But I feel fine. Perhaps some water.'

A maid came instantly to her side, delivering a glass of water. Helene nodded her thanks and took a sip before pressing the cool glass to her heated cheeks.

'Better now?' asked Caitrin.

Helene cleared her throat. 'Yes, thank you.' She shifted the focus from herself to Lady Sutton seated on her left. 'Lead with the first card when you're ready.'

'Hmm,' said Elspeth, frowning at the fanned cards in her hand. 'Ye did indeed shuffle these cards well, lass. Give me a moment longer.'

Helene sent another fleeting glance in Caitrin's direction, relieved to see Drumocher's matriarch studying her book and not Helene.

While waiting for Lady Sutton to start the round, Helene's mind slipped back to last night, pondering what Lachlan might have discussed with his mother in her chambers. No doubt Aila's brooch was the topic of choice, and Helene could not let go of its intrigue. Why did the family make such a fuss of it?

'Helene, 'tis yer turn.'

This time it was Grizel's voice to draw Helene back to the present. Helene made a quick study of three cards lying in a pile in the centre of the table, and since she could not best the jack of spades, she played her lowest card in that suit.

Lady Sutton won the trick and placed the cards in front of her. 'There,' she said with a triumphant grin to Grizel. 'Ye and I are off to a flying start.'

Three more rounds saw Helene and Agnes lose to their opposing team. Helene gave Agnes an apologetic expression, to which Agnes sighed and said, 'Our fate depends on the turn of a card.'

The next round began with the queen of hearts, which pleased Helene no end. 'Aha! At last.' She laughed and looked at Agnes across the table from her. 'Finally, fate sees fit to smile upon us.' She played the final card and trumped the trick with the king of hearts.

'Lachlan!' exclaimed Caitrin. 'Where have ye been?'

Helene's laughter died in her throat when she looked up to see Lachlan enter the drawing room. Long, confident strides brought him to stand at his mother's side and rest a hand on her shoulder.

'Mother,' he said to her with a nod.

Warmth spread from Helene's toes to her cheeks. He looked every bit the wild Scottish laird with his shoulder-length hair, windswept as if having ridden his horse at breakneck speed across the moors. His linen shirt was open at the neck, and suddenly Helene fought the desire to go to him and plant a kiss where his lifeblood pulsed at the base of his throat. Her gaze drifted and drank him in, from his right shoulder to his left, across the broad expanse of his chest, right down to the belted plaid resting on lean hips.

She reached for the water to quench her parched mouth and glanced up at him over the rim of the glass. The slow smile he bestowed on her said he'd read and understood every nuance of her hungry reaction to him. A reaction she hoped only he had perceived, but when his solicitous smile reached his eyes, the other women turned their curious attention on Helene.

Her gaze dropped to the table, and she scooped up the four-card trick, stacking them face down in front of her. She then studied the remaining cards in her hand. For every second the silence stretched, Helene's cheeks grew hot from embarrassment.

'Well?' Caitrin said, a tinge of amusement in her voice. 'What has kept ye and Cuthbert from us this morning?'

Helene let out a silent breath, pleased to think Lachlan was now the centre of attention.

'I had to settle a grievance between two clansmen beyond the castle walls, and Cuthbert agreed to join me for the early-morning ride.'

'And where is Cuthbert now?' Lady Sutton enquired.

'Right here, Mother.'

Helene's gaze flew from her cards to Cuthbert. He walked into the room with a cheerful disposition, dressed in a linen shirt, neckcloth, waistcoat, and jacket. Buckskin trimmed the inner leg of his tartan trews, and leather brogues adorned his feet. His fair hair was brushed back from his forehead and tied at the nape with a black silk ribbon.

Caitrin MacLanoch cast an appreciative eye over her nephew. 'Good to see ye advocating yer Scottish heritage.'

Cuthbert bowed. 'When they are at Rome, they do there as they see done.'

Grizel clapped loudly. 'Quoted from Robert Burton's *Anatomy of Melancholy*.'

Lachlan was not the only one to look at her with wide-eyed surprise. 'I'm impressed, sister. I see ye've been making use of our extensive library.'

'Aye,' she beamed. 'That I have, and for longer than ye ken.'

'Then perhaps we both might spend time together to discuss which books ye prefer to read.'

'Philosophy,' she said without hesitation. 'And aye, that would be nice.'

Lachlan's new-found admiration for his sister shone clear in his eyes. Helene found it a joy to watch ever since Grizel had stood up for herself after admonishing her brother the day of the picnic. The siblings appeared to share a deeper respect for each other.

Helene was unsure as to whether the same could be said between Lachlan and Cuthbert. She made a surreptitious study of each man, searching for any sign of angst or animosity between them. Outwardly, they appeared to be on good terms; however, the bruise marring Cuthbert's left cheek begged the question his mother now asked.

'Good Lord! What happened to yer face?'

'Well! Discussions between the two fractious clansmen turned physical. Unfortunately, one man's fist was faster than my reflexes, and I caught a blow to the cheek.' Cuthbert shrugged. 'They soon sorted their differences and walked away friends, albeit me coming off the worse for wear.'

Lachlan added, 'Serves ye right for stepping into the fray.'

'Quite so, cousin. Quite so.'

'Men!' Lady Sutton scoffed in disgust and threw down her cards on the table.

Helene did not believe Cuthbert's explanation, given his conspiratorial tone.

'Ladies, our time is now yers,' announced Lachlan. 'Are ye happy to see out the day indoors, or'—Lachlan's eyes lit on Helene—'would ye care to discover more of Drumocher's surrounding woodlands and secret caves?'

Only Helene understood the hidden suggestion in Lachlan's invitation. Its effect on her triggered the fluttering of her heart, and liquid heat pooled between her legs. Under any other circumstances, she'd have shamelessly jumped at the opportunity, but instead she kept silent, lowering her gaze to reshuffle her cards lest any of the women read the desire she felt for Lachlan mirrored in her eyes. Concern and fraught nerves resurfaced over how best to bow out gracefully from her summer sojourn in the Highlands.

'I confess I'm quite content to stay put for the moment,' said Agnes. 'Perhaps later I might do as Auntie Caitrin suggested and have a braw clansman sweep me off my feet and carry me off into the sunset.'

Grizel giggled.

Lady Sutton scoffed again.

Lachlan threw his mother a dark, questioning look.

'Ye ken 'tis not what I suggested at all, dear niece. What I meant was—'

'I know, Auntie,' laughed Agnes. 'I was just teasing you.'

A sharp rap on the drawing room door had all eyes turn to see a servant holding a silver salver upon which lay an envelope. Lachlan nodded permission for the man to enter the room. He proffered the tray to Lachlan, who took the envelope in hand and eyed the inked handwriting naming the addressee.

'When did this arrive?' he asked the servant.

'Just now, my lord. Both messenger and horse were a lather of sweat.'

Helene's ears pricked up at this. The messenger must have ridden post-haste to deliver what could only be an urgent letter. The servant bowed and exited the room.

'Well? Who is it for?' said Caitrin.

Lachlan's gaze slid to Helene.

Helene's heart lurched and worry churned her gut. He passed her the envelope, and she saw it was indeed addressed to her. Though she recognised the handwriting, it was written in such a way as to give her pause. In place of the usual controlled and steady script, it reflected duress in the person's state of mind, evidenced by the shaky penmanship and irregular size of each letter, an inconsistency in connecting strokes, and the unequal pressure in upward and downward strokes.

She flipped the envelope over to see the wax seal bearing the impression of a familiar signet ring. 'It's from my father.'

Lady Sutton smiled and nodded reassuringly. 'No doubt he's missing ye, lass.'

Helene excused herself from the card table for a moment's privacy to open and read the letter. She moved to stand by the window, acutely aware of the silence at her back. Her thumb slid beneath the seal, and a deep breath did nothing to calm her nerves. With jittery fingers, she unfolded the missive.

CHAPTER EIGHTEEN

HELENE, COME HOME!

Three words. Nothing more.

Three words—punctuated with an exclamation mark—delivered a directive and the expediency with which the order must be effected.

Three words that could only mean one of two things. Either something had happened to Prudence, or she was . . .

Helene's eyes snapped shut and cold fear shot up her spine. Her shoulders curled forward and tightened, hairs lifting along her arms. Trembling hands shook the envelope and parchment. They fell from her grasp, both fluttering down to lie at her feet. Black spots littered the edge of her vision and, suddenly light-headed, she swayed.

Lachlan's hand beneath her elbow steadied her. 'Are ye all right, lass?'

She fought to quell rising panic, the tightening in her chest, and the feeling of constriction around her throat. No, she wasn't all right, and her voice failed to say so.

His arm came swiftly around her waist, guiding her to sit down in a plush padded armchair away from the others.

Her onlookers fired forth a volley of questions.

'What's happened, Helene?'

'What news from yer father?'

'What is it? Ye've gone deathly pale.'

Lachlan raised his hand to stave off their advance and any further questions. He knelt on one knee before her and took her hands in his. 'Helene?'

His voice, soft and calm, was like salve to a wound. In his eyes she saw, and not for the first time, genuine compassion for her. She drew in a fortifying breath and pulled herself together, choosing to believe Prudence was well, that her father had finally agreed to bring Prudence home and that he'd accepted Helene's wish to be her sister's full-time carer.

Helene had been angling for a plausible excuse to leave Drumocher, and now she had one. Her father's brief missive, albeit devoid of detail, provided tangible justification why she must go. She glanced at the letter and envelope on the floor behind Lachlan, and as if she'd spoken her request aloud, he retrieved them for her.

'Thank you,' she whispered. She deftly folded and slid the parchment inside the envelope and spoke so that all might hear her. 'I must return home. Immediately.'

Agnes crinkled her nose. 'But why? You were to stay with us for the entire summer.'

'My father did not say why.' That, at least, was the truth of it. 'I can only assume the matter urgent and of a private nature. I apologise to you all for having to leave so soon.'

Lachlan's brows hitched together in a deep frown as he stood and stepped away from Helene. In his eyes she detected a hint of mistrust. Guilt had her look down at her feet before rising and offering up a tremulous smile in thanking him for having come to her aid.

Without argument, he said, 'I must oblige yer father's request and will immediately send word to the garrison to arrange a retinue of the king's men to escort ye home. I'll make the journey with ye.'

'No!'

'I swore to protect ye, lass, and so I *will* accompany ye.'

Helene reacted to his sharp tone. 'What I mean is, it could be days before troops and provisions are rallied and arrive here.' She held up the envelope. 'Your servant said the horse and messenger who arrived with this were a lather of sweat. Does that not tell you something of consequence has occurred? Otherwise, my father would not summon me home in so swift a manner.'

Helene grew desperate with every passing second. 'I've not a moment to waste. I must prepare to leave and begin the journey home. Today.'

'Today?' Caitrin's brows almost met her hairline. 'But, lass, we dinnae have the appropriate conveyance to get ye back to London.'

'I respectfully thank you for considering my comfort, but I don't need a carriage. All I need is a horse and an escort.' Helene looked beseechingly at Lachlan. 'If you insist on accompanying me, then surely the fastest route would be on horseback. A horse can travel where a carriage cannot, and I've no doubt you know routes and pathways to cut travel time by half.'

Lady Sutton voiced her protest before Lachlan could answer. 'Out of the question, lass. Ye're a young lady! Ye cannae be traipsing from Scotland to London on a horse and camping beneath the stars at night. And alone with one man, even if that man is the laird of Drumocher. Think of yer reputation. Good Lord! Yer father would have our heads for this.'

Helene gave Lady Sutton a placating smile. 'With all due respect, how is riding a horse alongside Lachlan any different to having trekked with him on foot to the shielings, where

I assimilated with cottars and their way of life? Besides, my father needn't know what mode of transport conveyed me to him. All that matters is getting me home by the fastest means possible.'

'Helene,' said Cuthbert. 'Regardless of the urgent circumstance by which your father calls you home, you must heed all precautionary measures. The Highlands, Lowlands, and south of the border are teeming with lowlifes and miscreants. Lachlan is indeed a force to be reckoned with when it comes to wielding a sword or firing a pistol, and'—his gaze flicked briefly to his cousin—'he's lightning-fast with his fists, but a man travelling with a beautiful woman is an invitation to be set upon. My cousin can hold his own, yet if a band of armed men were to attack, then Lachlan alone could not protect you.'

Helene had not expected Cuthbert's concern for her. Or was it all for show, Lachlan's safety being his one true concern?

'Well said, brother,' said Agnes. She made a sweep of her hand, gesturing to Helene's attire from head to toe. 'And how could you possibly be comfortable riding side-saddle for days over such rough terrain dressed like that? Imagine the discomfort of it all.'

Helene had the perfect comeback to counter each of their objections. 'Then I'll dress like a man, conceal my hair beneath a cap, and ride astride my horse.'

A gasp of feminine outrage vibrated through the air, and Lady Sutton looked set to suffer a conniption fit. 'Dress like a man?' Her voice rose even higher. 'A man?'

Grizel slapped her hands to her cheeks. 'Oh my! The adventure of it all. I should hate to see ye leave us so soon, Helene, and I do pray nothing untoward has occurred, but I applaud yer initiative. Ye're a woman of stalwart courage.'

'That's kind of you to say so, Grizel, but I'm simply doing what I must.'

Helene stepped forward and gripped Lachlan's upper arm. Her gaze bore into his, and in an emotion-choked voice, she said, 'Please. I beg of you. Say you'll agree to my suggestion. My slight build would fool anyone into believing me a young man and not a lass. I won't complain about a thing, and I'll explicitly follow your rules and direction every step of the way. I swear it. At journey's end we could slip unnoticed, and under the cover of dark, into my father's residence. He would not have summoned me home without a valid reason.'

Helene held Lachlan's steady gaze. Mistrust still lingered there. His pensive face and drawn-out silence indicated he would not agree to her request.

Before Helene resigned herself to defeat and disappointment, Prudence screamed in her head. *Get me out of here!* The haunting memory of her sister's white-knuckled fists clutching the bars of a locked asylum cell bolstered Helene's resolve to make one final plea. She swallowed and leaned in closer to Lachlan so that his broad chest hid her face from the others.

'Please,' she whispered. Only he could hear her. 'In return, I'll do anything.' Her gaze made a sinful sweep of his mouth. '*Anything* you ask of me.'

Hers was a desperate appeal, but was it tempting enough to stir and awaken the scoundrel in the Scot? She lifted her gaze to see his eyes dilate and darken, after which a muscle ticked along his jaw.

With a curt nod, he said, 'We leave today. As soon as I can arrange it.'

Helene's shoulders sagged in relief. 'Thank you.'

'Nephew!' Lady Sutton jumped to her feet. 'Ye cannae be serious.' She looked aghast at Caitrin. 'Sister! Will ye not say something?'

'Aye! I will.' Caitrin's chin tilted up. 'I support my son's decision. 'Tis nae a rash one, but proactive.'

Elspeth's mouth fell open. 'What? Ye consent to Helene dressing like a man and sallying forth to London, alone with Lachlan? 'Tis not the proper thing to do.'

'Proper?' Caitrin rose from her chair and stood one inch taller than her twin. 'Sometimes *proper* has nae say in happenstance. We women are made of sterner stuff, and the lass has proved herself in as much. She's up for the journey, and I ken my son will protect and keep her safe. If the earl's order is time-sensitive, then I'll not have him hold the MacLanochs responsible for any delay in his daughter's return.'

Lachlan reassured his auntie. 'Dinnae worry over how this might reflect on ye as Helene's chaperone. She might have travelled here with ye under the king's escort, but given the sudden turn of events, she'll return to London with me. 'Tis my decision, for which I take full responsibility.'

Cuthbert stepped forth. 'You must allow me to go with you.'

'Thank ye, but that willnae be necessary. Besides, ye must stay here at Drumocher and look after the family.'

'Then what can I do to help expedite your preparations for the journey?'

'Seek out the farrier. He and the groom will need to prepare my horse and one for Helene. Then have a servant gather my councilmen to meet in the great hall in one hour's time. Join me there, for I must inform them of my impending absence and that 'tis ye who'll stand in my stead until I return. Quarter day is nigh, so ye must oversee the collection of rents.'

'Of course,' said Cuthbert with a nod.

Helene caught Cuthbert's cursory glance before he spun on his heel and exited the room. Struck by guilt, her chin dipped to her chest. She'd come to Drumocher with one purpose in mind, and now, having achieved it, culpability weighed even heavier on her conscience. This tight-knit family rallied to do her bidding, and in so doing they, and the people of Drumocher, would be temporarily without their laird. The journey to London would not be without danger, and despite Lachlan's prowess as a fierce Highland warrior, she prayed there would be no adverse consequences for either of them, especially for Lachlan on his return home.

Warm hands grasped hers, and she raised her head to see Grizel softly smiling at her. 'I'll rally Cook to prepare as much food and wine as ye both can carry.' She turned and dashed away.

Lachlan addressed Helene with direct formality. 'How soon can ye be ready?'

'As soon as I source men's clothing.'

'I'll see to that,' volunteered Caitrin. She swept an assessing gaze over Helene. 'I'll have the clothes sent to yer room, lass.'

'You're most kind. Thank you.' This was all too humbling for Helene. Her thoughts filled with self-loathing.

Drumocher's matriarch glanced over to her sister. 'Best we all do not abandon Agnes. Do ye mind staying here to keep her company? I'll rejoin ye shortly.'

'Aye,' said Lady Sutton. She stayed Lachlan with a hand on his arm just as he turned to leave. 'A word before ye go.'

'Auntie?'

'Ye must show Helene how to protect herself with a *sgian-dubh*.' She swung her gaze to Helene. ''Tis a wee dagger small enough to conceal on yer person.' Then to Lachlan she added, ''Tis wise for the lass to ken self-defence. Promise me ye'll take all precautions to stay safe.'

'Aye. I promise.' He glanced over to Helene. 'Meet me in the inner bailey in two hours.'

Helene watched him go and swallowed at the chilling possibility of having to wield a weapon, yet at the same time she knew, without doubt, Lachlan's life was as much a priority to her as was her sister's. If required of her, she'd fight and defend them to her death.

Agnes struggled to stand on her feet. 'You must let me help you pack a few things.'

'Absolutely not.' Helene coaxed Agnes back down onto the chaise and sat beside her.

'But I feel like such a useless invalid.'

Helene clasped her friend's hands. 'There's nothing for you to do except promise me you'll continue to rest. When your ankle heals, you'll be up and about and enjoying the Highland summer, as you well should.'

Agnes squeezed Helene's hand. 'I'll do more than that. I'll pray for your safe return to London and that all is well for you and your family.'

Helene hugged Agnes close. 'Thank you, dear friend. That is the most I could ever ask of you.'

⁂

Lachlan scanned the inner bailey in search of Helene. He turned to Cuthbert at his side and said, 'What the devil is taking the lass so long?'

Cuthbert lifted one shoulder. 'I've no idea.'

'I'll see what's keeping her.' Lachlan strode with purpose in the direction of the great hall. Clan folk were quick to clear a path for their laird, except for one whose forward approach set the two men on a collision path.

Lachlan kept up his pace and shouted a warning. 'Out of my way!'

The tall, thin clansman stared him down and ignored the order.

'I said, out of my way!'

The man did not alter his course. Was he deaf? The distance between them closed with every step, and the bastard showed no sign of backing down. Defiance towards a laird, and in full view of his clan, must not go unpunished. Lachlan's hulking body would knock the gomerel to the ground, but that would not be punishment enough for the fool's dogged insolence.

Lachlan prepared himself, his right hand clenching into a fist as he strode forward. In the second he drew back his arm, his challenger pulled up short, cowering in fear with forearms raised and crossed to protect his face.

'Lachlan. It's me! Helene!'

In horror, Lachlan froze mid-manoeuvre. A reactionary reflex followed, and he recoiled from her, stumbling back a step or two. He steadied himself, sucked in a shuddering breath, and let it out on a rasp. 'Christ! Helene!'

If she hadn't have spoken to identify herself, he'd have unleashed on her the brute force of his fist. He suffered the burn of bile at the back of his throat with the mere thought of it.

'Forgive me, lass. I didnae ken it was ye!' His remorse-filled heart thumped inside his chest.

She whipped off the bonnet, and the weight of her plaited hair fell over her shoulder like a thick rope. 'Then my disguise worked. Did it not?'

He baulked at the triumph in her voice, aware of the curious stares of clansmen all around them. 'Aye, it did. Too well. Ye should have called out or warned me.'

She gave him a wide smile. 'But my idea was to evaluate the authenticity of my disguise and see just how long it took for you to recognise me.'

Relief over not harming her suddenly switched to anger, and he took hold of her shoulders in a firm grip. His mind's eye tortured him with the horrendous consequences had he not gained swift control over his actions. The sickening crack of her cheek bone. An eye dislodged from its socket. The perfect line of her straight nose smashed beyond repair. Split lips and a bloodied face.

His eyes shut tight, and he shook his head to rid himself of those heart-wrenching images. The worst-case scenario turned his stomach. His eyes snapped open, and his chest rose and fell with each laboured breath.

'One blow to yer head and I could have killed ye, lass!'

She stared at him in wild surprise, as if baffled by his stern outburst.

His racing heart skidded to a halt and anger left him when she softly cradled the palm of her hand against his cheek.

In a quiet voice, she said, 'I'm sorry, Lachlan. I didn't mean to cause you distress, and you're right. I took my disguise too far. I should not have done so.'

His eyes followed the gentle curve of her jawline, her rose-coloured lips, flawless delicate skin, and perfectly arched brows. His gaze fell into hers and fell deeper again until he was drowning in a sea of shimmering green.

He covered her hand with his and spoke on a strangled whisper. 'If ye'd have died by my hand, lass, I'd have plunged my dirk into my own heart.'

She gasped in shock at his candid declaration. In the next instant, she slid her hand from his cheek.

Lachlan cleared his throat, mindful of their growing audience. His gaze swept the bailey, warning curious bystanders to go about their day.

'Now,' he said to Helene. 'Let me have a good look at ye.'

She looked every inch a tall, gangly youth. In one hand

she held a lichen-green Highland bonnet made of wool. A waistcoat sat beneath a woollen coat, and beneath the former, a linen shirt with a stock tie, tied in a square knot and tucked neatly into the top of her waistcoat.

Lachlan's gaze sank lower to take in breeches and riding boots. The overall fit of her clothes was by no means tailor-made, nor did they appear remotely new. This, together with the earthy colours, would see her blend in and mark her as a Highlander of no particular means.

'Perfect,' he said, lifting his gaze to her face. 'My mother has done well in securing these clothes, because the last thing we need is to draw attention to ourselves. Except . . .'

'Except what?' she asked with a glint of concern in her eyes.

Even dressed as a man, her beauty transfixed him. 'Ye're a very pretty man.'

Cuthbert sidled up to them just as Lachlan uttered those words. 'You mean to say I have some competition?'

Lachlan gave him a wry grin. 'Ye cannae hold a candle to Helene.'

Cuthbert feigned great umbrage to the insult before turning serious. 'You are indeed a fair beauty, Helene. Should you cross paths with other travellers, then tug your bonnet low over your brow and keep your head down. Clean, manicured nails and small, dainty hands also give you away. Hide them in your pockets if necessary.

'Your voice will also betray you, so if there's any talking to be done, leave it to Lachlan.' He paused for a moment before adding, 'Safe travels. I wish you and your family well.'

Lachlan watched Helene with keen interest. She had no idea he knew of hers and Cuthbert's dealings and that she was now in possession of Cuthbert's promissory note. Why she needed the money was still a mystery, one he felt confident of solving when they reached London, if not before.

Her eyes flitted between the two men, and she appeared to be taken aback by Cuthbert's genuine sincerity. 'Thank you. I shall heed your sage advice.'

Lachlan glanced over her head and saw his mother and Grizel making their way towards them. He continued in conversation with Helene.

'If ye're going to complete the look of a Highland clansman, then there's a few more things we need to add to yer disguise.'

'Like what?'

'Ye'll need to wear a sword at yer side, even if ye dinnae ken how to wield one. No man travels without weaponry. I've a *sgian-dubh* to hide on yer person too, so I'll instruct ye how to use it when we make camp tonight.' He nodded to his mother and sister as they joined the trio.

Grizel pointed to the animal hide satchel strung over one shoulder. ''Tis from Cook. Inside ye'll find food pouches containing cheese, nuts, dried berries, smoked venison, oats, bannocks, and bread.' Her gaze shifted to her other shoulder. 'And in this one ye've flasks of whisky and wine.'

Cuthbert relieved her of the satchels.

'Son?' said Caitrin, pointing to Helene's clothes. 'What do ye think of my handiwork?'

'Ye've done well, Mother. In fact, I didnae recognise her at all until she spoke her name.' Lachlan refrained from admitting he'd come within an inch of assaulting Helene.

'Aye, weel, sorry for the delay. Helene has a small foot, and 'twas the wee boots I had trouble sourcing.' Caitrin gestured the way forward. 'We'll see ye to the stables and on yer way, then.'

It pleased Lachlan to see Helene take his mother's arm and walk companionably with her to the stables. He overheard her thank his mother for her warm welcome to Drumocher, for her understanding Helene's urgent need to return home, and for providing her with the appropriate attire.

'I do not take for granted your son leaving Drumocher on my behalf,' said Helene. 'I'm eternally grateful to you, to Lachlan, and your family and clan, and I apologise for the inconvenience of it all. If there's anything I can do to repay your kindness, then name it.'

'Ye can promise me ye'll return to Drumocher,' said his mother. 'For ye've nae had time enough to experience what the Highlands truly have to offer. Ye will promise me this, won't ye, lass?'

Lachlan strained to hear Helene's reply, drowned out by the excited whinny of his horse upon sighting its master. Lachlan glanced over his shoulder to see his mother smile and pat the back of Helene's hand. He surmised Helene had answered in the affirmative. An honest response, or was it one to appease his mother in the moment?

In the ensuing minutes, Lachlan strapped to Helene a leather sword belt, sheathed in the scabbard the lightest of rapiers, befitting her stature.

Helene embraced his mother and Grizel, repeating her thanks and her goodbyes, and said, 'I've already bid farewell to Lady Sutton and Agnes, however, please do reiterate my thanks to them both for escorting me here to Drumocher.'

'I'll do as ye ask, lass,' said Caitrin. 'Yer belongings will be loaded onto their carriage when they return home.'

Grizel giggled and swept admiring eyes over Helene. 'Ye make a fine-looking Highland warrior.'

'Well, if nothing else,' said Helene, 'these clothes are far more comfortable than being wrapped, strapped, and cinched in skirts and corsets.'

Lachlan gave her a leg up into the saddle and took from his coat pocket a *sgian-dubh*. ''Tis kept on the side of yer dominant hand,' he said. 'Ye might as well get used to wearing it now.'

He walked around to her right side. 'The blade is inside this safety sheath. I'll tuck it into the top of your woollen sock inside yer boot. The hilt will be visible, the idea being ye can quickly and easily retrieve it.'

He concealed the small stabbing knife in the way he'd explained, adding, ''Tis a functional blade aside from being used as a weapon, and it comes in handy when cutting bread and cheese, or fruit and meat.'

Helene grimaced. 'I hope the cutting of food is the only use I'll have for it.'

'Aye. Well. Ye can put it to the test when we stop to eat.'

Lachlan took Grizel in his arms and hugged her tight. 'Take good care of Mother, won't ye, lass?'

'Aye. Of course I will. And ye take care of yersel' and Helene.'

Lachlan felt the tickle of Grizel's breath by his ear when she whispered, 'I like her, ye ken. She's a brave lass. A verra *bonnie*, brave lass.'

She stepped out of their embrace and winked at him with a knowing smile. Lachlan had no trouble reading between the lines, but he was thankful Helene busied herself with the reins and therefore did not hear or witness the exchange. He then stepped into the circle of his mother's open arms and held her close.

'Stay safe and Godspeed, son.'

Lachlan pulled back and felt the gentle squeeze of her hands in his. 'Thank ye, Mother. I'll return directly home once Helene is with her father.'

'Take whatever time ye need,' she said. 'I daresay ye'll discover a few home truths about the lass between now and when I next see ye.'

'Aye. No doubt, and if needs must, I'll have a wee word with her father.'

She leaned in closer. 'And dinnae forget yer grandmother's words of wisdom when it comes to matters of the heart.'

One corner of Lachlan's mouth lifted in a half-smile. 'I willnae forget.' He planted a soft kiss on the backs of both her hands. As he turned towards his horse, Cuthbert took him aside.

'Is everything all right?' asked Lachlan.

'Of course,' said Cuthbert with one of his enigmatic smiles. 'I just had a quiet word with Helene and asked her not to inform my father of the mishap with Agnes and her sprained ankle. He need not worry. I also asked that she keep to herself any knowledge she might have of my *private* affairs.' He inhaled a deep breath. 'Now, rest assured I'll do you proud in your absence.'

'Aye. I ken ye will.'

'And . . .' Cuthbert switched to Gaelic in a quieter voice. 'Thank you for your understanding. You know of what it is I speak, and you have my eternal gratitude.' His gaze darted in Helene's direction. 'I wish for you to piece together the puzzle of your heart's desire.'

Lachlan laid a hand on Cuthbert's shoulder. '*Mar sin leibh an-dràsta.*'

'Aye, goodbye for now.'

CHAPTER NINETEEN

HELENE SHIFTED IN her seat. A thick sheepskin lined the leather saddle, providing soft cushioning for her bottom. Riding for hours on end was not something she otherwise engaged in, and so she had thanked Lachlan for his care and consideration regarding her riding comfort. The numbness she was beginning to feel would likely have otherwise been tenfold.

The journey thus far had seen them pass through verdant woodland. Helene pulled into her lungs the perfume of pines and crisp, sparkling mountain air. A cacophony of birdsong accompanied them along the way, from the very vocal stonechats to the strange popping noise of a capercaillie.

The sun's slow descent brought with it a drop in temperature, and darkness would cloak them in a matter of hours.

Lachlan led the way along what looked to be a well-trodden trail, its width at present only enough to ride in single file. At times, progress was slow, requiring their mounts to tread carefully along undulating ground or pick their way over roots growing over the path.

Helene admired Lachlan's physique at her leisure, this day being the first time she'd seen him dressed in anything but his kilt. Her gaze took in the muscular definition of thighs encased in dark breeches and knee-length boots. Like her, he wore a woollen vest over a linen shirt with a neckerchief. A coat hugged his broad back. His baldric and sword belt buckled over one shoulder and around the waist reminded her of the day they'd met when she'd fallen from the carriage and into his arms. The pin of the baldric buckle had caught the weave of her cloak, rendering them, quite literally, fastened together.

'Like bairns fused at birth,' he'd said.

She hadn't appreciated the humour in his comment at the time. However, she did now, and could not help but smile at the quip. She valued all she'd come to learn about the laird of Clan MacLanoch. He'd proved himself to be a man of worth, a fierce protector of family and his clan. He had a head for business and a heart brimming with compassion, kindness, honesty, and integrity. Try as she did to repel his magnetic charm, he was a man in whom she could find no fault.

Until this morning in the drawing room. One singular moment replayed itself in her mind, and the memory of it slapped her across the face. Her good opinion of the laird had been ruthlessly overturned when he'd agreed to be her sole escort to London *only* after she'd offered him her innocence.

And this from a man who claimed to have sworn off deflowering debutants.

Liar! Hypocrite!

Of her own volition, she was no longer pure of virtue after their time together when sheltering from the squall, so how stupidly naive of her to believe Lachlan thought more of her than just another carnal conquest. A lascivious indulgence. A prize to be won in a wager. Any guilt she harboured over retaining Cuthbert's promissory note turned to ash, just as if she'd tossed the parchment in a blazing hearth.

The MacLanoch laird had lived up to his reputation. Once a rake, always a rake.

Yet, contrary to this, in the bailey, he'd looked at her with eyes radiating distress and despair, confessing intent to take his own life had she died by his hand. Why? Because he cared so deeply for her that he couldn't live without her? Or because he couldn't face her father and suffer the disgrace of having to declare himself a murderer?

The man was a confusing conundrum of morality and vice. A timely reminder to metaphorically burn any emotional connection to him. She had no scope for him in her life, nor she in his. He was no more than a person whose job it was to escort her safely back to her life in London. Back to her father, and to Prudence.

Sweet Prudence. *Dear God, keep her safe.*

Another matter of consequence weighed heavy on Helene's mind. At what point during her journey home would Lachlan call in her debt and take her innocence? Tonight? Sudden trepidation rippled through her, swiftly followed by an involuntary quivering of excitement at the apex of her thighs. She squirmed in the saddle, mortified when she glanced up to see Lachlan watching her over his shoulder.

'Ye'll be pleased to ken we'll make camp up ahead,' he said.

She nodded and prayed he believed her discomfort due to being saddle-sore, not because her traitorous body reacted to the memory of his touch, yearning for more.

A few minutes passed before Helene cocked her head to the sound of rushing water. Soon, the path's downward gradient brought them into view of a narrow stream.

'Over there,' Lachlan said, pointing. 'We'll make camp on the embankment.'

Helene's gaze followed in the direction he pointed. She marvelled at the setting. Lush. Picturesque.

Secluded.

Helene swallowed the ball of nerves in her throat. She

watched Lachlan dismount, his boots thudding on the earth. He stepped towards her and raised his arms, ready to assist in helping her down. She did as he had, removing her feet from the stirrups and swinging her right leg over the horse's neck.

Strong hands latched firmly around her waist, and instinctively she braced her palms on his broad shoulders. Whisky-flecked eyes, rare and striking like that of a wolf, locked onto hers as if she were his prey to devour. She couldn't have looked away or fought for freedom if her life depended on it.

He lifted her down from the saddle, slowly and without breaking eye contact. Corded muscles flexed beneath Helene's hands, and heat from his skin radiated through his layers of clothes, penetrating deep into her bloodstream.

At what point he set her on her feet, she did not know, for she remained trapped in his gaze, trapped between the large hands spanning her waist, and hopelessly trapped in a vortex of intense sensation.

Mentally burning emotional ties to this man was one challenge, but any hope of nullifying her body's reactions to him was like asking the sun never to rise again.

His hands fell away from her waist, and yet the heat of his touch lingered. That heat sparked and flared inside her when his gaze dropped to rest on her mouth. Something surged inside her. Anticipation? Expectancy?

The moment his gaze lifted to hers, he took an abrupt step backwards. Had he seen her hunger for him in her eyes?

'I'll see to the horses.' He gathered up their reins and led them to drink at the edge of the stream. Next, he unburdened the horses of bedrolls and bundled supplies.

Helene sucked in an unsteady breath. One urge might be denied, yet another required her immediate attention. Nature called, and so she fumbled with the buckle of her sword belt.

'What are ye doing with that?'

Helene glanced up to see his quizzical frown. 'Removing it, and the baldric.'

'Why?'

Awkward embarrassment heated Helene's cheeks. 'I must tend to my needs, and I'll manage the process a lot easier if I'm not encumbered with all this leather and steel.'

Understanding dawned in his eyes. 'Aye. Well.' He started towards her. 'Let me help ye.'

This time it was Helene who took a step back. 'Thank you, but I'm quite capable of tending to my own needs.'

He stopped mid-stride, lips quirking in amusement. 'I meant, I'll help ye remove the sword belt and baldric.'

'Oh.' Helene's chin dipped down. 'I thought . . .' She shook her head, feeling more than a little foolish. 'Never mind.'

Lachlan's approach set her senses on high alert, and when he stood only inches before her, her gaze drank him in. From the bonnet worn flat across his head, to the dark autumn hair framing a face more handsome than any mythical God.

Her gaze fell from his face to watch large hands and nimble fingers unclasp the buckles, lifting the leather belts and armoury off and away from her body. She rolled her shoulders several times to exercise sore muscles.

'I'll set these aside for now,' he said, and nodded to the woodland behind her. 'Mind ye dinnae stray too far from here, and dinnae ever remove yer bonnet. Yer long hair will give ye away as a woman.'

Helene picked her way into the woods in search of privacy. The wide girth of a tree trunk doubled as a privacy screen. Noises in the underbrush rendered her skittish, and so she waited a moment or two, hoping that whatever creatures she'd disturbed had now scurried away. When all she could hear was the whisper of leaves in the canopy overhead, she released the buttons at her waist and then two more on the fall flap on her breeches. Men had it easy. All they need do was release their appendage and stand in one spot to relieve themselves. Women, on the other hand . . . She rolled her eyes and drew the breeches down, squatted, and emptied her bladder.

Upon standing, muscles in her legs and backside protested for having sat so long in the saddle. This was only day one of their journey. Lord knows how her body would ache by the time she reached home.

She returned to their camp to see the horses munching on lush grass beneath the shelter of a tall pine where they'd been tethered. Lachlan had dug a small crater in the ground where he presently crouched, lining its perimeter with rocks the size of his fist.

He'd divested himself of his coat and woollen vest, and Helene could not take her gaze from the way his linen shirt accommodated the width of his broad shoulders and the depth of his muscular chest. Sleeves rolled to his elbows exposed strong forearms. She suspected his physique was testimony to years of wielding the mighty weight of a broadsword and other such combative weaponry, and exercise.

'What can I do to help?' she asked.

He spoke without glancing up. 'If ye dinnae mind dirtying yer hands, then 'twould help if ye gather kindling for the fire.'

'Of course,' she said without hesitation, and watched him pull out a small axe from one of the leather bundles lying on the ground close to the firepit.

While retrieving twigs, dried leaves, and anything crisp enough to catch fire, Helene stole furtive glances at Lachlan. He searched for fallen branches and used the axe with gusto to chop wood for the fire. Since embarking on their journey today, conversation between them had been sparse, with no real substance. A comment here and there about Scotland's flora and fauna, Lachlan explaining what to expect of weather conditions during their journey for this time of year.

Something weighed heavy on Lachlan's mind. Helene could see it in his furrowed brow, in the grim set of his mouth, and she'd lost count of the number of times since their departure he'd rubbed the back of his neck as if beset by worry.

The only conclusion she drew about the cause of his distraction was his concern and regret over leaving his family without their laird. She was a burden to him, for sure. Helene consoled herself in knowing he did have a choice. He could have outright refused to travel solo with her to London, despite her desperate plea. He could have insisted they wait for a retinue of soldiers and a carriage to convey her, and him, back to London. Instead, the appendage between his legs and her offer of him taking her virginity had won out. That decision was on *him*. Not her.

In a battle of wills, Helene had succeeded, and if it meant the difference between ensuring Prudence's survival and well-being or mourning her death, then so be it.

Besides, the Highlands might be experiencing turbulent times, but Lachlan had an impenetrable stone fortress in which to keep his family safe. He had Cuthbert and councilmen to make strategic decisions for the welfare of their clan in Lachlan's absence, and he had an army of clansmen. Trained fierce warriors to guard, to protect, to fight and die for his family and livelihood.

Helene had herself. *Herself!* She was her sister's only devout protector, and she refused to feel any guilt over seeing the laird of Clan MacLanoch struggle with any internal war he waged with his personal decisions.

She laid down what she'd collected beside the firepit and watched as Lachlan carefully arranged layers of chunked wood, twigs, and kindling in the hollowed-out ground.

Attached to his belt was a leather pouch, from which he retrieved a small round tin. He flipped the lid with his thumb and took out a steel striker, a piece of sharp flint, and a two-inch length of cordage, which he teased into a bird's nest and placed amongst the fire fuel. With practised ease, he set sparks to the cordage. It caught alight, followed by the kindling. His gentle breath gave greater life to the flames.

Next, he produced a large blanket pin from the same pouch, through which he threaded thin sturdy sticks to form a makeshift tripod over the fire.

Within the space of half an hour, Lachlan had suspended from the tripod a small pot. Its boiling contents included stream water and root vegetables from their rations. Helene took the initiative to retrieve portions of food and smoked venison from the parcels Cook had packaged for them, and before long, she and Lachlan sat down to a satisfying and belly-filling meal.

Helene swallowed her last mouthful. 'Thank you.'

'For what?'

Helene gestured with a sweep of her hand to the fire and to their empty bowls. 'For all this. You make survival in the wild seem so simple.'

'Survival in the wild is not just about keeping warm or satisfying one's hunger.' His gaze went to the small weapon concealed inside her boot. ''Tis time ye learned a thing or two about using that *sgian-dubh* to defend yersel', but first we'll clean up here and pack away the remaining food else it attracts animals while we sleep. We also best prepare our bedding by the fire before it gets too dark.'

They worked together in the waning light, and Helene followed Lachlan's lead in foraging moss-like ground cover pulled from the woodland floor. This served as a soft mattress over which she laid the sheepskin from her saddle.

Lachlan explained, 'I ken 'tis primitive bedding compared to what ye're used to, but it helps ye stay warm and prevents the earth from sapping ye of body heat. When ye're wrapped in yer plaid blanket, ye'll be plenty warm. Now then, if ye'll follow me.'

He took several long strides away from their fire. Helene did as he asked and followed.

'Take yer *sgian-dubh* in hand,' he said.

Helene bent to the weapon tucked in her sock and unsheathed the sharp, single-edged blade. Her palm closed around the intricately carved antler horn handle, and an ominous shudder ran right through her. '*Sgian-dubh*. What does it mean?'

'In Gaelic it roughly translates to "black dagger". *Sgian*, meaning knife or dagger, and *dubh*, meaning "black". *Dubh*'s secondary meaning is "hidden", for obvious reasons.'

So intent was her focus on the blade, and the potential damage such a small knife could inflict, that Helene did not notice Lachlan approach and position himself close behind her. Only when his right hand suddenly closed around hers holding the knife did she react with a start like that of a victim caught by surprise.

'Shh,' he soothed.

His warm breath caressed her ear. Awareness of him at her back frayed her nerves and set her heart aflutter.

'Out here in the wild, we're nae different to any animal, bird, or insect. One preys on the other. Yer senses must always be on high alert,' he warned.

Right now, desire was her only sense on high alert.

'Everything, anything, and anyone can present a danger, and ye must have eyes in the back of yer head. Now, listen carefully. When attacking with a *sgian-dubh*, 'tis best to do so using the underhand.'

Without warning, his hand on hers thrust forward and upward in a stabbing motion. He repeated the frenzied, jerky movement several more times, and Helene's stomach lurched at the imagined sound of steel puncturing flesh. Desire dissolved into stark reality, and she gave Lachlan her full attention.

He brought his free arm around her left side and used both his hands to reposition her grip on the knife so that its tip pointed down. He then braced his left hand on her upper left arm.

'If someone surges up to attack ye, or if ye need to come down with a hefty blow on someone, then use overhand.'

Helene squeezed her eyes shut against her imaginary victim when Lachlan's hand on hers forced a merciless downward thrust. Once. Twice. Thrice.

Pray God she'd never have to put theory into practice.

'Do ye ken where on the body ye'll do lethal damage?'

Did she really need to know? Yes, she reasoned, because surely Lachlan would not be so cruel as to shock her with tactical violence simply for the sport of it. She shook her head in answer to his question.

He let go of her hand and pressed his fingers against her lower back. 'Focus on my touch.'

It was impossible not to.

Through her coat, she felt his fingers locate and trace the underside of her ribs. 'Here,' he said as he pressed. 'Beneath the last rib. Thrust the blade upwards and into the kidney.'

His hands fell away from her. 'Turn around.'

When she did, it was to see him tug his shirt from his breeches.

Helene swallowed and gave him a wide-eyed stare. Was that it? Lesson over? Why was he undressing? Did he plan to take her here? Now? On the stream's embankment?

He raised the garment high enough to expose the left side

of his chest. Helene fought the urge to lift her free hand and touch the dusting of dark hair over the expanse of hard muscle.

On his stomach she saw a thick, ragged white scar the length of her middle finger. Was it the only scar to blemish what she perceived to be the most perfect specimen of a man? Perversely, she longed to explore and examine every inch of his body, and to press a kiss to each healed wound that might have once caused him untold pain. She startled at the sound of his voice.

'Should ye find yersel' face-to-face with yer attacker, then plunge yer blade into his heart. Aim here.' He pointed beneath the breastbone. 'Remember to thrust forward and up, ye ken?'

She gave a barely perceptible nod.

'Do it,' he said.

Her gaze flew to his. 'Do what?'

'Attack me with the knife.'

She took a step back, deeply disturbed by the macabre order. 'I'll do no such thing!'

''Tis merely to practise yer skill with the *sgian-dubh*.' He took a step forward. 'Do it.'

Helene looked down at the knife in her hand, then back at Lachlan. If only to appease him, she gave the knife no more than a gentle, half-hearted nudge.

'Pathetic. Do it again.'

Her second attempt was no better than the first.

Lachlan exhaled on an exasperated grunt. 'I willnae break, lass. Again!'

His voice was sharper than the knife's tip, and she flinched at the scowl he gave her. He made her feel weak and hopeless.

'Christ, lass!' he said on her third go. 'Ye'd not hurt a butterfly with so feeble an attempt. Try again. With conviction,' he insisted.

Anger over his condescending tone gave power to the

driving thrust of her knife. His hand shot out with lightning speed and captured her wrist.

'Too high.' He let go of her hand. 'Do it again.'

She did, and again he caught her hand before the tip of the blade touched him.

'Take the knife in yer other hand.'

Helene complied. He then took her dominant hand in his and pressed her fingertips to his body. 'Aim here,' he said. 'Below the ribs. The heart lies beneath the ribcage, and that's what yer aiming for.'

With her next attempt, Lachlan made no move to catch her hand, and so her fingers stabbed muscle as hard as the steel blade.

'Spot on, lass, but use more force.'

Two fingers stabbed him again, and when she withdrew her hand his skin bore the imprint of her fingernails.

'Now use the knife and stab at me as if yer life depended on it! It's attack or be attacked! Always think in these terms.' His voice grew louder, harsher, with each word he spoke. ''Twas *ye* who wanted to dress like a man, so show me ye can damned well fight like one!'

The mocking remark, the uncompromising bite in his voice, and the heat of his skin was like tinder to the spark in Helene's rising anger. In a flash she switched the *sgian-dubh* from one hand to the other, and with all the force of her resentment she thrust the blade forward and up.

Lachlan's hand caught Helene's wrist in a tight, vice-like grip. Her gaze flew to his, where she saw in his widened eyes something akin to surprise, if not pride, like that of a teacher whose student had finally mastered the skill being taught.

'Well done, lass. This time, yer blade would have found its mark.' He still held her wrist, but his gaze flashed downward, then back at her in an invitation to inspect her aim.

Helene looked down. Blood trickled from the point at which the tip of the blade had pierced Lachlan's skin. Panic shot through her, and she gasped in horror. Her hand holding the knife flexed open, the weapon falling at her feet. Instinctively, she pressed both hands to the crimson-smeared flesh.

'I'm sorry! I'm so sorry!'

'Hush now. Ye needn't worry, lass. 'Tis but a wee scratch.'

'A scratch?' Her voice rose with her panic. 'I stuck you with a knife and you're bleeding!'

He took a step back out of her reach and untied the neck-cloth at his throat. He used it to wipe away the blood. ''Tis but a tiny puncture wound. I caught yer hand before ye could do any real damage.'

Beads of blood reappeared, and again he wiped them away.

'Come,' he said, walking towards the stream and beckoning her. 'Wash yer hands here beside me.'

They crouched at the water's edge, where Helene washed Lachlan's blood from her hands.

He drenched and squeezed water from the neckcloth and wiped clean his wound. 'See? 'Tis as if I'd nicked myself shaving.'

Air whooshed from Helene's lungs in a sigh of relief, and her chin dipped to her chest. The rough pads of his thumb and forefinger settled beneath her chin.

'Look at me,' he said, his voice calm. Gentle.

Helene opened her eyes and could not hide the glistening sting of tears.

'I'm not sorry for putting ye through that, lass, for 'tis imperative ye learn to protect yersel' as best ye can in any situation, not just here in the Highlands. We both ken what men can be like, even in what should be the most civilised of circumstances.'

He was right. She knew of several young innocents who'd

been forced upon, their reputation in ruins at the hands of so-called noblemen. How different those young women's lives would be had they the knowledge or skills to protect themselves.

Prudence. How would she protect herself if one of the asylum minders were to—? She quashed a strangled cry. It didn't bear thinking about.

Helene acquiesced with a blink, and Lachlan thumbed away the single tear falling down her cheek. He rinsed his neckcloth in the stream and gently wiped the day's grime from her face. That done, he pulled her to her feet, retrieved and cleaned the *sgian-dubh*, and handed it back to Helene.

Darkness had descended, the fire their only source of light except for the heavens above glittering with a thousand stars.

'Best ye get some rest now. We leave at dawn.'

Helene sheathed the knife inside her boot, pulled her bonnet tight on her head, and settled beneath the blanket on her makeshift bed. Somewhere in the distance a wolf howled. She tensed and pulled the blanket tight about her like it was a suit of protective armour.

'Dinnae worry, lass. Animals, insects, and the like will nae approach us while the fire burns, and I'll be sure to fuel it throughout the night.'

Reassuring words, yet Helene would have felt even safer if they were to share a blanket, with Lachlan's arms about her. Beneath lowered lashes she watched him tuck his shirt into his breeches and don his waistcoat and jacket. He spread the wet neckcloth over a nearby rock close to the fire, there to dry overnight.

He bedded down facing away from her, the fire between them. Helene glanced up from his strong, solid form to the dark mass of encircling trees standing like sentinels guarding them. A gentle breeze kicked up a murmuring discussion between the leaves. Like a lullaby, the soothing sound forced Helene's heavy lids to close over tired eyes. Her thoughts drifted to Drumocher. The stone fortress, and those who resided within it, had grown on Helene in such a short time. Her heart sank in knowing she'd never return to the Highlands, the shielings, to the MacLanochs and their clan.

The brooch came to mind. Grizel or Caitrin would surely have found it by now, sitting on top of the dresser in the bedchamber Helene had occupied. They'd return the heirloom to its rightful owner. Aila.

The last thing Helene heard before slumber claimed her was the soft, deep hoot of an owl.

CHAPTER TWENTY

LACHLAN HAD NEVER known a woman like Helene. They were nine days into their journey, and true to her word, not once did she complain. Despite the summer heat, getting caught in a sudden shower or two, or dealing with periodic encounters with swarms of flies, she hadn't voiced the slightest protest. Even the toughest of his clansmen would have found something to whinge about.

Helene demonstrated resilience through and through. Tolerance for the hard earth as her bed. Long days in the saddle. The absence of freshly laundered clothes. Going without a bath to wash away the day's sweat and grime at the end of each long day. Meals were hardly sumptuous, but rather bland and basic. Stewed rabbit, fish, root vegetables, and wild berries. Cook's rations of cheese, nuts, smoked venison, oats, bannocks, and bread had served them well, meted out sparingly and without waste.

Lachlan insisted on setting time aside each evening to hone Helene's skills with the blade, and to empower her with the means of defending herself from a physical attack. Hardly ladylike pastimes. Better she possessed some knowledge and skills in self-defence than none at all.

He glanced sidewards and down at her hands holding her

horse's reins. Those delicate hands were made for crafting needlepoint, for holding and reading books, for playing the pianoforte. Not for wielding a lethal weapon. Still, needs must.

They'd made good progress south through the Highlands, crossing into the Lowlands and forging on towards London. If he'd let Helene have her way, her dogged determination would have driven their horses harder, faster, and further. He reminded her the beasts would drop dead from exhaustion if pushed beyond their limits.

Time-saving tracks and pathways ensured they'd arrive at their destination in three to four days' time. Encounters with other travellers had been few and far between, and fortunately none saw through Helene's disguise. Passing her off as a deaf mute meant people made no attempt to engage her in conversation. Instead, all communication was through Lachlan.

He spent hours ruminating over what Helene was running to in London. What was so damned pressing and urgent that a woman of her breeding willingly suffered the indignity of traversing the countryside on horseback, and in so primitive a manner, rather than comfortably seated, as she rightfully deserved, within the plush interior of a horse-drawn carriage?

She might have pleaded ignorance as to the reason why her father wanted her home, but Lachlan was not so naive as to believe her. He'd witnessed proof of his suspicion in her telltale, if not distressing, reaction to her father's brief missive. She'd read between the lines and reacted adversely, the blood having drained from her face. Her pained expression, shallow breaths, the trembling of her hands, and her body on the verge of collapse were collective indicators of her being privy to an existing problematic situation. A worsening situation, by all accounts. Something confidential. Something secret. Something her father did not wish for Lachlan or anyone else to discover.

Helene, come home! Lachlan had glimpsed those three words when retrieving and handing the parchment back to her. It was only natural one might react with alarm or anxious concern over receiving such a cryptic command. A command that offered no deeper explanation. Helene's reaction indicated she understood the broader message within the context of that shakily handwritten note. Of that, Lachlan was convinced.

He'd shouldered many an affront and insult in his lifetime, most of which were addressed and settled with a sword, but never had he suffered such a cutting injury as the blow of Helene's bribe.

Please! The desperation in her whispered plea had shredded Lachlan to the core. *In return, I'll do anything.* She'd offered to trade her virginity for his services as her personal escort and guide.

Christ! Did she still think so little of him? Did she believe him to be idiotically shallow, so easily persuaded and bought? Had she not learned anything of his moral fibre since setting foot on MacLanoch soil?

If ever he were to bed her, it would be because she wanted him as much as he desired her. Not because she offered herself to him as a reward for his services rendered.

What was her situation that made it so dire, so desperate that she'd part her legs for him? It surely must have something to do with her furtive dealings with Cuthbert. And the money? What did she intend doing with it? What problem would it solve? It rankled not knowing.

Lachlan rubbed the back of his neck before lifting his gaze to assess the position of the sun. Four hours of daylight remained. Ample time to reach the abandoned church not far down the track. A nearby spring would serve their needs and provide water for tonight's broth, in which he'd use the last of the salted venison.

He glanced her way once again. She looked tired, weary, with shoulders slumped forward. He hated seeing her like this, hated not being able to make the journey more tolerable for her, and hated that she didn't trust him enough to share whatever burden she bore.

'We'll make camp soon, lass.'

She nodded, and in her eyes he saw relief.

Two miles on and Lachlan deviated off the path, leading them both into the protection of dense woodland. They reined in their horses, and he pointed to a stone structure almost completely shrouded in vegetation.

''Tis where we'll spend the night, lass.'

'An old farmhouse?'

'Nae. 'Twas once a house of prayer and worship.' He pointed to the south side of the building. 'There. Do ye see the graveyard beneath that cathedral of trees?'

Remnants of tombstones jutted out from the earth like broken, decaying teeth. Not one of them stood straight. Other headstones lay fractured among the tall grass.

'I see it,' she said. 'Those burial stones look ancient.'

'As is the church.'

'You've sheltered here before?'

'Aye.'

Lachlan dismounted, assisted Helene in doing the same, and then tethered the horses to a tree. 'Wait here while I check 'tis safe to go inside.'

He approached the entrance, where mangled rusty hinges hung limp from the timeworn stone. The wooden door had long ago disappeared, perhaps stolen and used on another dwelling, or pilfered as firewood to warm someone's hearth.

Lachlan ducked his head beneath the low archway and crossed the threshold. Inside, his gaze made a wide sweep of the empty building's two-cell structure with its small chancel.

Several birds, startled by his presence, took flight through narrow, paneless windows in the walls. Through those windows and the building's entrance, daylight illuminated the nave where once a congregation would have sat.

At one time, floorboards would have covered the hard-packed earth. They too had perhaps been repurposed. Animal droppings littered the ground here and there. Easy enough to clear away. The long grass, once cut, would soften the floor beneath his and Helene's bedding tonight.

He glanced up at the ceiling, still intact, and gave a nod of thanks to the medieval stonemasons who'd built the church. Tonight, Helene would sleep with a rock-solid roof over her head.

Lachlan stepped outside to see Helene rubbing her hand in one spot over her horse's shoulder. It put its head forward and down and exhaled a deep, fluttering breath through its nostrils. A response akin to a sigh.

'I see ye ken how to relax the horse.'

'I do. Something our stable hand taught me as a child when I learned to ride.'

'Well, ye keep doing what ye're doing,' he said with a smile. 'I'm sure the horse's muscles are as sore as ours after another day's ride.'

'I'll go fetch them a drink if there's water nearby,' she offered, still massaging her horse's shoulder.

'There's a brook a wee way into the woods over there.' He pointed. 'I'll come with ye.'

'That's not necessary. I'm sure I'll have no trouble finding it.'

Lachlan took this as her way of requesting privacy to tend to her needs. 'All right, then. I'll unsaddle the horses and prepare our camp inside the church.'

She merely nodded and retrieved two empty waterskins.

'When ye return we'll water the horses, and then I'll refill the skins, aye?'

She nodded again without looking at him and set off in the direction of the brook.

Lachlan watched her retreating. She'd grown quieter with each passing day, more withdrawn, and seemingly lost to her own thoughts. If only he could remove her oppressive cloak of sadness and raise a smile to her face.

☙

The rippling sound of water led Helene like a compass in the direction of the brook. The snap and crunch of twigs beneath her footfalls punctuated the air, and she heard the hum of insects, the chattering of squirrels, and the ever-present symphony of birdsong. A rabbit scampered beneath the underbrush ahead of her, followed by another.

Shafts of late-afternoon sunlight speared down through the trees, casting tall shadows on the lush forest floor. There was not so much as a whisper of a breeze, so that every branch, leaf, fern, or blade of grass remained as if frozen in time.

The peace and tranquillity of her surrounds, together with a lungful of fresh air, worked its magic to lighten Helene's disturbing thoughts. Obsessive overthinking about her sister's well-being had sent her spiralling down into depression. Would she, could she, ever atone for the darkest sin of her past?

Helene cast an appreciative eye up and down the babbling brook. For a moment, she closed her eyes to its soothing sounds, then lifted her lids to observe water rush, ripple, and trickle over and in between stones and rocks of all shapes and sizes, some covered in a green carpet of iridescent moss.

Mindful of the late hour, she set about filling the waterskins and laid them down on the grass. She shrugged out of her jacket and waistcoat, placing them next to the waterskins, followed by her neckcloth and woollen bonnet. She lifted her long braid and let out a deep sigh, relishing the feel of cool air on her ears and neck.

On her knees beside the brook, she scooped up and drank handfuls of crystal-clear water. She cleansed her face and wiped her hand behind her neck and down her throat, delighting in the tingling cold liquid running down between her breasts. If not restricted by waning daylight, she'd have completely stripped off to sit in the shallows and enjoy the bracing water sluicing over her entire body.

With her chin tilted skyward, Helene exhaled another deep sigh and closed her eyes, only to flash them wide open. Something seemed amiss. Her head cocked to one side, a knot of unease in her gut. The air was not only still, but silent. Unusually silent, devoid of the trilling or high-pitched rapid notes of birds and the buzzing of winged insects. Her surrounds had fallen eerily silent, save for the rushing sounds of water.

A chill worked its way up her spine. She stood, turned about, and stared down the length of a sword, its tip two inches from her face.

Helene froze, stricken by fear.

The gap-toothed, bearded, stocky brute holding the sword's hilt leered at her with unmistakable intent.

'Well, well. What do we 'ave 'ere, then?' he drawled. Small, deep-set eyes glimpsed her clothes on the ground. His free hand pointed to the tartan woollen bonnet. 'That there ain't the likes of what we Englishmen wear, now is it?'

Frightened, she stood like the deaf mute she'd pretended to be thus far on the journey.

'It be the kind what those heathen Scotsmen wear, eh?' Glittering grey eyes raked her from head to toe. 'But you ain't no man, are you, darlin'?' He lightly traced the tip of his sword from her right temple to the corner of her mouth. 'And you're a long way from home.'

Helene's heartbeat thrashed in her ears and her mind raced.

'Well, it makes no matter what you're wearing, darlin'. It's what lies beneath that interests me.' He licked his lips and took a step back, the sword still holding her in check.

'I ain't never poked a Highland lass before, but you'll do just fine. Your shirt. Take it off.'

Lachlan! Helene screamed his name inside her head. If spoken out loud, she risked being run through with a sword. *Think.* She had to think. If she could eliminate the threat of the man's sword, she might stand a chance of escape.

'Take it off, you heathen bitch!'

The onset of an idea kept Helene calm, and it was all she could do not to outwardly react or show any understanding of his terse command. She pointed to her ears and shook her head from side to side, then to her lips and mouthed the words, *'I can't speak.'*

Comprehension dawned, and his eyes rounded like trenchers. He gave a throaty laugh, and the look he sent her was a mix of pure evil, lust, and cruel subjugation.

'Even if you could scream, there's no one about to hear you.' He laughed again. 'I'll bury me cock in you more than once, me darlin', and then some more.' The sword dropped to his feet.

Helene schooled her expression to that of a trusting innocent and prayed he would fall for her ruse.

When he lunged at her, Helene was swift to react, lifting her arms and bracing her hands against the man's shoulders. She raised her right leg and kneed him in the groin. He groaned, his shoulders falling forward. Helene followed through with an elbow to his jaw, dazing him long enough for her to turn and run. She screamed Lachlan's name, startling and sending birds bursting from the treetops.

Just when she thought herself free of her attacker, excruciating pain seared her scalp and brought her to a standstill. He'd caught and wound her braid like rope around one hand, and his free arm grabbed her about the shoulders.

'Lying sawney *bitch!* You ain't no deaf mute,' he yelled in her ear. 'I'll fuck you 'til you're dead!'

Helene took a step to her left and swung her right arm down, hitting her fist with force between his legs. He yelped in pain and loosened his grip on her shoulders.

Helene broke free of his hold, doubled over, and snatched the *sgian-dubh* from her boot. Lachlan's words reverberated in her brain. *Attack or be attacked.* She spun around, and with what strength she could muster, she thrust forward and up.

Beady eyes widened in startled surprise.

Helene let go of the blade and recoiled in horror. He glanced down to see the knife protruding from his belly. Stubby fingers curled around the bone handle and yanked the knife free of his person. Shock registered on his face, then morphed into disbelief when he stared at the bloodied blade and then at Helene. He dropped the knife and clutched his gut. Crimson stained his clothes and hands. He stumbled forward and dropped to one knee, his eyes glinting with murderous resolve.

Helene spun on her heel and ran into a wall of hard muscle.

Lachlan! Thank God! She held on to him for dear life.

However, she was mistaken, and all hope of being rescued evaporated the instant her vision focused and she stared at an unkempt bearded face with the same deep-set grey eyes as the man she'd stuck with her knife. Wearing a battered tricorne hat, he stood tall, solid in stature, and fixed a grip on her shoulders so tight she thought her bones would shatter.

Attack or be attacked! Helene spiked her knee up. He

instinctively arched back. In a counter move, she raised her fist to deliver a hook to his cheek. He caught her hand in his and laughed hot vile breath over her face.

'Feisty little Scottish scum! Think you can stick a man like a pig and get away with it? I don't think so!'

He let go of her fist and slapped her hard across the face. Helene's head snapped to one side, and she lost her balance, stumbling backwards and falling to the ground. Air whooshed from her lungs. In the time it took her to catch her breath, he'd uncinched and shed his sword belt and strode towards her.

Lacking strength to rise and run, Helene dug her heels in the ground, hands clawing the earth in a frantic effort to scuttle back and away from him.

His heavy weight fell upon her, and a futile attempt to sit up was met with a splayed hand to Helene's chest, keeping her down.

Amidst the struggle to free herself, she heard a rasping voice to her side. 'Get off her. I saw her first.'

The man straddling her barked, 'You might have seen her first, little brother, but I'll have her first. When I've had me fill, she's all yours.'

Helene heard material rip, and the forest's cool air swept over her bared chest and stomach. Terror as she'd never known it sent her arms flailing as she struggled to buck him off. He caught both her arms, brought her hands together, and restrained her wrists in one large, hard-skinned hand. With his other hand he squeezed her breast so tight it made her eyes smart.

She summoned the last of her strength to scream Lachlan's name before seeing her attacker raise his arm, fist clenched. Helene closed her eyes and braced for the blow.

A roar rent the air. A sound unlike any Helene had ever heard. It was raw, primal, and spine-tingling. Her hands were suddenly free, and the unyielding weight pinning her down lifted. She opened her eyes to see her attacker rise above her and fly unceremoniously through the air to land atop his brother's writhing body.

There, standing at her feet, was Lachlan. A sob of relief escaped her hoarse throat.

In a flurry of movement, he reached down and pulled her to her feet, drawing the opening of her shirt together and covering her breasts. Pure rage emanated from his wild eyes, in the set of his jaw, and on the hard planes of his face. Every inch the enigmatic Highland warrior, Lachlan's war cry had been as chillingly lethal as he looked.

'Kill him, brother!'

The strained, pain-laced words came from the first of Helene's abusers. He sat on the ground, hands pressed to his belly to stem the flow of blood. The second man was on his feet. His lips curled back, baring rotten yellowed teeth. He spied his brother's sword on the ground and snatched it up, snarling like a cornered animal.

Lachlan pushed Helene behind him. 'Get back!'

She ran to hide behind the wide girth of an ancient oak only to stop in her tracks and wheel around. Terror struck her anew. Lachlan was unarmed. No sword. No pistol. No dagger. How would he defend himself against the man bearing down on him with sword raised and ready to cut him down?

Helene could only watch in horror as Lachlan stood there unmoving.

As the sword came down, he drew his arms to his chest, leaped out of the way, and disarmed the man. He kicked the sword in Helene's direction and threw the man face down on the ground.

His aggressor clambered to his feet and charged at Lachlan with a grievous growl. The sickening thud of their bodies colliding forced Helene's hands to her ears, and yet she couldn't look away as Lachlan delivered blow after blow, fuelled by revenge and retaliation.

She winced at the stomach-turning sound of his fist against bone and the subsequent grunts and groans of his assailant. The man's bloodied face from a broken nose left Helene feeling nauseated.

The beating ceased and the man crumpled in a heap on the grass. Lachlan's broad back heaved from the exertion of the fight. He stared down at the man and let fly with what sounded like a damning tirade in Gaelic. The man scrambled away on his stomach as if he knew Lachlan had marked him as a dead man.

Sudden movement caught Helene's eyes, and in a twist of heart-wrenching horror, the man Helene had stabbed teetered on his feet, having retrieved the other sword. He retracted his shaking arm, poised to hurl the weapon towards his brother.

Helene screamed a warning to Lachlan. He flicked his gaze towards her. In so doing, he didn't see the exchange of swords from one man to the other.

Helene yelled, 'Behind you!'

Lachlan swivelled and sidestepped the surprise attack.

Without thought for her own safety, Helene ran with speed and swiped up the sword Lachlan had previously kicked in her direction. She tossed it towards him, and he caught the middle of the long blade in his left hand before deftly grasping the hilt in his right.

Helene glanced at the man she'd stabbed—weak and immobile on the ground—and back to the duelling pair.

The hardened, seasoned warrior in Lachlan emerged. Sparks flew with the clashing and clanging of steel. His opponent was no match for Lachlan's strength, agility, and skill with a sword. Helene held her breath and felt Lachlan's wrath with the accuracy of each strike, cut, and slash to the man's body.

She stood as if in a trance, horrified by the sight of blood and the sound of torn flesh, yet at the same time perversely satisfied to watch her attacker's imminent demise. If not for Lachlan, she'd have suffered a fate she daren't imagine. How many women before her had suffered, if not died, at the cruel hands of these vile creatures?

Lachlan delivered the final blow, skewering the sword deep into the Englishman's chest. Helene's stomach heaved at the slushy sound of punctured flesh, and again when Lachlan withdrew the sword. The man made a gurgling sound and coughed up blood before collapsing to the ground. Eyes wide. Dead.

A shout of anguish escaped his dying brother.

Lachlan flicked cold, merciless eyes on the man, who could do nothing but spray loud caustic curses at himself and Helene. Insulting, offensive, and obscene. The stream of abuse continued as Lachlan approached and stood over him with sword raised, two hands on the hilt, ready to silence him forever.

'Wait!'

Lachlan swung his gaze to Helene, confusion in his eyes.

A sudden breeze kicked up, rustling dead leaves and pine needles on the forest floor and sending a shudder of movement through the branches. Shadows from tall trees loomed larger and leaned in, like a courtroom of ghosts summoned from the past. Insects chirped, the sound resembling a rapid drum beat in sync with Helene's hammering heart.

As her eyes bored into the man on the ground, she caught the sickly scent of wood rot. She held no pity, no remorse, and no regrets for having used her *sgian-dubh* against him in self-defence. Pity her blade had missed its mark. It didn't matter—he'd die nonetheless.

She'd never hated anyone except herself, but in this moment, she felt the full force of the emotion for the bastard who railed abuse at her, at Lachlan, at Scotland. Brutal words weighted with violence, hatred, and hostility.

'Helene?'

She heard impatience and bloodlust in Lachlan's voice, knowing he waited for a sign from her, a signal, like the age-old gladiator tradition of thumbs down for death.

Calm, she stepped up to his side, took from him the sword, and plunged it deep into her attacker's heart.

Blessed silence.

'*I* had to do it, Lachlan.' Her voice was soft, faint. 'For you. For me. For every man, woman, or child whom these two lowlifes have harmed or violated.'

Tender hands covered hers. Moments after Lachlan prised her fingers free of the sword's hilt, Helene's world turned dark.

CHAPTER TWENTY-ONE

HELENE AWOKE FEELING groggy and disoriented. The dimly lit space around her carried a mixture of scents: burning wood, herbs, and grass. She heard the crack and pop of a fire and the gentle simmer of what smelled like broth. Above her, she studied a grey stone canopy, not the usual umbrella of stars and treetops to which she'd become accustomed. Soft bedding lay between her back and the ground, and a blanket covered her clothed body from the chest down.

Gradually, she pieced together the clues to place her in the present. Memories of being set upon hit with the ferocity of the attack, and she sat bolt upright. 'Lachlan!'

His arms came swiftly about her before she'd called out his name.

'Hush now. Ye're safe, *mo ghràdh*.'

She went limp with relief in his arms, and in moments, the shock of the afternoon's events took its toll. She shivered as if in the thick of winter snow, her breathing erratic. Lachlan drew her onto his lap where he sat on the floor of the old church, his back against the wall, and held her, talking to her in soothing sounds of Gaelic. The low dulcet tones of his native tongue washed over Helene like a lullaby. There she stayed until her body no longer trembled and her breathing evened out.

Lachlan. Her anchor, her shelter, her saviour. She clutched him tight, inhaling the scent of his skin through his linen shirt. There was no doubt this man, the laird of Clan MacLanoch, would remain her sworn and devout protector until delivering her safely home. Already, she mourned being separated from him. Despair and loss added weight to her sorrows. How would she get through each day without him?

'Those men. Their bodies?' Asking the question left the bitter taste of bile in her mouth.

'Disposed of.'

'I'm sorry you had to do it on your own.'

''Tis not something I'd have asked ye to do. I worry only for ye.'

Dare she hope his worry for her equated to a deeper connection, and that he yearned for her as she did him? A futile and fanciful wish. She reminded herself for the umpteenth time it could never be. Despite efforts to quash intensifying feelings for him, there was nothing to be done but resign herself to silently bewail the anguish of missed opportunities and unrequited affection.

'I'll be all right, but had you not found me when you did . . .'

His arms firmed about her. 'Aye. That those curs so much as laid a finger on ye unleashed in me blind fury such as I've ne'er ken, and to see that man atop ye, and to ken what he was about to do . . . I wanted to rip his heart out with my bare hands.'

His chest rose and fell beneath her cheek, the hammer of his heart loud against her ear. His laboured breathing and raw rage told Helene just how much her near rape affected him. She leaned into the hand he used to gently cup her cheek.

'I'm sorry I didnae get to ye before he struck ye.'

Helene lifted her head from his chest to look Lachlan in the eye. 'It's done and over with. Those men are dead! A threat to no one, and I hope they burn in the deepest, darkest depths of hell.' Her words carried the venom of her conviction.

'Aye. That they will.' His thumb caressed her jawline.

They eyed each other in silence for a time.

He raised a brow. 'Ye're quite the feisty warrior, ye ken? Any Highlander would be proud to fight alongside ye.'

She smiled up at him. 'I learned from the best.'

He stared at her with curious intensity. In the next instant, as if remembering himself, he removed her from his lap to seat her on the bedding. 'Best ye cover yersel' with this,' he said, handing her the blanket.

Helene took it from him and looked down to see her shirt agape, with her breasts almost completely exposed. She shuddered with the memory of her attacker having ripped her shirt open. She hastily tucked the blanket beneath her armpits and accepted the bowl of broth Lachlan offered her.

''Tis slim pickings tonight. I didnae want to go out and hunt and leave ye here on yer own.'

'Whatever this is, it smells delicious.' She brought the bowl to her lips and sipped. Her eyes closed and she hummed a sound of appreciation. 'Delicious. Thank you.'

'Yer shirt will need fixing, but I'll deal with that when ye're done eating.'

Helene sent him a quizzical look. 'Fix it? With what?'

He winked and patted the pouch on his belt. ''Tis not just tinder and flint in here, ye ken?'

'You mean, you have buttons, a needle, and thread in there?'

'Aye. Bone buttons. And 'tis nae always clothes that need stitching, but flesh wounds.'

Helene gave an approving nod. 'Resourceful.'

'Practical.'

The man never ceased to impress Helene. She sipped the broth, taking in all the preparations Lachlan had made for their night's stay inside the church. He'd set their belongings and saddles alongside one wall and had laid out their bedding. She surreptitiously watched him crouch beside the fire to feed it more wood. She assumed he'd positioned the fire just inside the church's doorless entrance to repel and ward off any curious nocturnal animals.

'Thank you for the broth,' she said, setting the bowl to one side.

'There's more if ye'd like.'

'No, thank you. That was ample.' She spied and pointed to one of the full water bladders. 'Would you mind if I were to use some water to give myself a washdown? It's just that I feel as if my skin carries the filth of . . . of . . .' She looked away, unable to meet his eyes.

'Ye needn't say it, lass. I understand.' Lachlan stood, took up the water vessel, and placed it on the floor in the derelict chancel. 'Ye've enough firelight here, and I'll turn away to give ye privacy. In the meantime, I'll mend yer shirt while ye tend to yersel'. Hand it to me when ye're ready.' He sat down before the fire with his back to her.

Helene removed all her clothes and drew the blanket about her. She padded over to Lachlan and gave him her shirt, then picked up her neckcloth and returned to the chancel. She set the blanket down within easy reach and, standing naked, glanced over her shoulder to see Lachlan open the leather pouch and take from it a needle and thread.

She was surprised how comfortable and at ease she was standing naked in his presence. Perhaps because she knew him to be a man of his word and he would not turn to peek or take advantage of her in so vulnerable a state. Unabashedly, she wished he'd do so.

Multiple times she drenched the neckcloth with water, scrubbing the material over her face, neck, and washing her body all over. As she did so, her thoughts turned inward. Melancholic. Disconsolate. How ironic that she found herself in God's holy house wishing to be cleansed of having been sinned against, and of committing her own sins, the worst of which was taking a life, even if it was to protect her own. Purgatory awaited her. Of this, she was sure.

And then there was Prudence. How many times over the years, to no avail, had Helene clasped her hands in prayer, begging God's forgiveness? Begging Him to restore her beloved sister's health so that Prudence might lead the life she, and not Helene, deserved. Right now, Helene felt as empty and as abandoned as this building. How she longed to escape this hopeless sense of despair and loneliness, if only for a brief time. Lachlan had made her forget once before. Might he do so again?

'Yer shirt is ready when ye are.'

Firelight cast Helene's naked silhouette against the wall. She eyed it for a moment and, arriving at a decision, untied the leather thong binding her braid. Slender fingers combed the long wavy hair, fanning it out across her back. 'I'm ready.'

Lachlan's sharp gasp reached her loud and clear. The ensuing silence was punctuated by a whinny from one of their horses tethered outside, the piping notes of a common nightingale, and the hiss of a log fallen in the fire.

Helene waited in the hope he'd come to her, that he'd appease her longing for the comfort of his touch.

Another prayer went unanswered. Defeated, her chin fell to her chest only to lift again when the feel of linen touched her back.

Firm hands settled on her arms, and Lachlan's breath on the nape of her neck sent a shiver down her spine. Helene turned her head slightly to the side and raised one hand to cover his.

His voice came in a tremulous, hoarse whisper. 'I shall leave ye to button up yer shirt.'

'No!' Helene turned and slid his hand down to cup her breast. His large, warm palm seared her skin with the greatest of pleasure. 'No,' she repeated in softer tones.

He sucked in a breath. 'Helene.'

She heard strained emotion in his gravelly voice, but still she held his hand firm against her, unwilling to let him go. 'Have you forgotten my promise to you? I'm offering you your reward for taking me home.'

His gaze lifted from her breast to her eyes. 'Lass, the promise of bedding ye is nae the reason I agreed to see ye home.' He removed his hand from beneath hers.

'Then why?' The sting of rejection tinged her voice.

Lachlan bent to the blanket and concealed her modesty.

'I dinnae ken the reason for yer father's summons, but I daresay *ye* do. Bargaining away yer virtue for the sake of fast returning home made me realise how desperate ye were to oblige him. It was for that reason, and that reason only, that I agreed to make this solo journey with ye.'

The confession took Helene by surprise. She had indeed thought Lachlan to be first and foremost a libertine. *Fool!* She should have known better. Shamefaced, she said, 'My apologies. I believed it was only because of the offer to bed me that you agreed to escort me home. I've sorely misjudged you. Forgive me.'

'Och, Helene. Surely ye ken I care about ye and yer welfare. It's nae secret something troubles ye and that ye carry a burden ye're unwilling to share. I wish to help ye, if ye'll let me. I promise to listen, and I'll not judge ye, as ye've judged me.'

She deserved his reproof, but her heart broke listening to his softly spoken words, rich with understanding. Guilt formed a lump in her throat, preventing Helene from speaking. He turned away, no doubt because of her silence. Her gaze followed his retreating back as he seated himself in front of the fire, arms drawn around bent knees, head slightly bowed.

He'd left his family and clan to accommodate *her* needs, to go above and beyond for *her*, and without question. She'd given him nothing in return. She at least owed him an explanation. They were in God's house, despite its state of ruin and disrepair, and so it seemed fitting that, if she was going to bare her soul to Lachlan, then here, now, was the right place to repent the unvarnished truth.

Helene moved forward, each step heavy with guilt. She settled down beside Lachlan, her body and limbs concealed beneath her shirt and the blanket. She stared into the fire, inhaled a deep breath, and finally found her voice.

'I have a younger sister,' she began. 'Her name is Prudence.'

A pause and another deep breath. 'I was ten years old, and she eight. We quarrelled over a doll. Prudence grabbed it from me and ran from my bedchamber. I gave chase and caught her on the landing just beyond the staircase.' Another long pause. 'I prised open her hands and took from her the doll. She hit me.' Helene heard the quaver in her voice. 'I retaliated with a shove and . . . and turned my back on her to walk away.'

Helene's stomach churned with gut-wrenching remorse, tears banking behind her eyes. 'Prudence screamed. I glanced over my shoulder to see her tumble down the stairs. I heard her head smack the floor below and saw her lying in a little crumpled heap. Unmoving. Lifeless.'

Her voice cracked with the pain of reliving the past, and

her trembling shoulders curled over her chest. Lachlan's arms came about her, drawing her to his side.

'It all happened so quickly,' she said, her voice rising with the panic of that fateful day. 'I never meant to be so cruel to my sister.' Her pitch rose another degree. 'I never meant to harm her!'

'There now, lass. 'Tis not in yer nature to harm anyone or anything.'

'But I did harm her, and she's never been the same since.'

'She lives?'

'Yes, but the accident caused irreversible damage.'

'How so?'

'Without warning, her body convulses. Her arms and legs jerk uncontrollably, after which she is left tired and confused. The condition deprived her of a normal childhood and has completely ruined her life. She has no real friends to speak of, and no prospects of marriage and bearing children of her own.'

Helene's body quaked with repressed sobs after having purged from herself the dark stain of her unforgivable deed.

'Take yer time, lass. Nae need to rush the telling of it all.'

Helene accepted a cup of water from Lachlan and took two swallows. She was grateful for his steadying arms about her. No one, not even her mother when she was alive, had sought to console the distress of her guilt and suffering the way Lachlan did now. Helene had accepted full blame for her actions. It was her burden. Her cross to bear for the rest of her life.

She pulled herself together, ready to divulge further details. 'After the accident, friends and polite society were ignorant as to the cause and severity of her condition. They were led to believe Prudence was born with a weak constitution and that it was the family's physician who recommended her condition was best suited to fresh air and a quiet life with a distant cousin residing in the country.

'In truth, Prudence was removed to the country to be cared for by a childless couple who raised her as their own. Not only did my father pay them handsomely to keep quiet about my sister's identity, but he provided them ample financial support to care for and raise Prudence. As the years went by, my sister became the forgotten child. Society stopped asking about her, and the family never mentioned her to others. My father believed it was for the best. Out of sight, out of mind as it were.'

'Did ye not visit yer sister? I ask with nae censure, but rather, curiosity.'

'Yes, but after my mother died, those visits became less frequent. Father always claimed business matters consumed his time, and it was a trial to get my brother to chaperone me.'

Helene took another sip of water. 'I've written to Prudence almost every day since she first relocated to the country. Her letters weren't as forthcoming as mine. I'd plead in my letters for her to reply, but I sometimes wondered if her silence was deliberate.'

'Why would ye think that?'

'Perhaps it was her way of punishing me for what I did to her. For ruining her life. If that was her only reason, then I cannot blame her.' Helene drank the last of the water and set the cup down.

'The last eight months have seen her condition worsen. Her episodes have become more frequent and severe in nature. It reached a point where the aging couple could no longer provide the proper care and attention for my sister, and so Father was forced to seek alternate accommodation.'

'I ken 'tis not my place to say, but yer sister should be with family. Surely yer father could arrange for qualified and discreet carers to be always with her. Like a lady's companion.'

Helene made a snort of disgust. 'I begged him to do exactly as you suggest. I begged him to let me learn how to deal with and manage her condition. After all, I am her sister, and the cause of her affliction. I argued it was only right I be the one to devote my life to her.'

'And he wouldnae hear of it?'

She shook her head. 'Neither would my brother. They said if anyone, including servants—because they spread gossip faster than the Great Fire of London—were to encounter Prudence during one of her episodes, it would bring such shame and disgrace upon the family as to risk all of us being ostracized by society and the beau monde.

'My father is of the opinion that no one of sound mind would choose to associate with—let alone marry and breed with—myself or my brother if they knew we have a sister who is afflicted with the falling sickness. It's a condition whereby others, in their ignorance, believe that person to be insane and possessed by the devil. Better Prudence remain forgotten, he said, and out of sight.

'I even suggested I reside with Prudence and her foster parents. My father quashed that idea too. He's determined to marry me off, but I've refused every suitor he's pushed my way. I'll dedicate my life to no one but Prudence.'

'Might I ask where yer sister resides now?'

The heat of anger and stomach-dropping nausea thickened Helene's throat. If those parting images of Prudence traumatised Helene now as they had done at the time, how must poor Prudence be feeling? Helene could not begin to fathom her sister's condition and state of mind.

'The day before I left for Scotland, Prudence was taken to Bethlem Royal Hospital in London.'

Helene felt every muscle in Lachlan's body lock. Did he share her outrage at the injustice of her sister's plight?

'She's neither mentally nor criminally unwell,' Helene explained. 'She suffers from a brain disfunction that occurs at random, but she is not dangerous, nor would she harm anyone.'

Whatever Lachlan thought of Helene, her wrongdoing towards Prudence, or the situation at hand, he did not pull away, but instead continued to hold her close. For that, Helene was eternally grateful, for if ever she needed his strength and moral support, it was now.

'And what do ye surmise from yer father's missive about wanting ye home?'

Helene swallowed. 'I fear something terrible has befallen Prudence. Or worse.' She sniffed back more tears and choked out, 'I promised her I'd return and free her from that madhouse. I promised her we'd make a life somewhere together, no matter how quiet or simple a life it might be. I must fulfil that promise. I will *not* abandon her to live out her days in that madhouse!'

Lachlan dropped a kiss on the crown of her head. 'Ken ye this, lass. With or without yer father's permission, I'll ensure yer sister is released forthwith from that hell-hole of an asylum. And if yer father will not have Prudence cared for in her rightful home, then ye and yer sister have a home at Drumocher.'

His unexpected words, spoken with promise and steely determination, were Helene's humble undoing. She buried her face in her hands and wept.

'Dinnae cry, *mo chridhe*. All will be well.'

She looked up at him and shook her head vigorously. If she was going to confess all her sins, then she must tell Lachlan about the bargain she'd struck with Cuthbert. 'There's more,' she blurted. 'I've used and deceived you and your family in the worst possible way.'

'Hush now, *mo ghràdh*.' Lachlan turned his body towards her, cupping her face between his palms.

Helene tried again to speak the truth, only to be silenced with his thumb pressed gently to her lips. Soft kisses rained down on her head, her forehead, and her temples. Her eyelids fluttered closed. She revelled in his touch as his lips, like the soft beat of a butterfly's wings, kissed her tear-stained cheeks.

His mouth shifted to where a teardrop collected in the groove between her nose and the downward arch of her cupid's bow. There, he paused for the space of several heartbeats before brushing his lips over hers in a chaste kiss.

From somewhere in the grip of giddy sensation, Helene heard him say her name on a ragged breath. Before she could muster clarity of mind, his lips covered hers. She came alive, and like the release of a lock with the turning of a key, her mouth opened to him and welcomed the velvety touch of his tongue.

The kiss deepened and elicited from Helene a whimper of pleasure. His response, a groan, came as did the rumblings of the thunderstorm that had thrown them together in the rock crevice.

When suddenly he broke the kiss, any fear Helene had of him doubting what he'd just started, vanished the moment she opened her eyes to stare into his. The insight she gleaned from eyes flecked with gold and brown was that they mirrored her unsated desires.

Lachlan's chest rose and fell with quickening breaths, and he looked to be a man who would not deny his needs. He proved Helene right by possessively taking hold of her shoulders, slanting his lips over hers and kissing her with urgent fervour. She kissed him back, untutored in the art of seducing a man with her mouth, yet eager to follow his lead when he kissed her deeply, greedily, and with ravenous voracity.

Helene pressed her hands to his chest, and with fingers splayed, she traced the shifting wall of muscle beneath his shirt. Freeing the buttons, she tugged the shirttails from his breeches, and assisted him in shrugging it off. Another groan escaped Lachlan when she locked her hands behind his neck and pressed her breasts to his heated skin. His chest expanded beneath her, after which he raised his head and they drew breath in unison.

Before Helene could exhale, he'd lifted her onto his lap, sitting face-to-face, legs straddling him, her hands latched to his upper arms. She didn't care or know at what point the blanket and her shirt had slipped from her shoulders. All she knew and triumphed in was the wonder of being held by Lachlan, his hard thighs beneath her, his formidable body at her fingertips.

She dropped her head back and to the side, giving way to hot kisses across her shoulder, collarbone, and the dip at the base of her throat.

One hand supported her spine, and with the other he cupped her breast. Long fingers traced the pigmented skin surrounding her nipple before taking the hardened bud between thumb and forefinger and using enough pressure to fan the fire of excitement in Helene.

His mouth closed over her nipple, escalating desire with each sensuous glide of his tongue, alternately circling and flicking the taut peak.

His attentions turned to the other breast, first filling his palm with its soft weight, then using his thumb pad in an evocative caress across its hardened peak. Helene drew in a shaky breath, desire rising another notch when he paid homage to that breast as he'd done with the other.

Tangible awareness heightened with the exploration of hands caressing the dip of her waist, the sensitive curve of her hips, the swell of her bottom. One long finger slid deep into her soft centre. Her mouth fell open on an aroused sigh and her nails sank into Lachlan's shoulders. Her hips rocked slowly of their own volition, the movement primal, instinctive, seeking to satisfy the urgent ache inside her. His finger slid deeper and then withdrew, the rhythm in keeping with the tilt of her hips moving back and forth. Mimicking the act of intercourse drove Helene mad. She wanted him, needed him inside her.

Heavy eyelids lifted to study Lachlan. Firelight glanced off the hard-edged planes of his face, the breadth of his shoulders, the muscles in his arms, and the dusting of dark hair on his chest. Leashed desire, yet to be liberated, glowed in dark-amber eyes.

Keen frustration set Helene's body on fire. 'Lachlan. I want—'

'Aye, lass. All in good time.' His words were a breathy whisper against her throat.

He lifted her off his lap and laid her down gently on her back atop the softness of blanketed bedding. When he rose to his feet, Helene made a cry of protest, thinking he was going to abandon her, that he'd had a sudden change of heart. Instead, he divested himself of his boots and remaining clothes.

Helene's breath hitched. She stared up at him and drank in every inch of his nakedness in the fire's glow. He was all beautiful lean, hard muscle. She'd seen him naked from the waist up before, but when her gaze stopped dancing over the contoured muscles of his lower abdomen, his lean hips, and powerful thighs, it came to rest on that part of his anatomy so proudly hard, thick, and erect.

Lachlan MacLanoch was a virile vision of what could

only be more potent and powerful than the most stimulating aphrodisiac.

And yet, Helene acknowledged her moment of indecision. How on earth would or *could* her body accommodate him? She tore her gaze away to stare up at him and saw in his eyes he'd understood her concern. He made no further advance upon her. Helene knew, without question, he gave over to her the power of consent. Commit or abstain.

She parted her legs for him.

In a heartbeat, he dropped to his knees. 'Trust me, Helene.'

'With my life.' She gasped when he lowered and settled his face between her legs and pressed his mouth to her mound.

She tensed in shock with the first lave of his tongue against her soft folds. With the second and successive caresses, sensation struck with more force than a bolt of lightning. Strong, sharp, mind-melting.

Helene threaded her fingers through his hair, torn between pushing him away and experiencing the exquisite pleasure of him having draped her knees over his shoulders and trailing kisses up and down her inner thighs.

Between ragged breaths and her swirling senses, she decided on the latter. To savour Lachlan's expertise and experience all he had to give. To enjoy the set of his mouth once again on her swollen flesh, pleasuring her with intimate kisses and the gentle swirling of his tongue against her sensitive nubbin.

Again and again, he introduced her to new levels of sensation, laving at the entrance to her core, filling her with his tongue, pressing intimate kisses to delicate folds. He took her quivering body higher, to a fever pitch, and when he drew her back, sensation receding, he'd once again elevate her pleasure with each explicit touch, caress, and kiss.

Abruptly, he changed tack and trailed kisses from one side of her belly to the other, circling her navel with his tongue and sending her senses into a frenzy. He forged a path between the valley of her breasts, then suckled each peaked nipple. She twisted and writhed beneath him until his body pressed lightly down upon hers, his hips between her thighs.

He silenced her soft moans with gentle kisses, and she tasted her essence on his lips and tongue. In that same moment, he rose above her, arms straightened with his hands planted on the bedding either side of her. He pressed her thighs wide, and she felt the heat of his sex nudge where his tongue had probed.

Lachlan broke the kiss to stare down at her. Their gazes locked. She was wet with wanting, and when he nudged a little harder, Helene felt the intimate intrusion of the rounded head slip inside. She gasped and gripped his forearms.

'Take a deep, slow breath, *mo chridhe*.'

She did, the action giving her focus, and when she exhaled and her body relaxed fractionally, he inched further inside her. Another deep breath, another exhale, and he sank a little deeper. He withdrew and slowly re-entered her. Helene could feel her body stretch and adjust to receive him, her maidenhead the only barrier.

The repeated manoeuvre cost Lachlan. Helene could see it in his strained features, and she could feel the tension in his body and in the rigid muscles of his forearms. He seemed to battle for control against rushing the act or hurting her, but she knew that with pain comes pleasure.

'Do it now,' she whispered.

On the heels of her words came Lachlan's powerful thrust. He breached her, sheathing himself deep inside. Sharp pain lanced through Helene and she cried out, eyes clenched. Her body tensed. Inner muscles locked around his hard length. Light kisses fell upon her lips as she adjusted to the enthralling feeling of her body joined with Lachlan's.

He drew back. 'There'll be nae more pain now, lass. Only pleasure.'

Helene's eyes blinked open. He was right. The pain had passed, and in its place she felt his throbbing heat inside her. All tension ebbed from her body. With her gaze trapped in his, Lachlan eased himself slowly from her before sliding home inch by inch. Helene moved and matched the age-old rhythm.

Pleasure bloomed with the urgency building between them. Helene's soft moans grew louder, her breathing ragged. There came a point when she could take no more. If she could say so, she'd beg for her release. No sooner did she think it than Lachlan delivered one final thrust to tip her over a precipice, where she flew free.

Her body spasmed in shuddering waves. Intensity of sensation, in all its colours, ran its course. Only when the last tremor abated did she register Lachlan's guttural groan as he lost himself inside her.

CHAPTER TWENTY-TWO

LACHLAN AWOKE TO the sound of birdsong. Dawn's soft light filtered through the church entrance and window slits. He gazed down at Helene sleeping on her side, sated, soft, warm, and peacefully languid in his arms. He studied the long sweep of eyelashes against her sun-kissed cheek and marvelled at the stark contrast of midnight-coloured hair spilling over her pale-skinned shoulder and down her back. One small hand rested on his chest, and a long, lithe leg lay across his thigh. The lass was nothing short of womanly perfection.

Their intimacy had been prodigious and to the point of stealing Lachlan's breath, as it did even now just thinking about it. He'd made her body sing, responsive to his every kiss, touch, and caress, and when they'd both left this mortal plane in a sunburst of ecstasy, it was, for him, an experience comparable to no other.

He craved so much more for her, and from her. Sexual pleasures to be enjoyed were boundless, and he yearned to be her only tutor. He wanted her for the rest of his life, to explore and discover together limitless passion.

She stirred in his arms, sighed, and nuzzled her cheek against his chest. Her hand shifted, with delicate fingers splayed over his beating heart.

So subtle and simple were her soft sounds and movements that they shook Lachlan to the core. Emotion gripped him and galvanised the true depth of what it was he felt for Helene. In that moment of clear mindful focus, he acknowledged it for what it was.

He hadn't realised it at the time, but it was while making love *to* her that he'd acknowledged his love *for* her. He was in love with Lady Helene Beckett, and by God, he'd do whatever was necessary to prove himself worthy of her and to win her hand in marriage.

And yet, her life was complex enough without him complicating it further. Declaring his true feelings for Helene and wishing to whisk her away to the Highlands must wait. There was no point professing his love for her until they reached London and matters were resolved with her father and sister.

By way of courtesy and respect, he resolved to do the right thing by her father and ask the earl's permission to marry Helene. Ultimately, it would be her decision. He'd extend the invitation to have Prudence cared for and live with the MacLanochs at Drumocher. It would be cruel to separate the sisters either side of the border.

Lachlan didn't anticipate any objections on the earl's behalf, given the man was intent on sequestering Prudence away from gossip-mongers, believing they'd smite his reputation and social standing.

Quiet reflection in the wee hours of the morning clarified for Lachlan the whys and wherefores of Helene's actions and opinions during her stay in the Highlands. He recalled her overprotective instincts in the way she'd stepped in to champion Donnie, thinking him helpless and unsupported by his family and the clan; her cynical views on the institution of marriage and why she'd spurned multiple suitors, insisting she had no need of a husband and bairns; her offhand comment after she nearly drowned, saying her father would have one less female to worry about. She'd told Cuthbert she was spoken for. By that, Lachlan could only assume she'd meant her life and future belonged to Prudence. Now it all made sense.

Christ! The lass was sabotaging and sacrificing her own happiness and prospects in favour of her sister's. She was looking to atone for ruining her sister's life.

Lachlan suddenly felt the pull of Helene's gaze upon him, and he glanced down to see sadness in her eyes. His heart sank, fearing the worst.

'What is it, lass?' When she didn't respond, he asked, 'Do ye have regrets about last night?'

She sat bolt upright. 'No!' The blanket fell to pool about her waist, exposing creamy breasts. 'No. What we shared . . . What you did for me, *to* me, made me feel . . .' Her cheeks coloured and she averted her gaze. The deep rosy blush was enough to have Lachlan believe she'd enjoyed their union, as had he.

'What then?' he gently prompted.

'Last night, before we . . . I tried to . . . There's more I must tell you.'

'Go on.'

She hesitated before pulling the blanket up to cover her nakedness. 'I'm sorry. I'm so very sorry, Lachlan. I've used and deceived you and your family to my own end. In being completely forthcoming with the truth, I must mention your cousin Cuthbert. You see, he and I . . . we . . .' Again, she looked away and swallowed.

It pained Lachlan to see on her face and hear in her voice deep despair. He didn't doubt for one moment her genuine remorse. He took her chin gently between his thumb and forefinger and coaxed her to look at him. 'Lass, I ken about ye and Cuthbert.'

Her eyebrows rose above wide-opened eyes. 'You do?'

'Aye.'

'How?'

Lachlan's hand fell from her chin to settle reassuringly on her arm. 'It was Cuthbert who told me, but only after I forced the truth, *his* truth, from him.'

'When?' she stammered. 'How long have you known?'

'Late that night when we returned from the shielings, I saw Cuthbert at yer bedchamber door.'

Rage and intense jealousy surged with the memory of that moment, then died just as quickly in knowing Cuthbert was neither a threat nor a rival in Lachlan's hopeful pursuit of Helene. He kept his emotions at bay and voiced only the facts.

'I saw something pass from his hands to yers. Naturally, I was disturbed by the mysterious and improper timing of yer encounter. I had Cuthbert meet me by the loch early the next morning, whereupon I called him out on the matter. At first, he refused to engage, but when I threatened to confront and interrogate *ye*, he changed his tune to spare ye any embarrassment.'

She looked sheepish. 'What did he tell you?'

'That ye both struck a deal with me as yer pawn, each with yer own personal agenda.'

'Did he say what he'd hoped to achieve by entering the bargain?'

'Aye.'

'And?'

Lachlan watched her gently bite her lower lip, and something akin to hope brightened the hue of her emerald eyes. 'His revelations earned him a fist to his face.'

Her chin dipped to her chest. Curiously, Lachlan caught the hint of a bitter smile.

She met his gaze. 'It was *you* who struck Cuthbert? Not one of the two clansmen with whom you met to settle an apparent grievance?'

Lachlan raised a brow, and it took a few moments before understanding dawned in Helene's eyes.

'I see,' she said. 'You and Cuthbert were the two clansmen.'

'Aye. 'Twas a heated discussion between us, and I lost my temper. All is now amicably resolved.'

'Then you know about the promissory note?'

Lachlan sat up beside her. 'Aye, lass. A sum to equal yer dowry, nae doubt. Cuthbert revealed his truth; now trust me enough to tell me yers.'

Shamefaced, she said, 'I have no money of my own, so what I did, I did for Prudence. My intention was to bribe one of the asylum wardens with a handsome amount of coin so that he'd turn a blind eye long enough for me to escape with my sister. I was going to have a carriage waiting to take us to a little rented cottage deep in the country where we could live a simple life. A safe life. A *happy* life.'

Lachlan heard fierce determination in her voice, and her admission about the reason for the promissory note slid the final piece of the puzzle into place. It took courage and temerity to devise and want to execute such a plan, and to hold blind faith in the hope of seeing it through to the end. Deception aside, Lachlan loved Helene even more for her selfless intentions.

'So ye planned to run away?'

She bowed her head. 'Yes, I suppose I did.'

'It wouldnae have taken long for yer father to track ye down.'

'I know, but desperate times call for desperate measures,

and I can*not* leave my sister to the mercy of sadistic doctors who might subject her to all kinds of inhumane treatment. She is not mad. She is not a lunatic. When Cuthbert came to me with his proposal, I saw an opportunity and I named my price. I am not proud of what I've done to you and your family, and I pray Agnes remains in the dark about it all. She is my one true and trusted friend.'

Lachlan took both her hands in his and paused for a moment. 'Helene, I must ask, if yer plan was to succeed, who would ye turn to when the money runs out? Yer father? Yer brother? Or given what ye've discovered of Cuthbert's intimate personal affairs, would ye again use the threat of blackmail?'

Her head snapped up, and Lachlan clasped her hands tight when she tried to pull free of him. 'I'm verra sorry, Helene, but Cuthbert is family, so ye'll understand why I asked the latter.'

She raised her chin a fraction. 'I suffer the shame of having taken advantage of you and your family, and for coercing Cuthbert to hand over the promissory note. I did what I had to, but I swear to you I'd find another way to support Prudence and myself before I'd extort money from Cuthbert or anyone known to him.'

It distressed Lachlan to consider, if push came to shove, just what extreme Helene was prepared to go to if she did have to keep herself and Prudence safe and financially secure. He dismissed the concern, for he'd gladly settle on being their benefactor, anonymous or otherwise, if his plans for the sisters went awry.

'Thank ye, Helene. Unmasking Cuthbert could send him to prison or the gallows. If ye were responsible for that, I couldnae forgive ye, but I do forgive ye, and I understand why ye and Cuthbert did what ye did. Yers and his scheming was not born of malicious intent, but rather a need to do what ye thought best for someone else.'

Lachlan took her face gently between the palms of his hands and pressed a kiss on her lips. 'Ye're one remarkable woman, ye ken?' She smiled and his heart flipped.

'A woman, after last night, yes, but remarkable? I hardly think so.'

Her lips compressed together in an expression of holding something back. Lachlan debated over whether to suggest she speak her mind, deciding against it when she abruptly rose to her feet, gathered up her clothes, and dressed.

He followed her cue, mindful of her agitated brush strokes before she plaited her long hair and hid it beneath her woollen bonnet.

'Helene, we'll soon be encountering other travellers, so I'll need to replace our bonnets for English civilian hat wear. I'll situate ye in a safe place before we leave the cover of the woodland, and I'll make a trip into a local village to acquire us each a cocked hat. I'll purchase food supplies to last us the next two days until we reach London.'

She nodded her thanks and set about packing away their bedding.

Lachlan extinguished what was left of the fire's smouldering embers and cleared the ground of debris. Together, they left the abandoned church, belongings in hand, and Lachlan saddled and readied the horses for the day's journey. 'I'll go and refill the waterskins. Would ye like to come with me?'

'No, I'll stay with the horses. I'll be safe enough here.'

'Aye, well, I willnae be long, then.'

Lachlan made haste with fetching water. Just before he stepped clear of the woodland, he caught sight of Helene holding and staring down at a sheet of parchment. He waited, watching her fold and wrap the parchment in a square of thin leather. She then placed it in a pocket inside her coat and secured the buttons.

What he'd witnessed, and recognised, gave Lachlan pause. Did Helene still intend cashing in the promissory note? Perhaps she didn't think him sincere when he'd offered her and Prudence sanctuary at Drumocher? She'd have no need of Cuthbert's money, unless her intent was to stick to her original plan. Lachlan's heart felt as if it were shrinking. He walked free of the clearing. By the time he reached Helene, she'd pulled from her outer coat pocket a small, familiar-looking woven bag. She loosened the drawstring and took a whiff of its contents.

Lachlan tied the waterskins to each saddle. 'What do ye have there?'

'Herbs with which to make tea in the hope of remedying anxiety. Mairi gave them to me.'

'For ye?'

'Prudence.'

Her answer took him by surprise. 'Ye told her about yer sister?'

'No. When I realised Mairi was so knowledgeable with herbal medicine, I spoke to her of a friend in need.'

'I see. That friend being Prudence.'

'Yes.'

Lachlan couldn't bear seeing Helene looking so forlorn. 'Lass, if ye dinnae mind, I'd like to suggest we go directly to my uncle's house and—'

'You mean Viscount Sutton?'

'Aye.'

Lachlan's hand rasped over the stubble on his chin. He hadn't shaved in two days, having used the last of his soap. 'It would give us the opportunity to bathe and dress in fresh clothes. Ye're about the same size as Agnes, so ye can help yersel' to her garments. Her maids will attend ye. I'll attire myself from Cuthbert's wardrobe. Depending on our arrival time, we could then go directly to Bethlem. I'll deal with the administrators and get Prudence discharged. We can either take yer sister to the safety of my uncle's house, or we can return to yer home and to yer father.'

Helene's eyebrows drew together, and she shook her head. 'I know you mean well, and I thank you, but no.'

'Why not, lass?'

'Any association with my sister and her controversial illness is enough to damage your uncle, his family, and his family's good name. I will not be party to that. To do so would destroy Agnes's future, and Cuthbert's. I've destroyed one life. That's enough. It's best I go straight to my father to find out why he sent for me. Afterwards, I'll freshen up and deliver on my promise to free Prudence from that madhouse.'

'And if yer father forbids it?'

Helene raised her chin in defiance. 'Then I won't just threaten Father with exposing our family secret, I'll see it through.' She turned from Lachlan, slid a foot in the stirrup, and mounted up.

'I dinnae ken the full extent of what yer father is capable of, but if ye threaten him with that, he has the power to consign *ye* to Bethlem too.'

Lachlan's words caused Helene to visibly shudder. He rested his hand over hers holding the reins. 'For that reason, I'll face yer father with ye and not leave yer side, unless safe to do so.'

CHAPTER TWENTY-THREE

IT WAS LATE morning, midweek, when Helene arrived with Lachlan on the doorstep of her father's Grosvenor Square residence. Grayson, the usually unflappable, portly butler of senior years, turned a ghostly pallor when Helene tipped her hat high enough for him to see her face. With raised brows, he promptly stepped aside to allow them entry, knowing better than to ask questions, and quickly closed the door in fear of the landed gentry spying the Earl of Penforth's daughter masquerading as a man.

'Welcome home, Lady Helene.'

'Thank you, Grayson. I have with me the laird of Clan MacLanoch.'

Grayson bowed to Lachlan. 'Laird, I am at your service. May I take your hat and'—Grayson looked pointedly at Helene's and Lachlan's sword belts—'weaponry?'

'Aye, we dinnae wish to bear arms during an audience with Lord Penforth.'

'On the contrary,' said Helene, giving Lachlan a sidelong glance, 'it might not be a bad thing.' She removed her hat, releasing her hidden hair, which flopped down her back in one long braid.

Grayson took their hats in one hand and had them drape

their belts with weaponry over his free arm. 'Did you arrive with any luggage, Lady Helene?'

'Only what's secured to our saddles. Please bring those items in and have a groom attend the horses. They need a rubdown, feeding, and the best of care.'

'Consider it done.'

Without preamble, Helene asked, 'Is Father home?'

'Lord Penforth is in the library.'

Something in the butler's eyes and in his tone frayed Helene's nerves. 'Grayson, is everything all right?'

'That's not for me to say, Lady Helene.'

The long-serving butler could always be counted upon to be diplomatic. In this instance, his response rattled Helene to the bone. She swung her gaze across the hall towards the library.

'Shall I bring you some refreshments?' said Grayson.

'Not just yet, thank you. I must speak privately with my father.'

'As you wish.' Grayson bowed in his customary deferential manner and made himself scarce.

'This way,' Helene said to Lachlan.

They both garnered gaping stares from two passing servants who'd be all too keen to send tongues wagging below stairs. It made no matter to Helene. What set her on edge was the oppressive atmosphere in her home.

Home. How strange it was to be amongst the opulence of her father's London residence with its marble floors, chandeliers, mahogany furniture, and soft plush furnishings. She felt oddly out of place and already yearned for the wide-open spaces of the Highlands, sweeping, heather-covered moorlands and shimmering lochs.

She sent Lachlan a worried glance. He responded with an encouraging smile, affirming his moral support.

They came to a stop outside the library door.

'Are ye all right, lass?'

'No. My heart races and I can barely breathe.'

Lachlan took her hand and gave it a squeeze. 'I'm here for ye, lass. I've said it before, but I'll say it again. I willnae leave yer side unless 'tis safe to do so.'

She gave him an appreciative smile. 'Thank you. I take great comfort in having you here with me. Truly, I do.'

'Aye, well, shall we?' He rapped on the door.

'Enter.'

The deep voice reached Helene from beyond the door. She took in a deep breath, exhaled, then turned the handle and stepped inside. The latch of the door clicked as Lachlan closed it behind them. Helene saw her father in profile, seated in one of the leather wingback armchairs opposite the hearth. To her surprise, her brother, Robert, sat in the chair beside him. The men continued in muted conversation.

'What is it, Grayson?' asked her father, without troubling himself to glance over his shoulder.

Helene moved deeper into the room with Lachlan by her side. She opened her mouth to respond, but it was Lachlan who spoke first.

''Tis not yer butler.'

The assertive, commanding brogue had the two men twist their heads around to see who addressed them. In the next moment, they were on their feet. Their eyebrows rose in shock, their mouths falling open the instant they recognised Helene. Her sudden, unannounced arrival, and dressed as she was in men's garb, rendered the men speechless. Their questioning eyes darted between herself and Lachlan.

'Hello, Father.' Helene's gaze flicked to her brother, impeccably dressed as always, and sporting a fashionable wig, and yet something about him seemed off. She nodded a greeting. 'Robert.'

Helene readied herself to battle a barrage of questions, to be raked over the coals for entering and presenting herself in her father's house in such a manner as to cause scandal and self-ruination. Her spine stiffened, shoulders back, chin high. Let her father and brother come at her with their words of rebuke, but if they dared to utter one word of condemnation against Lachlan, she'd reach for her hidden *sgian-dubh* and hold it against their throats.

'What is the meaning of this?'

The indignation in Robert's voice had Lachlan take a menacing step towards him. Helene read the strategic manoeuvre for what it was. Something in her way of thinking shifted, almost throwing her off balance. From the outset, Lachlan MacLanoch had made a promise to her father to keep her safe during her stay at Drumocher and to ensure her safe return to London before summer expired. Lachlan had more than fulfilled his end of the bargain, and now it was well within his rights to leave, to walk away and return to his own family and clan in the Highlands.

And yet, here he remained. The hard set of his jaw, the tension in his body, and the closing and opening of his palms sent her father and brother a strong, clear message. He stood his ground, ready to defend and protect Helene against her own kin, just as she was preparing herself to defend him.

The realisation struck that it wasn't just deep affection she felt for the laird. No. Affection didn't even come close to qualifying her true feelings for him. It was love. She was in love with Lachlan. *I willnae leave yer side unless 'tis safe to do so.* Safe or not, Helene never wanted him to leave her side. She had no time to ponder this sudden revelation because her stomach tightened with the palpable tension in the stillness of the room.

Lachlan's gaze remained fixed on Robert. What must he be thinking, having now finally come face-to-face with her brother who'd treated her so cruelly after Prudence's accident? When Lachlan's gaze flicked to her father, his expression showed contempt for the man who'd always put self-importance and reputation before the well-being of his own flesh and blood.

Each man took the other's measure. Lachlan stood solid of stature, a head taller and with a broader back than the two men he faced. Helene glimpsed the subtle sagging of her brother's shoulders and shuffling of his feet. How satisfying it was to see her brother on the receiving end of intimidation.

Her father ventured forth, his eyes on her and with arms outstretched. Lachlan stepped aside to let him pass.

'Helene, my child.'

The words were warm and welcoming as his arms came about her. Despite having the privacy to bathe with soap alongside rivers and lochs during her journey, Helene was suddenly conscious of her clothes reeking of fires, horses, and mother earth. Whatever her father might have thought, he said nothing. His gentle embrace took her back to a time before Prudence's accident. To a time when Helene felt loved and cherished by both her parents.

When finally he pulled back, she noticed how much older he appeared. There were lines on his face she didn't remember being there before she left for Scotland. The grey in his hair seemed more prominent, and there were dark shadows under melancholy eyes. He looked to have lost weight. He used to stand tall and proud. Now, he stooped.

The dramatic change in him alarmed Helene, especially when he cupped her cheek with his warm palm and smiled in such a way as to convey fatherly affection. Something she hadn't seen or experienced from him in years. What had occurred in her absence to have brought about this marked change in him? Before she could ask, his gaze shifted to the man at her side.

'You can be no other than the MacLanoch laird.'

'Aye, Lord Penforth. I am Lachlan MacLanoch.'

Lord Penforth inclined his head. 'Thank you for bringing my daughter safely home to me.'

Her father gave a nod in Robert's direction. 'May I introduce you to my son, Robert Beckett—rather, Lord Atkins, his courtesy title.'

'Lord Atkins,' said Lachlan with a stiff nod.

'Laird,' returned Atkins.

Penforth turned to his daughter. 'The rigours of your journey would have been nothing short of a trial, in which case you'll want to freshen up and rest. While you do so, your brother and I will have time to acquaint ourselves with the laird.'

Each word her father had spoken seemed to Helene as if they'd been carefully curated. She could not accept his concern for her as genuine, nor could she understand his warm welcome, without him having yet passed judgement or uttering one word of censure about her unseemly arrival and appearance. Perhaps he was working up to it, but Helene had no time for procrastination, and she would not be a pawn in whatever game he played.

'First things first, Father. I received your missive summoning me home. Your brief words, and the way they were written, led me to believe something critical had occurred in my absence. Sending word to Fort Firth and awaiting the king's regiment to escort me home via carriage would have taken weeks and wasted time I believed I could ill afford. For that reason, I begged Lachlan for his personal escort and protection in seeing me safely home by the fastest means possible.'

Helene ignored her father's raised brow for having spoken Lachlan's name with fond familiarity. 'I am eternally grateful and indebted to Lachlan for agreeing to temporarily leave his own family and his clan so that I might stand before you now. Let me assure you'—she turned to look at Lachlan—'you will never meet a more respected and *honourable* man than Lachlan MacLanoch.'

Lachlan inclined his head in thanks of her praise.

Helene glanced back at her father. 'Secondly, I've decided, and will make it my priority, to house and care for Prudence myself. You need not concern yourself in this very moment with how I intend doing so.'

Her father's and brother's eyes widened in alarm at her having spoken Prudence's name in the laird's presence.

'Lachlan knows about Prudence and is privy to her condition and her whereabouts, but if you think to foil my plans, then think again, for I'll not hesitate to leak our family secret to your peers should I be forced to do so. I will fetch Prudence as soon as I bathe and change my clothes. Time is of the essence, so tell me, Father, what was your reason in summoning me home?'

Helene might as well have cut out their tongues with her *sgian-dubh*, for both her father and brother stood rooted to the spot in mute silence, arms slack by their sides, with neither of them meeting her eye.

'Speak your mind, Father. Whatever it is you have to say, it can be said in front of Lachlan. He is the *only* man I trust.'

This revelation pulled her father's gaze to hers, and Helene thought she glimpsed hurt, if not regret, in his eyes.

He did not answer her, and the oppressive silence weighed heavy on Helene. She refused to stand idle. 'Lachlan, if you can tolerate the present company for the next half an hour, I'll quickly ready myself and then we'll go directly to Bethlam.'

'Aye, lass.'

She turned to leave.

'Helene! Wait!' said her brother.

'Wait? For what?'

He gestured to the armchairs. 'Let us all sit. I'll ring for Grayson to bring tea. We've much to discuss.'

Helene cut her hand angrily through the air. 'I'll not sit drinking tea and making polite conversation while Prudence suffers indignity, injustice, and God knows what else in that lunatic asylum.' She took another stride towards the door.

'Prudence is no longer there,' said her father.

Helene froze. She twisted her head and shot a glance at him over her shoulder. 'What do you mean, she's no longer there?'

Her father's gaze fell at her feet. Helene looked to her brother for an answer. Even he could not look her in the eyes. Her heart pounded and she felt the blood drain from her face. Her insides turned ice-cold. She didn't see Lachlan move, but suddenly he was there by her side, hand on her elbow, supporting her. She stared at her father and heard the tremor in her voice when she asked, 'If Prudence is no longer there, then . . . where *is* she?'

What could have been only two seconds of unbearable silence had Helene cry aloud, 'Father?'

Sorrowful eyes met hers. 'She is abed in her room upstairs.'

Helene spun on her heel and ran from the room.

❧

Helene quietly pushed the door ajar and slipped inside the bedchamber. Sunlight streamed in through partially drawn velvet drapes, illuminating a vase of yellow and orange roses on the dressing table. Their glossy green tooth-edged leaves and sweet-smelling fragrance instilled in Helene an essence of calm and a feeling of raised spirits.

Her eyes came to rest on Prudence, sleeping on her side and facing the opposite wall. A bed-sheet covered the slender curves of her shoulder, waist, and hips, and black hair, an inherited trait from their mother, fanned out in long waves over the pillow and bedding.

Helene leaned back against the closed door, grateful for its support, and pressed a hand to her mouth to stifle an anguished sob of relief. Relieved to be finally home. Relieved to see her dear sister here, safe and protected in their father's house amidst comfort and care. As it should always have been.

With relief came hard-hitting concern. What had been the catalyst for her father in bringing Prudence home? How long had she been here, and had her father welcomed Prudence home indefinitely? Despite the need to know and understand the answers to those questions, Helene allowed herself to rejoice in her sister's return. It was the first time in more than ten years that they were all under the same roof. Was this not progress and a pathway to reconciliation?

Still, something seemed sorely amiss with her father and brother. It was as if the fight to estrange themselves from Prudence was gone. Between them, they'd exhibited a pensive expression, their voices flat, and at times, their inability to meet her eyes suggested to Helene they were keeping something from her.

Helene rubbed her temples. Fatigue messed with her mind. She inhaled and released a slow, deep breath before padding quietly over the plush rug towards the dressing table chair. Once the chair was carefully placed in position beside the bed, she sat down to watch over Prudence, eager to look upon that sweet face with its refined chin, full lips, perfectly symmetrical nose, and high cheekbones.

What she saw caused Helene's breath to hitch in her throat. Features pale and gaunt, with dark-circled eyes, Prudence's appearance gave rise to gnawing fear. This was not the young lady Helene had last seen at the asylum, but rather a shadow of that person.

She covered her sister's hand with her own. 'Prudence.' The name passed between Helene's lips on a strangled whisper, and her chin dipped to her chest.

'Helene?'

The weakened voice had Helene look into eyes that were once the colour of her own. Those green eyes had lost their sparkle. Prudence's lips stretched into a wide grin, and long lashes blinked in recognition of Helene.

'You've come home,' said Prudence.

Helene reached out and tucked a wayward dark curl behind her sister's ear. 'Yes, my dearest. Just as I promised. And finding you here is an unexpected and wondrous surprise.'

Prudence grimaced. 'Yes, I suppose it is.'

Helene wanted so desperately to press her sister into revealing all that had happened, and to explain how it came to be that she was back home in this house. Those were questions she'd ask her father, for in Prudence's weakened state, Helene sought only to give her sister hope for a brighter future.

'I did it, Prudence. My time in Scotland paid off, and I now have the funds to provide a life for us both in the countryside, just as we discussed. It won't be a lavish life by any means, but rather one in which I will be your full-time carer, and we'll live comfortably enough.'

Helene refrained from mentioning Lachlan's offer to accommodate herself and Prudence at Drumocher. While his intentions were genuine and honourable, Helene would never impose on his family and their clan. She was in love with Lachlan, but despite their shared intimacy and conversations, he'd voiced no claim on her heart. She could not live under the same roof as him and suffer the pain of unrequited love.

More importantly, she knew Highlanders to be much addicted to superstition, and she very much doubted the MacLanoch Clan would willingly welcome and embrace into their fold a woman afflicted with the falling sickness. Prudence would likely be branded a witch or possessed by the devil. Settling her in Scotland would be akin to writing her death sentence.

Prudence furrowed her brow and asked, 'How did you obtain those funds? You never did reveal that part to me.'

Cuthbert's promissory note rested safe inside Helene's inner coat pocket. If her father had plans to turn Prudence away once she was no longer confined to her bed, then those funds would be used for the purpose Helene had originally intended. 'You needn't worry about it now. I'll tell you someday.'

Prudence's stare strayed past Helene, and she wore an expression as if going back in time. The corners of her mouth lifted into a wistful smile. 'Someday might never come, so we must make the most of each day.'

Helene gave her sister's hand a light squeeze. 'Indeed, we must.'

'I thank God you made it home in time.'

'In time? Whatever do you mean?'

Prudence blinked several times before refocusing and sweeping her gaze over Helene as if seeing her for the first time. 'Goodness!' Her eyes widened. 'What are you wearing?' She wrinkled her nose. 'And what's that smell?'

Her sister's delayed if not comical reaction sent Helene into a fit of laughter. 'I wished to return home by the fastest means possible, and so Lachlan and I travelled here on horseback. It meant disguising myself as a man.'

Prudence looked suddenly confused. 'Lachlan?'

'Yes, the laird of Clan MacLanoch. His castle, Drumocher, is where I stayed in Scotland, as did Agnes; her brother, Cuthbert; and their mother, Lady Sutton.'

Prudence squinted. 'Yes. I remember now.'

'Lachlan is currently in the library, acquainting himself with Father and Robert.'

Helene saw that her sister was tiring. 'Rest now. I need a bath and a clean change of clothes. We'll talk more about it later, but before I go, is there anything I can get you?'

'Yes. Have Grayson ready the carriage to leave after the dinner hour.'

It was an odd request. 'Leave? To go where?'

'I wish for you and me to view the sunset from Spring Hill.' Prudence closed her eyes, and a serene smile lit her face. 'Do you remember we'd go there as a family when we were little, and we'd walk through the woods?'

Helene felt a pang of emotion, of loss and happier days. 'Yes, dearest. I remember it well. You and I would take off at a run, kick at leaves, and chase rabbits.'

A teardrop rolled down Prudence's sallow cheek. Helene suffered a stab to the heart over seeing her sister so visibly upset. She gently thumbed the tear away.

'We'd all sit on a blanket atop the hill, and together we'd watch the sunset. The sky looked as if an artist had used brush-strokes in a palette of reds and oranges. So beautiful. Magical.'

Helene refused to read the ominous signs of her sister's flagging health. 'Then we shall watch another magical sunset tonight,' she said with cheer. 'I'll ask Robert to chaperone us.'

'No. Not Robert.'

'Father, then?'

'No. I should like to meet your Scottish laird, Lachlan.'

Helene gave a laugh. 'He is not *my* laird, but it would give me great pleasure to have the two of you meet, and I'm sure he will most heartily oblige your request.'

Prudence's lips lifted in the briefest of smiles. 'Good. It's settled, then.' Her breathing slowed. Long, dark lashes rested on pale cheeks, and she appeared to be on the cusp of sleep. 'I have . . .' The words were a faint whisper.

'It can wait. Rest now. All will be well. You'll see, Prudence. All will be well.' Helene bent to her sister's hand and pressed a kiss to the soft skin.

'A secret . . .'

Helene stilled and waited, her ear close to her sister's mouth. *A secret?*

'To confess.'

This last word, spoken on a breathy rasp, sent Helene's heart racing. She drew back to look upon her sister's face, wondering if Prudence had spoken the words in a confused, dreamlike state, or whether she'd been lucid enough to speak her truth.

Moments passed in which Helene remained in the quiet of the room, her sister's hand in hers. A secret? A confession? What could Prudence possibly mean? Helene searched her mind for answers and came up with nothing. Instead, she wallowed in self-loathing as her memory punished her with the events of that fateful day long ago. If only she could go back and right the wrong she'd done to her sister. If only she hadn't fought with Prudence over a damned doll.

Helene pulled her thoughts together. The only way forward was to be strong for Prudence. That was the least she could do. That, and to see her sister received the very best of care to ensure her strength returned.

Helene exited the bedchamber and made her way downstairs to her father's library. The three men rose to their feet upon her entering the room. Sighting Lachlan was like imbibing a tonic that promised to cure her of all her angst and woes. He was her stalwart pillar of strength.

Concern for her lay bare in the creases around his eyes and in the grim set of his mouth. He seemed ill at ease, which made Helene question what the men had discussed during her brief absence from the library.

Helene glanced at her father. His stance looked altogether defeated, if not apologetic, with his arms limp at his sides and shoulders pulled low. Her gaze flicked to Robert. Where once her brother would have taken every opportunity to lord it over her with his jutting chin and arrogant superiority, he now bore an expression suggestive of guilt and repentance.

Lachlan approached and stood before her. 'Are ye all right, lass?'

No. She wasn't. She held herself like a tightly coiled spring and wanted nothing more than to lash out and rail against her father and brother. Had they not committed Prudence to a psychiatric hospital, where she was in danger of being treated in horrific ways, then she wouldn't appear as if she were on her deathbed. Helene had spent her life atoning for her crime against Prudence. How would her father and brother atone for their part in her failing health?

'Yes,' she stoically lied.

'Then, if ye dinnae mind, 'tis time for me to take my leave of ye and yer family.'

Without thought, she stayed him with a firm hand on his arm. 'Leave? For Scotland?'

'Nae, lass. To my uncle's residence. Viscount Sutton. He too lives in Grosvenor Square.'

Helene's hand flopped by her side, and she breathed a sigh of relief. 'Of course. Agnes and Cuthbert's father.'

'Aye.' He looked at her with kind and caring eyes. 'Yer sister, Prudence. Was she pleased to see ye?'

Helene thought it odd he didn't enquire after Prudence's health. Perhaps her father had already apprised Lachlan of those developments. She ran a condemning gaze over her father and brother. There'd be time enough to deal with them, but not in front of Lachlan.

'Yes, she was most pleased to see me, and as a matter of fact, she expressed her wish to meet you this evening. She would like to view the sunset from Spring Hill and asked if you'd accompany us in the carriage?'

Robert spoke up. 'I don't believe she's in any condition to travel. She—'

Helene cut him off with a sharp glance. 'If Prudence wishes to see a sunset, then a sunset she shall see. I will ensure her every comfort.' Her gaze slid back to Lachlan.

He placed one hand over his heart. 'It would be my absolute honour.'

'Thank you. Since the sun sets late in the evening, we'll head out after the dinner hour. Say, seven o'clock?'

'Aye.'

Helene smiled her thanks. 'I'll have Grayson retrieve your belongings and the horses.'

'Nae, lass. I'll speak to Grayson. Thank ye all the same.' He gave a nod in her father's direction. 'Ye have some catching up to do with yer family. If ye should need me before this evening, nae matter the reason, just send word. I'm not far away.'

There was so much Helene wanted to say to Lachlan. She wanted to throw her arms around him, feel his solid strength against her body, and press her lips to his, but with her father and brother looking on, she simply said, 'Thank you for everything. I'm most grateful and forever in your debt. If there's anything I can do for you, anything at all, you only need ask and I shall oblige.'

Helene yearned to lean closer and whisper three heartfelt words in his ear.

Lachlan bowed. 'Until this evening.'

She watched him leave the room, and when he'd closed the door, Helene sat in the chair he'd occupied. Bathing and a change of clothes could wait. She stared pointedly at her father and brother and gestured for them to sit.

CHAPTER TWENTY-FOUR

THE CARRIAGE MERGED with a stream of conveyances rumbling over cobblestones. Hooves clip-clopped, horses snorted, and harnesses creaked. Snippets of conversation from people strolling by filtered through the open curtained windows.

Lachlan sat inside the plush compartment opposite Helene and her sister, Prudence, whom he'd met not an hour ago. She'd been flanked by Penforth and his son, each with a supporting hand under one elbow and upper arm in assisting her down the stairs.

She wore a gown of silk brocade in ivory, yellow, and green, and her dark hair, covered with a little lace cap, fell at her back in curls with a braid pinned to the head. For all her fashionable finery, the lass lacked physical strength and looked poorly and pale. Lachlan could only surmise her ill-fitting clothes were a result of her having lost weight. Her eyes, a cloudy shade of green, had settled kindly on him when being formally introduced by her father.

Lachlan had respectfully greeted her with a low bow and engaged her in polite conversation. Though he'd given Prudence his undivided attention, he'd been all too aware of Helene descending the stairs behind her family. Being apart from her this afternoon had seemed like an eternity, especially after having spent so much time in each other's company since their first meeting in Scotland. He yearned to pull her into his arms, hold her tight, never again to leave her side.

Only now, inside the carriage, could he fully appraise Helene's appearance. She looked tired, drawn, and like Prudence, she'd dressed as befitting an earl's daughter, in a steel-blue silk mantua with the lappets of her lace cap framing her face. Her hair was dressed like her sister's, and Lachlan marvelled at their similar features. He assumed they resembled their mother in appearance, for neither of them had inherited their father's likeness.

Time spent alone with Penforth and his son earlier today had given Lachlan the opportunity to stand firm and have his say, leaving the men in no doubt as to his feelings for Helene. His declaration of love for her, and requesting her hand in marriage, had been met with utmost surprise. While not accepted, neither was his proposal rejected.

To Lachlan's chagrin, they'd outright refused his offer to care for Prudence at Drumocher. When challenged, they'd apprised him of Prudence's fast-deteriorating health and shared with him additional private information, recently come to light, about her childhood accident. Little wonder the two men were contrite in their countenance towards Helene.

Though it had pained him to have left her with her father and brother this afternoon, he'd done so in firm belief of her safety. Besides, some discussions were only to be had between family members. Lachlan was not family, and in understanding that, he carried the burden of guilt for being privy to crucial facts that Helene had yet to learn from Prudence. For better or worse, it would significantly impact the way Helene viewed the past, the present, and her future.

Distant jocularity, incongruent with the sombre mood inside the carriage, dragged Lachlan from his thoughts. His love for Helene deepened as he watched her lay, with meticulous care, a blanket across her sister's lap.

Prudence broke the silence between them, her voice soft yet assertive. 'My lord. I must admit to being a little disappointed.'

Her statement took Lachlan by surprise. 'Disappointed? With what?'

'You!'

Lachlan glanced at Helene. Her face fell, and the hand of failure squeezed his heart. Disappointing Prudence was to disappoint Helene. Something he wished to avoid at all costs.

'I'm verra sorry if I'm a disappointment to ye, Lady Prudence. Please do tell me in what way I've let ye down, and I'll do my verra best to make amends.'

She swept a critical eye over him. 'Well, I had hoped to see you dressed as a Highlander, kilt, broadsword, and all. Yet here you are, elegantly dressed in a grey wool coat with narrowed sleeve cuffs, matching breeches, and a white silk waistcoat.'

An unsteady slim finger pointed to his wrists. 'I'm sure cotton ruffled shirt cuffs are not the order of the day when traversing the Highlands on horseback.' She glanced down. 'Nor would be white silk stockings and black shoes with small silver buckles.'

Her frown deepened when she glanced up. 'And your hair! I'd imagined a wild, windswept look, not neatly tied back at the nape of your neck with a black ribbon. You are ruggedly handsome, indeed, but where is the barbaric clansmen I had hoped to meet?'

Her words of reproof rendered Lachlan absurdly speechless, his mind a complete blank. He blinked, unable to trust himself to string a coherent sentence together, let alone vocalise the words even if he knew what to say. He chanced a look at Helene, who looked as perplexed as he.

Prudence flicked her gaze between Helene and Lachlan. From one instant to the next, she burst into fits of laughter. 'Forgive me for teasing you. I only meant to lighten the mood between us so that we might relax in each other's company. If you could see your own face right now!' She clutched her belly as another trill of laughter escaped her.

Helene pressed a hand to her chest and laughed with what sounded like equal parts shock and relief. At the same time, Lachlan's shoulders shook with amusement before the rumbling in his chest morphed into deep, resonant laughter.

Prudence had taken him and Helene by surprise, and though her comic ruse was at their expense, she'd created a moment amidst great solemnity whereby laughter was especially welcome. Seeing the sisters laugh together was a joy to behold. The memory would stay with him.

Prudence struggled to catch her breath when her laughter subsided. Helene was swift to react. She reached into her reticule, produced a small flask, and held it to her sister's mouth. 'Sip slowly.'

Lachlan caught the scent of the familiar medicinal brew. 'Is that made from Mairi's herbs?'

'Yes, it's a relaxant.'

The elixir took immediate effect, and Lachlan made a mental note to personally thank and commend Mairi when he returned to Scotland.

'My lord?' said Prudence in a weak voice.

'Please, do call me Lachlan.'

Prudence smiled. 'Lachlan, you do not disappoint me in the least. In fact, quite the opposite.' She paused for a few breaths. 'Thank you for bringing my sister home to me.' She took hold of Helene's hand. 'I could not have been blessed with a greater gift.'

'Yer sister is indeed a treasure, and one I'm most reluctant to relinquish.'

Prudence's eyes widened when she looked sidelong at Helene. 'Dear sister! You blush.'

Helene used her hand to fan her face. 'Blush? You're mistaken! If my cheeks are flushed, it's because this summer evening is insufferably warm, as is this gown.' She hid her face by turning away to stare out the window.

Lachlan could not take his eyes off Helene, pleased his compliment had brought colour to her cheeks. When he glanced back at Prudence, it was to find her making a quiet study of him. She raised a brow, gave him a knowing smile, and then discreetly inclined her head in recognition of him having feelings for her sister. *Christ!* Was it so blatantly obvious that he was enamoured with Helene, or was it that Prudence, despite her frailty, was not only witty but also possessed a sharp mind?

Lachlan answered Prudence's questions about his homeland, its history, and its people during their journey to Spring Hill. On arrival, he spread blankets and cushions on the ground and placed several oil lanterns at the periphery. He assisted in comfortably seating Helene and her sister, whereupon he sat down to unpack and enjoy with them a sumptuous supper.

Helene took the lead in conversation, and it warmed Lachlan's heart to hear her speak fondly of his sister and mother, of Donnie, Aila and Ross, Greer and Mairi. She gave animated descriptions of woodlands and lochs, wildlife, and the shielings. Thankfully, the only danger recounted was her brush with death, first with the cattle stampede and then her near-drowning in the river.

'If not for Donnie shoving me into the water,' she explained, 'I'd have been trampled beneath a herd of Highland cows, and it was Lachlan who rescued Donnie and myself from the raging river.'

It was at this point in Helene's account of her adventures that Prudence leaned forward to lay her hand on Lachlan's sleeve. 'Who better to watch over and care for my sister than *you* and *your* clan?'

Prudence fixed him with a level gaze, and Lachlan had the distinct impression she'd chosen those words to convey a message stronger than her grasp on his arm.

'The light is fading fast, and the sun has almost set,' she said. 'Lachlan, would you be so kind as to give me a moment alone with my sister?'

Prudence's faltering smile worried Lachlan. 'Aye. Of course. Give me a shout when ye're both ready to leave.'

He stood, bowing slow and deep. As he straightened, he glanced at Helene, her expression pensive. He picked up one of the blankets and draped it about the sisters' shoulders.

'Thank you,' the sisters said in unison.

'Aye.'

Lachlan backed away and headed towards the lantern-lit carriage. He stopped and turned around, within clear sight of the sisters, yet respectfully out of earshot. The air was still, and fading light had long since triggered nighttime songsters like the bubbling exuberance of a nightingale, churring nightjars, and ever-present robins with their sweet, melodic war cry.

The sisters sat shoulder to shoulder beneath the blanket, their heads tipped to the darkening sky. Lachlan sensed Prudence had, without doubt, chosen this place, this moment, to disclose the truth of her accident to Helene. All he could do was wait and prepare himself for whatever Helene's reaction might be.

Already, his heart hurt and bled for Helene.

ℰ

The summer sun's descent cast a warm, golden glow upon the sky. Colours, pink and orange, merged, and streaks of fiery red painted a breathtaking masterpiece against a canvas of deepening blue.

'Doesn't it just take your breath away?' said Prudence.

'That, and more,' agreed Helene. 'Nature has a way of making one appreciate the little things in life.'

'Indeed, it does.'

The ensuing silence became unbearable. Helene had a deep sense of foreboding about her sister's mortality. Why did Prudence insist they visit Spring Hill tonight of all nights? Why not wait until she had regained her strength? Asking Helene to sit and watch the sun bid farewell to this summer's day was tantamount to Prudence making her final farewell.

Tears stung Helene's eyes and a knot cinched in her chest, making it difficult to breathe. She summoned the resolve to smile and speak positively of the future and of her sister's recovery. 'Prudence, I—'

'The laird, I think him quite the catch, don't you?'

Helene's gaze cut to Prudence. 'Lachlan?'

'I know of no other laird.' Prudence winked at Helene and then returned her gaze to the sinking sun. 'He is in love with you.'

'What? No!'

'Of course he is. It's obvious. Can you not see it for yourself?'

'How can you say such a thing when you met him a matter of hours ago?'

Prudence turned her head slowly to look at Helene. 'It takes but one moment to witness in his eyes the love he has for you, and if I'm not mistaken, you are in love with him.'

Helene's jaw dropped as she considered her sister with

utter dismay. True, Helene had been hard-pressed to take her eyes off Lachlan, dressed as he was in the height of London fashion, and so strikingly handsome as to make her eyes shoot arrows into any woman who dared look his way, but for her sister to read deeper into her feelings for the laird? How was that even possible?

'Well, do you deny it?' Prudence pressed.

Helene swallowed. Hard. She had not expected their conversation to take this turn.

'Speak the truth. Do you love Lachlan?'

Helene stole a look over her shoulder, satisfied Lachlan was indeed far enough away as to not hear a word spoken between Prudence and herself. 'Yes. Yes, I do.'

'You cannot know how happy I am to hear you've found love with a man who loves you in return.'

The look of relief on her sister's face was altogether a curious thing, but before Helene could pursue it further, Prudence's expression turned pitifully forlorn.

Helene flinched. 'What's wrong?'

'Did Father explain to you why the asylum discharged me?'

Helene's free hand formed a fist beneath the blanket. How could she forget her father's explanation?

Your sister had the most violent of episodes. Convulsions. Rhythmic, jerking muscle movements of the neck, face, arms, and legs. Her muscles stiffened and jerked, and her body arched so high off her bed as to make those responsible for her care believe she'd levitated by supernatural means.

'Yes,' answered Helene between gritted teeth. 'Father told me, after which I railed against him and our brother for neglecting you and sending you to that Godforsaken place! He and Robert should have been there for you. *I* should have been there with you through the throes of your turn. To be by your side when you awoke. To hold your hand and reassure you, knowing you'd wake dazed, confused, frightened, and all alone within the cold, clinical walls of that hell house!'

'Shh,' soothed Prudence. 'Do not despair for me.' She gave a triumphant yet feeble laugh. 'After my turn, not one of the wardens would come near me. They thought me possessed by the devil, and so I played on their belief to my advantage. Silly fools!' she scoffed. 'I threatened to curse them with the falling sickness if they did not send for Father.'

Helene unclenched her fist, and the hand at her sister's waist pulled her closer. Her body felt as frail as a bird's. 'You needn't worry about a thing from here on in.' Cuthbert's promissory note came to mind. 'I have the means to take good care of you.'

'Dear, sweet Helene. I do not deserve an angel for a sister.'

'How can you say that after what I did to you? Your life would have been so different had I not been so cruel as to push—'

Prudence pressed a finger to Helene's lips. 'You won't think yourself so cruel once you hear what I have to say.' She began to wheeze, and her body trembled as if from cold.

Helene made a move to stand. 'We must return home. Now!'

'No!' Prudence clutched Helene's arm. 'Not until you've heard what I have to say.' She dragged in a ragged breath. 'My violent turn was not the sole reason Father agreed to bring me home. I confessed to him the truth behind my fall, and I begged him to send for you so that I could tell you to your face. Before it's too late.'

Panic rose in Helene. 'Tell me what? And too late? Prudence! You're not making sense. What are you talking about?'

'You and I, we fought and squabbled when we were young.'

'As do all siblings.'

'Yes, but on that day when we fought over the doll, anger

and hate for you overcame me. I wanted to retaliate and have Mother and Father scold you.'

'And they did.'

'You did not deserve having them turn their backs on you, nor did you deserve Robert's cruel retribution.'

Helene shuddered at the memory of her brother having tied her to the tree and abandoning her amidst the storm.

'Dear sister, I did something sinister that day, and because of it, I've lived my life with deep regret. I was too much of a coward to speak the truth at the time, and with each passing day, week, month, and year, shame and guilt made it impossible for me to confess my sin.

'The falling sickness was God's just way of punishing me, of that I'm sure, and it's something I've come to accept. My spiteful actions impacted and shaped your life in more ways than I care to admit, but that shall no longer be the case. I must make my peace with God. And with you. I can only pray He, and you, will find it in your heart to forgive me.'

'Stop!' Helene's heart hammered. 'All this doom and gloom talk distresses me. Whatever you did, I forgive you. You need not tell me anything.'

'I must! And here's the truth of it. You didn't push me down those stairs. I *threw* myself down the stairs.'

Helene's head drew back on a gasp. She blinked, rapidly, and shook her head. 'No, no. I pushed you!'

'That much is true, but your *push* was not forceful enough to send me toppling down the stairs. When you turned your back and walked away, I ran to the landing and hurled myself over the top.'

Helene gasped again in disbelief. She stammered, 'Why? Why did you do such a thing?'

Prudence dipped her chin. 'At the time, I was a stupid, jealous, irrational eight-year-old sister.' She glanced up. 'After the accident, Mother and Father lavished all their love and attention on me, especially when I began to suffer from those turns. Years later, when Mother passed and Father sent me away because of my illness, I was angry at *you*.

'I concede it was misplaced anger, but I was too selfish to admit and hold myself accountable for my actions. In my twisted mind I believed that if I was to suffer and be estranged from our family, then so should you.' She glanced down, wringing her hands. 'If only you could know the depth of my shame and guilt.'

Helene closed her eyes and massaged her temples. 'Why now? Why has it taken you this long to admit your wrongdoing towards me *and* our family?'

Prudence swiped at wet lashes and her voice faltered. 'Being sent to that asylum was as good as being condemned to purgatory. I did not wish to die there and have my callous soul forever roam those cold corridors. It forced me to admit I'd strayed far beyond my moral compass. That, together with my insufferable condition, was my pathway and process to redemption.'

Gently, gingerly, Prudence reached out and held Helene's hands in hers. 'I'm so sorry, Helene. I'm so *very* sorry. I humbly beseech you to find it in your heart to forgive me.'

Helene slid her hands free of her sister's touch and wrapped herself in a hug. The years had seen her sink completely into a quagmire of self-recrimination, with every waking moment spent looking to atone for what she'd believed was *her* sin. A sin that had destroyed familial relationships between herself and her siblings, her father, and her late mother.

It was they who'd turned their backs on her. She'd lived like an outcast within her own home, always longing for life to go back to what it had been before her sister's accident. Back to playful interactions with Prudence and Robert, and when she'd enjoyed the loving smiles and attention of parents who were there to protect, support, and care for her.

She'd shouldered guilt, heartache, hurt, pain, emotional and mental stress, feeling disconnected and alone. To think of the extreme lengths she'd gone to in securing Cuthbert's promissory note. And all for Prudence.

The jolting reality of the confronting confession gave Helene the right to loathe, resent, and vehemently despise her sister, and yet, now was not the time to vent those feelings. Time Helene had, and so she suppressed deep in her heart a maelstrom of emotion, there to be later unleashed and processed with a rational mind. Tugging at her heart this very instant were her sister's sad, listless eyes and an expression of defeat and genuine remorse. Despite the wicked, deceitful deed, compassion rose in Helene, leading her to realise Prudence, in need of seeking absolution, was to be pitied rather than pilloried. Helene drew her arms around Prudence in an embrace. 'Forgiven.'

Prudence bowed her head and wept on Helene's shoulder, her thin body shaking like a brittle leaf on a branch. After a long silence, it occurred to Helene that from something bad had come something good. 'I must thank you.'

Prudence pulled back. 'Whatever for?'

Helene tucked a stray wisp of hair behind her sister's ear. 'If not for you, I'd never have met Lachlan.' Prudence startled Helene by pressing her palms to Helene's cheeks.

'I'm in no position to ask anything more of you, but please promise me one thing.'

'Anything.'

'Promise me you will not spend the customary three months mourning my passing. I am not worth it.'

Helene sucked in a breath. 'Your passing?'

'Promise me.'

Despite her sister's frailty, Helene failed in her attempt to pull Prudence's hands from her face. 'Don't be ridiculous! Nothing is going to happen to you.'

'Promise me!'

Desperation and chilling finality were laid bare in Prudence's narrowed eyes and pinched face. Helene heard the words her sister refused to say out loud, and in that moment, she could no longer protect herself from another truth too painful to accept. Only then, and with the heaviest of hearts, did Helene begrudgingly acknowledge Prudence's days were numbered. Through trembling lips, she whispered, 'I promise.'

Prudence sighed in relief and rested her forehead against Helene's. 'Make your feelings known to Lachlan, lay claim to him, for if you don't, Father *will* force you into a loveless marriage. Do you hear me?'

Helene heard her loud and clear. Her thoughts turned practical. Up until now, she'd staved off her father's attempts to marry her off by threatening to expose Prudence's condition. Without that advantage, there was no telling what he might do. If Lachlan did not declare his hand for Helene, then her saving grace would be to call in Cuthbert's promissory note and support herself for as long as the money would last.

Prudence eased back, smiled, and thumbed away Helene's tears. 'Come now, the last vestiges of day are fading fast. Let us enjoy what's left of this magnificent sunset.'

Helene resettled her arm around her sister's waist. At the same time, Prudence tilted her head to rest on Helene's right shoulder.

In glancing up at the evening sky, Helene was happily reminded of her journey from Scotland to England with Lachlan, sleeping out in the open beside the fire. Always she'd look towards the twinkling heavens and wonder what existed beyond the vast universe.

The sun sank below the horizon, plunging the world into darkness, save for the illumination of the lanterns on the picnic rug.

'Look!' Helene pointed with her finger. 'Did you see that, Prudence? A shooting star!'

When her sister gave no response, Helene shifted her gaze to see Prudence had closed her eyes, her face as serene as her smile. No longer did she clasp Helene's hand. Prudence's hand was limp, the palm open, fingers curled back and relaxed. Her head felt heavy on Helene's shoulder, so too her body propped up against Helene's side. A chill, colder than an arctic wind, shot up Helene's spine.

CHAPTER TWENTY-FIVE

PRUDENCE WAS AT peace. Helene, not so.

Grief overcame her in continuous suffocating waves since laying her sister to rest eight days ago. There, at the foot of the grave, she'd stayed with Prudence until the last shovel of soil had been turned.

With grief came anger, and like Pandora's box, it lifted the lid on emotions, unleashing pent-up tumultuous hostility because of her sister's violation of righteous principles. The dire consequences of one long-lived lie were too many to count.

Now, perched on the edge of her bed, Helene stared without seeing the opposite wall of her bedchamber. Though the room was awash in glorious afternoon sunshine, she saw only darkness. In her hands she bunched the material of her voluminous skirts. Ten years she'd been made the scapegoat for Prudence's misdeed. Ten years of missed opportunities, of thinking herself worthless and unworthy of anything and anyone. Unworthy of life itself. She'd seen fit to forgive her sister, but Helene grappled with how to process and reconcile what Prudence had done to her, as well as coming to terms with the injustice of having lost a sibling who was too young to die.

Nothing good will come from dwelling on the past, or giving life to ill feelings. Easy enough to say, but her father's words at the private family funeral gave her no measure of help or healing, especially having been spoken with a stiff upper lip. At the time, his meek apology to Helene for his uncharitable, misguided rejection of her all these years fell on deaf ears.

In the same private family dialogue, Robert had voiced profound apologies for his wrongdoing towards her and had seconded their father's advice. Little comfort, and too late. Nonetheless, it would be erroneous not to concur with her father's counsel. Indeed, what purpose would be served to recount and dwell on the past?

Closed eyes and deep breaths settled and calmed her nerves. Images, unbidden, sprang to mind. Mountains, moorlands, rivers, and lochs. Those images helped her to see her way forward, and she clung to hope, to the one person who might make a difference in her life. Someone who'd help her digest and surmount the hurt in her heavy heart.

Lachlan MacLanoch. The man who'd irrevocably captured and won her heart.

Granted, had it not been for Prudence, Helene might never have found her way to the laird, nor might she have known what it was to love a man so freely, so deeply, and so completely. For that, she'd be ever grateful to her sister. If this was fate's way of atoning for all Helene had suffered, then she'd accept it as a precious gift, just as she'd gifted Prudence forgiveness, and in honouring her sister's final promise, Helene would gladly gift her heart to Lachlan if only he were here to accept or refuse it.

Lachlan. Why had he not called or come to see her? Was he already on his way back to Scotland, his clan, and his family?

This past week had plunged her too deep in her grief to

go in search of him, and when she was not alone in her room, weeping, there were visitors to face, those who came to pay their respects and convey their condolences after word spread of the earl's long-forgotten poorly younger daughter who'd come home to die.

Helene buried her face in her hands as another wave of grief split her soul in two.

There came a sudden, sharp rap on the door. 'What is it?' she called, without turning to see who entered the room.

'Lady Helene, Lord Penforth requests your immediate presence in his study.'

Helene recognised the maid's voice. 'Thank you. I shall be down in a moment.'

The door clicked closed.

Helene stepped over to the washbasin, splashed cold water on her face, and dabbed it dry with the linen cloth. She glanced at herself in the looking glass. Her eyes were red and swollen, her face pale, strained, and puffy. What was so urgent that her father needed to see her now? It couldn't be more visitors, not at this late hour of the afternoon. Besides, if anyone had come to see them, they'd be received in the drawing room, not her father's study.

Helene made her way down the stairs, her black muslin mourning skirts shushing with each step. At her sister's insistence, she'd be sure to shuck the drab, dreary clothes soon enough. For now, whilst under her father's roof, she'd adhere to social mores for the bereaved.

One hard knock on the library door, and his voice bid she enter. She slipped inside and closed the door behind her. 'You wished to see me, Father?'

'Yes. Come sit awhile.'

Helene sank down onto a seat opposite him.

His elbows rested on the arms of his chair, and he

thoughtfully studied his steepled, long-fingered hands before his face. 'I've had two more formal requests for your hand in marriage.'

Helene stiffened.

'You'd needn't look so affronted. Both men came to me before Prudence passed.'

A prickling along the back of Helene's neck sent her into a panic. It was exactly as her sister had predicted. With Prudence fresh in her grave, their father was set to marry Helene off into what would be a loveless marriage. That would never do. Never! Not for Helene. 'Father, I—'

His raised hand cut her off. 'I've made a decision with regard to which one you will marry.'

Will marry? Those words struck fear in Helene's heart. Her mouth opened to protest, but again, her father cut her off.

'He has proved himself to be a man of integrity, a man of honour. He is a powerful man in his own right and financially secure.' Penforth blew out a breath. 'I've encountered many oath-breakers in my time, but not him. He is—'

'A peer of the realm, no doubt. And what's in it for you?' Helene could not hide the sarcasm in her voice.

'I was going to say, he is a man of his word and can offer you a good life. He's earned my respect, and I hold him in high regard. I've given him my blessing, as has your brother. Robert and I firmly believe this man is the one for you.'

Anger propelled Helene to her feet. Blood rushed to her cheeks, and her fists clenched by her sides. 'And what about *my* happiness, Father? Have you or Robert ever factored that into your matchmaking checklist? I'd sooner be left to shrivel up on the shelf than be shackled to a man unknown to me. A man who has yet to earn *my* respect and *my* high regard.

'Your marriage to Mother might have been one of financial and social gain, but if I cannot marry a man of my choosing, a man whom *I* love, then I shall not marry at all. Tell your man I refuse his hand!'

Penforth raised his eyes to hers. 'You can tell him yourself. He awaits you now, in the drawing room.'

Helene sucked in a breath and stared in dismay at her father. How she despised him. His placid, nonchalant demeanour inflamed her ire.

'If you had the slightest care for me or my opinion, you would not have contrived such a deliberate set-up. Be assured, Father, I have absolutely no qualms in facing and refusing the man who awaits me beyond these walls. I understand I am a burden and a disappointment to you. I have been ever since—' Helene choked on her emotion, unable to finish the sentence. She inhaled a deep, shuddering breath. 'I shall leave tomorrow and make my own way in this world.'

Her father's silence and expressionless stare galled her. Not one word of objection. No offer of financial assistance. No thought to ask where she might go or whom she might turn to. She was on her own. Just as well she still had Cuthbert's promissory note in her possession. She turned smartly on her heel and strode towards the door.

'Helene!'

Her father's commanding voice brought her to a halt, yet she didn't turn to face him.

'You might find this difficult to believe, but it's because I do love you, and wish only for your future happiness, that I give this union my heartfelt and genuine blessing.'

That longed-for spoken word from her father's lips almost brought Helene undone. She wanted so desperately to believe it true, that he did indeed love her as a father should love and cherish his daughter. It was one thing to tell her how he felt, and yet it was another to demonstrate proof of its meaning. She continued towards the door.

'Helene!'

Her hand paused over the latch.

'If you refuse him, I'll—'

'You'll what, Father?' She snapped her head around to glare at him. 'Send me to an early death and banish me to Bethlem? Just as you did with Prudence?' Helene pushed through the door, leaving her ashen-faced father to deal with his demons.

The footman, seeing Helene stride with determined intent towards the drawing room, hurried to open the door. She swept into the room, and at the same time as the door shut behind her, the man standing by the window with his back to her whipped around.

Helene came to a halt. Confused, her gaze made a clean sweep of the room. Only she, and *he*, occupied the room. 'Lachlan?'

He stared at her for long moments before greeting her with a stiff bow. A tailor-made coat of expensive cloth hugged his broad frame. Breeches encased powerful thighs, and sunlight streaming in through the window gave his highly polished buckled shoes that extra gleam. His russet hair was unbound, falling to his shoulders, giving him that wild Highland appearance, just the way she preferred it.

Optimism sent her heart aflutter, and a quickening in her entire being forced from her a silent prayer that Lachlan was indeed the expectant groom her father had spoken of. 'What brings you here?'

His approach was slow, almost hesitant. A wintry sadness clouded his eyes, with worry etched in the crease of his brow. At the point of standing toe-to-toe with Helene, he gently cupped her cheek with the palm of his hand.

''Tis ye who brings me here. I've been worried sick wondering how ye've been faring.'

Helene instinctively leaned into his touch. 'I feel better now that you're here with me.' Tears pooled behind closed eyes.

In the next instant, Lachlan pulled her close and held her tight. 'Christ, lass! I cannae imagine the heartache ye've endured.'

She clung to his hard warmth. 'Made all the more unbearable in thinking you'd returned to Scotland without saying goodbye.' The confession slipped out before she had time to think. One large hand cupped the base of her skull, and the heat of Lachlan's lips pressed to her crown. She revelled in the sensation of his caring gesture.

'Goodbye? Nae, *mo chridhe*. Ye should ken me better than that by now. It killed me to stay away from ye, but I did so at yer father's request. Understandably, ye and yer father and brother needed time and space to lay Prudence to rest, and to say whatever need be said between ye.'

Helene rushed to say, 'I didn't do it, Lachlan.' She held back a sob. 'I didn't push Prudence down the stairs.'

'I ken all about it, lass. Yer father enlightened me as to the truth of it all.'

'I feel so broken. So damnably angry and sad about everything.'

He pulled back and thumbed the tears from her cheeks. 'Aye, and ye've every right to feel that way. It will take some time before yer heart and mind heals. I ken what that feels like.'

Helene clung to him, the room silent save for the ormolu clock marking time on the mantel shelf. She wished for this moment to last forever, never to remove herself from the security of Lachlan's protection. She gave a soft whimper when he set himself slightly apart from her and took her hands in his.

'Helene. I've something to say.' He swallowed. 'Forgive me, but . . .'

His long pause and averted gaze put Helene's expectations

on high alert. He didn't look at all like a man who was about to propose. Perhaps he'd changed his mind, or her father had it all wrong. A tight knot formed in her gut, and she braced herself for yet more despairing disappointment.

'Considering the sobering circumstances, what I have to say is ill-timed.' He swallowed again before meeting her gaze. 'I want to take ye away from here, to Scotland. I want ye to be my wife.'

Breath escaped Helene on a gasp, and her legs almost buckled beneath her. Her jaw slackened as Lachlan went down on bended knee.

'Lady Helene Beckett, would ye do me the great honour of becoming my wife?'

A tingling surge in Helene's chest spread outwards. Her heart raced beneath her breast, and a million butterflies danced a reel in her stomach. She felt breathless and giddy with euphoric delight, and a flush heated her face and neck. She tipped her head back, eyes closed. Her mind emptied of all concerns and worries. Never had she dared to believe her wish would come true.

'Well?' he said in a congenial voice. 'Are ye going to answer me, lass?'

A resounding yes was on the tip of her tongue, but in the second it took to drop her head forward and meet his golden-brown gaze, stark realisation clamped her mouth shut. Something Lachlan had said, together with things her father had said, tolled like bells warning of impending doom.

Considering the sobering circumstances. A man of honour. A man of his word. I've encountered many oath-breakers in my time, but not him.

Elation evaporated in the blink of an eye. There'd been no declaration of love for Helene, nor the slightest hint of affection in Lachlan's proposal. She slid her hands from his and retreated a step.

Lachlan looked bewildered and surged to his feet. 'What is it?' When Helene gave no immediate reply, he said, 'Helene, granted, my timing is poor, but—'

'What was it you agreed to?' Her voice was stoic. Flat.

'Agreed to?' Lachlan cocked his head to one side. 'I dinnae understand.'

'In your handwritten oath to my father. What penalty did you agree to in the event my virtue was compromised or ruined whilst under your protection and care?'

Mortified understanding dawned on his face. 'It doesnae matter, lass.'

'Answer the question.'

He shook his head and repeated, 'It doesnae matter.'

Helene bit back, 'It matters to me!' She retreated at the same time as Lachlan took a step forward. 'Answer the question.'

Lachlan looked away, his lips pressed together in a thin white line. 'Dinnae do this, Helene.'

'You committed your signature to a legally binding agreement with my father. Didn't you?'

'Aye.'

'Why and what for?'

He looked at her again. ''Twas the only way yer father would agree to ye travelling to Scotland with Agnes, Cuthbert, and my auntie. I didnae want to disappoint Agnes. She had her heart set on ye staying with her at Drumocher for the summer.'

'I see. You tout yourself to be an honourable man, and I know you to be just that. So tell me, Lachlan MacLanoch. What did you agree to do if my reputation was in any way tarnished or sullied whilst under your protection?'

His hands formed fists by his sides, and the muscles along his tight jaw twitched. 'Marry ye!'

His admission hit Helene like a punch to the gut. So, his marriage proposal was as sincere as Lucifer preaching God's word. In a tight voice, she said, 'I'm sorry, Laird MacLanoch, but I cannot, and will not, marry you. You are free to go and do as you please.'

With head held high, Helene turned for the door. Lachlan's hand clamped down on her wrist, staying her.

'I dinnae accept yer answer.'

'I have nothing more to say to you!'

'*I* have plenty to say to ye!'

'I don't care to hear it! Now let go of me.'

'I ken what ye're thinking, and ye'd be wrong about it. No one kens what's happened between us and—'

'Then you're off the hook on that account.' Her indignation flared and she narrowed her eyes on him. 'It must be that the rumour mill is in full flow over me returning home dressed as a man, alone with you, and as we both know, rumours are enough to drive the nail in the coffin when it comes to a lady's character and virtue. But you needn't feel it's your honourable *duty* to marry me. I herewith absolve you of any further responsibility over me. Consider your oath null and void.'

Lachlan snapped, 'I dinnae ken about any gossip or rumours, and I dinnae care if they exist. Even if it were the case, that blasted oath is not the reason why I asked ye to marry me.'

'No? Then why do you want to marry me?' she pressed. 'For my dowry? To establish connections here in London?'

He flinched as if Helene had struck him hard across the face. She bore the brunt of his brutal stare and challenged him with an angry glower. His mouth opened to speak, not once but twice, but still he said nothing. *Scoundrel!* She broke free of his grasp, marched four steps towards the door, and came to a sudden stop. Her gaze snapped to her left shoulder. She could have sworn a gentle hand had settled there. *Prudence?* Helene shook her head. Grief played havoc with her thoughts. She took another step forward.

'*Love*, Helene!'

His words at her back brought her to a standstill.

'I asked ye to marry me . . . because I'm in love with ye.'

Helene's breath caught in her throat.

'I've loved ye from that first moment when ye fell from the carriage into my arms. When ye defied me in front of my clan and championed wee Donnie that day in the great hall. Every day since, I've fallen deeper in love with ye, and I cannae stand to be without ye.'

Though she still stood with her back to him, she heard him take one soft booted footfall towards her.

'When ye went to see Prudence in her room the day we arrived here, I spoke with yer father and brother and offered for yer hand in marriage. Not because of any damaging gossip or rumour or an oath, but because I'm genuinely in love with ye. I made that very clear to them. I also took the liberty of speaking on yer behalf, in saying I was certain ye had feelings for me. Yer father informed me of another suitor who keeps pestering him for yer hand. Ultimately, yer father chose me over the Duke of Wentworth.'

Helene almost keeled over. Marriage to the duke—the ultimate advantageous alliance—would have opened all manner of doors for her father, and yet he'd slighted the duke and championed Lachlan. A lump lodged in her throat. Though it was impossible to believe, her father had forgone his selfish ways in favour of accommodating her future happiness and well-being.

Despite all Lachlan had confessed, she had to ask, 'And if my father had chosen the duke over you?'

'I wouldnae have given up on ye! I'd have wanted to hear

yer decision, and if it were me ye chose, then I'd do everything in my power to refute yer father's wishes and make ye my wife. I'd have stopped at nothing short of kidnapping ye.'

Helene heard the determination in his voice and sensed him drawing nearer.

'There's something else ye need ken. When I offered for yer hand, I suggested taking Prudence with us back to Scotland, but yer father wouldnae hear of it. He explained why, saying she didnae have long to live.'

Helene's head dropped to her chest before glancing at Lachlan over her shoulder. 'Why didn't you declare your love for me *before* I refused your offer of marriage?'

Lachlan paused for long moments. 'Five years ago, I weathered the betrayal of an unfaithful fiancée, who subsequently took her own life to be with her paramour in death. He was a Jacobite, and she . . . Ross and Aila's granddaughter.'

Helene gasped and spun around to face Lachlan. He'd never spoken to her of any past relationships, but then, neither had she taken the time to ask.

'As their laird, I've always reassured them I dinnae hold them responsible, but to this day they carry the shame and stain of their granddaughter's actions. When ye and I visited Aila and Ross on our way to the shielings, I told them I was finally free of the past and that 'twas ye who'd won and now owned my heart.'

Helene listened in stunned silence, recalling with distinct clarity the moment inside the cottage when conversation between Aila, Ross, and Lachlan had taken a sobering turn and tone. Although she'd understood not a word of Gaelic, she'd sensed an element of sensitivity around what was being said and had wondered why they'd each cast a furtive glance her way.

'The truth behind Aila gifting ye her brooch was akin

to giving us her blessing. The heirloom was her most prized possession.'

Helene pictured the brooch where she'd left it on the dresser in her bedchamber at Drumocher. Dismayed, she asked, 'Why did you wait until now to tell me all this?'

'Ye asked me why I didnae declare my love for ye before ye refused my offer of marriage? I need ye to understand that all those years ago, I thought I kenned what it was to be in love—except, it wasnae love at all. It didnae have the depth nor breadth of what I feel for ye. My heart howls in despair when I think of my life without ye, and I was too goddamned scared to admit it to myself, least of all admit it to ye.

'If I were to single-handedly fight one hundred men, I'd be fearless, but being honest about my feelings and laying my heart at yer feet, there to be cherished or stomped on, absolutely terrified me. Call me a coward, but there ye have it.'

The sincerity in his eyes, his face, and the pain in his voice cut Helene to the quick. She could relate to and understood the source of that pain, how a single event in one's past maintained a stranglehold on the present. Rejection. A debilitating emotion, and one associated with loss.

'Lass, put me out of my misery.' It was a plea, no less. 'If ye dinnae love me as I love ye, or if ye dinnae want me as I want ye, then I'll leave this very minute and return home to Scotland. If ye say aye to being my wife . . . well then, I swear I'll spend the rest of my days earning and deserving yer love.'

Helene saw reflected in his eyes the same hope she'd harboured in them forging a life together. This man, a battle-hardened Highland warrior, had laid bare his underlying vulnerability in the purest and most honest way. She had one last question. 'Had you not been in love with me and scandal broke, would you still have married me as per your oath?'

'Aye, lass. Honour is my all, and how blessed am I to have

fallen in love with the lass whom I'd pledged to safeguard and protect?'

Elation returned, flooding Helene's heart to the point of bursting. She moved slowly to stand within an inch of him, inhaling a fragrant blend of citrus soap, freshly laundered linen, and a pleasing scent uniquely his.

She stared into the depths of his darkened eyes. 'I love you, Lachlan MacLanoch, and my answer is *aye*. I wholeheartedly accept your marriage proposal.'

He stared at her with a mixture of relief and disbelief before cupping her cheeks in his hands and pressing his mouth to hers in a searing kiss. A kiss claiming her as his.

All too soon, he pulled back. It took Helene a few moments to catch her breath, to open her eyes and see his face in clear focus.

'I will love ye for all time, *mo chridhe*. This I promise ye.'

'And I, you.' She caressed his cheek and smiled up at him. '*Mo chridhe?* You've said it often to me. What does it mean?'

''Tis a term of endearment—my heart.'

Helene eyed him in wonder. 'All this time, and I never knew.'

Lachlan took Helene's chin gently between his thumb and forefinger. 'I've spoken many an endearing word to ye in Gaelic. Ye just ne'er kenned what I'd said.'

'In that case, you must teach me.'

'Aye, that I will.' He brushed his lips over hers. 'Yer father wishes to see ye wed here in London, before we return to Scotland.'

Helene nodded. 'Prudence made me agree not to see out the customary mourning period, so the wedding shall be an expedient and small affair. Just you, me, my father and brother.'

'Then tomorrow, I'll obtain a special marriage licence. As soon as we are wed, we can be on our way. We'll travel home in comfort, by coach, and under escort this time, and we'll overnight in the most comfortable inns. I'll not have my newly wedded wife dressed as a man and travelling on horseback.'

Helene let out a laugh. 'My backside is still recovering from that ordeal.' She laid her cheek against Lachlan's chest. 'I should like to have a second wedding at Drumocher, and in keeping with your Scottish traditions.'

Lachlan chuckled over her head. 'It will be nae small affair. I can tell ye that!'

It pleased Helene to know they'd arrive back in Scotland before summer's end, and before Agnes and her family returned home to London. She tipped her face up to meet Lachlan's eyes. 'At our wedding, I want to be draped in the cloth of your clan.'

His broad smile showed how much this pleased him.

Helene found her home in Lachlan's tight embrace, in the warmth of his mouth pressed to hers, and in his kiss. A kiss as fiercely possessive as it was achingly tender.

EPILOGUE

LACHLAN SAT AT the table upon the dais in the great hall. The skirl of bagpipes and the swirl of the plaid never failed to stir his blood, and yet those very sights and sounds, here amidst his wedding celebrations at Drumocher, paled in comparison to feelings roused in him at the sight of his newly wed wife.

Helene MacLanoch. His bonnie bride. Her radiance burned brighter than the myriad candles ensconced on walls, in chandeliers, and on tables. Pride filled his heart as he watched her follow a set sequence of steps in a Scottish reel with his mother, auntie, Grizel, and Agnes. The sweet trill of her laughter rose above the cacophony of conversation and merrymakers.

Lachlan cast his gaze over the crowded hall, and amongst the dancers he spied Mairi and Greer, Donnie, and his parents. A sense of clan cohesion and unity filled the air. Never had Lachlan felt so content and so gratified with life.

He turned his head, again drawn to his wife. She was dressed in a gown of MacLanoch plaid, with a contrasting embroidered silk petticoat and stomacher. A sprig of heather adorned her upswept hair, and several long tendrils framed her face. A dainty thin strip of lace graced her neck, the ends tied in a bow and trailing down her back. Lachlan smiled, his heart bursting with love and devotion for her.

'She is indeed a true beauty,' said Cuthbert, seated beside Lachlan.

'Aye. That she is.'

'You know, you never did thank me.'

Lachlan reluctantly dragged his gaze from Helene to look at his cousin. 'Thank ye for what?'

Cuthbert raised his brows and spread his hands wide. 'For playing Cupid and landing you a wife! I'd go so far as to call it the *perfect*, perfect match. Wouldn't you agree?'

Lachlan took a moment to reflect on the lengths his cousin had gone to in bringing Helene to Drumocher. 'Aye,' he said, nodding. 'Ye're right, Cuthbert. How remiss of me. Ye did indeed matchmake me with a true treasure.'

Lachlan laid his hand on Cuthbert's shoulder and gave it a squeeze. 'Thank ye, cousin. If not for ye, I'd not be the happy and fortunate man I am today. Ye found me the fairest and most captivating bride, and for that, I'm truly grateful. *Slàinte mhath.*'

Cuthbert followed Lachlan's lead in raising his glass. '*Do dheagh shlàinte.*'

After taking a sip of wine, Lachlan asked, 'Do ye recall the tail-end of our conversation and yer parting words in the library on the day ye arrived at Drumocher?'

Cuthbert winked. 'Imbibing your finest red comes first to mind.' He then tilted his head back with an upward gaze. Suddenly, he grinned, snapped his fingers, and looked Lachlan in the eye. 'I goaded you into playing one last throw of the dice.'

'Aye, and ye said, "May the best man win." Yer enforced risky wager of the hearts between Helene and me paid off. Acclaim is all yers, cousin. Not only were ye best man at my wedding today, but also the best man, and deservedly so, as winner of that wager.'

Cuthbert laughed and slapped Lachlan on the back. 'Oh, I don't know about that. I'd say we both came up trumps.'

A frown formed on Cuthbert's face when his gaze strayed to the dance floor. 'Although, having said that, tradition demands from my job as best man to prevent anyone from stealing your prize, including the young man who's now taken your wife's hand in his.'

Lachlan's protective instincts kicked into battle mode. He reached for his dirk, shot up from his seat, and whipped his head around to see who dared to attempt kidnapping his wife.

Cuthbert howled with laughter. 'Sit down, man. I hardly think Donnie will make off with your wife tonight, and if Helene sees you threatening the young lad with a blade again, then your marriage will be over before it begins.'

The sound of Lachlan's heartbeat thrashed in his ears. The mere thought of someone running off with his bride was more than he could bear. He cursed his cousin in Gaelic for the unnecessary worry, which made Cuthbert laugh even more. That prompted Lachlan to sit down and drink the rest of his wine with the hope it would instantly calm his nerves, but one look at Helene and his heart resumed its peaceful pulse. Seeing her elegantly master the steps of the Strathspey, hand in hand with young Donnie, simply warmed his heart. The lass was indeed a precious find, which led him to ponder his cousin's marital plight.

Lachlan leaned in close to Cuthbert, even though the melodic harmonies of fiddles and bagpipes would prevent others from hearing what he wanted to say.

'Helene and I will do everything in our power to ensure yer personal happiness. To comply with yer father's filial demands, we'll give thought to whom ye might marry. Perhaps a lass who wishes to protect a secret such as yer own?'

Cuthbert dipped his chin and gave Lachlan an appreciative

smile. 'You will, of course, both attend my wedding, with you as my best man.'

'Of course. We wouldnae miss it for the world, and 'twould be my honour to stand at yer side as yer best man.' Lachlan indicated Cuthbert's kilted attire with a sweep of his hand. 'Ye look quite the handsome Scotsman in the MacLanoch cloth, ye ken. And 'tis refreshing to see yer fair hair unbound and untamed.'

'Yes, well, as I quoted once before, "When they are at Rome, they do there as they see done."'

'When ye get married, which I daresay will be in London, to which *Roman* attire will ye proclaim yer allegiance? England, or Scotland?'

Cuthbert shrugged. 'Perhaps both. Only time will tell.' He waved Lachlan away. 'Now go and dance with your wife. Her adoring eyes are on you with a clear invitation.'

Lachlan rose to his feet, his height and stature as striking as his Highland wedding regalia. He wore a hip-length black velvet jacket and waistcoat. A kilt of MacLanoch tartan sat around his waist, signifying pride in his clan and lineage. A shirt with frilled, embroidered cuffs and a diamond stock pin enhanced his overall elegance. His plaid, woven in the same autumn hues as the kilt, was draped over his coat, gathered at the shoulder, and pinned with the green jewelled brooch that had belonged to his late father. Candlelight caught the healthy shine of his shoulder-length russet hair.

As he left the dais and made his way to the floor, the music steadily petered out, the crowd withdrew to line the walls, and a hush fell over the great hall, with Helene at its core. All eyes were on the MacLanoch laird in excited anticipation of his next move.

Lachlan focused solely on his wife, and it pleased him to see her green-eyed gaze levelled on him. He stopped but two steps in front of her and drank in the sight of her remarkable beauty. He placed his right hand over his heart and made a slow bow. 'My lady.'

When he straightened, Helene dipped a deep curtsy. 'My laird.'

Lachlan offered her his hand, palm up. When his wife reached out to rest her fingertips on his palm, Lachlan bent and pressed a kiss to the back of her hand. He glanced up. 'Shall we dance?'

'Aye.' Her radiant smile said it all.

Lachlan signalled the musicians to recommence playing the Strathspey, then fixed his unwavering gaze on the centre of his world.

Helene.

ACKNOWLEDGEMENTS

To my husband, Bryan, I am deeply grateful for your unwavering support and constant encouragement, which have sustained me throughout my writing journey. Your belief in me and my passion for storytelling has been a steady source of strength.

To my daughter, Skye, thank you for your enthusiastic support and for contributing your insights to the development of one of my characters. Your input added depth and authenticity that I truly value.

Sincere thanks to my wonderful writer friends in the HOGS (Hearts of Gold) critique group, and to my fellow friend and author, Anthea Laurelton. Collectively, your thoughtful feedback, camaraderie, and shared love of the craft have been both inspiring and invaluable.

ABOUT THE AUTHOR

Vanda was born in Papua New Guinea, where she spent her early childhood, before later settling in Australia. At the age of eleven, a holiday in England sparked her fascination with the days of old. Castles, ruins and discovering Jane Austen novels inspired a lifelong interest in all things historical, a passion that later kickstarted Vanda's desire to write historical fiction. Her locale and global visits to faraway places inspire her to create fictitious characters and dramas set against authentic and geographical backdrops. Vanda's debut novel, *The Pirate Lord*, and follow-up, *The Prodigal Laird*, both reached #1 on Amazon Australia's bestseller list.

Vanda has degrees in child and adult education and worked as a teacher of literacy and numeracy. She has also worked in the banking and recruitment sectors. The Gold Coast is home to Vanda, her husband, their children and grandchildren, where they enjoy walks along world-renowned beaches or a quiet getaway to the lush hills of the Hinterland.

If you'd like to know more about Vanda, her books, or to connect with her online and via social media, you can visit her website www.vandavadas.com

www.ingramcontent.com/pod-product-compliance
Lightning Source LLC
LaVergne TN
LVHW041107080826
845145LV00007B/1714

* 9 7 8 0 6 4 8 1 8 7 1 3 4 *